The Point

By G. Nykanen

~~~

Published by G. NYKANEN
Copyright © 2014 G. NYKANEN
All rights reserved

ISBN: 10-0989878457
ISBN: 13-978-0-9898784-5-6

ALL RIGHTS RESERVED. This book contains material protected under International and Federal Copyright Laws and Treaties. Any unauthorized reprint or use of this material is prohibited. No part of this book may be reproduced or transmitted in any form or by any means, electronic or mechanical, including photocopying, recording, or by any information storage and retrieval system without express written permission from the author.

This is a work of fiction. Any resemblance of events to real life, or of characters to actual persons, is purely coincidental.

*This book is dedicated to MR.
Thanks for your inspiration.*

Chapter 1

"What time are you leaving in the morning?" she finally asked, hoping it would be late so they would have the morning together.

"About nine," he replied.

She'd been hoping he'd confess his love. She was searching for any sign that he felt as connected to her as she did to him. Nora watched the candlelight dance, her hand firmly clasped in Jake's, as she considered what she should say next. She'd long awaited this connection, to experience the level of intimacy they shared.

I'll just say it, she thought.

"I ..." She froze, trapped by his caring eyes, so blue and charming. She tried to spit it out but couldn't.

"I hope you can come up to see me this summer. It'll be a long break without you."

She was sickened by her cowardice but held on to hope. *Maybe he'll say it now,* she thought, *now that I got the ball rolling.* She looked to him with eagerness. She focused on him as though she were willing the words to spill from his lips.

Jake knew that look, the *I love you* look; he'd seen it before. The only problem was that this time he felt it too. *I can't say anything. Not yet.*

"I have to focus on work this summer. There is also something important..." Jake trailed off as though he were about to disclose something else. He wanted to tell her: he wanted to explain what a ball-buster his father was and how he had a plan to appease him. How he was

The Point

going to work hard over the summer to clear the path so they could be together. *What if I can't pull it off?* he thought. *I can't tell her, I can't risk the heartache it'll cause if I don't succeed.*

Jake grasped both of her hands, holding them tightly at his chest.

She shifted closer, smiling sweetly with anticipation. *All right*, she thought. *This is it, he's about to say it.*

"I have two jobs lined up," Jake explained.

"What? Wait a minute… I thought …" Nora trailed off. She was caught off guard.

"You can't find one long weekend?" she asked, trying to cover her shock and disappointment over Jake's denial of the "L" word.

"I'm afraid not," he replied.

"What if I came to see you?" she pushed, realizing this was her last chance to convince him to connect over the summer.

Jake felt nauseous, his insides twisting as he watched her come to terms with their separation. *Be strong,* he thought, *she'll understand when you see her in the fall. When she realizes why you did it, all this will be forgotten.*

"That wouldn't be a good idea. I have some personal issues, and my work will be all-consuming. I have to focus and finish up a few things, but I can't wait to see you next semester."

Chapter 2

The warm May wind filtered through the small opening in the window of the late-model Rover. Nora picked up speed as she entered the ramp onto I-75, her long, dark-blonde hair twisting in the breeze.

She glanced at the brass compass nestled in the console amongst her loose change. It had been passed down from one generation to another. Her father gave it to her, just as his father had given it to him. It had long been a Reynolds family tradition to hand it down to your first-born son. Well, William Reynolds was blessed with only one child, and it wasn't a boy.

"It will always help you find your way," her father had told her. Well, it hadn't helped her find it with Jake. She ran her fingers over the aged brass case, its presence somehow providing a deeply needed comfort as she struggled to understand her love life.

She began to think about Jake and how their farewell had left her with more questions than answers. They'd never discussed whether or not they were exclusive, whether what they had was serious. *Am I available?* Nora thought. *I don't feel available.*

She stopped dating once she became intimate with Jake. She assumed he did the same. Perhaps that was naive of her. "You know what they say about assuming something," she said to herself in the rear view mirror. "It makes an ass out of you and me." She squeezed the steering wheel, shaking it with frustration! "Jake, Jake, Jake, Why did you do this to me?" she asked, once again referencing the mirror, her mouth turned down into a pout.

The Point

She decided to focus on what lay ahead, like her best friend Lucy and all the upcoming festivities her cozy beach town provided. "I've gotta stop talking to myself in the mirror; it's making me look crazy."

She hunkered down, the pedal to the metal, as she sped along the highway eager to get home. The university was at the very southern end of this vast Midwestern state. So, it was seven hours due north, then across the bridge (Iron Bay was just one of many towns on a peninsula in the northern most section of the state) and then another three hours down rural, winding roads, with nothing but pines and mosquitoes for miles.

"It's about time. I think this drive gets longer every time," she whined as she passed a sign that read "Iron Bay 15 miles ahead."

She searched for the local radio station.

"Q101.3 WIBP The Bay." *You really feel like you've made it home,* she thought, *when you hear that familiar jingle.*

Iron Bay was a quaint little town. The radio station played songs chosen by the residents of the surrounding counties, so it was forever stuck somewhere between 1983 and 1995 (as far as musical tastes were concerned).

The small northern city of about 20,000 was supported by the only major medical center in the region and a small state university (you know, the kind with a direction in the title). The name Iron Bay came from the iron-rich ore mined and exported from the area.

The town had two sections, the original downtown area founded in 1837 and a section called "the Village." The Village was a collection of small shops, restaurants, and friendly pubs. It was the part of town that catered to the college crowd, provided by Northern Bay University.

The lower harbor consisted of a marina, where the locals moored their sailboats, and a large park where the city's festivities were held. The harbor was also home to a few upscale eateries and Prell's Fish Market, where the townfolk could purchase the catch of the day, pulled directly from Lake Paramount.

Nora took in the familiar sites of her beloved hometown.

"A sight for sore eyes, and a relief to my sore ass," she giggled as she pulled into the driveway.

The sun was still shining as she pulled up this late evening; its warm glow was bathing the facade of her home in an ethereal light. (Iron Bay was so far north it didn't get dark until ten-thirty in the summer.) The house was nestled on a wide, tree-lined street on the east side of town in a neighborhood known for its sprawling manors and grand Victorians.

Nora's mother had always dreamed of owning a house on the east side. She truly appreciated the history in these old homes. "They just don't build 'em like that anymore," she would offer while she admired the old gems around town.

William Reynolds, Nora's father, was the proprietor of a sporting goods shop downtown. He outfitted the town folk and tourists with sporting gear for any season or occasion. He also guided fishing trips and tours of the surrounding wilderness. William doted on his wife and daughter, like any proud husband and father would. Elizabeth was his best friend, and he told anyone who would listen how wonderful she was.

One summer William overheard his fishing-trip client having a spirited debate on his mobile phone about an investment property he had to "unload." The hefty

The Point

man sat at the campfire squawking about the "fixer-upper."

The only thing William snagged the whole fishing trip was the fixer-upper, and he was delighted by the joy it brought to his wife.

Elizabeth took great care to restore every detail. She hunted to find just the right fixtures and furniture. She wanted the house to be something that could be handed down to her daughter.

Now, here it stood, the only physical comfort of her mother that remained. Nora paused in the driveway, admiring the home her mother had built for her, while vigorously rubbing her sore butt with both hands.

The cedar siding was a light gray, and the age of the home was apparent from the many scraped and painted layers. White gingerbread trim dressed each window. She stood, one palm to each cheek trying to massage away the pins and needles, while she took a moment to analyze how it felt to pull up and see her home, its charm heightened by the late sun of the spring evening.

The front door, a deep red in color, opened as her father appeared.

He was short in stature, thin but fairly muscular for a man of 50. He waited on the porch while his daughter rubbed away the long drive, his arms crossed over the buttons of his plaid shirt, and his wiry brown hair stiff and resistant in the spring breeze. William's expressive eyebrows were raised above his smiling blue eyes as he questioned his daughter. "Were you speeding? I didn't expect you til' ten."

"I got started earlier than expected," she answered, still massaging away the many miles between school and home.

He'd nudged his daughter to go downstate and partake in the true college experience, not wanting her to be limited by going to school from home. After she left, the emptiness was crushing, not unlike what he'd felt when his wife passed.

William had enjoyed his daughter's calls home. They were filled with stories about wild parties and crazy professors; the excitement she felt was tangible even over the phone. Refusing to let his loneliness diminish her chance for the experiences life in the city provided, he took great care not to let his daughter know how devastated he was by her absence. He suffered in silence, worried she would return home simply to spare him the pain of being alone.

Twenty-one now, she was a grown woman with only one more trip downstate, one last semester in the fall.

As she approached the porch, thoughts that should've been focused on her father were focused on Jake. They'd met in an economics class; he was the graduate assistant. The two would catch each other's glances, often exchanging a smile. One day Jake handed back a quiz with his number attached.

Her daydream was interrupted by her father's eager greeting.

"Oh, how I've missed you, Nora." He approached with arms outstretched, grinning from ear to ear.

"I've missed you too, Dad. It's so nice to finally be home."

She had to try and put Jake aside to focus on her father and Badger. The tiny canine was jumping around on the porch and excitedly circling her feet. Badger, although only 12 pounds, was hurling himself at her legs

The Point

with enough might to knock her backwards. "Whoa, little dog," she soothed as he continued to demand her attention. Scooping him up with one arm, she commenced rubbing her face on the top of his little head.

"I didn't get that enthusiastic of a greeting," her dad jabbed.

Nora smiled, her chin resting atop the dog's head. Although she'd missed her father and his quirky sense of humor, she'd missed her little dog most of all.

Badger was her closest companion and had been just a pup when her mother was ill. Elizabeth, Nora, and Badger would spend hours curled up on the sofa. They sat, spending quiet afternoons just existing in each other's presence.

She kept nuzzling, enjoying his kinky gold fur. It twisted in every direction, his short tail curled upward to form the letter "C." She stroked his unruly coat while catching up with her dad.

"Been keeping busy?" she questioned.

"Oh, some fishing and what not. Oh, and beer on Friday with the fellas," William answered. "Are you hungry?"

"Not really." She yawned. "I had a burger when I stopped for gas at the bridge. I'm just tired and looking forward to hitting the sack."

"Well, let's get your stuff in from the car and get you tucked in," her father insisted.

He helped his daughter gather her bags, and dropped her and her belongings at her bedroom door. Delighted they were both under one roof again, they stood in the hallway a few minutes more exchanging anecdotes. "Alright, that's enough gabbing," he finally announced. He leaned in and turned his cheek toward his daughter.

He twisted his mouth to the side as though to give her more room to plant a kiss. He pointed at his face, "Right here," he said.

She grinned, warmed by his silliness, and kissed him on the cheek, "Goodnight Dad. Love ya."

"Love you too, my dear."

He shuffled to his room, peeking around the doorframe to give one last wave.

Nora returned the favor before closing her door.

It's been a long day, she thought while heading into the bathroom. She stood in front of the mirror and examined her face. "You need to get some sun," she said to her reflection as she pulled at her cheeks.

With a fair complexion and a petite build, she resembled her mother, but her blue eyes seemed to reflect a hint of mischief, a trait she inherited from her father.

Shuffling around, she unpacked her things. "A place for everything and everything in its place," she chimed as she placed the compass safely in her nightstand drawer. She took a moment to admire it nestled amongst the other bits and bobs one accumulates in a bedside table. She slid the drawer closed and finished her nighttime routine before slipping into bed.

Her feet slowly slid between the cool sheets as she tipped her head back onto the pillow. Her long locks spilled out all around her.

She began drifting off only to have her burgeoning slumber interrupted by her furry companion. After hopping onto the bed, Badger began raking at the quilt's edge, wanting Nora to lift it and allow him to burrow underneath.

"All right," she yawned as she raised the blanket, granting him passage.

The Point

Badger tucked his head under, finally settling when he found his favorite space between her knees. Curling up, he rested his head on her shin. They both fell fast asleep, contented by the familiarity of sharing the bed.

Nora slept heavily until morning. She only stirred when the sound of the birds singing their a.m. tune drifted through her open window along a crisp morning breeze. She remained curled in her bed, relishing the feeling of the cold draft on her face while the chorus of robins and chickadees serenaded her.

The lovely avian melody was rudely interrupted by the music of Hall and Oates. The dreadful ringtone version of "Maneater" pierced Nora's still sleepy ears as she reached for her phone.

"Little early for a call isn't it, Luce," Nora mumbled as she glanced at the time on her alarm.

"Good morning to you too," Lucy replied cheerily, unaffected by her friends sarcasm.

"What shall we do today?" she asked Nora excitedly, no doubt already fueled by caffeine and hairspray. "It's a lovely day to go down to the harbor and shop for the catch of the day."

She knew Lucy didn't mean whatever had been pulled out of Lake Paramount. "Isn't it a little early for harassing guys at the dock?" Nora asked her enthusiastic friend.

Lucy sighed. "Fine. How about breakfast at the Light House instead?"

Nora agreed that eating breakfast, not fishing for hunks, would be a better start to their day. She got out of bed, went through her usual morning ritual, and headed downstairs. Her father had departed early to open the store. He left a note:

Here's some mad money.
Stop by the store if you have time.
Have a great day. Love Ya, Dad

Forty dollars was tucked under the paper. She smiled. *Mad money* was a tradition established by her mother. "Everyone needs a few extra dollars, just in case they feel the need to get out and do something crazy," Elizabeth would say with her eyes rolling and her fingers twirling.

Nora folded the cash and stashed it in her pocket before trying to procure a morning beverage.

"Nothing," she sighed as she rummaged through the empty fridge. "Good thing I'm off to the diner," she said to Badger as she grabbed her bag and keys. He looked up at her, his large eyes dark and glossy. He twisted his head to the left as he tried to make sense of her ramblings. "You be a good boy, I'll be home later." Badger lingered a moment to stare at the back of the closed door, before trotting to the sofa to find his favorite guard position.

The seats in the Rover were cold. Nora winced as the chilled leather met her bare legs. "Holy hell!"

She'd donned a pair of shorts this morning, *obviously an optimistic and misguided attempt to will the day to be warm,* she thought. The far north mornings of this peninsula were still frigid, even late in May. Nora snapped the heat on to combat the chill.

The car slowly warmed as she drove to meet Lucy.

~~~

The Point

The friends sat and faced each other, picking up right where they'd left off after Christmas break. With forks in hand, they chatted between bites.

Lucy spoke in her usually animated fashion, her long, wavy red hair, professionally tousled, bouncing as she waved her hands, excitedly telling tales about love found and lost, *and* found and lost, at school out West.

"There are too many tanned and toned guys, and too little time." Lucy stated before prying into her friend's love life. "So, tell me about Jake. What is *that* like?" she asked with a devilish grin, her hands now folded under her chin.

"Are you fishing for details, Lucy Jane Meyer?" Nora asked sarcastically.

"Of course I am. Be specific, and use all the dirty words," Lucy commanded jokingly.

"Let's just say that he was giving and attentive." Just the thought of Jake made her warm all over.

"You look a little red, Nora. Is that because just thinking about him has you worked up?"

She didn't get into it. It was too early for tales of heartache over Jake; she just kept the conversation light, returning her attention to her good friend.

"You're incredible, Lucy. I guess I'm just not as experienced as you."

"Funny, and true," admitted Lucy as she nodded from behind her coffee cup. She went on to tell Nora about a guy she'd hooked up with when she got back into town. "He's intellectual and attractive." Lucy winked. "But also down-to-earth and wealthy." (Lucy usually just went for attractive, uninterested in other qualities.)

"Must be serious if you've spent enough time with him to realize he's *intellectual*," Nora said with a grin.

Lucy shot her a glaring look then said, "He's having a party this weekend and asked me to recruit some single ladies to attend."

Mulling it over, Nora eventually agreed to show up, all the while wondering if she truly qualified as single.

"What are your plans for today?" Lucy asked. "Do you wanna do some shopping or catch a movie? You don't want to cruise guys, *so*, we'll have to find something else to do."

"I probably should drive out and visit my mom, I couldn't get out there at Christmas, too much snow. I just don't feel like I can put other activities first."

"Okay," Lucy conceded. "I understand. Do you want me to go with you?"

"No," she replied. "I want to go alone."

After gossiping a bit longer, Nora decided she should get going. "The drive out is a long one, and I'll need to do some grocery shopping before I can head home after. I tried to have some tea with milk this morning and found half an onion and a bottle of ketchup in the fridge."

Lucy giggled. "I guess your dad isn't much of a shopper."

"He just eats out most of the time. He hates to eat alone, says it's too depressing. I think it gives him the opportunity to flirt with the waitresses."

Parting with a hug, they agreed to touch base later in the week about going to the party.

Nora headed home.

~~~

"Let's go outside," she called to Badger as she opened the door. He came barreling toward her, his short legs a blur as he dashed to the backyard. She took

The Point

pleasure in gathering a bouquet of forget-me-nots from the shady garden while Badger took pleasure in relieving himself in the shady garden.

Elizabeth Reynolds had been an avid gardener, leaving several lovely flowerbeds positioned around the Reynolds' home. What were once glorious floral displays (featured yearly on the city's garden tour) were now a bit weedy and overgrown.

These have really been suffering in your absence, Nora thought as she surveyed the area. "I need to straighten out this mess," she voiced to Badger. "Mom would not be pleased with our laziness," she assured her little dog, who was now bounding past the shed in pursuit of some poor creature.

A sweetly scented breeze swirled around while she returned to picking, pushing warm air from the sunny side of the yard into the shaded flowerbed. The morning's chill ebbed as she worked, the sun warming the May afternoon. She held the bouquet in her fist, admiring it from every angle. She didn't want to visit her mother without a small tribute, " What's lovelier than this fresh bunch of blue and purple blooms?" she asked rhetorically as Badger sped by.

Chapter 3

Elizabeth Reynolds had been laid to rest under a large maple tree in the back-west corner of a small rural cemetery. She had suffered from a sudden ailment that affected the lining of her heart. It had gone undetected until she fell ill just before Nora's sixteenth birthday. Elizabeth passed, quickly and quietly. She didn't suffer, just simply slipped away while resting on the sofa one afternoon.

Nora kneeled before her mother's headstone, the long grass climbing up around her. Picking a piece, she fidgeted, weaving the blade between her fingers. "I miss you," she said quietly. "I picked these from the shady garden." She motioned to the forget-me-nots she'd laid on the base of the headstone upon her arrival. "Badger helped," she added with a small smile, the memory of him darting about bringing some comic relief.

Several moments passed as she sat remembering her mother's warm smile and quirky spirit. She thought about how it felt when her mother would braid her hair or hold her when she was sad. Elizabeth had been a petite but sturdy woman. Nora knelt, remembering that it had seemed like her mother could do anything.

A picture of her mother's fine brown hair, pulled back and tucked under a baseball cap, drifted into focus. The wispy strands of the ponytail poking out of the back, her deep brown eyes peeking out from under its brim. She thought about how gentle her mother's hands were, how delicate her touch was, even though they were rough from hard work.

The Point

Time seemed to stand still as she sat listening to the wind rustling in the leaves of the surrounding forest, memories of her mother flooding over her. Closing her eyes, she soaked in the sun's warm rays while contemplating what her life would have been like if things had turned out differently.

This quiet moment was interrupted by the sound of a shovel scraping through the rocky soil.

Turning toward the disturbance she saw a strapping young man, tall, maybe six feet. He was struggling to push the tip of his shovel into the ground. His work boot–clad foot was stomping wildly on the shovel's top edge.

"Miserable rocky ground!" The handle on the shovel broke with a loud crack under the pressure of his full weight.

"Fuck! Piece of shit shovel!" He realized he'd caught her attention. "Oh, I apologize," he said smoothing his hair. "Had I noticed you were sitting there, I might have tried to exercise some self-control." The handsome man before her was flushed from the laborious digging, thus hiding the blushing he was no doubt doing.

"No worries," she said. "I don't mean to ask an obvious question, but aren't there machines you can use to dig graves these days?"

"I'm not digging the grave," he replied. "I'm digging the footing for the headstone."

"Oh," Nora replied. "Can't you use some sort of digging apparatus for that?"

"No," answered the young man. "The footing must be dug to size and provide a level base. It's a fine process; machines are too clumsy. This *is* the apparatus," he added jokingly, while giving the broken shovel a shake.

She was now feeling a bit flushed herself. This was a very attractive guy. He was tall, with thick blonde hair. His jaw line was strong and angled; he had a rugged, unshaven appearance. His dark brown eyes were a strange and beautiful contrast to his lightly colored locks.

At some point during his struggle with the rocky ground he'd abandoned his shirt. Now he was before her, his muscular chest heaving with every breath. *I'm so glad I left Lucy behind*, she thought as she admired his form.

"I apologize again for disturbing your visit."

"That's okay," she replied with a comforting tone.

"Must be someone very special," stated the man as he gestured toward the flowers.

"Yes, my mother," she answered.

"Sorry for your loss."

"Thanks, she died when I was fifteen."

"It must've been hard growing up without a mother."

"Yeah, but my father is wonderful, so that helped."

She wanted to keep talking, and run, all at the same time. She found it hard not to stare, captivated by the masculinity before her. Finding herself caught in an awkward moment of silence, her cheeks started to feel flush as the embarrassment crept in. "I should go and let you get back to work."

Turning quickly she headed back to the car. She turned the key, ready to put some distance between her and the awkward situation. "Schwaaa," the engine coughed. *Oh no*, she thought, as the Rover made a noise one could only describe as retching.

Observing her from a distance, he contemplated her attributes. *Motherless, raised by her father, seems*

The Point

trusting... delicious, he thought, *how flawed, how gullible, is a girl who's lost her mother?*

"Can I help you?" he asked, popping his head into the driver's side window.

"Holy hell!" She jumped.

"Sorry, so sorry," he chuckled, entertained by her reaction.

"You scared me, my heart is in my throat," she gasped, her hand planted on her chest.

"Really, my apologies, I didn't mean to scare you... Dane Buchman," he said, as he held out his hand, transitioning swiftly into an introduction.

"I'm Nora. Nora Reynolds."

He shook her hand, taking her all in. *She has an innocence, a sweetness, about her*, he thought.

Realizing that his gaze might start to seem creepy, he released her hand abruptly.

"Well, Nora, pop the hood: let's see what's wrong."

He investigated the contents of the Rover's front end for a considerable amount of time. She began wondering what he was doing, his actions shielded by the Rover's hood.

"How's it going out there?" she asked.

Peeking his head around he answered, "Well, I think you should let me drive you home."

"Is it bad?"

"I can't be sure," he answered, rubbing his forehead with the back of his forearm. "I don't know much about cars."

"Why'd you look under the hood if you didn't know what you were doing?"

"Just trying to seem manly, help the damsel in distress," he answered coyly.

Dane's eyes, fun and flirty, were intoxicating. She peered into them and mindlessly said, "Yes, perhaps you could drive me home." *Was that me*, she thought. *Did I just agree to a ride from this stranger?* Her mouth was clearly speaking without direction from her brain.

"Great, I would love to give you a ride. Let me bring these tools back to the shed."

He pointed over to the cart. It had a rack on the back for the various shovels and spades used to prepare the stone sites and tend to the grounds. They walked over to where he'd been struggling, and he motioned to the vehicle.

"Have a seat."

"Thanks," she smiled.

As he loaded the tools, she was watching him in the rear view mirror. He filled the rack and then bent over to retrieve his shirt. He was well built, his muscles flexing as he pulled on the flannel. Nora watched intently as he buttoned, his strong hands moving over his muscular chest.

"I just have to drive this hotrod back to the shed," he announced as he claimed the driver's seat.

"Okay," she answered, his statement breaking her trance.

It's amusing, she thought, *that he referred to the cart as a hotrod.* She was so attracted to him that he could have had the personality of a cardboard box and she would still have found him entertaining.

She caught herself thinking about her feelings for Jake as she sat next to this fine male specimen. Nora's attraction to Jake had grown over time. She felt comfortable with him; even their first moments together were easy. He was a safe place, a place where she took shelter. Dane, on the other hand, had her feeling worked up, not like herself.

He pulled in front of the shed and parked alongside one of the other carts. He exited the vehicle and came around the other side.

"May I assist you from the vehicle, miss?" he asked as he held his hand out to her.

"Oh, of course you may, sir," she replied, playing along. As she grasped his hand, every nerve in her body was at attention; she hoped he'd never let go.

A professional womanizer like Dane easily read a woman's body language. He could sense her attraction by the neediness in her grip.

Leading her into the shed, he pushed open the squeaky door, never releasing the hold he had on her hand. Once inside they followed a hallway to a small office.

Dane Buchman, Grounds Supervisor was etched on the door.

"You're the boss," she stated. "That's impressive."

"Not really. I went to school to be a landscaper, and worked here in the summers. After graduation I was offered the job. I took it, thinking it would be temporary."

"What were you hoping to do instead?" she asked.

"My uncle runs a construction business that's been in our family since Iron Bay was founded; I was hoping to get in there."

"Why haven't they taken you yet?"

"Family politics," he offered, his tone tinged with contempt. "I've worked here for three years now, trying to save up to start my own landscaping business."

"You've done a great job, the grounds are beautiful," she said, trying to sound encouraging.

"Thanks," he replied.

He led her toward his desk, breaking his hold on her hand but not her attention to his every move.

"Let me grab my keys and we can go," Dane said as he pointed toward the drawer. As he reached past her, she found herself conflicted, hoping he *was* and *wasn't* going to make a move.

As he brushed against her, she tensed up. The feeling of him close to her caused her to hold her breath.

Dane felt Nora flex, her muscles tense; he knew he could move in.

He stopped suddenly in front of her and pulled her close. In one swift movement, he was closing the door while simultaneously spinning her around so she was pressed against the desk.

He reached and pulled her head up toward him, kissing her hard on the mouth while locking the door behind him. The sound of the lock clicking made her realize he wasn't just looking for a quick smooch.

This is crazy, she thought. *I've just met this guy; he could be a serial killer.* She wanted to stop him *and* didn't want to stop him.

His hands were under her shirt and over her breasts. The forcefulness of his touch was frightening and exhilarating.

Dane picked her up and placed her hard onto the desk. He pressed his legs against her knees, forcing them apart so he could move closer to her.

She slid her hands under his shirt, running them along his muscular back.

Suddenly she realized it was just two nights ago that it was Jake's back under her hands, and guilt washed over her.

The Point

"I'm sorry," she apologized. "I lost myself in the moment, I don't know what came over me."

She didn't want to share with Dane the real reason for her sudden shift in gear.

"I'm really sorry for leading you on. Perhaps you could just forget this happened and give me that ride home now," she continued, choosing to be direct.

"Of course, but I don't think I want to forget this happened." He smiled, hoping to put her at ease. He didn't want to scare her off; he was interested in getting to know her better.

Chapter 4

The lengthy ride back into town gave Nora ample time to contemplate what had taken place in the office. Any attraction that sudden and primal has to be bad news, she concluded. The term *animal attraction* kept swirling around in her mind.

It'll be best if I distance myself, she decided. *Best not to let him know where I live.*

"Could you drop me off downtown, I need to take care of some business."

"Yeah, wherever you need to go."

He followed that statement with, "Perhaps we could have dinner sometime?"

She prepared to hop out of his truck, her fingers quickly pulling the handle as she said, "I'm busy, but I'll call you." She hurriedly shut the door and jogged down the sidewalk, quickly taking shelter in the library.

"You didn't get my number!" Dane shouted, his words colliding with the inside of the already closed door.

Standing inside of the library, she peeked at an angle through the window until he drove off. "Whew," she exhaled, relieved to be free of the awkward situation. Now that the coast was clear, she left the library and headed toward her father's shop. She hoped a little face time with dad would be comforting. Besides, she needed to tell him about the Rover.

"Oh crap!" Nora growled as she stomached the realization that she'd have to eventually retrieve her vehicle.

The Point

Reynolds' Sport and Tackle was nestled on the corner of Lake and Lincoln. It was one of many small shops lining the main street in town. Her father's store was on the crest of a hill and if you stood in front of the shop, facing east, you could see the lake stretching out past the harbor.

The bell above the doorframe jingled as she entered the store. To the right was a display of kayaks and life vests and to the left was a giant cutout of a vicious-looking bear. It was growling, with paws outstretched, and the banner read "Black Bear Outer Wear. It's Fierce!"

The small store was crammed full of miscellaneous supplies: boots, jackets, snowshoes, paddles, fishing poles, anything and everything. There wasn't a bare space on any surface in the whole store.

She walked up to the counter and peered through the glass at the fishing flies. A little sign read, "Hand-tied right here in Iron Bay."

Her father called out from the back, "How can I help you?" He rounded the corner and saw that she was standing at the counter. "Oh, it's you," he said with a smile. "I thought you were a customer."

"Well, some of these fishing flies look pretty nice," she joked.

"Perhaps they would make for some lovely earrings."

She smirked, rolling her eyes at her father's attempt at humor.

"My Rover has died and is at the cemetery."

"Funny that it chose to die there."

"Ha-ha, Dad."

"I'll see about sending a tow truck out there and have it brought to the shop," William added.

"Thanks for taking care of it. I was worried about getting it." She continued to explain that statement by saying she feared the car would break down again on the way home. She didn't want to get into how she was avoiding the grounds supervisor because she had an uncontrollable urge to jump him.

"No worries, my dear. I'll take care of it."

She smiled at her father, relieved she didn't have to return for the car.

They sat and talked about mundane things for a bit (like her father's inability to shop), then she decided to head to the market to pick up a few groceries.

"Is there something special you'd like me to make for dinner?" she asked.

"How about Mom's beef stew?" her dad requested excitedly.

"Beef stew it is. How about some grocery money?" she requested with her hand outstretched.

"Is a hundred enough?" he asked her.

"Yeah, I think that should do it for now."

He opened the cash register and handed her five twenties.

"You might need these as well," he added with a jingle as he shook the keys to his truck.

After giving her dad a kiss on the cheek she headed out, deciding to drive by her favorite beach on the way.

The water sparkled in the afternoon sun as Nora cruised the avenue along the lakeshore. She could see a few people wading under the watchful presence of the lower harbor lighthouse. Summer was just getting underway, and the still-cool temps meant the tourists

The Point

hadn't arrived. For the locals, on the other hand, any temp above fifty degrees meant swimming. She took a right turn, away from the lake, and headed back toward town.

Making quick work of the shopping, she headed home with the loot. She enjoyed cooking her mother's recipes for her father. They would sit, eat, and reminisce.

Nora was over the stove stirring the stew when her father came in from the shop. Badger was doing his usual arrival dance at William's feet.

"How was your walk home?" She asked.

"Just fine," he replied. "The stew smells incredible."

"Thanks, it's just about ready."

They sat down at the kitchen table and began to eat and chat.

"So, seeing anyone special at school?" he asked, between bites.

"Just Jake. You seeing anyone?" she asked her father.

"No. Just not interested in any of the gals around here. I think your mother may have been the only fish in my sea."

"Things were getting sort of serious with Jake," Nora shared. "But we parted without clarifying the situation."

She was waiting for some sort of response from her father when the sound of her phone got her attention. "Excuse me." She got up from the table and headed to her purse, fishing it out of the bottom of her bag.

"Hello."

"Hey," Jake returned. "I see you made it home. I was curious. I hadn't heard from you."

"I was busy settling in," she lied. "I'm in the middle of dinner with my father, can I call back later tonight?"

"Sure," Jake replied.

"Talk to you later." Nora hung up. She was uncertain how speaking to Jake had made her feel. Returning to the table she decided to discuss it with her dad.

"Two days ago I was sure I was in love with Jake. I was hoping he would, well, at least acknowledge that we were an *Us*. All he offered was he'd miss me, and he'd see me next semester."

"Why didn't you just tell him how you felt?" her father asked, uncertain what he was missing.

"I wanted him to say it first. I wanted some romance, you know, a grand romantic gesture. You always did that for mom."

"Yeah, but I was a fool for your mother. She had a way about her that just... Oh, drove me to go through great lengths to keep her around."

Nora loved the way her father talked about her mother. All she wanted was to be loved the way her father had loved her mother. It was the basis for every relationship she'd ever had and, until two days ago, Jake was well on his way to being that guy.

"Well, anyway, I met a guy at the cemetery when I was visiting mom. He drove me to town, and then asked me to dinner. I blew him off because of my feelings for Jake."

"Wow. That's quite the load of info," William said, trying to absorb it all. He picked up his buttered bread and folded it in half. Just as he was about to take a bite he pointed it at his daughter and said, "It couldn't hurt to have dinner with this new guy, if Jake's been vague.

The Point

You're young, try not to get too bogged down." He took a big bite out of the bread then held his finger up, a gesture that clearly established he had more to say. "It's summer. Try to enjoy yourself, Nora, life is short."

"Thanks, Dad." Nora said with a grin, grateful for her father's limited but attentive parenting style.

Even though her father had offered a fine suggestion, she still felt like she needed some clarification. She picked Jake's number out of her contact list and hit "call." She realized it was late and hoped he wasn't already asleep.

"Hello," a female voice blurted on the other end. "Hello, who's this?"

She could hear the woman questioning Jake. "Who would be calling you this time of night?"

Nora hung up. That was all the clarity she needed. *No wonder he couldn't get away*. She called Lucy.

"That bastard," Lucy exclaimed. "I can't believe he'd do this to you."

"I'm such an idiot. I was smitten and didn't consider the possibility that there was someone else. He never tripped my suspicions."

"Most men are bastards; he just happened to fall into that very wide category. Put him out of your mind and, instead of looking for true love, settle for true lust. Sometimes Mr. Right Now can be a pleasant distraction."

"How do you do it? I can't help but feel connected. I have difficulty separating the physical from the emotional." Nora hoped her friend had some nugget of wisdom that would clear up her struggle with morality.

"Yeah, I forgot, you were raised by stable devoted parents, and I was raised by Kitty and Derek Meyer. They probably got their parenting advice from white wine labels and soap operas. Don't get me wrong, they never abused me or neglected me or anything, and coming from one of the wealthiest families in town, I definitely can't complain, but the moral fiber at my house was a little thin."

"They seem sweet, and you turned out okay," Nora tried to assure her friend. "You definitely have the best hair in town, so at least there's that."

"True, true," Lucy said with a smile, jokingly giving her hair a toss. "I'll just have to live vicariously through you when it comes to being virtuous. Wow, all right, that's enough self-exploration for one day, let's get back to discussing the party. There will be plenty of eligible bachelors to abuse. Cooper's in construction, so imagine the pool of guys he must know."

"I just don't know if I'm in the market yet, I'm still in shock."

"Well, just go and keep an open mind," Lucy suggested. "You never know what might happen."

Nora went to bed feeling a bit sad that she'd lost what she had with Jake. *How had so much slipped away in such a short time, she thought. Perhaps there's a silver lining: with Jake out of the picture, I can feel free to date and explore the local possibilities.* "Who am I kidding?" she confided in Badger, taking his little face in her hands. "I miss Jake, I don't want to explore."

Just as she turned out the light, the phone rang.

"You called?" Jake inquired.

"Yes, I did, and a woman answered." She waited for the reply to this.

"It was my father's assistant," he explained.

"What's she doing at the house so late?"

The Point

"We're putting together a project. I've been working two jobs, and one is for my father…"

"I hung up on her, I assumed she was with you," Nora interrupted, uninterested in his explanations.

Jake was silent for a few moments.

I wonder what he's thinking, she thought.

"I hope you have a good summer."

"You too, Jake."

The call was over. No frills or feelings expressed. She set down the phone and curled up. Tuesday night she was in Jake's passionate embrace; now it was Thursday, and he seemed like a stranger.

Chapter 5

"Hello, Mr. Reynolds, I'm here to pick up Nora."

"Of course. Come in." William greeted as he opened the door wide, gesturing for Lucy to enter.

Nora came bounding down the stairs. She threw her arms around her dad's neck. "Don't wait up; I'm probably staying at Lucy's."

"Have a good time, and don't get your name in the paper," William commanded.

"Will do, Dad." She gave her dad a kiss and led Lucy out the door.

"Why does your dad always say 'don't get your name in the paper'?"

"Because you get your name in the paper if you're arrested or dead. It's his way of saying be careful," Nora explained.

"Your dad's a strange fellow," Lucy declared.

The two friends admired and complimented each other on their outfit choices while they drove to the party. "I see you wore a skirt for easy access, just like I did," Lucy teased.

"You are *so* bad, Luce. I just wanted to look nice, not provide access."

"I wanted to look nice," Lucy continued with a mischievous grin, "*and* provide access."

"You're such a slut, Lucy Jane Meyer, what would your mother say?" Nora scolded, continuing the witty banter.

"Safety first," Lucy chimed, as she waved a condom she'd pulled from her bag.

The Point

They were still laughing about Lucy's unapologetic promiscuity when they pulled into the driveway at the party's location. The house was a newer build, located in a swanky subdivision out by the Cherry Creek River.

The river was one of the larger waterways that fed into Lake Paramount. The house was an immense grand ranch. It appeared to be one sprawling story from the front, but the house was cleverly built into a hill, so from the back you could see that it was two stories.

The kitchen was like something out of a magazine. Filled with the finest cabinetry, it had counters constructed of gray granite and stainless steel appliances that gleamed in the soft light of the decorative industrial light fixtures. French doors opened to a deck that looked out over the landscaped back yard, which was bordered by the river. Stairs cascaded down to a lower deck that was positioned off the lower-level family room. The bottom deck stepped down to a stone path that wound to the river's edge. The view was beautiful.

"So what's the name of this guy you have taken the time to get to know?" asked Nora as she and Lucy admired the view from the top deck.

"His name is Cooper Buchman, and this is his house."

She turned and shot Lucy a look. "Buchman!" Nora felt ill. *Maybe it's just a coincidence,* she thought. "Does he have any brothers?" she asked, dreading the answer.

"No, he's only mentioned his parents and a sister."

"Good," she said with relief, dropping her guard.

"Fancy running into you here," a familiar voice breathed from behind her.

"Dane." She tried to sound indifferent as she turned to face him. He looked amazing! He was freshly shaven and was wearing dark jeans and a tight black dress shirt. The sleeves were rolled up; his muscular forearms causing the rolled cuff to pull tight.

Rugged Dane was sexy, but cleaned up? Nora doubted she had enough self-control.

"Sorry about flaking out on you Thursday, I was conflicted about something, but that has resolved itself. I hope you can forget it."

"I thought nothing of it. Women are often prone to squirrelliness."

What an incredible smile. Nora swooned.

He held out his hand. "Let's get a drink," he ordered.

"Sounds good," she complied.

He led her to the lower deck where they both grabbed a beer before descending down to the river. A cobblestone-type patio sat adjacent to the water's edge, and upon that was a large stone fireplace.

The area was staged like an outdoor living area. Benches and chairs were arranged and covered in lovely pillows and cushions, creating cozy conversation areas.

There was a large fire burning, and everyone was talking and carrying on. Cooper introduced Lucy to Dane. "This is my first cousin Dane, our fathers are brothers," he explained.

Lucy introduced Nora to Cooper. "This is my best friend, Nora, she's like my sister," she added, while throwing her arm over Nora's shoulder.

Cooper looked smart and sharp but caring. His wide, bright smile was friendly and comforting. He had the same angled chin as Dane, but his eyes were blue. There was softness about them. Nora saw why Lucy was so taken with him.

The Point

"Can I talk to you for a minute?" Lucy asked as she grabbed her by the hand and led her away from the crowd. "When did you meet Cooper's cousin?"

"At the cemetery, he helped get home when my car broke down. We had a bit of a brush-up." She told Lucy all about the Rover and the desk and the awkward ride home. Lucy sat uncharacteristically speechless for a few seconds and then said, "I didn't know you had it in you."

"Well, I guess I don't, because I did stop him."

"Well, the night is young." Lucy smiled. "Anything is possible."

Nora flashed a grin at Lucy and turned to head back to the party.

The night progressed, and Lucy and Cooper got a little drunk. The canoodling had escalated as they drifted into that blissful place where their focus on each other caused the surrounding crowd to fade out of existence.

"Get a room," a voice called from the distance.

They came up for air and realized that they were close to making everyone on the back patio voyeurs.

"Oh, excuse us," Cooper said as he rose, leading Lucy to the door. "We're just going to step inside, go back to your booze and banter—there's nothing to see here." He waved his hand, comically gesturing at the onlookers.

Dane and Nora were now sitting close, continuing to discuss random topics. She could feel the tension between them building now that Lucy and Cooper had left them alone. They'd been such a welcome distraction from the building desire she seemed to have for Dane.

He reached over and put his hand on her knee. "I'm going to grab another beer," he said. She heard the words but could only focus on the feeling of his palm on her bare knee. "Actually, why don't we both grab a beer and take a walk?" he suggested.

"Okay," she quickly answered, her resolve dissipating.

Taking her hand, he led her to a tub filled with beer on one of the nearby benches. They selected their beverages and turned to walk along the river.

The Cherry Creek River was a main tributary of Lake Paramount. It was quite large and provided a generous sandy bank. They chatted and sipped, enjoying the night air, walking until the sound of the party faded in the distance. Dane sat down, placing the beer on the ground. He tugged Nora's hand, directing her to sit on his lap. "I wouldn't want you to sit on the cold sand in your skirt," he said.

"Oh, thanks," she replied.

He placed his arm around her and pulled her so her back was up against his chest. She reached over and set her beer next to his. He pulled her hair away from her ear, proceeding to kiss and nibble at her lobe. Goosebumps began to spread as her flesh reacted.

Gently he tugged at her hair to position her mouth next to his before kissing her.

She melted. He had her. Pleased with his latest find, he placed both hands on her thighs and began to run them over her knees. It was chilly and his palms felt hot on her cool skin. He reached under her skirt and put pressure on each thigh. Now she sat straddled over his legs, his hands exploring beneath her accessible skirt. *I love these naive girls*, he thought as he manipulated her, getting her into position for his deed. *Sex has such power over them.*

The Point

What am I doing, Nora asked herself as Dane helped himself. It was an out-of-body experience; she was on the outside watching as he had his way with her.

She worried what was next. *I've never moved this fast before*. This time she'd thrown caution to the wind, with a total disregard for safety.

She stood up and began to gather her things; the pangs of shame were now rolling in. Dane turned her around and began to gently brush sand off her bare bottom. "You were incredible."

"I've never had an experience like that before," she confessed.

"You did have an innocence about you," he agreed. "Let's get dressed; I'm going to take you home with me."

She was relieved. The worry that he'd just wanted to dine and dash began to fade. She pulled on her clothes and took his hand.

He was sure to coddle her delicate psyche on the journey to his house. He knew all too well that she was a flight risk. Nora wasn't the first nice girl he'd taken advantage of; they were prone to come to their senses and flee. He'd perfected the dance over the years, sex them up, then make them feel appreciated; *they just don't want to feel like they've done something smarmy.*

"You're a wonderful girl, so tender and loving," he reached over and rubbed her cheek. "I can't wait to get you home and treat you right."

Nora was skeptical. *Is this for real? Is this how real men talk to women?*

She thought about her father and how he talked to her mother.

I guess it isn't too different than Dad...

Chapter 6

The east side, she thought as they pulled into his driveway, *home is just a few blocks away.* Although she considered bailing, running home as soon as the car came to a stop, that thought proved fleeting as he sweet-talked her, unknowingly (well, as far as she knew) convincing her to stay.

Dane's house was on the northeast side of town, two blocks from the city beach. It was a Craftsman with richly colored cream trim and new siding designed to look like cedar shakes. He led her up the stairs and through the front door. The house was beautiful.

"I had it completely remodeled," he explained. "It was dated when I bought it—gold appliances, shag carpet, the whole thing." Now it was a nod to modern decorating, with sleek lines and neutral colors.

"Looks like a magazine photo in here," she said, complimenting him. "Just like your cousin's house." Cooper's place had been spectacular as well.

Dane nodded in compliance with her observation as he led her toward the bathroom, not wanting to pause for conversation. He wasn't interested in talking about his fine taste in home design; he was interested in something else entirely.

Nora was in awe of the bathroom's beauty. It was a brilliant white. Tumbled marble covered the floor and white subway tiles ran the perimeter of the room. There was a pedestal tub on the left wall and an espresso brown vanity with two vessel sinks on the opposite side. On the

The Point

back wall was a walk-in shower. It was magnificent. The shower had travertine-lined walls and a stone basin.

"Wow," she exclaimed. "This is where you broke the bank."

"Never mind that, let's get you out of those dirty clothes and rinsed off."

He guided her to the center of the room; then guided her out of her clothes. He pulled off his shirt as he walked toward the shower to turn it on.

"Please, get in." He offered, his hand gently guiding her.

Stepping under the falling water, she tipped her head back rinsing her hair.

He stood before her in all his glory, watching as the water ran freely through her long golden tendrils. "Turn around," he commanded.

"Why?"

"Trust me."

After some fidgeting, there was a lovely fragrance combined with the feeling of his hands in her hair. He gently massaged her scalp as he shampooed. He spun her, forcing her to face him. Now disoriented, and her balance lost, he reached behind her. Grasping her rear firmly, he pushed his tongue into her mouth and her back against the wall of the shower. The force drove the small of her back into the travertine.

"Oh." She tried to voice her discomfort, but his mouth was locked firmly onto hers, her complaint unnoticed.

Looking at the pain on her face he held tight, forcing her to the shower floor.

He finished his carnal task before apologizing. "Oh, did I hurt you?"

"You pushed a little hard at the end there," she explained.

"Did I? I'm so sorry."

He knew he'd hurt her, and that's what pleased him.

She was shivering; the hot water was being deflected by Dane's back. He stood and reached down assisting Nora to her feet.

"I feel a bit wobbly," she admitted. "Too much excitement, I guess."

"I best get you to bed then." He reached out of the shower and retrieved plush white, towels. After wrapping her in one, and himself in the other, he wandered to his bedroom. She followed with some apprehension, her arms tucked inside of the towel for warmth. "I'm ssssso ccccold," she shivered, her bottom lip trembling wildly.

"Get in, I'll keep you warm." Dane dropped his towel and climbed into the bed. He lifted the covers, motioning to the spot next to him. Nora sat on the edge, struggling to scoot in elegantly while wrapped in the towel.

Finally, she flung the damp towel onto the floor and settled next to him. He turned on his side, pulling her back to his chest. He wrapped her up in his arms, the cold slipping away as his warmth surrounded her. Just as she began to relax, she felt a pang of guilt as her mind wandered to Jake. *Maybe he's holding someone else,* she thought.

Although she felt a powerful attraction to Dane, she now felt awkward next to him, out of place. It was the same feeling she would get when she was at sleepovers as a child. Unfortunately, Mom wasn't around to save her from this uncomfortable situation.

"Is everything alright?" he probed as she began to pull away.

"Just thinking that I should go home," she answered.

"Are you uncomfortable?" he asked, squeezing her a little tighter. She was surprised by his observation. "Why don't we get up and have a snack?" he suggested.

"Okay," she answered.

He climbed out of bed and crossed the room, his bare behind ghostly in the dim light. He entered the rather generous closet, closing the door behind him, obscuring her view of its contents.

This was the inner sanctum, the one place he never let people stray. His closet was sacred, only he was allowed to cross its threshold.

He ran his hand over the wide bar pulls as he made his way to the proper set of drawers. He donned fresh undergarments, admiring the perfectly starched crease in his shorts, before procuring something to lend to his latest piece.

He kept a drawer of old items he would allow girls to wear should the need arise.

He returned dressed in a crisp white T-shirt and the boxers.

"Here you go, my favorites," he lied, keeping the illusion alive.

"Thanks, these look comfy." She pulled on the *favorite* sleeping clothes of her hot admirer, gullibly eating up every situation he fed her, slipping ever deeper into his trap.

Rubbing her arms she basked, enjoying the way it felt to be inside of his shirt. She slipped into the pants, pulling the drawstring tight, before hiking up the legs.

The clothes hung loosely on her petite frame, but she was glad to be warm.

She followed him to the kitchen, the shirt's long sleeves dangling at her sides, the pant legs puddled at her feet.

The kitchen was small but well equipped. Two chrome stools sat at the granite island, facing a small television, which was mounted on the wall by the refrigerator. He pointed to the flat screen and asked, "How about some TV?"

"Mmm-hmm," she nodded in agreement. He turned on sports highlights, not her favorite but she still felt relieved. Sleepover anxiety at Grandma's house had always been alleviated by a snack and late night TV.

Funny, she thought with a shrug, *now a grown woman, and that still seems to be the remedy.*

"What should we eat?" he asked.

"P.B. and J," Nora answered. She was smiling, finally feeling a little better.

"Excellent choice," agreed Dane.

They sat in the kitchen, talking and sharing stories. It was effortless. They compared favorite ice cream flavors and discussed books they had and hadn't read.

"Tell me about your family, what are they like?" she asked.

"Let's not talk about me, I want to focus on you." He smiled, dodging the subject.

Nora talked about Lucy and childhood and happy times. Dane shared anecdotes involving Cooper and their youth. He avoided talking about his mother and father, and she left out sad stories of her mother's passing. Without realizing it, they talked through the night. The

The Point

light of the breaking dawn started to peek through the Roman shade on the kitchen window.

"It's morning," she said with disbelief. "I can't believe we stayed up all night talking."

"Time flies when you're having fun," he offered generically.

"I should get going, my father will worry." Nora knew her father wasn't expecting her, but she was ready to go, and a worried father seemed like a fine excuse.

She headed toward the bathroom to get back into her own clothes. She hung Dane's sweats on a hook behind the bathroom door.

"Do you need a ride?" he called from the kitchen.

She did dread walking home the six blocks in the chilly May morning. "That would be great."

He led her out to the garage, making sure to keep contact, his hand placed gently on the small of her back.

"I didn't know you had another car," she said, admiring its beauty.

"This is my sexy car," He explained. "The truck is for every day, this is for important occasions."

"Why didn't you drive the *sexy* car to the party?"

"Cooper lives out in the woods—too many chances for damage to occur with the dirt roads and branches."

He escorted her to the passenger side door and helped her in. "The truck is good, but after last night, you deserve to ride in this car all the time."

Dane closed the door and made his way to the driver's side, sickened by how cheesy that last line was. He cringed, *she probably saw right through that one*. He jumped in and surveyed her face for a reaction to his bullshit. Instead, she was looking out of the window at all of the gym equipment in his garage.

It wasn't just a few weights lined up with the tools; the garage was finished like a professional gym. The walls were painted, and mirrors were hung parallel to the lifting station. There was a large flat screen mounted in the back corner and a water cooler next to a small fridge recessed in the wall.

"This is quite the setup," she stated as she motioned to the equipment.

"I like to work out," Dane said as he sat back in his seat, relieved that she was distracted.

"Doesn't it get cold in the winter?" she asked.

"Not at all. When the doors are closed, the electric heater keeps it pretty warm. Plus, once you get movin' you don't feel the chill, if there is one."

"You must be really dedicated to fitness."

"That's how you get guns like this," Dane said as he kissed both of his biceps while flexing.

She laughed at his antics. He smiled as he backed out of the garage, relieved she was smitten enough to let his bullshit slide.

The drive to her house was a quick one. She lived on the same side of town, just six blocks south. He pulled into the driveway. "Beautiful house," he said, looking up through the windshield.

"My mother loved old houses, she fixed it up herself."

"Huh," he replied, with a distant look in his eyes. "You don't say." She smiled at him. "I want to see you again. I think we might have something here," he admitted, surprising her with his openness.

"Thanks for everything, last night was amazing," she said shyly, wringing the handle on her bag.

The Point

She reached for his phone, which was resting on the center console. She entered her cell number and placed the phone in his hand before leaving the car. "See you later," she said, closing the car door.

Nora waved as Dane pulled out of the driveway. She walked around to the back door and stepped into the kitchen. The Kit-Kat clock was swinging his smug tail over the stove. "Don't judge me," Nora said to the Kat, her finger pointed at its bouncing eyes.

She went to her room and climbed into bed, shoes and all. Badger was there waiting, happy to see her and eager to join her under the covers. Looking up at the ceiling, she contemplated the events of the night before, realizing she felt torn and confused by her feelings for Jake and her passion for Dane. Nora was unaware that she was ignoring the subtle signs of trouble he'd unintentionally provided. She reached for her phone, eyeing Jake's name on her contacts list. She missed him. Guilt began to swell.

"I should just call," she said to herself.

Without another thought she touched his name, and the phone began to ring.

"You've reached Jake, leave a message."

Chapter 7

She kept Jake tucked in the back of her mind, her loneliness masked by the company she was keeping with Dane.

Two weeks had passed and the budding relationship seemed to consist of brief phone calls and intensely physical escapades, which *were* great. *Who doesn't like rolling around on the beach in the dark,* Nora thought as she stirred milk into her Darjeeling. Her hand continued to blend, the spoon clinking slowly and methodically against the bottom of the ceramic cup. She stared blankly into the rolling eyes of the Kit-Kat clock. *He makes me feel incredible when we're together, but I feel so empty when it's over...I need substance.* She stopped stirring, realizing she'd drifted off.

"Why are you always judging me?" she snapped at the smug plastic feline, her stirring hand now jabbing the spoon in its direction.

The Kat continued to arbitrate, his tail wagging with a tsk-tsk, like the finger of a grandmother in mid-scold.

"I know, I know," she conceded to the ticking custodian, her conscience burdened by the sins of her flesh. *I need to stop being such a slut,* she thought, unwilling to say that out loud (especially in front of the Kat).

"I just need to talk to him...clear this whole situation up."

Nora set the cup in the sink and grabbed her keys. "Be back soon," she assured Badger, who was licking crumbs from under the table. "And keep an eye on that

The Point

Kat until I get back," she ordered, with her thumb pointing in the clock's direction.

"We'll continue this when I get back," she stated to the Kat with rebuke, her palm flat and moving in a circular motion, a gesture meant to clarify what *this* encompassed.

She was still thinking about the cold, rolling eyes of the Kit-Kat clock as she rounded the block to Dane's house. Her mother had found that clock in one of the local shops. "Don't you just love the curious look on his face?" she asked, like she already knew the answer. "Its like he sees and knows all."

Nora grinned as she pulled up to Dane's house. The driveway was filled to capacity, forcing her to find a spot on the street. The memory of her mother's whimsical nature was still fresh in her mind as she negotiated her way through the assortment of cars and pickups. She knocked on the door and was greeted by an unfamiliar male face.

"Can I help you?" asked the rather rotund fellow at the door.

"Yeah, I'm Nora, I'm here to see Dane."

"Dane!" The guy shouted from the front door, "Nora's here."

She stood on the porch looking into the crowd, while the rotund fellow peered down her blouse. Dane waved her in, a beer bottle gripped in his hand. "Come on in," he invited, his bottle pointing the way.

She stepped in, and the peeping doorman closed up behind her, now admiring her ass as she walked into the room. He nodded to Dane. A nod that said, "Nice piece of ass." Dane gave a subtle nod back, which meant, "I know."

Nora was unaware of the signaling going on between Dane and his friend. She was all too aware that all eyes were on her. *Great!* She thought, *ogled by ten guys in matching sports garb.* She gave a little wave then nervously smoothed the back of her hair. They quickly got their fill and returned to sipping their beer and watching the game between conversations.

"I really need to talk to you," she said, her resolve dissipating as she stepped closer to him.

"Alright," he answered, grabbing her hand to lead her through the living room.

"What's going on today?" she asked as she looked over at the gathering of testosterone.

"The Cubs are playing, so the guys are over."

"That would explain the hat." She pointed to the blue baseball cap atop Dane's head; a red "C" was embroidered on the front. He removed it, and used it to gesture toward the hall.

She followed him into his room and plunked her ass heavily onto the bed. *How to approach this*, she wondered, *just spit it out I guess*.

He strolled over and parked himself next to her, curious what was next.

"What's on your mind?" he asked, helping her along.

"When I left school," she began, "I was involved with someone. I thought I loved him, and he said he would miss me, but I haven't heard from him since. I wanted him to tell me how he felt, where we stood, what our relationship meant to him. He never did." She paused to catch her breath and maybe gather some more nerve. She snatched the beer bottle from his hand and guzzled some liquid courage, hoping it would wash down the

The Point

lump in her throat. "Now I find myself tangled up with you, and this morning I realized that our time together might just be physical... shallow." She winced when she said the word shallow. *Shit, it hadn't sounded as harsh in my head.*

Dane had sat and listened quietly to her. He reached over and placed his hand on her knee. "I've relished every moment, Nora. I'm hooked."

He had enjoyed the last two weeks with her. She was easily charmed and fantastically fuckable. He already knew her type: the good girl tripped up by the urge to give into desire. He'd been waiting for Nora to show her particular weakness, and here it was: she was looking for a man to declare his love. Fantastic.

Women were just playthings. He didn't have a great deal of respect for the fairer sex; in fact, none at all, thanks to the volatile upbringing his mother had provided. Dane could never trust a woman to get what was in his guts, so he just used them up and moved on.

He liked to play games and, in this moment, decided Nora had dealt him a winning hand. He gazed deeply into her eyes. *If you only knew what I have in store for you, he thought. I better gain your trust, better turn on the charm.*

"I have treasured this time we've shared. You're an incredible girl."

Dane was always generous with his compliments. He found that charm and flattery often led girls to do things, or put up with things they usually wouldn't. He wanted her to feel like she was the most beautiful woman he had ever seen, always commenting on how her hair moved in the breeze or the way her skin looked in certain light.

Keep her distracted; string her along, his little voice reminded him. He scooted closer, rubbing her thigh. "My feelings for you have grown these last few weeks. I might be falling in love with you," he said with a pout, his eyes looking up from under his brow.

Overcome, she hadn't realized how she'd longed to hear those words. He leaned in and kissed her, pulling her close to him, his embrace engulfing her. She suddenly felt safe, loved. She held him, kissing him deeply, passionately. He slowly guided her so they were lying on the bed; he gazed intently at her.

"I hope you feel the same about me?" he asked in a hushed tone, his lips brushing hers.

"I think I do," she whispered.

He gently pressed his lips upon hers, softer than he ever had before.

Dane seemed so tender in this moment, so vulnerable. "I love the way it feels to make love to you."

She was swept away.

He knew she was hooked. *The naive ones always fall the hardest*, he thought as she pushed herself against him with an all-too-familiar longing. He could feel the desire in her body language. *Gotcha*, he thought, as he took control and took what he wanted.

He held her, stroking her cheek in this quiet moment of manipulation. Sex was a powerful tool, and he knew it.

A knock at the bedroom door broke the silence. "Hey, are you coming back out, you're missing the game."

"Be right out," Dane yelled at the door.

She'd been so preoccupied with the situation, she had completely forgotten about the living room filled with his friends. He hopped up and began putting on his

The Point

clothes. His demeanor quickly shifted from loving partner to one of the guys.

"Oh my God," she uttered with embarrassment. "What'll your friends think? I don't wanna do the walk of shame."

"You have nothing to be ashamed of. You're my girl, not some frat-house floozy. Besides, they don't know what we were doing. Maybe we were just having an important conversation," Dane reasoned as he zipped his pants.

She was thrilled to hear him call her his girl. *Is this what love really feels like? Maybe I hadn't loved Jake at all.* Love or not, she knew she liked the feeling of being recognized by Dane.

She put herself back together, trying not to let her thoughts wander toward Jake at this crucial juncture.

Grabbing her hand just as she reached for the door handle, he stayed in character, "I meant what I said, sweet tits. You're my girl."

She loved to hear him say those words. (*Maybe not the sweet tits part*, but the open recognition of their attachment (although playful pet names *were* a bonus).

As they entered the front room, some of the guys turned and looked. For the second time today, all eyes were on her. She knew *they knew*. Dane was standing behind her. He placed his finger to his lips, gesturing to his pals to keep quiet. He stood behind her, air-thrusting his pelvis and performing other rude gestures involving his tongue and two fingers.

The guys looked on with amusement as she stood smiling nervously into the crowd, unaware that Dane was behind her miming dirty details to his friends. One of the guys distracted her by starting a conversation. "So Nora, how long have you two lovebirds been an item?"

"We just met really, dating off and on for a few weeks."

The friend smiled. Suddenly his glance darted over her shoulder, causing her to turn and look. Just as she shifted to try and see what had caught his attention, Dane stopped his shenanigans and crossed his arms at his chest. He cleared his throat and made the introductions.

"Nora, these are the guys, and guys, this is Nora." She blushed, overwhelmed by his focus on her. "She's my girl," he added.

I will never be tired of hearing that, she thought. He had her take a seat on the sofa next to the gangly fellow who had started the conversation to distract her while Dane was gesturing. "My name is Matt, by the way," he said.

"Hi, Matt," she returned.

Morning transitioned to afternoon. The beer was flowing like wine, and Nora was enjoying chatting with Dane's friends. She'd learned that Matt, the gangly one, and Brian, the rotund one, were his best friends from high school. Most of the other guys were friends of friends, or members of the fantasy ball club. Dane hadn't really mentioned his friends or family before; it was nice to finally see this side of him.

The day wore on, and one by one the guys left. Soon the house was empty. She began cleaning up. Dane grabbed her, hugging her from behind. "It feels right having you here, doing domestic things for me," he said as he reached down and smacked her ass.

She smiled as she reached back to rub her stinging cheek.

The Point

"I need you to clean up the kitchen for me. I got up early to host this get together and now I'm a little drunk and tired. You clean while I rest," he commanded.

"Where are the mop and broom kept?" she asked, agreeing without complaint or question. Telling her where to find the supplies, Dane smiled; she was working out well.

She went to work while he went down to his room. He left the door open so he could listen to her move about the kitchen, sweeping and mopping. After half an hour he went to inspect her work.

Standing behind her in the kitchen doorway, he leaned on the wall. Pointing to the corner by the stove he hassled her, "You better clean it again; I can see some dirt in that corner."

She ran the mop into the corner once more.

"It's still dirty. Get down on your hands and knees and scrub it," he ordered.

That was the limit. Shooting him a look, she snapped back, "I think it's as clean as it's going to get."

Dane had found her threshold for the day.

"I'm not a fifties housewife who scrubs on command and obeys her man."

"Life's short. You have to take what you want when you want it, no hesitation," he said with certainty.

"Are you *sure* you want me?" Her head bobbed as she shifted her weight to the other foot.

"I already have you," he replied coldly, his tone absolute.

Dane pushed her toward the sofa. She landed on her rear end with a bounce, the springs squeaking in protest. Kneeling down, he crept toward her. He grabbed the bottom cuff of her shorts and pulled.

He lifted her up and flipped her around. She found herself on all fours, facing the arm of the sofa, the brown tweed just inches from her nose.

"Woo! You're wearing me out!" Dane exclaimed as he tossed his head back.

She glanced at him from over her shoulder, "I doubt that very much."

Dane took what he wanted, then brought her to the bathroom where they soaked in the tub and talked.

"What are your parents like?" she asked. "You haven't talked about them."

"That isn't important."

"Of course it is," she pressed.

"My parents are great, they have been together forever. There isn't much to tell." Dane glossed over the details. His parent's relationship was twisted and difficult, and his relationship with his mother was miserable.

"That's nice to hear," she said, pushing bubbles toward Dane.

He smiled, his toothy grin guarding the ugly truth.

"My parents were very much in love. They fought sometimes but they always seemed closer afterward. Dad was lost when Mom first died, but he's better now." She sighed, the memory of her father's pain still fresh in her mind. "I hope to find the same happiness my parents found someday," she admitted.

Ignoring her admission, he tried to change the subject. "Does your dad get out and chase the ladies?"

"Dad doesn't date, although I wish he had someone. He said Mom was the only fish in his sea."

Dane smiled, thinking that any fish was better than no fish.

The Point

"Why the grin?" she asked, playfully splashing in his direction.

"Just thinking how cute you are when you talk about your parents," he fibbed, suddenly aware that his thought might not be well accepted.

Tiring of the small talk, he wanted to steer her toward a more physical activity. He began sliding his hands over her thighs under the bath water. The bubbles made the water viscous, allowing his hands to slip freely over her skin. She tipped her head back, the edge of the tub pressing into her neck.

He got up, resting on his knees. She opened her eyes, her curiosity stirred by the jostling of the bath water.

"Lie back, and close your eyes, sweet tits."

She did as he requested with a smirk, her pet name still amusing.

He continued caressing her, his left hand now positioned to pleasure her while she leaned back, with her arms resting on the rim of the tub.

Dane rubbed himself vigorously, straightening his thighs, getting as close to her as he could without her sensing the further shift in position.

"Keep your eyes closed," he commanded. "No peeking."

She squeezed them shut tighter, the focus of her attention on the hand he had between her legs not the one he had between his. Unaware he was pleasuring himself, she arched her back, ready to cross the finish line. He sat back quickly, the water surging, rinsing away any evidence that he'd raced her and won.

"No more," she stated as she was drying off. "No more for today. I might need some ice as it is," she motioned, a pained look on her face.

"At least I know I've left you satisfied," he said, secretly pleased with her discomfort.

"You weren't satisfied this time," she said, running her finger down his chest toward his navel.

"I love watching you; that's satisfaction enough." He was pleased. He'd played his naughty game and won, and she was none the wiser.

"I should head home. I didn't tell my dad I'd be staying out, and maybe he should meet you before I start sleeping over."

"I want to meet him soon. Tomorrow, if possible," Dane ordered.

She was happy that he was anxious to move their relationship forward. "I'll give you a call tomorrow and set a time for dinner."

He saw her to the door and gave her a deep, slow kiss (always playing his angle). "See you tomorrow," he called as she headed to the Rover. She turned and smiled, blowing him a little kiss.

She had butterflies in her stomach as she pulled out of the driveway. Finally, love.

Chapter 8

Perhaps it's a stomach bug, she thought as she hurried to the bathroom, a sharp pain running the length of her right side. Nora tried to pass whatever was ailing her for several minutes, "Ow, ow, ow," she stammered. "Crushed glass, I'm peeing crushed glass." After dabbing her bottom with tissue she stood to flush. "Oh my God," she uttered. To her horror, she found the bowl stained red.

~~~

The ER was quiet.

"Sunday morning is definitely the right time to find yourself at the hospital." Nora commented to her father as she looked around the empty waiting room.

"Fill in this section," the nurse instructed, while pointing to a highlighted area with the capped end of a ballpoint pen. Nora collected the clipboard and the pen.

"The doctor will see you shortly," the nurse assured her before scurrying from the waiting area. Nora sat with her father at her side. Glancing up from the paperwork, she glimpsed a worried look on her father's face. *I haven't seen that look since Mom was sick,* she thought.

"I'm sure it's nothing serious," she comforted, trying to put her father at ease.

Changing the subject she said, "I wanted to tell you, I've been seeing the guy I met at the cemetery. He'd like to join us for dinner. I wanted to arrange that for today, but..." Nora motioned, pointing to the clipboard, making the point that plans had changed due to the current circumstances.

Her father smiled. "Glad to hear you've found someone." His grin was weakened by the worry on his face.

Just as they started to discuss the new man in her life the nurse called, "Nora Reynolds." Nora looked around the room, entertained by the fact that the nurse called out to her as though she were sitting in a crowded waiting area.

She got up, patted her dad's hand and said, "I'll be right back."

Nora handed over the clipboard and stood amused as the nurse contorted her face in a series of strangely contemplative gestures. Nora tried not to grin as this very thorough, and clearly enthusiastic health-care professional inspected the form. When the nurse had finally finished scouring the contents of the clipboard, she tucked Nora into her room. She waited only briefly before a young doctor popped in. She was in her early thirties, slender, with a polished conservative look to her. Her hair was sandy in color, and bobbed just below her jaw. It was parted far to the right and tucked tightly behind her left ear.

"Hello, I'm Dr. Smith," the physician said, holding out her hand in a professional manner.

Nora shook the good doctor's hand, pleased that she was a woman.

"What seems to be the problem this morning?" the doctor inquired.

"I woke up with this pain in my side," she explained as she traced the area with her hand. "And there was blood in my urine."

"I see," replied the doctor. "Are you still in pain now?"

The Point

"Yes," she answered. "The pain runs down my right side and ends around here," Nora again explained by motioning, pointing toward her pelvis.

"Have you been sexually active recently?" Dr. Smith asked.

"Yes," she answered shyly.

"Could be a urinary tract infection but the pain usually isn't so severe. Let's run some tests, including a pregnancy test, just to figure out what we're dealing with."

"I can't be pregnant. I take the pill…I just had my period?"

"Did your partner use a condom every time?"

"No, not every time. We were caught up, we didn't even think about it," she replied honestly.

"Nothing is one hundred percent, Miss Reynolds, and sometimes a seemingly benign action can interfere with birth control's effectiveness. I think we should screen for sexually transmitted diseases as well."

Dr. Smith turned to a computer kiosk nestled in the corner. She typed swiftly, ordering tests and making notes. She must have sent a message to the comically serious nurse, because she returned ready to take action. She moved about the room, preparing trays and opening and closing cupboard doors; every movement performed measured with purpose.

After Nora had provided all necessary samples, she stretched out on the table. Focusing on the fluorescent lights, she prayed for a negative pregnancy test while the doctor took a look below to make sure things were okay.

"Alright," The doctor said as she removed her rubber gloves with a snap, "We're all finished, everything looks fine. I'll come back when the tests are in."

"How you doing, hon?" William asked his daughter as he peeked his head into the open door.

"Alright, just waiting now, you can come in and wait with me?"

William shuffled in, sitting in the corner. He was happy to be closer to the situation and no longer left wondering and waiting alone.

She cringed as another wave of pain stabbed through her side. Her father stood in reaction to her discomfort. "I'm alright, Dad, just a spasm, it stopped already." He returned to his seat. "What the hell taking so long? They always keep you waiting."

Time had come to a standstill. Nora and her father sat silently. The sound of the industrial clock over the door ticked, its clicking cutting through the stale air in the sterile room. They'd been lulled into a trance, both staring blankly at the shifting hands of the noisy clock.

Dr. Smith burst through the door, "You have a kidney infection."

Nora looked to her father and was glad the doctor hadn't come through the door and announced she had an STD with that much enthusiasm.

"How will that need to be treated?" Nora asked, still a bit startled by the good doctor's entrance.

"Hospitalization and observation," answered Dr. Smith. "We'll give IV antibiotics and something for the pain. At least one night, it'll give us a chance to make sure the infection is clearing and not the result of something more serious."

The doctor could tell by the look on William's face that he was racked with worry. "Your daughter will be fine," the doctor added, trying to put him at ease.

The Point

After transferring her to a room on the third floor, her father skipped home for some pajamas and magazines. Once he was off she called the nurse.

"Could you please tell me the results of the *pregnancy test*?" For some reason she couldn't say those two words out loud. Instead they slipped through her lips in a whisper.

"I'll check your chart." The nurse lifted the clipboard off the foot of her bed, while lifting her eyebrows in response to Nora's need to whisper.

"*Negative,*" the nurse whispered.

Nora was so relieved. "Oh, thank God," she sighed, rubbing her forehead. With that peace of mind came the realization that she'd left Dane hanging. He was probably wondering why she hadn't called. Fumbling around at the end of the bed, she tried to reach the plastic bag of belongings packed by the nurse downstairs. Finally snagging the handle of her purse, she pulled it toward her. She had started looking for Dane's number in her contacts when the phone rang.

"Hello," she answered.

"It's about time," Dane said with some frustration. "I thought you were ignoring me." His irritation didn't come from worry that something might have happened to this girl he was supposed to love, but that he didn't want to be ignored when he was expecting attention.

"I woke up this morning in need of a trip to the hospital. I have a kidney infection," she said, trying to explain.

"Are you all right? Is it serious?" He asked, trying to play the part of the concerned boyfriend and conceal his previous irritation.

"It's probably the result of a urinary tract infection gone wrong from all of the sex we've been having."

"What room are you in?"

She gave Dane all the pertinent info before he ended the call with, "I'm on the way." He hung up feeling like he'd really sold her his feelings of concern with the *I'm on the way* bit.

He was right. She was touched by the amount of concern she heard in his voice.

William walked in and interrupted her daydream.

"Dane just called, said he was on his way."

"I look forward to meeting this new fellow of yours."

She smiled at her dad. William Reynolds had a soothing way about him. Just the presence of her father was comforting. Her mother used to say that it was his best quality.

Nora was nodding off, her hand snugly tucked in her father's, when Dane turned the corner into her room. He walked right past her father, who was camped by the window in an uncomfortable vinyl chair.

Rushing over, he kissed her on the mouth. "How're you doing, S.T.?" he asked with a wink.

She grinned, knowing S.T. were the initials for a pet name best not said out loud in front of her dad.

"A kidney infection, apparently, can be very painful," explained Nora.

"What's the plan?" he asked, managing to sound sincerely concerned.

"Well, antibiotics and observation is what the doctor said. Oh, and pain medication," she slurred as she pointed to the fresh IV hanging over the bed. She was awake and interacting but did so while lying very limply. She would

The Point

raise her hands, only to let them drop heavily as though she had no command of her own muscles.

"That would explain your relaxed state," he joked.

He turned to Nora's father. "Dane Buchman," he introduced himself, while firmly shaking William's hand.

"William Reynolds," Nora's father said, looking Dane firmly in the eye.

"Great to finally meet you," Dane said emphatically, knowing the fun with Nora could really begin now that he had the dad in his back pocket as well.

Her father sat back down, sizing Dane up all the while.

They sat watching while she slipped in and out of consciousness, sedated by the powerful pain reliever being delivered intravenously. The nurse came in regularly to check vitals and help her to the bathroom. The day ticked by.

Finally, visiting hours were at an end. "I guess I'll get going." William kissed his daughter on the forehead. "Good night, my dear. See you tomorrow."

"Good night, Dad. I love you."

"Love you too," he returned with a sincerely loving smile on his face. Dane observed, turned off by the disgusting display of emotion, as well as fascinated by the ease with which this man mustered such sincerity. William started for the door. He turned back and wished Dane a good evening. "I hope we can get together for dinner soon," he added as he departed. "Oh, and take good care of my daughter."

Her father gave her a wave and left the room.

"I thought he'd never leave," Dane said with a hint of contempt.

"Why did he need to leave?" she asked, perplexed by Dane's tone, wondering if she'd imagined it.

He dodged her observation, redirecting with something distracting.

"I've never had sex in a hospital. I thought it might be fun."

"I don't think I'm feeling up to it," she said, surprised he would ask.

"What if I close the curtain and you just give me a handy?" he asked while pulling the curtain closed around her bed.

He walked up to the gurney's edge and began to undo his pants. She slapped at Dane's zipper with her limp hand and said, "You're such a joker, Dane."

Dane wasn't joking. He had thrown it out there to see if she would bite. Since she didn't, he figured he'd leave and find his entertainment elsewhere.

"I'll come back tomorrow after work." He kissed her and headed for the door. He left, disappointed that she was too out of it to help him check his *"sex in a hospital"* box but knew he could round up some tail at one of the local bars to stave off his craving. *There's always some townie out at the pub looking for the attention of a handsome guy,* he assured himself.

As he contemplated which bar to pick up his evenings entertainment from, Nora drifted off, feeling fortunate to have two incredible men in her life.

The night slowly ebbed. Beeping, rumbling, shuffling: the night had been filled with interruptions, from vitals' checks to hospital noise. "How do they expect you to get any rest around here," she grumbled as she covered her head with the pillow, the protective plastic barrier crunching from under the pillowcase.

The Point

"TV is all that can save me now," she decided as she flipped through the few available channels. The shows stacked up as the night moved along, eventually flickering unwatched as Nora drifted off.

"Good morning," a cheery voice greeted while pulling open the pale green hospital drapes. "I have your breakfast here, do you need to use the restroom?"

Lifting her heavy lids, she nodded at the pleasant nurse who then helped her to her feet. She grumbled as she shuffled to the restroom. "It's too early."

She dropped her bottoms and sat. "Holy shit!" she squealed.

"You okay in there?" the nurse asked with her cheerful tone.

"Yeah, just chilly in here," Nora replied. Propping herself up, she levitated over the toilet seat, its surface too cold to comfortably support her cheeks. She peed, a shiver coursing through her body. *Hope that went better today,* she thought as she stood to flush. There had still been some pain, but the blood had cleared. Things were heading in the right direction.

William arrived, filled with anxiety over the health of his daughter. He couldn't help worrying that she would come in here for some seemingly simple ailment and discover that she was actually going to die. *It happens,* he thought as he rode the elevator to his daughter's floor. *It happened to my Elizabeth; she was weak and tired. When the coughing started we thought she had the flu.*

William's heavy thoughts followed him as he walked the hallway. By the time he arrived at his daughter's room, he was riddled with anxiety. He was sure he would enter the room to find her clinging to life.

"Hey Dad," she called as he entered. She smiled widely as she waved him in. He had to choke back tears of relief as he wrapped his precious girl in his arms.

"Good to see you feeling better," he said as he patted her on the back, taking a moment to compose himself before releasing her from his embrace.

She filled him in on the progress, unaware of how close to breakdown he'd just been.

The doctor made an appearance late that morning, finally uttering the words they'd wanted to hear. "You're being discharged."

"And everything is alright?" William inquired, wanting to know that there weren't any surprises hiding, some rare illness lurking, waiting to strike.

"I expect a full recovery," Dr. Smith assured the obviously anxious father. She went on to explain that based on the subsequent test, the infection had been responding to the treatment, "You'll continue with an oral antibiotic for two weeks. You might still experience some discomfort, so I'll include a script for codeine. You're free to go."

"Thank you, Dr. Smith." Nora said, relieved to be on her way.

William sat in the rigid vinyl chair, his limbs dangling loosely. "Well, that shaved a few years off of my life. I thought… You know what, never mind. Let's get you home."

Nora reached over and touched her father's arm. "I'm not going to die. It's just an infection. I'm already getting better." She knew her father had expected the worst.

Her first act upon arriving a home was to call Dane. "This is Dane, leave a message."

"Just got home, call when you can." She hung up and climbed into bed. It felt great to be back. Badger jumped up to commandeer a spot, greeting her enthusiastically. She relaxed, stroking his wiry fur as they both drifted off comfortably.

Chapter 9

Dane pulled his phone from his pocket, the display notifying him of Nora's incoming call. He let it go to voice mail. He was dismayed by her illness only because it cut into his fun. *Perhaps this will help,* he thought as he watched the parcel truck arrive. The office supplies were being delivered, and Beverly was unloading a shipment of paper and toner. He was plotting to take advantage of her. Bev had made deliveries to Dane before and he had often fantasized about bending her over in the back of the delivery truck. He'd had brief conversations with her in the past and knew she was an easy target. He had tested the waters, flirting with Beverly, fishing for weaknesses.

She was deliciously self-conscious, and you could tell by looking at her that she had been around the block. Beverly wasn't particularly attractive but she had muscular legs and an athletic build for a woman in her late thirties. Dane was confident that his good looks would be a welcome treat for this butterface. He stood behind her, admiring her backside. He trolled for an opportunity as he offered to spot her. "Let me help you." She was teetering on a ladder, shifting boxes from the top load.

"So, are you married, Bev?" Dane inquired as he supported her by resting his hand on the back of her leg.

"Divorced," she clipped.

"Sorry to hear that," he replied.

"I'm not sorry, he was a bastard," she declared.

Dane watched Beverly shifting, her muscular legs leading up to her firm behind. He reached up and ran his

The Point

hand up her thigh and under her shorts. Beverly dropped a stack of boxes to the trailer floor and jumped down from the ladder. "What do ya think you're doing?" she asked, her eyes piercing his.

Her tone was direct but not angry. He was pleased by her reaction. He took a chance, hoping she wouldn't flip out. He figured he would just tell her he thought she was falling if she reacted poorly.

"What are you playing at?" Bev asked.

He decided to go for broke; she hadn't freaked out yet. "I was hoping to pull that door shut and bend you over one of these boxes."

Bev looked Dane up and down. She bit her bottom lip as she sized him up. She slowly walked over to the truck doors and pulled them together until just a sliver of daylight was peeking through.

It wasn't as dark as he had hoped, but he was surprised by how quickly she took action. She walked toward him, unbuckling her belt as she waltzed, a hungry look in her eyes. Bev had never had a man as attractive as Dane come onto her before.

"You're a treat, she complimented. "I usually end up with middle-aged divorcees with beer guts and comb-overs. This is an opportunity I just can't pass up." She was hungry for some quality male attention and Dane was the main course.

He suddenly realized that she intended to control the situation and he needed to put an end to that fast. He began undoing his pants as she approached. He tried to be forceful and command Bev to perform. She slid from her shorts and dropped to her knees.

"Impressive," she said as she admired Dane's *gifts*. "I bet you get all of the girls," she cooed. Beverly the truck driver rolled her tongue and blew Dane with a level of expertise he'd never before encountered

"Wow, impressive!" He leaned back, his hand on the top of her head.

She pulled back and wiped her mouth as she stood, an action that spoke volumes about her character. "Sometimes us older gals know tricks the younger ones don't."

Grabbing her, he pushed her against a pallet of printer paper. She leaned in, the shrink-wrap sticking to her bare abdomen as she lifted her shirt out of the way. He hoped his abrupt movements would be shocking to her. Instead, she welcomed them. He moved in, pressing against her back. After gathering her hair, he pulled it, hard. Her head jerked back with a snap.

"You like it rough?" he asked as he looked at his left hand, his fingers entangled in her bleached blonde hair.

"Fuckin' right I do," she answered, with anxious labored breath.

He was surprised by the sincerity of her tone, and he worked hard to punish her for being demanding, every thrust harder than the last.

The friction from her body was causing the shrink-wrap to squeak.

"More," she ordered.

He was tired of her demanding ways. This game wasn't fun anymore. He needed her to submit.

He pulled out and began to jerk off.

"What are you doing?" She tried to turn over but he stopped her, holding her in place by her hair.

"I'm almost done," he uttered. Then with a gasp he climaxed. "I've just delivered my load all over your back," he whispered in her ear. Bev was outraged. She stood up, Dane's *delivery* running down the crack of her ass.

With a twisted, satisfied little smile, he stood back and began pulling himself together.

"Motherfucker!" she exclaimed. "You bent me over and got me all worked up just to jerk off on my back?" She picked up her shorts and began whipping him with them as she chased him out of the truck.

Chapter 10

Noise from the street below wafted through Nora's window on the warm evening breeze. She'd fallen fast asleep when she returned from the hospital and hadn't stirred until now.

She checked her phone. Dane still hadn't returned her call.

She headed downstairs and called for her father.

"Dad."

"I'm in here." Her father's voice drifted from the kitchen. He was standing at the stove, stirring an unidentifiable liquid.

"That's not dinner, is it?" she asked with her nose wrinkled. "It smells like hot garbage."

"No love, it's sealant for the canoe." William smiled at his daughter and pointed to the refrigerator. "There's a sub in there from the grocery deli."

She sat down with her sandwich and a glass of milk. "Why the canoe concoction?" she asked.

"I received a reservation for a trip out to the falls. Fishing and hiking for five days, starting Wednesday. I won't be home until Sunday. I wouldn't usually take a reservation on such short notice but it's a returning customer, big spender from Commerce City," her father explained.

"That's all right, I'll be fine," she said, trying to put her father at ease.

"Ask Lucy to spend some time with you. I don't want you alone while you're sick," her dad suggested.

"I'll find some company," she assured him.

The Point

Nora went out and sat on the porch to call Lucy. She was excited to hear about Nora's budding romance, especially because Dane was the close cousin of her latest catch. Nora was a bit surprised to hear that Cooper was still tickling Lucy's fancy. "He must be quite the guy if he's still holding your interest, Luce."

"I've never been with anyone like him before. He's talented, relentless. My knees shake a little at the thought of it," Lucy confessed.

"I know the feeling," Nora replied.

"I guess Dane has his own gifts then," Lucy inquired, digging for details.

"Yes, he does," Nora answered, smiling at the thought. "Are you able to stay with me a few days this week? My dad has to lead a fishing party out to the falls, and he'd rather I not be alone while recovering."

"I wish I could, but Cooper is taking me out of town for a long weekend. I'm sure Dane will keep you company."

Nora agreed that Dane might be interested in nursing her back to health. She wished Lucy a wonderful weekend and called him.

"How are you this evening?" she asked, pleased to have finally reached him.

"I'm a little tired, lots of digging today. We put in a new row of shrubs at the entrance," he lied. The truth had nothing to do with shrubs. After his adventure with Bev, he closed up shop and had some beer with the guys, anxious to share his story about violating her in the delivery truck.

"My father has to lead a fishing trip this week and doesn't want me to stay alone. I asked Lucy, but she's going out of town with Coop. So, I was hoping you would want the job," she explained.

"Yeah, I could do that," he answered, excited about the prospect of getting her alone for an extended amount of time. "Why don't you just stay at my place?" he suggested, wanting to explore her tolerance for the toys in his trunk.

"Okay, I can pack a bag for Badger and me."

"Who's Badger?"

"He's my little dog," she explained.

"No. No dogs. We better stay at your place," Dane sniped, his lips stretched over his teeth in a gesture of disgust. *There goes the trunk of toys,* he thought. Good thing she couldn't see him; she was already put off by his tone.

I can't believe he was so disgusted, thought Nora. *Could I love someone who doesn't like dogs?*

Dane realized his error by her sudden silence; he could just imagine the look of twisted contemplation crossing the face of his recent plaything.

"Besides I have never been to your house. I would love to see it," he tossed out, trying to defuse the situation. "It looks like your mother must have done an incredible job by how lovely the outside looks."

Still somewhat bothered by Dane's aversion to the dog (but touched by his interest), she tried to focus on his desire to see her home. "You could come over Wednesday after work," she suggested.

"Sounds good," he replied.

Tuesday was uneventful. William put his friend Tom in charge at the shop and spent the day caring for Nora while preparing for his excursion. After dinner father and daughter reclined, rocking in the old porch

The Point

swing, the chain squeaking in time with the dangling of their feet. They talked well into the evening until William decided they both should head up to bed and get some rest. "I'm going to hit the hay and so should you. I have to get up early and head out, and you are sick, my dear," William reminded his daughter.

"I'm not *that* sick, but I could use some rest. It's been a long couple of days," she conceded. They went in and closed up the house, clicking off lights as they worked their way upstairs.

As she sat in bed, her mind raced with thoughts of Dane and Jake and how quickly things had changed for her. She was excited about tomorrow and had a hard time settling down even though she was drowsy from the codeine. Although Dane was currently the man in her life, when she closed her eyes at night, Jake's was still the last face she saw.

Jake had cared for her last semester when she came down with the flu. He took care of everything from feeding to washing. She rarely had to ask for anything; he could preempt any scenario, knowing just what she needed when she needed it.

Nora slept restlessly and awoke to the sound of her father struggling to load the canoe. She pulled on a sweater and slid into her flip-flops before heading outside to assist him.

"Let me grab the other end," she insisted.

William appreciated her help but didn't want her to pull anything, given her recent trip to the hospital.

"I can get it, the last thing I need is you hurting yourself right before I need to leave town," William lectured as he strained to hoist the canoe himself.

"You worry too much, I'm fine," she assured her father, while lifting the opposite end.

"Look at that," she said with that *I told you so* tone in her voice as she tightened the strap holding the canoe in place. "I didn't even chip a nail."

"Dads worry about their girls, give a guy a break." William said, peeking around the tailgate of the truck. Backing away from the vehicle, she nodded in satisfaction with the state of the canoe. After a few more trips back and forth from the shed, crates and packs filled with supplies, William was finally prepared and ready to head out.

"Take it easy, and don't get your name in the paper," Nora told her father before giving him a farewell hug.

"I'm supposed to say that to you," he said with a smile.

"I'll be fine. I'm an adult, remember." She closed the truck door.

"Doesn't matter, all I see is my little girl," William reminded her with a grin.

Nora waved from the porch as her father backed out of the driveway, his truck loaded to the hilt for the fishing excursion ahead. When he was out of sight, she headed back into the house with Badger at her heels. The little dog followed her closely to the kitchen, where she prepared a cup of tea before curling up on the sofa. Nora pulled a cream afghan from the basket under the coffee table and covered her legs.

Badger saw this as an invitation and nudged her hand until she lifted the throw, allowing him to climb under and burrow into her lap. She leaned forward,

The Point

retrieving her cup of tea, and took a big drink to wash down the latest round of pills.

"Yech!" she exclaimed as she coughed, trying to clear her throat of the bitter powder the large chalky tablets had left behind on their way down.

She leaned back onto the sofa, her head resting on its overstuffed cushion. She traced the pattern in the stained glass light fixture with her eyes while thinking about Dane.

"Maybe it will be fun to play house for a few days," she said to Badger while patting him beneath the blanket. He grunted in complaint, not wanting to be bothered while so happily curled beneath the covers.

"Excuse me," she apologized, amused by the attitude of her dear companion.

She shifted, resting her head on the arm of the sofa. Once again causing Badger to sigh with irritation. She reached under the blanket and rubbed his kinky fur while trying to relax. She'd underestimated the toll the kidney infection had taken on her. She was a bit sore.

The day passed slowly, the pace set by watching television and dozing on the couch. Dane finally called to inform her that his arrival time would be around six. "I just have to stop home and grab my stuff."

Nora rushed upstairs. She'd been lounging around all day and didn't want him to see her so disheveled. As she entered the bathroom she was dismayed by her own appearance. "Ugh," she groaned, sticking her tongue out at her reflection. "Oh Nora, how you've let yourself go," she joked.

Her wavy hair had been swept back into a ponytail, which now had been pulled and smashed from sleeping on the sofa. Earlier it was smooth and perky; now it was askew, its many stray hairs protruding in every direction.

The creases in her cheek (left by the throw pillow she'd pressed her face against all afternoon) complimented her *lovely* hairdo.

She made quick work of improving her appearance by smoothing her unruly mane and splashing her face with some cool water. As she exited the bathroom she realized she better tidy up her room. Towels and clothing were strewn carelessly about, along with the many pairs of shoes she'd kicked off and never returned to their proper place, which was the bottom of the grand wardrobe that served as her closet. She straightened out her covers and stuffed all the stray clothes into the hamper. On her way out, she turned and looked back. *How strange it's going to be to share this room with a man,* she thought.

Dane arrived and rang the doorbell. Badger lunged, his head exploding into a shrill and repetitive bark. Something about the sound of the bell flipped a switch in the dog's mind, transforming him into a raving lunatic. Nora walked to the door. Badger was hopping up and down in front of it, barking rapidly. She scooped him up and let Dane in.

"Does it bite?" he asked, pointing his index finger at Badger's snout.

"Not usually," she joked from under one raised eyebrow.

He tentatively reached for the dog. The dog decided to show Dane his teeth. She'd never heard Badger growl so viciously before.

"Badger!" she scolded, giving the little dog an extra squeeze under her arm to try and settle him.

The Point

"He's never acted like that before," she said, trying to reassure Dane. "It's great to see you," she said, leaning forward to give him a kiss while trying to keep her little dog out of biting range.

"Yeah it's good to be here," he issued while eyeing the tiny attack dog.

"Follow me. I'll give you the nickel tour," she motioned with her free hand.

Nora conducted the tour with Badger tucked firmly under her right arm the entire time.

"How cute is this?" Dane said under his breath with a hint of sarcasm while exploring her bedroom. She missed it. She was busy setting Badger down on the bed. She sat beside her little dog stroking his wiry fur, as Dane looked around.

He peered into her on-suite bathroom. "I thought you said your mother redid this house?"

Nora suddenly felt defensive. "She did."

"Why does it still have such old-fashioned fixtures?" he questioned, gesturing toward the bathroom with his thumb.

"She restored the house and tried to stay true to its original beauty. She loved the history of it," Nora explained, her eyebrow raised in annoyance.

Dane continued his inspection, pulling open her bedside drawer. "What does my girl keep in here, I wonder?" he asked in a silly and quizzical tone.

Many things were scattered in the bottom of the drawer: hairpins, rubber bands, tacks, loose change, a fashion magazine, and the compass.

"This isn't an artifact I thought I'd find," he said as he held up the compass.

"It's a family heirloom. I'm the fifth Reynolds to hold it."

"Really," he chimed, unaware that his tone was mocking. Nora continued her story, while trying to read Dane's reaction.

"My father gave it to me after my mother died. I was supposed to get it before I went to college, but I guess he felt death was a larger separation than the separation of going away to school."

"Isn't that precious," he sneered, finding it difficult to be sincere. She hoped his reaction was just the result of discomfort caused by discussing the death of her mother. She took a moment to contemplate his behavior before dismissing it and moving on.

Although a little hurt by his insensitivity about the compass, *not to mention his comments about the house*, she decided that his difference in design tastes and difficulty with death weren't reason enough to find fault with him.

"What're you making?" he asked out of the blue.

"What do you mean?" she asked, uncertain what he was talking about.

"For dinner," he scoffed slightly irritated she wasn't tracking the conversation.

"I wasn't planning to make anything because I haven't felt well," she shot back, surprised that he missed that point.

"What are *you* making?" she asked him sarcastically.

"Takeout!" he exclaimed, frustrated with her and her neediness.

"Ah, our first fight," she giggled, not realizing he was actually irritated.

The Point

Nora smiled and agreed that takeout of some sort would be fine.

After a small discussion, they settled on pizza and sat quietly, watching an old movie while enjoying a slice.

"Are you done?" he asked, as he stood holding his hand out toward her plate.

"Yeah, thanks," she said as she stacked hers on top of his.

Dane brought the plates to the kitchen and dropped them into the sink. He watched as they slipped into the sitting water, coming to rest on other dishes already soaking from earlier.

Inspired, he strolled back to the sofa, his hands clasped behind his back as he schemed. Nora had scooted over and was now leaning on the left arm of the sofa.

Lunging, he pushed her over. He began poking at her as if to tickle her. He smiled devilishly as he pawed at her.

She squirmed off of the couch, and out from under his outstretched arm. She took a left around the coffee table, her hand supporting her sore side.

He tried to snag her legs as she headed for the kitchen.

Taking chase, he followed her. Badger was unpleased, and in hot pursuit of this aggressor, nipping at his heels as he followed Nora. She squealed with anticipation as he caught up to her and cornered her in the kitchen. He had her pinned in the space where the counter met the wall. Badger tugged viciously at his pant leg. *I would punt you, little dog, but I don't want to upset my playmate,* he thought, while trying to gently kick him loose.

"Go lay down!" Nora shouted at her ferocious pet. He released the hem of Dane's jeans and curled up under the kitchen table, still keeping a watchful eye.

Dane leaned down and kissed her hard, grabbing the back of her head and pushing her mouth against his. Nora could feel his teeth against her bottom lip.

He pulled away and grabbed her abruptly, wrestling her to the ground. His movements were quick and forceful.

This is taking a dark turn, she thought. She became defensive, twisting and squirming, trying to wriggle free of his powerful embrace.

That's right, he thought, *keep struggling. I like it when you struggle.* A tingling spread through his groin. *I'm really starting to enjoy myself.*

She could feel the pain in her right side growing as she tried to free herself. Badger began to growl deeply, his teeth clearly visible from between his thin black lips. Dane glanced over his shoulder, taking notice of the dog's warning. He stopped wrestling and pulled Nora off of the floor. He grabbed his crotch, making an adjustment to what had begun to grow, while eyeballing the dog. Locking Nora in his arms, he kissed her softly, trying to put her at ease. As he kissed, he walked— the sink's edge his destination. Soon she was disarmed, no longer tense and ready to struggle.

Watching over her shoulder, he led her, his lips the guide, until her back met the sink's edge. He peered down at the stale water, which was gray and murky from a day's worth of soaking dishware.

Laughing, he pushed her shoulders back, forcing her head into the cold slurry. The edge of the plates brushed her cheek as the filthy liquid soaked into her hair. Panic

The Point

was rising in her throat as water rose to the corner of her eye.

She began hitting Dane in the arms, twisting, trying to free herself. She shrieked, her voice cracking under the strain. Badger lunged, once again growling as he yanked violently at Dane's leg. Water spilled into her mouth, she began to cough.

Dane let go.

"Are you having fun yet?" he asked, knowing damn well she wasn't.

She was speechless and on the verge of tears, but to Dane this was just a jovial game of grab-ass.

"Oh, did I hurt you?" he added, interested to see what she would say.

Didn't he say that in the shower too, she thought as she stood before him, tears welling up in her eyes, dishwater dripping from the end of her ponytail.

"Too much activity seems to have aggravated my already sore side," she said stoically, trying to hide her true feelings. Afraid her apprehension about this behavior would seem like an overreaction, she needed to believe that he was just messing around, and what had just taken place was meant to be silly, not diabolical.

Dane approached her and wiped the tear from her face. She stared, her eyes locked on his, while she choked back a flood of emotion. He grabbed the dishtowel from the refrigerator handle and handed it to her. "Your hair is dripping."

She snatched the towel from his hand, then grabbed the end of her hair with it and squeezed. "I'm going to take a shower," she uttered, her voice low, her gaze distant.

She trudged up the stairs feeling hurt and confused by his behavior. The pain in her side was momentarily masked by what might have been shock.

He was experiencing *feelings* of his own. Something about her caused a stirring deep inside of him. Dane often felt deep desires after an incident like this. Something about these domestic struggles caused his favorite parts to tingle. He reached down and gave his crotch another squeeze, "Thank you, Nora," he whispered to himself, "it feels like I'm going to have a good night."

She was the first woman in a while who played along so well. She was giving emotionally, *and now I'll make it sexually*, he thought.

Standing at the bottom of the stairs, he gave her a moment to get into the shower before heading up to take advantage of her in her vulnerable state.

Waves of emotion washed over her as she removed her wet clothes. She wanted to pretend it was all right, but found herself filled with doubt about Dane and his behavior. She reached in and tested the water temperature, tears streaming down her face. She stepped through the curtain. The hot water was soothing. She stood there, the steam billowing around her, thoughts of her struggle with Dane still looming. No matter how she tried to spin it or rationalize it, she couldn't get to a place where it was okay.

She tipped her head back and ran her fingers through her hair, rinsing away the bits of food left by her dip in the kitchen sink.

The shower curtain drew back. She opened her eyes to find him standing before her, fully erect. "Turn around, sweet tits. I'll wash your hair," he directed, once again taking charge.

The Point

She reluctantly turned. Dane took the shampoo from the caddy and worked up a lather massaging her scalp. "Sorry if I was too rough," he offered apologetically while washing her hair.

Discomfort over the situation twisted inside of her as his large, strong hands moved from her hair to her breasts, the lather causing his fingers to glide effortlessly.

Dane's hands made their way down, the bubbles from the lather running along her legs to the drain. Nora felt as though she was on the outside looking in. It was surreal to have been so recently violated by an action and then let the perpetrator have his way with you.

She found herself struggling with the desire building inside of her. Dane's hands were sliding closer and closer. It was too easy for him to manipulate her. She wondered what message she would be sending if she were to give into him after what happened.

*Have some self-respe*ct, she thought as she grabbed his hands, pushing them away, ending his exploration. She turned and stared at him sternly while rinsing off. She shut off the water and exited the shower.

Dane stood alone in the tub, a grin spreading deviously across his face as he contemplated the challenge that had just been put forth.

Nora threw on her bathrobe and ran, climbing into her bed. Emboldened by the perceived challenge, he followed.

He hovered above her, using the covers to pin her down. She looked up at him, excited and afraid, the blanket pulling tight.

With a wild look in his eyes, he sat up quickly and tore the blankets from her. He grabbed the bathrobe and flung it open, exposing her. He forced her legs apart and slipped between them, kneeling in front of her.

He stared her down, his gaze and position unbroken, as he used her as a tool for his own pleasure.

Did I allow this, or did he just force himself on me? she wondered.

"You surprise me Nora. I didn't think you would be up for another chase after the incident in the kitchen." He smiled. It was a twisted, satisfied smile.

Unwilling to believe she'd just been assaulted (he said he loved her, right?), she tried to rationalize what had occurred.

In that moment of contemplation, she realized he liked games of control. Although her revelation was somewhat of a relief, she worried what that might mean in the long run.

The high from this latest sexcapade ebbed and returned her attention to the pain coursing down her side. She turned to Dane. "I'm really uncomfortable," she groaned while rubbing her side.

"What can I do for you?" he asked half-heartedly, now stretched out on the bed beside her, his eyelids heavy.

"My pills are in the bathroom."

She was hoping Dane would come to her aid. She waited for a reply.

"Are you asleep already?" she scoffed, her request for care still ignored.

"Not yet," Dane replied from behind closed eyes. "But I'm really comfy, thanks for getting it yourself."

With her jaw dropped and her foot tapping, she found herself unsure how to respond. She gawked at him a moment more before leaving his side.

The Point

She entered the bathroom and took her pills: codeine, antibiotics, and birth control. (After these last few weeks with Dane, she definitely didn't want to forget that last one.)

She returned to the bedside to find Dane sleeping greedily. She picked up a pillow and the quilt draped over the back of her rocker. Giving him one last glance, she headed downstairs.

She hoped that a little late night television would distract her from the emotional turmoil she was currently experiencing. Down in the dark and quiet of the living room, with the television silently flickering in the background, her thoughts wandered toward Jake.

He made her feel safe and loved. He never uttered the words *I love you*, but his actions spoke volumes. "I wish he was here now," she confided to her precious pet.

~~~

"What are you looking for?" she called from the living room, her slumber interrupted by his racket.

"Coffee!" Dane shouted back.

She made her way to the kitchen doorway and stood, wedging her arms in the opening. "We don't have any," she stated.

"Why?" he asked with a perplexed tone.

"We're tea drinkers." She added, "I'll put the kettle on and make you a cup."

Dane sat at the kitchen table. He strummed his fingers on the placemat, occasionally tracing the flowered pattern while he waited.

She finally slipped the cup of steaming liquid across the table.

"Thanks," he said, the word drained of all meaning.

They sat facing each other, sipping their tea. Dane seemed less than pleased with his morning beverage choice, grimacing after each sip. "I really need a cup of coffee. I'm going to head to work early and pick some up on the way." Dane pushed his chair away from the table. He kissed her on the forehead and then headed out.

Chapter 11

Thursday and Friday brought more of the same. Dane had an insatiable sexual appetite paired with a mean streak. Just when Nora thought she'd made sense of his behavior, he'd undermine her confidence and leave her wondering if her feelings, or reactions, were justified.

She tried to get through Friday night by suggesting they get drunk and play cards, a popular north-woods pastime.

Dane ran out and purchased a case of beer and she produced a bottle of root beer schnapps from the liquor cabinet. "Grandpa Reynolds always drank schnapps with his beer," she shared with him. (Of course, he lacked any kind of normal response to Nora's family anecdotes, mostly because sociopaths lack empathy.)

The couple hunkered down at the kitchen table, face to face, playing Rummy and drinking methodically. She sipped beer after beer, pulling intermittently from the schnapps bottle. She soon felt the warm flood of drunkenness wash over her.

"How you feeling, Nora?" Dane asked, a devious note in his voice.

"Fine. I'm still kicking your ass!" she exclaimed, tapping at the score sheet to her right.

"I think it's my turn to score," he added, stretching his leg out under the table. He ran his foot along her inner thigh, digging his big toe into her crotch.

She pushed her chair back abruptly, almost tipping over as the back legs hit a crack in the wood floor. "Hey, keep your toes to yourself," she slurred.

Dane licked his lips. She was clearly impaired, and this would be a great opportunity to push her sexual limits.

"Let's go upstairs, I have something I'd like to show you," he said as he held out his hand, giving her a false sense of safety.

She was extremely woozy. The booze, paired with the codeine in her system, had really taken its toll.

Trustingly, she grabbed his hand, gripping his arm for support on the way up the stairs. They reached the top and she fell to her knees, laughing as she sloppily began to crawl to her room. Her hands slapped the floor as she inched forward. "I'm *sooo* drunk," she giggled. "Did you know that's the mating call of a blonde," she hiccupped.

Dane tried to help her up. She swung wildly at his hand from the floor. "I can get there myself, you dick," she demanded.

"Aren't we feeling sassy?" he scolded playfully, pleased by her level of intoxication.

"Yes," she stated with a slur.

She continued crawling, eventually making it to the bed. She pulled herself up over the edge and flopped onto her stomach, arms spread out in front of her, her legs splayed sloppily to the floor.

"You've put yourself in a fine position for me to do terrible things to you, Nora."

"What's left?" she garbled from the side of her mouth, her face pressed against the comforter. "You've already done so much."

"There are so many possibilities," he informed her as he wrung his hands with delight. He went to explore the contents of his overnight bag. He had stashed a few toys, just in case an occasion was to arise.

The Point

She was motionless, her eyes closed, with a small bit of drool escaping the corner of her mouth.

It was slightly disappointing that she'd passed out. He'd taken advantage of an intoxicated girl or two in his day, but never one that was incapacitated.

He stood behind her, contemplating his next move. *Can I do this,* he thought. *It's not much different than getting them drunk to the point of being pliable...* Dane moved forward, running his hand up her thigh. She was still, unaware. Something deep inside of him stirred. The tingle he so often experienced expanded with the speed of light, rocketing through his entire body.

Stripping down, he folded his clothes tidily onto the rocker, his urge to fling them off hurriedly in direct conflict with his compulsive desire for control.

Now hovering above her naked and aroused, he felt like a kid in a candy store, excited by the many choices before him.

Dane placed some gadgets he'd fished from his bag in a row on the end of the bed. He pulled her pants off and then rolled her panties slowly past her ankles, watching the fabric twist and roll past her soft, pale skin. She stirred, rubbing her nose then falling back to sleep.

Carefully he slipped his hands under her, gently lifting, pushing her forward.

Selecting two zip ties from his line-up, he closed one around the radiator, creating an anchor point, and the other through that loop and around her wrists.

How tantalizing! A drunken blonde, naked from the waist down, zip-tied to a radiator.

He slowly, carefully negotiated her position until her legs were spread and bent at the knee, allowing him access.

Dane wanted, no needed, to take his time, trying to put out the fire that now burned, trying to satiate the hunger he now felt. He clasped his hands over his mouth, his ecstasy hard to stifle. He'd been worried that her lack of reaction would hamper his excitement but he'd experienced quite the opposite. "Violating you, Nora, fucking you while you were unaware, has brought me someplace I've never been before," he whispered into her sedated ear.

Wanting to forever remember this deviant and erotic moment, he dismounted and rounded up his cell phone to snap a photo of her unconscious and zip-tied form for his perusal later.

He cleaned up, tucking all paraphernalia back into his bag of tricks. Cutting her loose, he pulled her onto the bed so her head was on the pillow. He slipped her bottoms back on and tucked himself in next to her.

Still at half-mast, he thought about what he'd just done to his unsuspecting date. He eventually drifted off, looking forward to hearing what she'd remember in the morning.

~~~

"My aching head," Nora mumbled, faced with a terrible hangover. She looked over at Dane, who was sleeping blissfully. *How did I get to bed*, she thought as she continued to contemplate the events of the night before. Gingerly she traipsed to the bathroom, her head pounding with each step. She sat to urinate, and found things a bit sore and swollen when she went to wipe, not to mention other *left over* evidence that sex had taken place.

The Point

I don't remember fooling around, she thought as she stormed over to Dane.

"Wake up!" she shouted while shaking him violently.

"What is it, sweet tits?" he asked groggily as he rolled toward her.

"What did we do last night, what did *you* do to me?" She demanded with a tinge of worry in her voice.

"We got a little drunk and came up here to fool around," he answered.

"I don't remember agreeing to that. I vaguely remember climbing the stairs," she stated, her tone perplexed.

"I assure you—you were into it. You even got a little extra freaky." He patted her on the hand as he tried to reassure her. *This is fun!* He thought, *I hope she asks how freaky.*

She pulled her hand back. "I don't remember. What do you mean by freaky?"

Dane hopped up, thrilled she asked, excited to dig the surprise out of his bag. He enthusiastically brandished the toy. It was bright orange; the phony flesh quivered as he anxiously displayed it.

"My God!" she exclaimed. "Did you use that on me?"

"Just at first but then I took over," he assured her.

She knew the orange device was the reason she was so sore. "I let you use that on me?" she said, disbelief in her voice.

"Yeah, and you loved it, and I loved watching you." Dane smiled, a truly unnerving smile.

She went back to the bathroom and stood against the closed door, thoughts whirling around in her mind as she held her head in her shaking hands. She couldn't remember any of it. *Would I let a man penetrate me with a thing like that?* Glancing at her reflection in the bathroom mirror, she felt like she didn't even know who *she* was anymore. He'd twisted and manipulated her, until she couldn't recognize herself.

She ran a bath, hoping a long soak would help cleanse her of the filthy feelings crawling inside of her. Just as she leaned back into the tub, he burst in with another disturbing device gripped in his hand. The bizarre, bulbous item was just one more shock to her system, and he knew it.

Slipping down, she dunked her head under the water. *I can't believe what I've done*, she thought while floating below.

"Please get out so I can bathe in peace," she requested as she resurfaced.

Dane didn't listen. He pulled off his drawers, and slipped in behind her. Wrapping his arms around her he tried to offer some comfort, "People use toys all the time, there's no shame in it." He rubbed her breasts as he sweet-talked her. "Why don't we get out of this tub and do some more experimenting? You'll see how enjoyable it is, my sweet tits." He tweaked her nipples.

Nora was disgusted with herself.

"I'm too sore. I need a rain check," she replied.

"Maybe I'll get ready to go then," he offered as he tried to manipulate her, using his departure as leverage.

"That's a good idea. It'll give me a chance to rest before my dad gets home."

He didn't expect her to dismiss him so quickly; but then again, he had violated her.

~~~

The Point

William returned late Sunday morning, happy to see that his daughter was feeling better. He was full of tall tales about his fishing adventure. She listened intently as her dad spun a yarn about big fish and the physical prowess of the modern outdoorsmen.

"So how was your week?" her father asked, his attention now focused on her.

"Well," she began, "Dane stopped in to keep me company and…" She realized the toll he'd taken on her psyche. *What's wrong with me,* she thought. *By the time I edit for content, there's nothing left to tell.*

Her face was now twisted with contemplation. *How do I fill in the blanks?*

Dirty dishwater, can't tell him about that. Possible sexual assault, probably shouldn't mention that.

She also couldn't mention how he'd shut her out of the house in the rain. Afraid to make a scene, she only knocked and shouted a few times before she realized he wasn't going to let her back in. Her first thought was to seek shelter in the Rover, but she feared the neighbors would see her in the wet T-shirt crossing the front lawn. Thankfully, the shed was open and heated due to her father's attempts to tie fishing flies and paint decoys.

"Everything alright my dear?" William asked. "You look ill."

"Yeah, yeah, I think I'm just a little tired, not quite myself yet," she answered.

"You go have a rest, and I'll go have a shower," her father said while lifting his right arm sniffing his own pit. "I can't stand my *own* smell. A few days in the bush makes you appreciate modern plumbing. I love the outdoors, but I also *love* a hot shower," William finished with a nod, punctuating how sincere his love was.

"You are a bit ripe," she admitted while wrinkling her nose.

William removed his ball cap, which actually advertised camping gear, not baseball, and tapped his daughter on the head with it, "I'm heading up, see you in a bit."

"Will do," she answered as her father walked away. She was thankful she no longer had to try and detail her time with Dane.

She decided to call Lucy and see how her weekend went. Maybe her dear friend could help her sort out the mess her love life had become.

"My weekend was incredible," Lucy chimed on the other end of the phone. "We should get together, and I'll tell you all about it. Then you can tell me all about Dane." Lucy exaggerated his name, dragging it out. "Meet me at the diner in thirty?"

"See you in a few," Nora agreed.

~~~

The Light House was a small greasy spoon enjoyed by many locals. They only served breakfast and lunch, and it was a popular spot for those trying to cure a hangover.

Choosing a booth by the window, she waited for Lucy to arrive. She watched the town folk stroll by, her thoughts once again drifting to Jake. She knew she was in the middle of something intense with Dane, but couldn't help thinking about Jake and his gentle ways. She never woke up wondering if *Jake* had mistreated her... she missed his sensitivity. Just as she was about to be swept out into a sea of thought, Lucy appeared in the window. She was smiling and waving, her fingers wiggling next to her cheek.

The Point

She burst through the door, twittering about her long weekend with Cooper. "Cooper took me to his family's cabin. We spent the first couple of days alone talking and fooling around in front of the fireplace, and everywhere else."

"Has Cooper heard anything from Dane?" Nora interrupted, wondering if he'd said anything about her.

"Cooper hasn't mentioned him, in fact he never mentions much about him at all," Lucy added, wondering why her friend seemed so frazzled.

"I'm so happy that Cooper is treating you well," Nora continued, trying to turn the attention back onto Lucy. She realized that, for the first time, her best friend was in love.

"He's so wonderful. His parents and sister joined us for dinner on Sunday. I loved them. His mother was so warm toward me. She told me I was the best girlfriend Cooper's ever had."

Nora smiled and listened to Lucy rattle on. She was pleased that her good friend had finally found Mister Right and had given up on Mister Right Now.

She wondered how Lucy had fooled around with so many guys for so long and not seemed any worse for wear. *Why is Lucy able to separate sex from emotion and I'm not*, Nora thought.

"Tell me about your time with Dane," Lucy said as she paused her chatter about Cooper.

"He's a handful," Nora declared. She leaned in, pressing her shoulders against the table's edge, her hands clasped in her lap. " He was the first guy I ever had sex with, where it was just the sex I wanted. I couldn't admit that to myself until just now. I was drawn to him, it was chemical or magnetic or something, but something about him drew me in. I'm hooked, and now, repelled...it's so confusing. He's done things, terrible things, or at last I think they were terrible... I need you to help me sort it out."

"Could you elaborate?" Lucy asked her curiosity now piqued.

"It started at the river the night of Cooper's party. Wait, I take that back, it started at the cemetery. I knew him ten minutes and I almost let him give it to me on his desk. That's the kind of power he has over me. Anyway, after the party it was night after night of us hooking up. We only talked enough to decide when and where we would hook up again, sometimes we would pretend to date by seeing a movie first."

"So far it doesn't sound so bad, you found a sexy guy and enjoyed his many gifts. You're not the first girl to open her legs to a stranger just for orgasm's sake, Nora." Lucy grinned and nodded, assuring her friend that she'd done it herself.

"Although somewhat comforting that you condone my sluttiness, that isn't the whole problem."

"By all means, please continue," Lucy offered, her hand waving in a rolling gesture.

"So, riddled with guilt over my relationship consisting of sex and no substance, I confronted him. He'd mentioned we had something; I wanted to know *what* that was."

"Why didn't you tell me about all of this sooner, it's too good to keep to yourself," Lucy joked, trying to put her friend at ease.

"Funny. Will you just let me finish, please?" Nora barked, hoping to spit it all out before she lost her nerve.

The Point

"Sorry, I'll be quiet until you're done." Lucy pulled an imaginary zipper across her lips and folded her hands, ready to listen.

"He confessed his love for me, said I was his girl, even introduced me to his friends, and told them we were together. I was overjoyed… excited, that he was so open. Then things took a turn. He changed, the sex changed. It started to get weird. He was rough, joking around, doing perceivably mean things then wanting to fool around afterward. I haven't felt sure about him since."

"Once he said he loved you, he probably just figured there was trust there; he felt comfortable letting his freak flag fly," Lucy provided with a level of certainty. "Sexual appetites are complicated, maybe his cravings desire something a little extra spicy."

Nora hadn't looked at it like that. "Maybe you're right. I was worried about some of his behavior, but it did all connect to sex in the end, maybe that's just what he wants sometimes."

"Did he hurt you?" Lucy asked, concerned by what her friend had just eluded to.

"Not exactly. He horsed around, wrestled, played a few pranks. One night we had sex, but I didn't remember. I was upset in the morning when he divulged that we'd used some toys. He enjoyed reminding me by presenting them to me. I guess I was worried that he took advantage of me."

"I can't be sure, but it just sounds like he has a freaky side. Believe me, I've had my fair share of freaks, but then, I'm a bit freaky myself." Lucy was always willing to make her friend feel better by admitting to her own demons. "Are you afraid it's just too much, and you'd rather end it?" Lucy asked, concerned for her friend's well-being.

"No, I think you're right. I probably just overreacted to his freaky side. I think I'll just take a break from Mr. Buchman and see if I can talk to him about it once I feel up to it."

"Distance makes the heart grow fonder...of other people," Lucy quipped, once again baring her wide grin.

Just as the conversation about Dane ended, the waitress crept over and started to refill Lucy's coffee cup. She poured but didn't watch what she was doing, instead she stared at Nora.

"Is there something I could help you with?" Nora finally asked, hoping to get the gawking to stop.

The pasty, thin woman stood motionless, her large vacant eyes holding Nora's gaze.

"I'm sorry, but I kind of overheard you two talking." Her voice was raspy and quiet, yet emitted a bit of a high-pitched whine. She talked slowly, "Were you and your friend referring to Dane Buchman?"

"Yes, why?" Nora questioned.

"My BFF Kaitlin dated him for a while about two years back." She paused.

Lucy shot Nora a look, which in a split second conveyed how crazy she thought this waitress was.

The waitress continued, "He did mean and terrible things to her. She couldn't get help from the authorities, so she moved away just so she never had to see him again. You should be careful." The waitress finished and slowly turned away. She shuffled back to the counter and stood there, looking out the window.

The Point

"Thanks for the info, you nut," Lucy said in a hushed tone. "Holy shit, she's not playing with a full deck."

Nora agreed, "She's obviously touched." It didn't change the fact that Nora found a ribbon of truth in what she had said.

"Wow, Dane has made an impact in the past as well," Nora chimed.

"Don't believe everything you hear. That waitress was more than a little flaky—she might be wrong."

"I hope so; it certainly sounded like she knew, though," Nora countered.

"Besides, maybe he just dumped her friend and she's holding a grudge. Dane is quite the catch, and some girls might take rejection from him pretty hard. I know you're worried what she said is related to his behavior. Just tell him to ease up," Lucy recommended.

"Yeah, I'll just stick to my previous plan. I probably shouldn't put too much weight on info given by that space cadet," Nora reasoned as she gestured toward the waitress.

Chapter 12

As Nora took time to lick her emotional wounds, Dane returned home to take stock of his new and deepening desire.

He sat before the mahogany-dressing mirror mounted to the back of his closet door. This wasn't any closet but a temple, a monument to his ego. He sat in his finely upholstered leather chair, surrounded by his crisp shirts and polished shoes.

Resting his elbows on its rolled arms, he peered into his own eyes searching for any sign that he should deny this new and building urge.

He'd always known he was different than the other kids, unable to find pleasure in the usual activities. He always felt the need to spice things up, give them his own twist. For instance, a game of baseball wasn't fun unless you accidentally broke a few windows, or nailed a line drive into some kid's chest. The heavy thud of the ball making contact with the breastbone always gave the game more depth for Dane.

As he matured his mischief escalated, never quite reaching a criminal level, but definitely skirting the boundaries. He often borrowed things without asking, like booze or the virginity of a teammate's girlfriend.

It was electric, he thought as he continued to examine his own face. Still reeling from the charge he felt when he tied Nora's unconscious body to the radiator. He'd often pushed the limits of decency with women, testing their physical and emotional limits, but only what they'd allow, or at least that's how he'd spin it when they started to complain. *I've never taken without asking or at least disclosing, to some degree, my intentions,* he rationalized. *To be honest,* he thought, *I've had some complaints in the past, but that's to be expected when you're living outside of society's established comfort zone.*

With a silent nod he agreed with his reflection, then reached into the duffle bag resting at the chair's side. "Let's have a look," he said as he scrolled to the photo of Nora on his phone. "Oh my sweet tits," he whispered, taken aback by the flutter he felt deep in his gut.

The sight of her, the feeling of taking without asking, caused his insides to lurch like a parasite finally nourished enough to be felt by the host.

He held his abdomen with one hand and dropped the phone to squeeze his now shifting penis with the other. He rose to his feet, stepping toward the mirror. "I hear you in there; I feel you stirring. How will I satisfy you?" he asked, as though this manifestation were a living, breathing thing.

Just as he began to sink comfortably into his delusion, he was brought back to the surface by a call from Nora.

"Kaitlin never meant as much to me as you, and besides, she didn't *get* me like you do. Not to mention how hot you were. You were wild, you should drink more often!"

Now it might seem like Dane was trying to smooth over the situation out of fear he might lose Nora. In fact he cared less about how she felt and more about whether she felt wronged enough to contact the authorities.

"I was a little hurt by you," she divulged.

"I promise I didn't mean to hurt you. It was just a little fun." *End it or get over it,* he thought to himself, *just don't call the cops.*

"If we're going to be together, we need to communicate more," she lectured.

Dane rolled his eyes. He knew there would be some work involved in toying with her. He'd been doing it for years, but it had become exhausting trying to pretend, especially now that he'd found that his true desires didn't involve their cooperation at all.

Perhaps I'll branch out and explore this new yearning, stock up on tranquilizers, and never have to fake that I care again.

Dane decided to stifle the dark urges he'd recently discovered, and for the time being, go back to business as usual playing poor Nora. *Well, until she becomes too much of a pain in the ass anyway,* he thought. Most girls followed the same pattern, and by Dane's calculations, she would soon be at the end of her rope, *and then I'll cut her free and indulge my new desires.*

Setting aside the silent request of the parasite, he suggested dinner and a movie.

"We'll go out, then hit the beach." He was ready to slip her back into old routines, hoping to get her comfortable so he could use her for his fun again.

"Not this time," she stated. "I want to get outdoors and do something beside fuck you at the beach."

Dane was surprised. She'd never stood up to him like that before, let alone swear with such conviction. "I want to go camping or hiking... something I would usually do in the summer."

She was the daughter of two outdoor enthusiasts; her father owned a sporting goods store. She had spent the

The Point

last four weeks wasting her summer and now wanted to get out there. With a bit of fuss, she finally convinced Dane to embark on an outdoor adventure.

"Let's pack up some gear and head out to Paramount Falls. We can spend the night. We could ask Lucy and Cooper to join us."

"All right, but just the one night," Dane agreed, his answer filled with ambivalence. He was really tired of working so hard just to get off.

Excited by this development, she immediately got Lucy on the phone. It didn't take long to convince her best friend to be her double on this date.

Chapter 13

Nora turned down the last of the many dirt roads needed to arrive at their destination. She pulled into the gravel lot, stopping the Reynolds' Sport and Tackle truck in front of one of the many cut timbers placed to designate parking spots. A wooden sign was erected at the head of a narrow path to the far right of the lot. The heavily wooded area seemed to condense at the trail's start.

"That's the marker to the trail head," Nora explained as she pointed it out. "Each trail is marked with a number and a rough map of the trail system."

"Where's the campground?" Dane asked as he returned from examining the map.

"You have to hike into the falls' base and make camp in the forest near the water's edge," answered Cooper. "I've been there before. It's a challenging hike but well worth it."

"Let's load up and get started," Nora added, eager to be on the way.

Cooper and Lucy helped each other strap on their packs and apply sunscreen to each other's noses. Nora made sure her compass was in her front pocket. She always took it into the woods, just in case. Once she confirmed its position, she began to don her pack, struggling while Dane sat on the tailgate looking at his phone.

"Can you believe I'm still getting service out here?"

Nora looked at him with disappointment. Reading her less than subtle cue, he hopped up to finish gathering his gear.

The Point

Each couple grabbed an end of the canoe, pulling it from the truck, and headed into the forest. The trail greeted them with soaring evergreens. Swaying in the wind, the trees rustled and creaked, humming their own special tune.

As the couples hiked, the warmth of the afternoon sun heated the pitch and provided the sweet scent of pine.

This is what I've been missing, Nora thought as she walked. *I've neglected my inner outdoorsman.*

Badger was also an avid outdoorsman and trotted along the path, nose down, tail wagging.

Cooper and Lucy walked behind Dane and Nora. You could hear them talking in sweet tones. Nora glanced over at Dane, hoping to get eye contact. Oblivious, he trudged forward, a look of indifference on his face. He hiked along, occasionally kicking a rock from the trail.

"Isn't this beautiful," Nora offered. "Look at the way the light filters through the trees onto that marshy clearing."

"That is lovely," Lucy agreed. "Will you take our picture?" Lucy asked as she nudged Cooper, urging him to set down the canoe.

They trotted over to the marsh, hand in hand, and sat at its edge on a fallen tree.

Nora and Dane eased their end of the canoe to the path. Nora retrieved her phone and got into position to snap the shot. It really was a lovely spot for a photo. The sun's rays were shining through the canopy onto the marsh, which was covered by silver grass with wispy hair like strands. Each strand was curled ever so slightly and was in fantastic contrast to the bright green of the moss on the fallen timber. Lucy and Cooper sat close, her head on his shoulder. They both were smiling widely, love glinting in their eyes.

"Alright, you lovebirds," Nora sighed her happiness for them tinged by her disappointment with Dane, "let's get back on the trail."

The hike took another hour and, as they took their last steps, breaching the small rise before the falls' clearing, the hike proved to be well worth it.

Nora signaled to her companions to set down the canoe. They gasped in unison at the breathtaking view before them. (Well, everyone except Dane.) Nora had been to the falls many times before, but it was just as beautiful every time. Badger trotted over to join her, dropping his bottom onto her foot. His tail swished over her shoe as she breathed deeply, tipping her head back, taking a moment to appreciate the atmosphere created by the falls' natural wonder. A fine mist was in the air, and the drone of the water against the rocks was music to her ears. *This is just what I needed,* she thought, suddenly feeling centered.

The others were intuitively silent, as though they had telepathically agreed to spend a moment enjoying the sounds of nature around them.

The path opened to a clearing, carved by the rise of the falls and its large pool of crystal-clear water. Large rocks could be seen lying beneath its surface. Some were jutting out, covered in the same bright green moss from the trail. A river ran off of the pool to the right and cut through the densely wooded landscape. The falls cascaded down a series of stone steps. The water on the many rocky ledges was shallow. In the summer, the water ran slowly enough that you could walk, using the falls as stairs, to the top where the river pooled before dropping.

The Point

With the collective moment of silence over, it was time to make camp. Badger had already abandoned Nora's side and was on the hunt. He was chasing bugs, bounding and snapping wildly in the air, hoping to catch one of the many flying or hopping critters that inhabited this heavily forested area. He would stop occasionally and drink from the crystal pool, water dripping from his shaggy dog beard. Once he had his fill, he would trot away, his tongue hanging wildly from his mouth.

Lucy was in awe of the falls' natural wonder. Cooper placed his arm around her, "I'm glad I'm the one you were with the first time you saw it," he whispered to her while rubbing her cheek with his thumb.

Nora looked to Dane for some hint of what he was feeling, envious of the affection Cooper so easily showered on Lucy.

The look of indifference was still planted on his face. She went over and hugged him. "Isn't it incredible?" Nora asked, hoping for a connection.

"Yeah, I guess so. What is truly incredible is the swarm of mosquitoes trying to take off with me," Dane complained.

Nora put her pack on the ground and fished out the bug spray. Dane proceeded to soak himself while Cooper and Lucy helped Nora set up the tents. A pile of firewood, collected by the previous campers, was still piled by the pit.

"Is it okay to use that," Lucy asked, not wanting to snitch someone else's resources.

"It's kind of an unwritten rule, we can use it, and then replenish before we go." Nora explained.

With tents erected and the fire built, camp was ready and the relaxing could begin. Nora manned the fire while

Cooper and Lucy took a stroll down to the water's edge. Dane had already made himself at home in the tent, his phone planted firmly in his hands. He peered through the screen and called to Nora. "Why don't you come and join me, sweet tits?"

"Why don't you come out here and we'll take the canoe downstream?" she countered.

"I'd rather you join me in here," he said again, this time raising his eyebrows suggestively.

"I'm watching the fire." She was warming her hands with Badger spread out at her feet, exhausted from the frolicking.

"You can see the fire from here," Dane assured her.

"I know what you want, Mr. Buchman," she said, trying to sound playful.

"I haven't held you in a long time. I miss the way you feel, the way your hair smells."

Dane was always able to charm her. He had a gift for saying just the thing she wanted to hear. It had been a while since she was close to him, and how quickly one can forget ill feelings when they are young and in love.

She caved to Dane's sweet talk and entered the tent. He zipped the opening shut behind her. "If you do that I can't see the fire anymore," she teased.

"I have missed you, Nora," Dane said as he pushed himself against her. "You feel incredible."

" I hope you can enjoy your time here, you haven't seemed very interested, and it's important to me because I want us to be happy." Dane had to dig deep; he hated camping, and he really struggled to care about her feelings.

"I was just disheartened by the state of our relationship, but now that I know we're okay, I promise

The Point

to be more involved. I'll try to be a better sport about the camping."

Nora rolled on top of Dane, straddling him to kiss his neck.

I guess that worked, he thought to himself, *I'm back in the game.*

They spent most of the afternoon tangled up in their tent.

Cooper and Lucy returned from their adventure at the water's edge and figured they would follow their lead.

Badger had left the fireside and taken a post at the tent door, he wasn't guarding Nora from what was lurking in the forest, but what lurked behind the flap of the tent. He growled every time Dane shifted or grunted.

"I am sooo hungry," Cooper called from behind the flaps of his canvas abode. "Fetch me a meal, woman," he joked while tickling Lucy.

"Stop it, Coop!" she squealed.

"I guess spending the afternoon in the throes of passion after that long hike has really worked up some appetites," Nora added as she exited her tent.

"I could eat," Dane chimed in.

"I guess cooking is women's work out here in the north woods," Nora sniped as she tossed another log on the fire.

"And collecting more wood is men's work," Cooper offered while tugging on his cousin's shirt, hinting they should get on it.

With the division of labor established, the girls prepared dinner while the guys scouted for more firewood. As night fell, the four sat around the blaze talking about the hiking they missed out on, and the canoeing they didn't do because they chose *other* activities instead.

"Still a fine way to spend the day out at the falls," Cooper stated as he held Lucy tight.

"We could always stay tomorrow too," Nora suggested. "It'll give us a chance to ride down river, see some of the sights."

Dane had done what he'd promised: he schlepped out here, he tried to be nice, he'd even wiped away his look of indifference. *If she thinks I'm staying out here another night, she is terribly mistaken,* he thought.

He led her to the water's edge, a terrible plan twisting in his polluted mind. "This truly is an incredible natural wonder," he waxed. "I think staying another night is an amazing idea."

"Really, I'm so happy...wait until you see what's down river. It's a spectacular journey." Nora was excited by his interest.

Just when she seems really happy and comfortable, I'll strike. Then she won't want to stay, Dane grinned, pleased with his dirty plan.

Nora *was* happy. Dane had really changed his tune, and the camping was everything she'd hoped it would be. She didn't realize he was just setting her up, waiting for the moment he could pounce.

The couples sat around the fire, trading stories. Cooper had fantastic childhood tales about Dane and himself. Nora looked at Dane; he was smiling, firelight dancing in his dark eyes. Happy he was enjoying himself, she leaned over and whispered in his ear, "I knew you could have fun here if you tried."

The Point

He had been waiting for the right moment to act, and this was it. He stood up abruptly and pushed Nora over, pinning her to the ground.

"Let me up," she squealed.

"No," Dane answered sternly. "I haven't had any fun yet."

She began squirming, trying to wiggle free of his hold. Badger was growling, wildly biting at his ass. He freed one hand to swat at the dog.

"Let her go," Cooper barked.

"Stop it, Dane, you're scaring her," Lucy added while scooping up Badger, removing him from harm's way.

Dane just grinned as he leaned over her. He reared up. She tried to turn out of the way, groaning, trying to escape. Dane let go, a burst of saliva spraying her in the face. She tried to turn away, causing the spit to run along her cheek and into her ear.

Standing up he grinned, pleased with his childish prank. He dusted his pants, while Cooper and Lucy swore at him, "You're such a dick! What the fuck is wrong with you?"

He absorbed their insults without a care, delighted by how disgusted she felt.

"You jerk!" Nora shrieked, "That's so gross. I can't believe you did that. The spit got in my ear," she began to cry, "There's dirt in my eye."

Badger was hopping mad as well. He'd squirmed free of Lucy's hold and was bouncing up and down, barking in Dane's direction.

"Just in case you were wondering…I wasn't having fun, Dane!" she shouted.

She worked to calm her little dog while wiping the spit from her face. She wasn't physically hurt, necessarily, but something about the helplessness he'd made her feel had taken its toll.

Dane was suddenly inspired. He knew exactly what he was going to do next. "I'll show you fun," he chortled devilishly while lunging toward her.

Grabbing her, he threw her over his shoulder.

"Put me down," she yelled as she pounded his back with her fists.

Cooper recognized the mischievous grin on his cousin's face. Cooper himself had fallen victim to Dane and his warped sense of entertainment in their youth. "Come on Dane, put her down," he bargained.

"I don't think so, cousin," he sang as he trotted toward the water. "Her hair is dirty."

"Please Dane, don't," Lucy pleaded for the sake of her friend.

Cooper wasn't sure how to physically disarm Dane without harming Nora.

"Help her," Lucy implored, as she started running, goading Cooper to follow suit.

Badger was already on Dane's heels, chasing Nora's screams through the night. Dane had moved quickly, disappearing into the darkness. Her cries could still be heard, muffled by the roar of the falls.

"Oh my God, is he going to hurt her?" Lucy asked Cooper as they ran.

"No, just scare her, and probably toss her in the lake for his own enjoyment. He's always done shit like that. He can be a bit of an asshole," Cooper answered, the moon illuminating the worry on his face.

The Point

Lucy knew Nora had just recovered from her earlier struggles with Dane. She was sure this wasn't going to help his relationship with her, but perhaps that wasn't a worry of his. "He's so stupid. She's just recovered from the damage he did when he stayed with her," Lucy snapped.

"What do you mean?" Cooper asked sounding perplexed.

"He's hurt her before," Lucy whispered, rubbing the stitch in her side. She was having a hard time holding a conversation while running to her friend's aid.

Lucy and Cooper reached the shore. The ambient light from the moon lit the open area at the water's edge. They could see Dane holding her over his shoulder, enjoying her useless struggle against him. He was marching back and forth, spanking her on the bottom, and threatening to throw her in. Nora, still fighting, sunk her nails into Dane's side, digging, hoping to be released.

Dane stopped. He stood facing the water. She could see Cooper and Lucy approaching from behind. She let go, holding her hands out toward Cooper in an attempt to gain assistance. Just as she released, Dane grabbed her by the waist and flung her into the water.

Nora's back hit the surface with a loud smack, her elbow grazing a large boulder submerged just below the pool's surface. She began to sink.

Badger bounded into the water, paddling, trying to reach her. She resurfaced, the pain in her back lessened by the sting of the cut on her elbow. "Go, Badger," she sputtered, trying to send him back to shore. She could hear Cooper and Lucy shouting to her.

"Nora. Nora, are you alright?" Cooper trudged into the water to help her to her feet.

"You are such a dick, Dane!" Lucy exclaimed while glaring at him and flipping him off. She ran over to her friend.

"Let's get you back to camp." Lucy wrapped her arm around Nora's shoulders and started walking her back to the tent.

Cooper trailed behind, interrogating Dane, looking for an explanation for his behavior.

"I don't see what you're all in a twist about. I just wanted to have some fun. I joke around to spice things up a bit, and everyone gets angry. That doesn't seem fair." Dane was sarcastic, unapologetic.

"There aren't words for how ridiculous that is," Cooper sniped. "We aren't kids anymore!"

They trudged back to camp, Badger shaking his coat and licking his paws intermittently on the way.

Lucy broke out Cooper's first aid kit while Nora got out of her wet clothes. She searched her pockets for the compass; it was gone. *No, no, no,* her mind raced as panic started to rise, *I have to find it, I have to.* Nora threw on something dry and exited the tent with a flashlight.

"Thank God!" She sighed with relief.

Luckily the compass had fallen when Dane had initially flung her over his shoulder. It was resting in the sand next to the log they'd been sitting on. She put the compass back into her pocket, composed herself, and put on a brave face.

Embarrassed that she'd put herself back in this position with Dane; she just wanted to make the best of it and get through the night. "Boy, you really got me that time," Nora sniped, barely acknowledging Dane.

The Point

"Well, at least you're being a good sport," Dane said, while glaring at Cooper.

Lucy cleaned and bandaged the cut on Nora's elbow. It was sore and bruised, but it looked like it wouldn't need medical attention.

"The water is rocky. Maybe next time you can wait until daytime to chuck me in so you can avoid the rocks," Nora suggested sarcastically.

He was surprised to hear something so sassy come from her. She was surprised, too. She realized that hiding her disgust was harder than she thought.

"I'm going to get some sleep. I've had enough excitement for one night." She thanked Cooper and Lucy for their help and wished them sweet dreams. Curling up in her sleeping bag, she held the compass watching the point of the needle search for its location. Dane slunk in behind her, being sure to zip the dog outside of the tent.

"Where's Badger?" she asked.

"Lucy took him to sleep with her."

He couldn't get close to her with that mutt in the tent. "Unzip your bag; we can use it as a blanket and curl up together," Dane suggested.

"I think I'm going to sleep in it alone. You can put yours next to mine," she offered, honestly feeling like that was even too close for comfort.

Dane crawled into his sleeping bag, disappointed that she seemed unlikely to engage in any more sexual congress. This was especially disappointing because he so loved getting a little after a good scuff-up. Watching as she fell asleep, he tried to keep his twisting desires at bay. He tried squeezing his crotch; he hoped the tingle he was experiencing would dissipate. Instead, he found himself waiting for her to be defenseless. He lingered for what seemed like hours, his excitement growing.

Finally, her breathing slowed, and her eyelids began to flutter as she slipped deeply into her slumber. He unzipped her bag, inching it along, trying to open it silently. Slowly, gently, he lifted her shirt. Her bare nipples stiffened in the cool night air. Dane brushed his hand over them, the sensation causing his own stiffening. She stirred and rolled to her side. Dane, undiscouraged by her shift, gently slid his hand down the back of her sweat pants. He could feel her bare buttocks. He felt free to molest Nora in her sleep: fair payment, he felt, for the lousy act of camping.

She awoke, acutely aware of what was happening. She was stifled, paralyzed by the flood of negative emotion. Anger, horror, and resentment all washed over her. Tears began to roll as she realized that he *had* assaulted her that night she was drunk, just as he assaulted her now. She shut her eyes tightly, trying to hold back the sobs of fury and frustration.

"Are you awake," he asked suddenly, tipped off by the heaving caused by her silent desperation.

Guilt was suddenly heaped on top of the many other complicated emotions, *why didn't I stop him, I just let him violate me.*

"I didn't mean to hurt you," he whispered as he stroked her arm. "It was an accident. I didn't know you would hit a rock," he tried to explain. He knew he'd just crossed a serious line but hoped he could sweet-talk his way out of any trouble he might be in. "When you turned your back to me, I thought you were dropping a hint. We always make love after we wrestle."

The Point

Nora felt ill. He was just following a pattern of behavior that she hadn't bothered to break him of.

"Your actions have consequences. It's only fun for you! I didn't want you touching me, I was angry and hurt…you just took advantage of me."

"You know you wanted to. I could *feel* how much you wanted it." He tried to spin it, rubbing her ass as he tried to dig his way out.

Chapter 14

August was just around the corner, and Nora tried to fill her time with *typical* summer activities while she backed away from Dane. She realized being with him was like drinking too much; you end up hung over, filled with regret, and vowing to yourself you'll never do it again.

She and her father had hiked, fished, and canoed their way through most of July. Dane fell off the radar, leaving her without care, taking up with his buddies, drinking and womanizing: their usual idiocy.

She was scarred. He'd left her feeling uneasy about her entire sense of self, and Jake was in the distance, leaving her to wonder if she was just some gullible girl with a sign on her back that said, FUCK ME instead of KICK ME.

William Reynolds tried to entertain his daughter but knew she was struggling with something. *Maybe a time-consuming task would help get her mind off of whatever is eating her*, he thought.

"I could really use some help down at the store," he suggested one day.

"You aren't going to try and inventory everything again, are you?" she asked, worried, remembering the work it entailed the last time.

"I need a new inventory for the insurance company. The adjuster visited and said the place seemed to have more merchandise than before," her father explained.

"Okay, I'll help." She smiled.

The Point

Nora contacted Lucy, needing to confide in her about her internal struggles. The emotional baggage, packed by Dane, was still weighing her down.

"I just feel so screwed up, and obviously my dad is on to me; that's why he asked me to help at the store."

Lucy had been spending most of her time with Cooper and felt bad for neglecting her friend during her time of need. She was about to spend another weekend at the mountain and decided to squash her guilt by asking her friend along.

"You should come with us, Nora. It's beautiful up there... perhaps you'll run into an attractive guy who can take your mind off of your troubles for awhile."

"Thanks for the invite, Luce, but I'm going to stay in town and help my dad at the store. I don't want to be the third wheel up there and, besides, I'm steering clear of men for a while."

"Okay, but let me know if you change your mind, and say hi to your dad for me."

"I will." Nora promised.

Nora prepared to spend the next few days helping her father inventory his store while Dane planned to head out to Mt. Hematite to frolic with his friends. Mt. Hematite (Hematite is a type of ore), *the mountain* to the locals, is about two hours west of Iron Bay.

It sounds like a camping and skiing destination, and if you head up the hill into the forest, it is, but it also has a series of small towns at the base that cater to tourists. There are bars and casinos, in addition to a gentlemen's club called Bouncing Betties.

Apparently, a Bouncing Betty was a land mine utilized during World War Two. An army post was erected at the far west base of the mountain in the lead-up to the war. The years passed and the post closed. Betties was opened in the late nineties in the old officers' club, a sexy nod to the WWII era. It's *Betties*, not *Betty's*, because there is more than one "Betty" at the club.

Dane wasn't headed out to some cabin for hiking and fishing with the boys. He was going to gamble and wet his whistles at the club.

Nora woke up Tuesday morning ready to head to her dad's store.

She entered the bathroom preparing for her usual morning ritual, "Oh, oh my," she heaved as she trotted, her hand clasped over her mouth. She sat on the floor next to the toilet, sipping a cup of water, wondering what she could have eaten the night before.

The feeling passed and she finished up. With her hair pulled back and the store apron on, she headed downstairs for a quick bite before heading out.

She opened the fridge, and found the smell of yesterdays catch, a bit much for her touchy stomach. "Wow, feeling a bit green this morning, boy," she said to Badger as she turned her head out of the fridge, only to lock eyes with the Kat. She chuckled about the relationship she and her father had formed with the clock.

"I think it knows what I'm thinking," her father would often joke while rolling his eyes in time with it. Nora knew how he felt. She enjoyed loving to hate the Kat. Its personification was becoming a treasured tradition.

"I think I'll skip breakfast today," she informed Badger as he sat listening intently, waiting for a handout.

"Here you go, boy." She tossed him a treat from the jar on the counter before heading out to the car.

The Point

Once at the shop, she found herself up to her elbows in sporting goods of all sorts. She began counting boots and waders, which led to poles and lures.

It was already noon by time she looked up from her work. Lucy walked in just as Nora began to contemplate trying to stomach some lunch. "You feeling okay, Nora? You look a little peaked?"

"Funny you should say that. I was a bit green this morning but I think it was the leftover Chinese I ate last night," she explained while rubbing her belly.

"I just wanted to see you before I headed out. Are you sure you don't want to come with us?" Lucy invited her dearest friend one more time.

"Yeah I'm sure, go have a good time. I'll see ya when you get back. You two have fun."

Lucy hugged her friend and headed out the door, her signature wave following her. Nora returned the wave; she appreciated the invite, but would rather take the lunch order from her dad and head down to the deli.

"I'm grabbing lunch, you want the usual?" she called to the back.

"Yeah, you know what we want," a voice assured her from somewhere behind the wall. She took advantage of the warm summer afternoon and strolled to the deli armed with the sandwich order. The fresh air had lifted her spirits and all but eliminated any lingering illness.

"Let me get that for you," she offered as an elderly gentleman reached the door at the same time. She pulled it open, allowing the old guy to shuffle in before her. As soon as the smell of the bread and onions hit her, she had to dodge the senior citizen and sprint to the ladies room. Nora dropped before the toilet and began vomiting violently. Fear ran down her spine.

She stood slowly and wiped her hand across her mouth as panic welled up inside of her twisting guts. The harsh fluorescent light of the rest room flickered as she splashed cool water onto her face. *It's just food poisoning,* her inner voice supplied, trying to quell the rising fear.

She placed the order and picked up the sandwiches.

"I need to run an errand," she called to her father and his friend, and she dropped the sandwiches on the counter. "Be right back."

"Alright," her father answered as she ran out the door. Her mind was racing. *Maybe it's nothing, maybe it's the early stages of another infection, it can't be, it just can't be.*

She walked into the pharmacy and headed straight for the women's care aisle. Nora grabbed three pregnancy tests. She wanted to be sure. The checkout line was long. She grasped the boxes tightly, looking at her feet. She shuffled forward, following the person in front of her, never looking up.

She felt a hand on her shoulder.

"Hey," Lucy greeted. She had stopped in to pick up a few things for her weekend with Cooper. "Fancy seeing you here."

Nora motioned to the stack of boxes in her hands. Lucy stood next her, speechless. "Maybe it's nothing, maybe it's stress or food poisoning."

"Yeah," Nora agreed, knowing deep down it wasn't food poisoning.

Lucy followed Nora to her house. She sat in Nora's room while she went into the bathroom to take the first test.

The Point

She came out, the white stick in her hand. "Now we just wait a few minutes."

Time crept by, every second more painful than the last. Nora watched as a pink plus sign appeared. She handed the stick to Lucy. "Oh shit," she hung her head and cried. "How could this have happened? I'm on the pill. I never forgot it. I take it at the same time every day."

"Maybe it's a false positive; try another test."

She took the last two tests to the bathroom, willing every last drop of urine from her bladder. Lucy sat and waited. She'd been in there several minutes before Lucy opened the door.

"They're all positive." Nora cried.

All three tests were lined up on the floor in front of her. She sat, her back against the toilet—three different brands, with three different-colored plus signs. "Positive! Positive! Positive! What am I going to do?" she exclaimed.

"First, you should see a doctor and make sure you're okay," Lucy said.

She took her friend's advice.

Nora looked to Lucy, her hand over the receiver of the phone, "The doctor's office can get me in tomorrow," she sighed, the short wait a strange burden. "I'm on hold while they answer another call."

She placed the phone next to her mouth, motioning that they had returned. "Well, I felt sick, so I took a home test." Lucy watched as Nora nodded, responding with the occasional "Uh-huh," and "Okay."

The call ended. Nora turned to her friend, "They assured me that these home tests are very reliable. Holy shit, I can't believe this happened."

Lucy hugged her as she wept. "It doesn't seem like it right now, but it'll work out. You're going to be okay."

She wanted to believe Lucy was right but, right now, things looked very dark.

"I hate to leave you," Lucy said to her. "Let me call Cooper and cancel our plans."

"Don't do that, Luce, I'll be alright. You shouldn't miss out on this time with him," she tried to assure her friend.

Lucy tried to bring her some peace of mind before she departed. "I don't feel right leaving you. Call if you need me; I'll head right back."

She appreciated Lucy's offer but knew that not even the company of her best friend was going to ease the discomfort of this situation.

As Lucy departed for her romantic weekend, Nora tried to put her troubles aside and return to her father and his inventory issues. She'd have to save her grief and worry until later.

The rest of the day was agonizing. She tried to focus on the inventory, hiding the fact that she was carrying this terrible secret. Her thoughts raced as she counted and itemized the many fishing gadgets and gizmos strewn about her father's store. *How did this happen? What am I going to do? What will my father think? Why did it have to be Dane?*

As she worked the feeling of despair grew inside of her, along with Dane Buchman's child.

She felt a hand on her shoulder and turned to find her father standing behind her. "Why don't you head home, honey, you look tired." Nora realized she was just sitting on the floor, a pile of fishing lures in front of her.

The Point

"Oh, thanks, Dad, you're right, I'm not feeling real well. Maybe it would be nice to get some rest."

William thought his daughter was just emotionally drained from a spat with Dane. He didn't realize she was dealing with much more than that.

She kissed her father on the cheek and assured him she just needed some rest. She got into the Rover and started driving, deciding to head down to the beach for some quiet reflection.

McKinley Cove was an inlet on Lake Paramount. There were several large rock formations jutting out from the beach's edge and an old lighthouse standing high above, warning oncoming vessels of the impending danger of the massive rocky point.

She parked the Rover on the roadside and walked the narrow sandy path down to the water. Trees and brush impeded the walkway. Thick blades of grass and straw peeked up through the sand; their sharp tips poked at her bare feet as she tiptoed down the path, her flip-flops dangling from one hand.

Eventually the trail ended, and the trees gave way to the open beach of the cove. The cool water rolled in foamy waves over her feet as she stopped to dig her toes into the wet sand.

She looked out onto the open water. The lake was glistening in the afternoon sun, the light dancing on the ripples as the small waves gently licked the shore. She sat, sifting the sand through her fingers as she buried her feet, her muscles relaxing under its warmth. She reclined and thought about the trouble she was facing.

Having this baby would mean being tied to Dane for the rest of my life. Would it be selfish to have an abortion just to be rid of him? Do I want to keep this baby? If I do, how will I take care of it?

Sitting for a long time, she contemplated her future.

She tried to relax, her shoulders sinking into the sand, her head resting on her arms. She closed her eyes. The bright sun filtered through the forest on the beach's edge, casting shadows of the foliage onto the beach.

She suddenly felt very calm. Time in this place always brought clarity and resolution. She could hear the distant sound of children laughing as they played in the water around the corner. The chorus of the children's happiness and the lapping of the waves lent ease to her current discomfort. She sat up and decided she would go home; she knew what to do.

She returned to the Rover to find several missed calls from Lucy. She had frantically been trying to reach her to make sure she was okay. "I feel terrible about leaving you, please call as soon as you get this."

Nora returned her call.

"Oh my God, are you alright?" Lucy asked.

"I was at the Cove clearing my head, but I'm okay."

"I'd be freaking out if I were you," Lucy confessed.

"Believe me, Luce, I was on the edge but I found my way. I think you were right. It'll work out, I'll be fine," Nora asserted, starting to believe it herself.

"I can head back if you need me to stay with you." Lucy offered again.

"That's not necessary, enjoy yourself, I'll be fine.

Chapter 15

Nora prepared for her appointment placing the compass in her pocket. *If I've ever needed direction, today is the day.*

Lucy was on her long weekend with Cooper. She hummed a happy tune while she searched her bag for just the right outfit. She'd become quite smitten with Cooper and wanted to wear something special to show him exactly how she felt.

Cooper loved to take Lucy to the family cabin. There they could hike and fish, and Cooper could spend time admiring Lucy's beauty. She especially loved it when he was chivalrous. She wasn't crazy about the outdoor activities but knew that it gave him many opportunities to save his damsel in distress.

Lucy had packed several options suitable for outdoor activities, jeans, shorts, sweaters, and a pair of Merrell hiking boots Cooper had given her as a gift. She also packed some lingerie she knew he'd find adventurous in the bedroom. Smiling, she sat alone on the bed in the cabin's master suite, searching her bag, selecting the skimpiest piece.

Slowly her thoughts drifted to her friend and the hardship she was facing. *I wondered if Nora is going to tell Dane.* She felt sorry for her dear friend. Dane had turned out to be a real nightmare, and Nora would be tied to him forever. Lucy thought about how Dane had treated her friend at the falls and the stories Nora had told her about other times he'd been rough, not to mention the warning from the waitress at the Light House Café. *I should have given her better advice,* Lucy thought, worried that she was somehow responsible, even if just slightly, that her friend was in trouble.

Cooper entered the room to find Lucy crying. He fell to his knees in front of her.

"What's wrong?"

"Nora's in trouble, I feel terrible for her," Lucy cried.

"Is there something we can do for her?" Cooper asked.

"No, I don't think so, but I wish we could."

"Maybe we can, just tell me, I'll take care of it. I hate to see you like this."

She put her arms around him. He made her feel safe and loved. She began to cry harder. The thought that she had this man who cared so deeply for her, made her feel worse for Nora.

Through the sobs and the sniffles, Cooper only made out the word pregnant. "Are you pregnant?" Cooper froze.

"Not me, Nora."

"Nora is pregnant?" Cooper confirmed.

"Yes, and it's Dane's."

Cooper sat in disbelief. He rubbed Lucy's back and said, *"I* would be good to you."

"I know you would," Lucy said with a smile.

"Dane, though," Cooper started to explain, "Dane is a loose cannon, I'm not sure he's the fatherly type."

Cooper went on to tell Lucy about Dane. "He's been a longtime victim of some emotional abuse at the hand of his mother." He went on to explain how Sharon Buchman, his own aunt, had screeched and screamed and ranted at her only son, telling him he was evil and worthless.

The Point

Dane was a mischievous boy, but by Cooper's account, not diabolical in any way, just a little more rambunctious. Dane found more trouble than average, but nothing criminal.

Sharon was a hotheaded woman, her ill temper legendary in the Buchman family. Stories of her rage had spread far and wide; everyone in town knew about it.

Sharon not only belittled and demonized her own son, she would lay into anyone who held still long enough.

"She relished the chance to verbally assault anyone and everyone for any reason at all." Cooper explained. "Dane's behavior took a dark turn in middle school." Cooper continued. "He started acting aggressively toward girls. Grabbing asses and lifting skirts, even if it meant cornering them or trying to hold them down. That's when I personally noticed a drastic shift in his behavior. He was later denied a place in the family business, paid off instead of employed, because of his behavior; my father worried that he'd be a liability. He feared Dane would harass the female employees. I never saw him hurt anyone, just kind of act like a jerk. I'm sorry I didn't tell you this before. I guess I just didn't think my own cousin was capable of truly hurting someone."

"I understand," Lucy assured him, "I should have taken his behavior more seriously as well. Nora came to me confused, and I just didn't think to warn her."

What Cooper didn't know was that his Aunt Sharon was more responsible for Dane's worsening behavior than he thought. She didn't take well to her only son reaching puberty. He'd found one of his father's nudie magazines stashed in the basement and snuck it up to his room, curious about sex and women, as any thirteen-year-old boy would be. Naturally, he found the eye-popping content arousing.

His mother arrived home from work and caught him masturbating. She ripped the magazine from his hands and began to beat him with it. Sharon Buchman screeched mercilessly at her young son, telling him he was depraved and disgusting as she brutalized him. He fell to the floor, cupping his bare genitals as his mother's fist, clenched tightly around the pages, came down on him again and again.

Cooper didn't know what led to his cousin's obvious slide; all he knew was that he stopped hanging out with his childhood friends, the same friends he once shared with Cooper. The two cousins used to be close but, as they grew older, Dane became more violent and his entertainment needs exceeded Cooper's comfort level.

High school was when Dane discovered that the discomfort and humiliation of his dates was titillating. Cooper stepped back, distancing himself, while Dane migrated toward a group of friends who shared his disdain for the fairer sex.

"He has no respect for women, probably because he has no foundation for respect, based on his mother's irrational behavior," Cooper deducted. His analysis was based on the screeching, not realizing his aunt's abuse went much deeper.

Lucy thought it was sexy when he spoke so eloquently.

"I'm a lucky girl," she whispered as she cuddled closer.

"Maybe there's hope for them," Lucy confided. "He apparently professed his love to her, telling all his friends

The Point

that she was his girl. Maybe he really cares about her and will step up."

"Maybe." Cooper added, "But I'm pretty sure the only person he loves is himself."

Lucy was suddenly stricken with sadness by her friend's predicament. She dissolved into tears,

"It seems so unfair that someone as wonderful as Nora has been stricken with another hardship, and I haven't had any. I have you and my parents… sure, my mom is keeping the local vineyard in business, but at least she's alive. Nora is motherless and now pregnant. Left to struggle without a mate." Lucy broke down, sobbing wildly into Cooper's chest. He tried to comfort her. She pulled away, her makeup smeared and her nose dripping uncontrollably. Cooper looked down at his shirt to find she'd left quite the spot.

"Do you need to blow your nose?" he asked snatching some tissues form the nightstand.

"Uh-huh," Lucy nodded, a clear string of mucus hanging from her red, swollen nose. She blew it, while Cooper patted her back.

She put her arms around him. He made her feel safe and loved. She broke down again.

"What's the matter now?" Cooper asked, flabbergasted by the new breakdown.

"I'm so lucky," she sobbed.

Chapter 16

Nervously flipping through an old magazine, Nora shifted in her chair trying different positions: legs crossed, one foot tucked under her rear, leaning forward, knees up, anything to find comfort. She looked up from her fidgeting, to find a few of the other women watching her squirm. "Just can't seem to get comfortable," she tried to explain with a fake laugh and a shrug. Her spectators had no response. They just went back to perusing their own outdated magazines.

"Nora Reynolds," the nurse called.

"Here," Nora responded, thankful to be exiting the purgatory of the waiting room.

The nurse was a short, plump woman of about 50. Her hair was trimmed above the ears and was dyed two shades of red. She was wearing cat-eye glasses that hung loosely on a chain against her teal scrubs. Her nametag read Terri Clark, RN. Nora followed her, trying not to stare at her generous hindquarters that alternated, each side rebounding with every step.

"You had your yearly check-up in December, so what brings you in today?" the nurse asked while motioning for her to sit on the table.

"I think I'm pregnant," she answered, still trying to break the trance induced by the nurse's ass.

"What leads you to that conclusion?"

"Three home tests came back positive," Nora stated bleakly.

"Well, let's get a urine sample and find out for sure."

The Point

Nora made quick work of her task, and returned to the exam room. What felt like an eternity passed as she watched the second hand on the clock tick by.

The doctor appeared and, without warning, blurted, "You're pregnant."

"Are you sure?" Nora asked.

"One hundred percent."

Nora was quiet, the certainty of it a bit much to absorb.

She'd been seeing Dr. Majors since she was fourteen. Her mother brought her in the first time she had her period.

Dr. Majors was a tall woman, almost six feet. She had an athletic build. Her mostly blonde hair was flecked with gray. It was snipped into a precise, short, layered bob. She'd been an army doctor and her straightforward manner and dry sense of humor reflected that fact. Nora couldn't help wondering if all the female doctors in Iron Bay had their hair cut by the same stylist. *Her hair is almost identical to the doc at the ER,* she thought.

"Were you trying to get pregnant?" Dr. Majors asked interrupting Nora's fixation on the hairstyle choices of the area's medical professionals.

"No, I was on birth control. I don't know what happened," she answered.

"Did you forget to take it?"

"No, I even made it a point to take it the same time every day."

"Have you been ill, perhaps on antibiotics?" Dr. Majors asked.

Nora's heart sank. "Yes, I had a kidney infection. I was on antibiotics for two weeks."

"That'll do it. There should have been a warning on the bottle."

"I didn't realize that could happen," Nora confessed.

"How long has it been since your last period?"

"I had it a week before the infection, so about five or six weeks ago," Nora guessed.

"Was it a normal period?" the doctor asked.

"A little short, maybe a little light, but I still had it for three days."

"Well, let's give you the once-over to make sure you're okay."

"Alright," Nora conceded.

Nurse Clark came in and prepared the usual instruments. The doctor and nurse left the room so she could undress. She removed her clothing and thought about what she intended to do. She already felt attached to the child inside of her. It was a strange feeling to know you were carrying a life. She might not want to be with Dane, but she wasn't going to give up this baby.

Nurse Smith and Dr. Majors returned. The doctor checked reflexes and pressed on her abdomen. "Any tenderness?" the doc asked.

"No," Nora answered.

After a thorough physical exam, the doctor talked to Nora about how to move forward.

"You seem to be in good health. I recommend you make a choice about a plan of action sooner rather than later. You shouldn't wait too long, one way or the other."

"I would like to keep my baby," Nora said assertively.

"Then let's see if we can hear the heartbeat today."

The doctor pulled over an ultrasound machine.

The Point

"This might be a little cold." She squirted gel onto Nora's abdomen and began gliding a device over it. Dr. Majors pushed and swirled. The doctor used the keyboard to capture areas on the screen. She clicked and captured then swirled some more. All Nora could discern were bubbles and black spaces.

The doctor landed on one spot in particular and called for her attention. "This is the spot your baby is developing in."

The doctor was pointing at what looked like a black bubble amongst a mass of other dark matter. "This is the baby's gestational sac."

"What about the heartbeat?" Nora asked.

Dr. Majors used the keyboard to do more clicking and measuring. Soon she turned the screen toward Nora and pointed to a slight flicker on the edge of the gestational sac.

"Oh my God." Nora was overcome. "I can't believe that's my baby."

The weight of this moment, combined with her compromised hormonal state, brought forth a flood of tears. Nurse Clark handed her the tissue box. "There, there, it'll be alright," she comforted in a limited and institutional manner.

"I know it will." Nora sniffled.

The brief moment of comfort was dashed as she realized the possible harm that may have occurred due to the many things she'd done not knowing she was pregnant. Nora voiced these concerns to Dr. Majors.

"Did you do street drugs or drink to excess regularly?"

"No, I didn't do either of those things," Nora stated confidently.

"Your baby is well protected in there at this early date. Most normal activity has no effect," the doctor assured her no harm had come to the baby.

"Just take care from now on," the doctor urged.

Nora made her next appointment and left the office, feeling better than ever about her situation.

Once she saw the heartbeat, all she cared about was having her baby and loving it as much as her parents had loved her.

After a brief stop for some prenatal vitamins, she went home to prepare a special dinner for her father. She fretted over telling him, but knew he would help her and love her no matter what; that was the very thought that saved her from the darkness on the beach.

She practiced what she would say while she cooked, passing it by Badger, "Dad, I'm pregnant... Guess what, Dad, I'm knocked up," she joked. Badger groaned. "You're right, I probably should use the first one."

~~~

It was closing time at the shop, and William Reynolds left work with a spring in his step and a song in his heart. He really enjoyed having his daughter at home, and looked forward to the dinners she prepared.

He waltzed through the front door; unaware of the bombshell his little girl was preparing to drop on him. Badger was excited to see him. He bounced and twirled, "Alright, alright, little dog," William said as he scooped him up and began to rub his belly. "Are you happy now that I've given you a proper greeting?"

William placed Badger back on the floor.

"Something smells incredible, Nora."

"Mom's special meatloaf," she called from the dining room.

The Point

William appeared in the doorway. "What's the special occasion? You set the table and everything."

"I just wanted to set the stage for an important conversation," she replied.

"I'm intrigued," he said from under raised eyebrows.

She brought the food to the table while her father washed up. He returned and sat with purpose, wondering what his daughter was up to. "So, what's this conversation about?" her father queried.

"I—I'm not quite sure where to begin," she stammered nervously.

"Just start at the beginning and say it fast, like you're ripping off a Band-Aid."

"Okay."

She took a deep breath and spilled. She told her father, in limited detail, about her affair with Dane. She told him about the cruel pranks and poor treatment. "I don't want to be with him anymore, and that's complicated by the fact that…I'm pregnant."

The word *pregnant* escaped her lips at the same time she began to cry. The tears were running down her face as sobs poured from her uncontrollably. She was taken by surprise by how emotional she'd suddenly become.

William sat quietly, his mouth hanging, his eyes wide and fixed; it was an expression not too different from the trout he often pulled from the lake. "Well, uh…" He stumbled, "You're a grown woman, Nora. I realize you weren't planning this, but we'll get through it. You know you'll always have a place here; this is your home and I'll always have room at the business for you; you don't have to worry about money or security."

William got up from his chair and approached his daughter. He pulled her up and held her, stroking her hair. "You'll be fine, honey. Do you think that Dane will do right by you and the baby?"

"Being with him was a mistake. He isn't who I thought he was, I wish he wasn't the father." She began another wave of crying, her small frame shaking with every sob.

"Take some time to sit on this situation and form a plan. Know that I'm here for you," her father said with his most comforting voice.

"I knew I could trust you to understand; what would I do without you?"

Nora and her father sat quietly for a moment. William began putting food on his plate. He piled mashed potatoes for himself and then leaned over the table and gave his daughter a pile too. "You're eating for two now," William stated as he heaped.

She looked up from the growing pile of potatoes and smiled. Once again he'd managed to make her comfortable in an impossibly uncomfortable situation.

"You've done a fine job making Mom's meatloaf," he complimented as he chewed.

"Thanks, Dad." She went on, "I'm sorry I've gotten myself into this mess, you must be so ashamed of me."

"It's not an ideal situation, but you'll make a fine mother," her father promised. "You're not the first young woman to fall victim to a charismatic young man. Your mother didn't have a chance when I came calling; I was irresistible."

"I love you, Dad."

The Point

"I love you, my dear." William continued, "I'm sorry this guy hurt you. I wish you'd have said something."

"I just didn't know if what was happening was really that bad. Now, when I say it out loud, I can't believe I kept going back."

"Sometimes we're too close to a situation to see it for what it really is," her father wisely offered.

"I'm afraid to tell him. Actually, I don't want to tell him."

"This is a small town and you'll have to tell him eventually, but I suppose you have at least until you're showing to decide how to go about it."

"You're right. I'll just wait and hope the right situation presents itself. I'm not sure when I'll tell him, so let's keep this quiet for a while."

"Okay, hon."

Chapter 17

"Come on, Lucy, pick up, pick up, pick up," Nora chanted as her friend's phone rang.

"This is Lucy, you know what to do."

"Crap, hoped you'd pick up…give me a call when you get this; it's official, so please keep it quiet, good news travels fast around here and I don't want Dane to find out. Give me a call when you finally get out from under Cooper, Be careful or you'll end up like me."

She hoped Lucy was having a good time.

Nora tapped the phone to her chin as she contemplated the timing. "When did you get planted, little seed?" she asked, while looking down at her belly. "Let's see," she said as she pulled up the calendar on her phone. Sure enough, it all added up, "It must have been the camping trip." She looked down at her still flat abdomen and said, "You were conceived in a tent." Although saddened by the fact that Dane was the father, she grinned at the thought that her child was created while camping. *What a fitting beginning for a Reynolds,* she thought.

Nora's calls went unanswered because Lucy was preoccupied, blissfully indisposed, in fact. Cooper was the man of her dreams, and now she was alone in this grand cabin with him all to herself.

Cooper had planned a weekend of hiking and romantic dinners, but Lucy wanted to keep him in bed; it wasn't as if he was complaining.

After she brightened up (thanks to Cooper's tender care), she slipped out of her jeans and into some lingerie. They hadn't left the bed since.

The Point

Taking a break from their marathon of lovemaking and mutual exploration, the two decided that they should pause for some sustenance. "What you got to eat out there?" she asked.

"Let's take a look," he said as he hopped up and scurried to the fridge, his bare cheeks the last thing to round the corner.

"Crap!" he called from the darkness of the open refrigerator. "It seems I'll need to drive down for some ice, our food is going to spoil. Is there anything else you'd like to have?" he asked.

"Just more of you," she replied.

"Well, you stay here and prepare yourself for more of me. I'll be right back."

Cooper readied himself for the drive to town, "Wait here," he said to Lucy, who was sitting on the sofa, wrapped in one of the crisp white sheets snagged from the luxurious master bed. Lucy lifted her hand to the side of her face and wiggled her fingers, her signature wave. "Hurry back to me."

~~~

Cooper started down the mountain on his expedition for ice. With his window opened wide and the radio off, he enjoyed the sound of the crickets harmonizing with the peepers as they sang their evening melody.

The luxury sedan he was driving was technically carrying him down the winding road, but if you had asked him, he might have told you he was floating on a cloud. *You're a lucky son of a bitch,* he thought as he glimpsed himself in the rear view. The thought of Lucy wrapped in that sheet awaiting his return was fueling his feelings of good fortune.

Cooper parked along the street and headed into the general store. It was a quaint sort of shop, exactly the type of retail outlet one would expect to find tucked on the main street of a rural northern town. The tight aisles were lined with open wooden shelving, each crammed with dry goods and canned foods. Dust could be seen floating against the light cast by the old incandescent fixtures.

He moved toward the counter with purpose, eager to complete his task of procuring the ice and returning with haste to his cotton-draped goddess.

Cooper approached the fellow perched behind the counter. "Hey there, I need a couple of bags of ice."

The old guy was a man of few words. "Out...broken."

Cooper had stopped here a handful of times before, always enjoying what a character the old guy was. His beard was long and twisted, its configuration clearly unintentional. Course and unruly-gray hairs poked out from under his flannel, fur-lined cap. It was a winter hat, the kind with flaps that drop down to cover your ears. He simply expanded the hat's functionality by tying up the flaps during warm weather. His wire-rimmed glasses were balancing precariously at the very end of his bulbous red nose.

Cooper decided he would take the opportunity to get to know the old man. *A character like this must have an interesting personality,* he thought as he approached the old man. "What's your name?" he asked. "I see the sign reads Johnson's General Store; is that you?"

"Ernie Johnson." He nodded.

"You a Buchman?" the old fellow asked.

"Yeah," Cooper answered, now interested how old Ernie here knew his name. "How'd you…"

"It's the jaw," Ernie interrupted, shedding some light on the basis for his guess.

"Cooper, I'm Cooper Buchman.

"They have ice at the Silver Dollar across the street," Ernie offered.

"Thanks." He exited the shop, still digesting his odd exchange with good ole Ernie.

He strolled over to the Silver Dollar. A row of motorcycles was lining the curb adjacent to the shady watering hole. Cooper glanced at them as he approached. "Sounds like a rough crew," he whispered as he reached the door; a dull roar was clearly audible from the sidewalk.

He stepped inside to find the seedy establishment unchanged since his last visit five years ago. A long, lacquered, pine bar sat to the left, stretching in a curve from one corner to the other. Its chipped finish was reflecting the dimmed lights recessed in the grimy and nicotine-stained ceiling tiles.

The walls were covered in mirrors advertising various cheap beers, each of them claiming their brand was the best by using terms like, *smooth* and *refreshing*.

Several burly men were belly-up to the bar, with women, some looking a little less rough than others, chatting in cliques behind them.

Cooper approached the bartender; she looked him over, her expression clearly asking *what's a guy like you doing in here?*

"I need to buy some ice," he explained, immediately registering her look of confusion.

She nodded and disappeared into the back. He stood at the bar, looking around the dark and crowded room. He enjoyed people-watching, and there was definitely a slice of life in this place. As he took in the local sights, he noticed a man who looked a lot like Dane camped in a corner booth getting fresh with a very unhappy-looking girl.

Cooper walked toward the back; he couldn't believe what he was seeing. Dane was lying back in the seat, a thin blonde at his side. Her shirt was partially open and her breasts were bursting forward, a single button between them and freedom. "Come on, baby," Dane pushed, "No one can tell what we're up to...I promise," he said persuasively as he pawed at her.

"Stop, you fuckin' deviant," she hiccupped.

This chick looks as though she's been drinking since breakfast...the day before, Cooper thought. Her eyeliner had smudged and smeared, creating the appearance of dark circles. The expression on her face was that of indifference, with an underlying disconnectedness.

A small physical struggle was taking place as she argued with him.

He approached and Dane smiled. He raised his right hand in greeting, his drink still firmly gripped in it. "Hey, Coop, what a surprise. What brings you in here?"

He was at the edge of the table now. He could see that the struggle was due to the young woman trying to keep Dane's left hand out from under her skirt. It was hiked up and clearly revealing all she had to offer. Dane's pants were unzipped and he realized that they'd been back here, testing the limits of indecency in the Silver Dollar. Cooper wasn't sure there were any limits in this place.

The Point

"What are you doing?" Cooper asked.

"Wetting both my whistles." Dane smirked.

"What about Nora?"

Dane raised an eyebrow. "What about her? She hasn't been tossing me anything, so I came up here with my boys to get a little, and have a little fun."

"Where are your two henchmen now?" Cooper asked.

"They went back to the room for some *alone time* with a few of the girls."

Disgusted by Dane's behavior, he thought about how upset Lucy was due to her best friend's situation and became angry with him. Not only did he come up to the mountain after finding out Nora was pregnant, he doubled down and was cheating as well. "How could you do this to her in her condition? She thought you loved her." Cooper was livid.

Dane's expression changed. He leaned forward and decided to cautiously probe his cousin for more information.

"What does her condition have to do with anything?"

"I always knew your morality was questionable, but fooling around on your pregnant girlfriend, after everything else you've done. You're unbelievable. You should be home right now taking care of her, assuring her you aren't a complete dick!" he sneered through clenched teeth.

"I know." Dane jumped in. "I just freaked out. I'm a selfish asshole." He put his drink down and zipped his pants. He was floored by Cooper's disclosure. *He obviously thought I knew*, Dane thought while planning his next move.

"I don't know what I was thinking," he said, trying to sound apologetic. "We'd been distant because of my behavior. I should go home and try to get her to talk to me."

"Yes, you should."

"My baby needs a father; she needs, no, deserves a good man."

"Yes she does," Cooper agreed.

Dane could tell by the look on Cooper's face that his ploy to seem reformed was working.

"And no more pranks or rough-housing. She wasn't having fun before, and now you could harm the baby. Also, you're not a bad guy deep down. Ease up a little, maybe you could find happiness with her."

Dane started to spin Cooper in the right direction. "Listen cousin, you have opened my eyes to the error of my ways. I'm going to sleep this off and head home first thing in the morning. I'll swear off booze and broads up here at the mountain, and try to be the best I can. *Just* don't tell Lucy you caught me here with my pants down. She'll tell Nora and then Nora will get all upset. Think of the baby. She shouldn't get all worked up in her condition. I swear I'll behave, just keep it quiet."

"Okay, I won't tell Luce, but I want you to wake up in the morning and head straight to Nora's side," Cooper commanded.

Dane assured his cousin that he'd keep his word.

Cooper grabbed his ice and gave Dane one last look of disapproval.

Chapter 18

"That bitch!" he shouted as he slammed the steering wheel. "She did this on purpose."

He couldn't see himself as a father. He liked to do what he pleased, who he pleased, when he pleased. He would forever be tied to Nora Reynolds. He didn't want to be tied to any woman, for any reason; he never planned to be. As far as children go, he didn't want any, ever.

If there was one thing he knew, he was no good; his thoughts were deep and dark. It now took all his energy to curb his real desires, and no woman should ever bring one of his offspring into the world. *My mother's legacy ends with me,* he thought as he drove, exceeding the speed limit, needing to see her, wanting to deal with it quickly. "Perhaps she won't want it, if I give her a reason not to," he stated to himself.

Dane thought about how she didn't like to play his games. *Maybe I'll play one so twisted, commit an act so diabolical, that in the end she won't want to look at that child and see my face looking back at her.*

As he drove and plotted, Nora slept. She'd had a rough few days and was finally was getting some greatly needed rest. She was awoken from her deep and blissful slumber by the ringing of her phone.

The light from the street lamp illuminated Dane's front seat, exaggerating the dark under-eye circles left by his drinking and late night driving. He examined the bags in the rear view mirror while he waited for her to pick up.

She rolled toward her bedside table and watched the phone light up with each ring, Dane's name flashing across the screen. She stiffened, afraid to speak to him now that she knew what she knew.

Maybe he found out somehow, she thought.

She realized the only people who knew were Lucy, her dad, and the staff at Dr. Major's office. Perplexed by this late night call, she answered out of curiosity. "Is everything alright?" she asked.

"Did I wake you?" Dane wondered.

"Yes, but that's okay. What is it?"

"I was out at the mountain with my friends and realized I needed to see you. I missed you and wanted to be with you," Dane confessed convincingly. He waited for a reply, wondering when and how she was going to tell him she was knocked up.

Nora sat quietly, contemplating her next move. She hadn't quite figured out how to tell him or how to explain she wanted to keep the baby without him around.

It's time to make it sound realistic, he thought to himself, *better add a little detail*. "I was up there with Brian and Matt, watching them womanize and carry on, and realized I was tired of it and I wanted to come home to you. I've been a real dick to you, a *real* dick, and I'm sorry. I love you so much, please give me another chance."

She couldn't believe this outpouring. *Maybe he'd had a change of heart and realized the error of his ways. Maybe I should give him another chance, now that I have the baby to think about.* Nora knew she should send him away but what if, *just what if*, he *really* was trying to change then maybe they could be a family.

"It's good to hear you missed me," she admitted.

"I want to see you right now," Dane said.

"Are you already in town?" she asked.

The Point

"I'm down the street."

She couldn't believe that he'd driven back in the middle of the night to be with her. She rushed downstairs, phone in hand, and opened the door. She ran out onto the porch and grabbed the post at the top of the stairs, leaning to see if she could catch a glimpse of his car. She spotted it at the corner of the next block. She was stunned. He really was down there! Dane's yellow Charger was highlighted by the streetlight, his shadowy figure barely visible from this distance in the dark. "I see you," she said.

She watched as Dane appeared from inside the car. He began to walk toward her. He knew he had to sell it to get the reaction he wanted in the end. His walk became a run as he sped toward her. She was confused by her feelings as he hopped the steps on the porch wrapping her in his arms.

She leaned her chin on his shoulder. Although touched by this romantic gesture, she still felt she should be cautious. He had a way of manipulating her, and she had someone else to worry about now. Remembering that she'd promised herself to never wake up filled with regret again, she moved forward cautiously.

"It feels so good to hold you, Nora."

"I can't believe you're really here," she commented in disbelief.

"I want to start over, no games," he stated.

She was surprised he'd used that term specifically.

"I don't mind a little horsing around, but you took it too far," was all she could say.

"I know, I'm sorry. I promise to try and tone it down, sweet tits."

She was glad to hear it. She sat on the porch with Dane, talking and holding his hand. Dawn approached and she began to get a bit chilly. "You should head home. I'm cold and need to get back to bed."

"I'll just come in with you," Dane pushed, not wanting to leave any room for her to come to her senses.

"I don't know how my dad would feel about you staying in my room."

"I don't want to leave. I need to be with you, we've spent enough time apart," he pleaded.

She led him inside and sat next to him on the sofa, pulling one of the throws over her legs as she curled up next to him. Badger trotted downstairs and immediately began to emit a low growl, flashing his teeth at Dane. He reached down and called sweetly to the little dog, "Come here, boy, come here." Badger was unfazed by his phony affection and continued to snarl.

"Badger," Nora scolded. "Come here and sit down." She called him to her lap, patting her leg, motioning for him to jump up. Badger crossed the room with caution, eyeing Dane from over his shoulder before jumping and settling in her lap. She soothed the little dog, stroking his fur and speaking in hushed tones, "You be quiet now, little dog, be nice."

Dane reached over and began to pet him too. She was pleased by his attempt to be kind to the dog, especially considering his previous aversion.

She dozed off with Badger in her lap and Dane at her side, thinking about how nice it would be if he really had reformed and they could be a family.

He looked to his side, Nora asleep with that mangy dog curled in her lap and his bastard lurking inside of her. He closed his eyes, waiting to start the next day and begin

The Point

quickly moving this situation forward. *I'll take care of you tomorrow, yes I will.*

William Reynolds awoke, surprised to find his daughter sleeping with the enemy. He went into the kitchen and began preparing breakfast loudly, hoping to rouse the two and extract some information.

Nora sat up, aware that her father was intentionally banging pots and pans to get her attention. "Good morning, Dad." She yawned as she stepped into the doorway.

"Good morning to you. When did your company get here?"

"He called last night, desperate to apologize, wanting to see me."

"I don't think you should trust him, he's hurt you." William whispered to his daughter.

"Not intentionally really, just during some misplaced roughhousing. More like a kid who doesn't know his own strength," she tried to quietly rationalize.

"Be careful, he's a wolf in sheep's clothing."

"I will, but at the very least, I need to feel it out," she said.

"Don't tell him yet, wait until you're sure," her father suggested.

Standing in the kitchen doorway, she contemplated her father's advice.

She walked over to the sink to fill the teakettle, the sight of the dirty dishes soaking from the night before serving as a reminder of Dane's cruelty, and a trigger for a bout of morning sickness. Clamping a hand over her mouth, she stemmed the tide of vomit as she ran down the hall to the powder room.

She hurled as silently as possible, only a narrow wall separating the powder room from the living room where Dane was snoozing.

As she washed up, she was hoping he was still asleep on the couch. She didn't want to find an excuse for this sudden illness. He was smart; he'd catch on. She crept past the living room doorway to find him still asleep, his head resting awkwardly on his hand as he leaned on the arm of the sofa.

He wasn't really sleeping; he was lying in wait, gathering intelligence, waiting to strike. He waited until she was back in the kitchen before rising and following her. He walked up behind her, "Good morning, Mr. Reynolds."

"Good morning, Dane," William replied.

"Did you have plans with your daughter today, sir, because I would like to take her out," Dane asked.

She looked at her father as if to say, *I told you he changed.*

William looked at his daughter like *she* was crazy. "I don't have plans with Nora today. She's free to do whatever she'd like."

"Well, I hope she'd like to spend the day with me. I've behaved badly in the past and would like to make it up to her." Dane decided to be direct.

William looked at his daughter, a bit surprised by Dane's admission of bad behavior. "I expect you'll bring her back in one piece then?" William asked somewhat rhetorically.

"Yes sir," he replied with the sincerity of a snake-oil salesman. He let that lie escape his lips so convincingly. It was so believable, his whole act, that their reaction to him had only emboldened his sense of empowerment.

The Point

She smiled, delighted by the banter between Dane and her father.

"I'm going to run home and get ready, then I want to spend the day with you. What should we do today, Nora? Anything you want."

"How about the Cove? We can bring Badger, he loves to run in the sand and chase waves."

"McKinley Cove it is," Dane agreed. He kissed her on the forehead and headed toward the door, a skip in his step. Nora and William viewed his bright demeanor as proof he was repentant and working toward change. Dane flounced out of the Reynolds' residence with a spring in his step, high on his own power, convinced no one had ever been as fine an actor or manipulator. The inflated sense-of-self he was experiencing was making him aroused. "You're incredible," he said to himself in the rear view mirror as he pulled out of his parking spot.

The drive home gave him a few moments to plan how he'd prepare for the day ahead. "Lifting, masturbating, cruel fun," he grinned giving himself a wink in the rear view mirror, satisfied with the order of tasks on his list.

He backed into his garage and exited his car, closing the carriage doors so he could do a little lifting and admire his physique. Dane removed his shirt and straddled the weight bench with a 50 lb. dumbbell in each hand. He sat facing a large mirror mounted above the mini-fridge.

He watched himself intently, enamored by his good looks and cut build. He was pleased. Pleased with his fine looks, pleased with his charming ways, and pleased with his ability to manipulate that stupid bitch and her doting dope of a father. "Oh what fun we'll have today," he mouthed to his reflection as he curled the weights.

Dane was incredibly turned on by the thought of duping Nora and her father into a false sense of security. He headed into the house to wash up and prepare for the day he'd planned with her. He stepped into his closet and rounded up his best beach clothes. He selected a pair of leather flip-flops from the shoe display next to those crisp shirts and headed toward the bathroom.

Dane stood in his travertine shower, the warm water running down his muscular chest as he viewed his reflection in the chrome of the shower fixture. Dane watched his freshly-pumped bicep bulge as he pleasured himself feverishly.

Chapter 19

I'll spend a couple of months feeling him out to be sure he's truly trying to change his ways, she thought as she sipped her tea. *The life inside of me is the most important thing now, and I can't let Dane Buchman manipulate me anymore.* Unfortunately for her, he'd already manipulated her by getting her to see him at all.

"What ya thinkin' about over there?" William smiled at his daughter from across the table.

She was deep in thought, her teacup clenched and pressed against her lip. "I was just thinking, that I need to be cautious with Dane, really slow it down. I need to be sure he's really trying to change his ways. I can't risk him acting the way he did before around me, or the baby."

"I'm glad to hear you say it. He did seem softer today, but be careful. Better keep your little secret awhile, don't tell him until you're comfortable," her father advised.

"I chose the Cove because, this deep into the summer, there'll be plenty of other people around. He can't have too much fun with me when there's a crowd. Safety in numbers, I think," she said.

"You can have fun in a crowd at the beach," William said to her with a perplexed tone.

"*Having fun* is what he called it when he got rough and played his pranks."

"Oh, well, be careful then, and stay close to other people," William reminded her.

"I will, it'll be fine." She dropped her cup and saucer in the sink and went to get dressed. She knew deep down Dane was troubled but hoped he really could be in love with her and ready to reform. *How hard could it be to grow up a little and stop getting off on that over-the-top behavior?* She continued to mull those thoughts over while she pulled back her hair and checked her outfit choice. She stood before the mirror, exposing her midriff by lifting the sundress she was using as a swimsuit cover-up.

Cupping her belly with her hand, she stood amazed by the thought that a tiny life was growing inside of her. Despite the presence of Dane's genetic material, she loved it. Suddenly Badger's frantic barking interrupted her moment of quiet reflection. Dane was at the door and ready to go.

She stopped at her nightstand and tucked the compass in her front dress pocket before grabbing her beach bag and heading downstairs. She stopped on the landing to find her father holding open the door, Dane standing on the porch.

William had a worried look in his eyes.

"You be careful, Nora, and you," William said, as he pointed at Dane, "Take good care of my little girl."

"Will do," he answered as though he were accepting a military order, two fingers pressed to his forehead, offering a salute.

With his hand placed gently on her back, he walked her down to the car. She turned back to the porch, offering her father one more wave before beckoning to her little dog, "Come, Badger," she called.

William waved back, his heart heavy with worry, as the little dog hopped down with an extra spring in his step. He sat at the foot of the stairs, his little tongue flapping as he panted in the late morning heat.

The Point

"Let's go for a ride in the car, Badger." Badger trotted excitedly behind her. A wide smile across his little doggy face; he loved to ride in the car.

Dane wasn't crazy about the dog riding in his car; so he focused, trying to keep the objective fresh in his mind. *It's a short ride, just keep your cool, remember she thinks you're a new man, besides, how much damage could one little dog do to the car on a ten-minute ride?*

The drive to McKinley Cove was a quick one. She only lived three blocks west of the short road that wound down to the cove.

When they arrived, the lot was full. Late summer brought consistently warm days, and that meant plenty of people came from far and wide to enjoy the natural splendor Lake Paramount provided.

Dane helped her out of the car and proceeded to procure a cooler from the trunk. She was surprised to find he'd taken it upon himself to pack something for them. She'd brought a beach blanket, a few snacks, and two water bottles. He'd packed a whole lunch and assorted refreshments.

They started the walk down the path with Badger leading the way. He wove in and out of the brush and long grass excitedly. Soon the trees opened to the beach. Badger broke into a run, his tail wagging, as he bounded, heading straight for the water.

Ahead was a wide swath of sandy beach, crawling with beach dwellers. There were women in floppy colorful hats and toddlers in saggy swim pants. Kids were splashing and running and screaming.

The crowd thinned as they trekked right. The beach narrowed and became dotted with rocks, which progressed in size until they met the edge of the massive glacial formation the Iron Bay Lighthouse was built on.

This thinner, rock-lined beach was the one Nora often visited. "Let's sit in my favorite spot," she said, motioning to a bend just beyond the other bathers.

She led the way, picking an area in the sand between two of the smaller rock formations. It wasn't private in that you could still glimpse the other beach dwellers from this viewpoint and hear the occasional laughter and shouting of children at play, but it was just removed enough that someone looking down from the main beach might not quite make out what was going on.

This is perfect, he thought. Initially he'd been worried he wouldn't have the privacy to take the appropriate action, but she'd chosen the perfect setting for his treachery and she didn't even know it.

After spreading out the blanket, she flopped onto her stomach scrolling through the messages on her phone. Dane stretched out beside her. "Ahh, what the..." he complained as he fumbled with his pockets. "My keys are jabbing me," he explained while pulling them and his Droid and wallet from his shorts. Nora peeked at him from over her phone, a look of quiet consternation creeping across her face. His tone had been momentarily sharp, and it was making her nervous.

He turned to his side and propped his head up with his hand. He smiled, trying to put her at ease, worried by her concerned look, and more importantly that she would talk to Lucy and all would be ruined. Placing his hand on hers he asked, "What you looking at?"

"I left Lucy an important message yesterday morning and she never got back to me. I'm a little worried," she answered honestly.

The Point

"Lucy's fine. She is tangled up with Cooper out at that *pretentious* cabin. She'll probably call on Monday morning to dish all the details," Dane replied.

"Yeah, you're probably right, I'll just leave her alone."

Yes, leave her alone, he thought. *I don't want her or my cousin ruining my chances of dissolution.*

"So, how have you been?" he asked, making small talk.

"Good."

"Are you sure, because I thought I heard you getting sick this morning, worshipping the ole porcelain god," he probed.

A small spike of panic jumped into her throat. *I thought he was sleeping, what else had he heard?* "No, just clearing my throat, it's a bad year for allergies." She knew that excuse sounded ridiculous.

"Oh, that's good. I wouldn't want my girl to be sick."

He wondered why she wasn't anxious to tell him. He decided to force her hand. Dane opened the cooler and popped open a couple beers. He handed her one. *She'll cough it up now,* he thought. *She wouldn't want to drink and harm the baby.*

She grabbed the beer, acutely aware that she better fake drinking it or he'd be even more suspicious. With the bottle to her lips, she decided to take a drink small enough to be harmless but big enough to look legitimate.

Dane looked at her, then at the beer. He grabbed the back of her head and planted a kiss on her, driving his tongue into her mouth, verifying she'd actually drunk it.

Was I just taste tested? She knew he was suspicious.

"Wow, that was a surprise!" she exclaimed, reeling away from him.

"Just felt like I needed to break the ice," he said as a cover.

"How about less kissing and more talking?" she suggested.

"What are we going to talk about?" he asked as he leaned in, batting his eyelashes flirtatiously.

"Why don't you start?" she said.

Dane grew tired of this game. It wasn't fun to play by her rules. Grabbing her abruptly, he squeezed, staring into her blue eyes. Nose to nose he held her, horror building inside of her as she watched the pupils in his dark eyes dilate; the parasite stirred.

"Say it!" he commanded.

She remained quiet, unsure of how to react.

"Say it, tell me your filthy secret," Dane directed forcefully.

"I don't know what you're talking about," she said, fear welling up inside of her. She began screaming for help.

This sudden outburst took him by surprise. For a split second he lessened his grasp to peer over her shoulder, checking to see if she'd garnered the attention of the nearby beachcombers with her screeching.

Taking advantage of the slack in his grip, she pulled back from his grasp, pushing at his chest as she stood to run. He lost his balance and fell backward, giving her a head start. She ran, "Badger! Badger!" she shouted as she headed for the safety of the others.

She peered over her shoulder to see how close he was. She stopped cold, her steps so short and sudden that she almost toppled over. "Oh, no, no, no." She was

The Point

horrified to find Dane standing at the water's edge, sneering smugly in the distance, Badger dangling from his right fist.

Instead of chasing her when she fled, he had headed straight to the water's edge where Badger had been happily snapping at the incoming waves. Now the little dog was squirming and kicking wildly trying to break free of Dane's grasp.

A wave of nausea was forced forward by her sinking heart. *He wouldn't, would he?*

She started back toward him, hesitating, looking back to the safety of the crowd behind her, *but Badger*, she thought.

Dane placed his finger to his lips signaling she remain hushed, as he squeezed Badger a little harder, causing him to let out a squeal. She nodded in agreement. She knew any noise from her meant the end of her precious little dog.

She wanted to run. The safety of the beach crowd was only a few hundred yards away. She looked at Badger, his neck clenched tightly in Dane's large hand. She wanted to believe he wouldn't really harm him.

"I'll tell you whatever you want, just put Badger down."

She held her hands out as she approached, gesturing to Dane to lower the dog. His grasp tightened, Badger's whining now taking on an unsettling rattle.

"I was trying to find the right time to tell you."

"It seemed more like you were hoping to hide it. You did a very convincing job pretending to drink that beer."

"I just found out myself, I hadn't decided what to say to anyone yet," she tried to explain.

"YOU aren't going to tell anyone. YOU are going to end it, or I will end this varmint's life."

He held up Badger and shook him to drive home his point. She loved Badger; she was sickened by the decision before her. *Do I run, and risk the life of my beloved dog, or stay to retrieve him and hope he just wants to play one of his games?*

Dane turned and headed toward the lighthouse. He was running with Badger flopping helplessly in his grasp. He was tall and made quick work of completing the climb up the bluff's rocky face. His stride easily breached the large crevices and high ledges. She moved forward, ignoring the little voice that was telling her to let Badger go and head for safety.

That little dog was a living reminder of her mother. They loved that dog. He was only a puppy when Elizabeth was sick. They'd cuddled up with the tiny thing, enjoying the closeness he spurred. His presence at that time was a distraction from the looming truth of her impending death.

Badger would curl up between them, his little chin resting on her mother's chest, as they would pet him. They shared what they knew would be the last of their precious moments together with Badger at their side.

She still liked to sit and pet the little dog, because if she tried very hard, she could still imagine her mother's hand next to hers, stroking his wiry fur.

I have to save him, she thought as she struggled to climb to the bluff's top. Her petite build made it difficult to follow Dane's path. She veered to find a shorter shelf of rock. She climbed, her abdominal muscles burning from the stress of pulling herself, her legs weakened from the strain of the steep hillside. Shaking and out of breath, she finally reached the crest. Dane was standing at the bluff's edge, Badger hanging over the side still emitting a low whine.

"I want to play, have fun with you, I do, but please put Badger down. My mother gave him to me not too long before she died. We used to curl up with him while she was sick. Please, just put him down. I'll discuss whatever you want. "

He wasn't interested in fun now. He was interested in her ending the putrid life inside of her; nothing good could come from it. He needed to make her see.

The look of desperation on her face paired with the whining mutt in his grasp, were arousing. Dane reached down and adjusted his groin. His favorite toy was tingling with delight at her misery. He had a delicious thought: *kill her dog and fuck her, all in one day!*

She had a look of desperation plastered to her face, which made the parasite twist in his gut. *Perhaps I'll snap its neck first, really drive home the point.*

"Please, Dane," she pleaded.

Moving closer, she stood in front of him. The edge was now just a foot to the right. She turned her head, glimpsing the steep drop to the ledge below. Lake Paramount was splashing over it. Vertigo induced by her weakened pregnant constitution, caused her to weave. She tried to steady herself as he continued to threaten her.

"You will end that pregnancy, nothing good can come from a child of mine."

"You don't know that," she said, trying to use a comforting tone.

"I have to disagree. My mother's made it her mission in life to make sure I know I'm no good, and she isn't wrong. More importantly she isn't any good either, so the odds aren't on the kid's side."

"Mothers are wrong sometimes. No one does the right thing all the time. Maybe she was doing the best she could with the tools she had?" She was desperate to make Dane see.

"That's where you're wrong, sweet tits. I'm not just evil because she mistreated me. I was always dark inside, because she was dark inside. It's genetic, you see."

"You don't have to do this. I know you could be loving. I've seen a glimpse of it, what about all the sweet things you said, the tenderness we shared early on?"

"ALL AN ACT!" Dane shouted. He steadied himself and continued in a hushed tone. "You're thinking— Perhaps with the proper nurturing, I would have been able to control my urges, curb my behavior, see the value in treating people well, but my mother was wicked and I like being wicked, and you will not give life to a child like me and, more importantly, a child like my mother. No to mention, I don't want you to! I don't want to be tied to you, or anyone!"

She suddenly realized he was not to be swayed. Panic surged and anxiety took hold as she realized this was a no-win situation. He was probably going to kill Badger or her or both.

Shifting, she prepared to run. Lunging, she tried to catch Dane unaware, hoping to snatch the dog before escaping to safety. The plan failed as she lost her footing on the loose rock and debris. Dane reacted, dropping Badger, his small body falling to the rock landing below.

She lurched as the dog went over, the impulse to grab him was overpowering. She slipped over the bluff's edge, grasping wildly at anything to keep her from

The Point

plummeting to her death. Her fingers caught a lip in the rock; the snag halting her fall. Her legs crashed violently into the face of the rock wall.

Now dangling by one arm, she looked over her shoulder at the steep drop. Dane, a strapping man, would have had no problem hauling her petite frame to safety, but he hesitated.

"Help! Pull me up!" She was crying.

He got down on his stomach and scooted a little closer to the edge. He peered down at the little dog's lifeless body, "I was going to break his neck before I dropped him; you've interrupted my plans," he said to her while brushing dirt from her cheek. " My leverage over you has shifted. I guess I'll have to bargain with *your* life instead."

The fingers of her right hand were stretched over the edge of the rock, her knuckles white under the strain. Dane peered over the edge at her, panic flashing through her tear-filled eyes; her face was white as a ghost. He placed his hand on hers. She was relieved, needing to believe that he was going to help her.

Hesitating, his wheels began turning as he contemplated how to best satiate the parasite now squirming, demanding to be fed.

"Help me," she cried, her voice trembling.

"Is that a quiver I hear in your voice, sweet tits? Is the fear of falling causing you the most discomfort right now or is it the strain of dangling by one arm?"

"Please, just pull me up…pleeease," she begged as she tried to fling her free arm up to help grip the rock.

Dane just looked down at her, his dark brown eyes vacant.

"Please, Dane," she pleaded, unable to swing her other hand to the ledge.

"You *will* give me what I want," Dane delivered, his tone stale.

"Yes, anything," she promised as she felt her hand slipping from under his.

"I'll make sure you do."

Fear flashed across her face as Dane's words registered. A pernicious grin spread across his face as he pushed her hand from the edge.

Hitting the rock ledge below with a loud smack, the shallow water of the shelf sprayed out around her. She landed on her side, her arm shattering on impact as it cushioned the blow to her head. The pain was brief as the shock of the fall took hold.

Consciousness ebbed as she watched the swell of the small waves push against the rock edge, her little dog's lifeless body lying nearby. She tried to move her arm, reaching toward Badger. His wiry fur, now soaked, was shifting and swirling with the rhythm of the lake.

The wash of the water lurched over the ledge gently rocking her as she drifted off. A deep darkness blanketed her as the light of consciousness left her body.

Dane peered down, his mouth agape as he viewed the motionless form lying below. A crimson pool was spreading from under her, its volume exaggerated by the water's presence. The blood was swirling and spreading in the constant wash of the surging lake.

Standing on the cliff above, he placed his palm flat just below his rib cage. A strange, vibrating warmth was spreading through him. The warmth spread through him as her blood spread in the water below.

The Point

As he stood above, relishing the satisfaction of satiating the parasite, he spotted the very tip of a sail jotting around the Point. He considered fleeing but knew they'd search for him. "The boyfriend is always the first suspect," he complained to himself.

What to do: he had to think of something fast. He surveyed the bluff's edge, searching for the fastest way down. Scrambling, he looked for a place to descend the large rock formation. *How to get down there the quickest?* he thought as he paced, tracing the edge of the bluff's crest, looking for an answer. The climb was too steep; he'd have to drop too far. He turned and faced the beach, *too far to run back and swim around to the end of the Point; it'll take too long.*

He peered down the side of the cliff, and found his answer just to the left of the ledge Nora landed on.

There were large rocks jutting out of the water on either side, adjacent to the ledge where her body was now resting. Dane searched for a spot that cleared those rocks. There seemed to be a small opening to the left but the boulders were large and still visible under the water.

I'll have to wait for a swell to make the jump possible.

The sailboat can't be far now, he thought. He looked out to the open water and focused on an incoming wave.

He counted as he watched it roll into the span between the rocks.

"On three," Dane said to himself.

He focused on the next wave and counted, "One, two, three."

He jumped, arms at his sides, feet straight.

He hit the water just as the swell broke at the Point's base. Dane emerged, unscathed, in awe of his own greatness. Swimming around, he pulled himself along the Point's edge until he found a space between the large boulders lining the ledge she'd landed on.

Dane pulled himself up onto the landing, his clothes soaked and hanging from his frame. He sat a moment, catching his breath then looked over at her body. "Hey," Dane yelled to her. "Hey, sweet tits, you alive?"

She didn't respond. She was motionless except for the gentle sway of the lake rocking her.

He crawled over, quickly stooping by her side. He watched her hair floating in the shallow water as he reached to feel for a pulse. "Are you dead?" he asked as he pressed his fingers to her neck. "No, not yet anyway," he said aloud, his fingers detecting a faint pulse.

He peeked to the right around the bend to see if the boat was about to round the Point. It was close; he still had a few moments. The vessel wouldn't be far off when it rounded, maybe twenty feet or so. Dane knew he'd have to do the best acting job he'd ever done.

"Let's give these people a show," he whispered to her unconscious body. "I'll pretend to give a shit about you and you pretend to be terribly injured." He grabbed her face and squeezed her lips as if to make her talk. He used a girly voice and said, "Okay Dane, whatever you say, you stud."

He grinned, greatly pleased by his own sense of humor. As he removed his hand from her mouth he wiped it on her dress, using the wet fabric to remove the bit of blood he'd picked up when he grabbed her, his nose was wrinkled in disgust. His eyes had drifted to her breasts,

The Point

which were clearly visible through the wet sundress. It seemed her bikini top had been displaced during the fall.

"It's a shame this is the last time I'll get to enjoy these." Dane cupped her right breast. "I have some stirrings, Nora," he said as he reached for his crotch, adjusting his growing member. "I bet you aren't in the mood. Headache right?" Once again, Dane was taken by his own sense of humor, enjoying a private chuckle. "Man, I wish I had my phone. I could take a photo of you lying here to add to the collection."

He noticed a bulge in her pocket. "What have we have here, Nora?" he asked as he pulled the compass from her pocket. The face had been chipped. The needle floated, once again searching for the proper direction. The point settled; it was aimed at Nora. It was actually pointing northeast, but that's not what Dane thought. *It's pointing at her, like it wanted her to be there*. He turned it over; it was engraved with the letters MWR. He looked at her. "Is this a precious family treasure?" He was really enjoying himself. "What a lovely token to remind me of this day; thanks, sweet tits."

He sat rubbing the smooth crystal face, his thumb catching on the chip caused by the fall. Dane thought about what he'd done: *You had no choice, it had to be ended.* He nodded in agreement with himself.

The last of his humanity emerged to wrestle him, but the parasite won.

He was more monster now than he'd ever been before. He peeked one more time and found the approaching vessel nearly at the turn. He got on his knees and picked her up, cradling her in his lap. Dane poked himself in both eyes, and began screaming for help. By time the sailboat was at the end of the Point, he'd worked himself into quite a lather; his face was red, a small layer of perspiration developing, and both eyes watering from the jab he'd given them. "Help!" Dane shouted. "Oh my God! Help us!"

He kept yelling, trying to seem hysterical. He ripped off his shirt and began waving it wildly.

A man on the passing vessel waved back. Dane could faintly hear him yelling. The echo of the water's wash against the rocks muffled the man's voice. "I've called for help."

Dane wondered how this would end. If she died, she couldn't say he dropped her. If she lived, he couldn't be prosecuted for murder. If she lived and he got away with it, he won. He realized he really did want help, but only so he could win his own game.

The guy on the boat jumped into the water and swam over. He was wearing an orange life vest and carrying a first-aid kit. *Wow,* Dane thought, *he's ripped for an old guy.*

He had a sharp, educated look to him.

"What happened here?" the stranger asked as he approached, breathless and dripping.

Dane tried to stay in his hysterical mode. "Ohhh my Goddd, Ohhh my Goddd," Dane cried, exaggerating the words. "The baby, and, and, she was dizzy…I tried to catch her." Dane shook his head, trying to look remorseful.

He brushed her cheek and then looked into the gray eyes of the old guy, trying to sell it.

"Help is on the way; my wife contacted the Coast Guard." Dane looked out to the vessel and saw the form of a woman. She seemed to be watching from the boat's deck with binoculars.

The Point

Dane rocked her back and forth, the water sloshing around them.

"Let's put her down, we shouldn't move her, she could have internal injuries."

Listening to the fellow, he placed her on her back.

"My name is Dr. John Peterson," the gentleman introduced himself as he removed the life jacket. "I'm just going to take a quick look."

Of course it would be a doctor out sailing with his wife on their yacht, Dane thought. "Is she dead? Oh my God, is the baby going to be alright?" Dane thought that last line sounded *really* convincing.

"I can't tell that. She's breathing but it's shallow. What happened, how'd the dog get down here?" The doctor asked, looking back, motioning toward Badger as he fumbled around in the first aid kit.

He didn't like the way the dear old doctor asked that question. His tone hinted of accusation, almost as though he could picture him flinging the varmint over the edge. "She carried the little thing everywhere, she was holding it when she fell." Dane wondered if he'd buy it.

"My wife has a little dog, she keeps it in her purse." The doctor shook his head.

I have him, he thought. Luckily, the fine doctor could appreciate the attachment of a woman to her little dog.

"She lost her balance and began to slip. I, I grabbed her, and she went over just as I caught her arm. Badger fell from her grasp. She reached back quickly trying to stop him, she shifted, her hand slipped from mine, it just slipped. I can't believe she fell. Christ! It's all my fault," he offered, trying to fill his voice with despair.

Dane was really pleased with that story. He even thought the delivery was fabulous, the stammering, and then blaming himself—genius! He buried his head in his hands, peeking through his fingers to see if the doc was buying it.

Dr. Peterson was busy assessing Nora's condition. He'd covered her the best he could with an emergency blanket and had struck a flare. Her lips had begun to turn blue. "Hypothermia's setting in, but the cold water could be slowing any internal bleeding and helping stem some of the swelling," the doctor offered encouragingly.

He hoped the doc was right. He wouldn't want to miss out on challenging Nora on her version of events. He also didn't want to face possible murder charges if she expired. The parasite had enjoyed letting her fall, but he was sure it wouldn't enjoy lock-up; it couldn't thrive in prison.

Finally, the Coast Guard arrived to whisk Nora to safety. The vessel was larger and anchored just beyond the good doctor's yacht. Dane could see a smaller vessel speeding toward the Point, a few responders on board.

The emergency personnel worked with a quickness only years of training could produce. Commotion made it difficult for Dane to control the situation the way he would have liked to. He'd hoped to lay more groundwork but was able to get one of the men to retrieve Badger's body. "Please, she'll want to know he was buried in the garden," Dane pleaded with the young seamen out on his first rescue.

"Of course, sir," the young recruit complied, scooping Badger's lifeless body from the wash at the rock's base and wrapping him in a blanket.

The Point

That was the only additional play Dane had time for; the doc had already relayed whatever information he'd gathered about Nora's condition. They'd strapped her to a stretcher and whisked her onto the motorboat. The junior officer directed Dane to join them aboard the skiff as they transported what they thought was his injured wife.

"What happened, sir?" the officer questioned loudly as they raced toward the cutter, the whine of the boat motor making it difficult to hear.

Dane didn't want to shout and act at the same time, so he just opted to bury his head in his hands and pretend to sob instead.

The pretend grief was enough to deter the questioning. No one questioned him further until they reached the cutter.

I hope I can keep up the act, he thought as he sat at the back of the Coast Guard cutter as it skimmed along the water. The crew had transported Nora below to assess her injuries, trying to stabilize her. There were a few more questions, but thankfully they were only to better assess Nora's injuries. Dane was starting to feel pretty confident about his acting. He was fairly sure no one suspected he was responsible.

The cutter pulled into the Coast Guard station, where an ambulance was waiting to transport her to the Iron Bay General trauma center. Dane departed the vessel and was escorted to the ambulance by one of the paramedics.

He rode to the hospital with her, the crew believing he was her significant other. Words of encouragement were offered to him. Everyone was hugging and consoling him, buying that he was concerned about losing her.

Perhaps a decent person would have shrunk at the scope of this situation, but Dane Buchman wasn't decent. All he thought about was getting back to the beach to retrieve his phone. *I really don't want to lose that photo of Nora spread out on her bed, tied to the radiator.*

Chapter 20

It was move-in weekend at the U, and Jake was eager to find Nora. As he fought his way down the crowded corridors past boxes and futons and freshmen, he practiced what he'd say, "I love you and worked to appease my father...No, that makes me sound weak. I wanted to get back here to tell you why I was distant... No, it should be something touching, but honest." Jake stopped short, causing a traffic jam. He dropped his head and ran his hands through his hair.

"She is never going to forgive me," he conceded.

"I'm never going to forgive *you* if you don't move your ass," a snide voice quipped.

Oh no, he thought, his shoulders suddenly to his ears as he cringed, now acutely aware that he'd been working through his issues out loud.

He slowly turned to find a rather swarthy girl peeking form behind a stack of boxes. She was the first in a line of many held up by his moment of self-reflection.

"Oh shit, so sorry. I'm just really nervous about seeing my girlfriend. I have to apologize to her and try to make her see why I did what I did," he tried to explain.

The impatient *and* burly young woman surveyed Jake, her sarcastic and judgmental eyes scanning him head to foot, "From the looks of ya, I imagine you spend a lot of time apologizing."

"Yeah... I'll just get out or your way." He waved as he backed away.

How do I confess, then persuade her to forgive and forget, he thought as he continued to walk, scanning the dormitory for signs of her, all while trying to avoid another run in with frumpy co-eds. *How do I make her believe that what I did, I did for us...for our future. That the steps I've taken, were steps to appease my father, not to step away from her.*

His father was a powerful and persuasive force in his life. *A pain in my ass*, Jake thought as he searched. He'd spent the summer taking a full load of classes and working for his father, all so he could graduate early and become a member of his father's financial consulting firm.

"The only way I'll condone you tying yourself to some girl at your age is if you've proved your worth to me, son. You want into the family business, the family fortune? You'll do what I say."

Jake resented his father for putting him in the position he was in. *Why couldn't he just be more understanding? Give his only son a break?*

He'd caved to his father's demands and gambled with the love he felt for Nora. Now all he could do is hope she'd forgive him.

On the third and final floor of Nora's hall, he searched every door. They were all labeled, each girls name next to a frilly design, probably chosen by the resident advisor. No sign of her. He ran into Jen Matson on the second floor, Nora's suitemate from last year. "Have you seen Nora?"

"No, I haven't seen her around."

"Have you heard from her at all?"

"Last semester, before she left. She mentioned she was staying in this hall again; she should be here somewhere."

He pulled out his cell and scrolled through his contacts list. He selected her number. It went straight to

The Point

voicemail. Jake called and he kept calling. Nora never answered. He headed over to the Admissions Office. He'd worked there as a student employee and was on a first-name basis with all the ladies who ran the department.

Jake bellied up to the counter and told the current student employee that he would like to speak to Veronica Bates.

The girl gave him a slight smirk and picked up the phone. "Ms. Bates, there's a... What's your name, sir?" The girl asked as she covered the receiver of the phone.

"Jake McAllister."

"There's a Jake McAllister here to see you... Uh-huh, yeah, okay," she answered to the voice on the other end.

He tapped his fingers on the counter as he waited.

"You can go in now," she instructed as she hung up.

He walked into the office and greeted Veronica with a question. "Can you tell me if Nora Reynolds registered for classes this fall?"

"You know I can't share student information, Jake."

"I know, but it's very important."

"I'm sorry, but it's university policy; I could lose my job."

"No one would ever know. I just need to know if she's on campus before I drive upstate to find her."

"Why this girl?" Veronica inquired.

"I love her, and she hasn't arrived. I'm really concerned." He had the sound of desperation in his voice and it was heartbreaking. Ms. Bates surveyed the pathetic look on his face and suddenly felt the need to help him out.

"I have to step out for a brief moment, but I'll be right back," Veronica said loudly as she winked and walked toward the door. She flipped her dark hair over her shoulder. "Don't touch anything," she added, making sure the receptionist heard her. Veronica winked again, her lashes batting as she closed the door behind her.

He made haste and hopped behind the desk as soon as she exited. He accessed Nora's file, "She hasn't registered," he whispered in disbelief. "No funds dispersed, no deposits made... what happened to you?" he asked rhetorically as he searched. He reached down and let his hand graze the contents of his front pants pocket, *Why aren't you here*, he thought. He couldn't imagine what could have happened to her to keep her away.

Jake called the office as he traipsed to his car. "I'm headed out of town unexpectedly, forward my calls and e-mail to my cell, and under no circumstances tell my father that I've left."

"Will do, Mr. McAllister," Jake's assistant complied. He ended his call to the office and dialed Nora's number. "Come on, Nora, pick up," he prayed, just wanting to know she was all right.

"This number is no longer in service," the automated voice assured him.

He tossed the cell into the BMW's console and started north.

His mind was swimming with gruesome scenarios, and his heart was burdened with worry over her absence. *Car wreck, illness, hit and run, abduction... You hate me. You hate me and you changed your number.*

The Point

The drive was lengthy and provided plenty of time for reflection. He pulled into Iron Bay so distracted by his thoughts he almost missed how lovely it was. The street leading into town was lined with an abundance of flowers. Sidewalk to curb, blooms of all heights and colors graced the side of the street. As you looked ahead, you could see the small town positioned on the rise of a hill, the streets stacked with old buildings, kept in good repair, a proud display of the history of Iron Bay.

To the right stretched Lake Paramount, its blue water sparkling in the descent of the early evening sun. He pulled into the Vacation Gas Station.

The sign read <u>Vacation Gas Station, Where filling up is a holiday.</u>

The humidity was settling as the cool air dropped in, reaching the dew point. The fluorescent lights on the canopy hissed while collecting the first bugs of the evening. He took it all in as he reached for his card to pay at the pump, *Wow,* he thought, *card reading technology has yet to reach this particular gas station.* Jake filled up and then went inside to pay.

"Will there be anything else?" the attendant asked.

"Yeah, you wouldn't happen to know the Reynolds family, would you?"

"Will Reynolds owns the sporting goods shop downtown. I get my lures in there." The friendly guy smiled while he gestured toward his head, a few lures stuck into the face of his hat. "Why ya askin?"

"I just drove up from down state and was hoping to pay them a visit." Jake was surprised he found a lead this easily.

Then the man in line behind him touched him on the shoulder and said, "The Reynolds' live on East Ridge, gray house, red door."

" Oh, that's great! Thanks for telling me, I'm really looking forward to seeing them."

"They've had quite a few visitors lately. I reckon they wouldn't mind us steering folks toward 'em."

Jake was floored by the abundance of information found at a Vacation Gas Station in Iron Bay. Nora had always joked about how small her hometown was, but Jake thought she was exaggerating. He finished his transaction. "Thanks again, I really appreciate it."

"Ah, Christ. Think nothing of it." The attendant assured him.

They must not fear crime because they divulged the info without a second thought. I guess she meant it when she said Iron Bay was the kind of place where people didn't lock their doors. Jake couldn't believe his luck.

He stepped outside and pulled out his phone to access a map of the area. He was standing at the tail of his sedan trying to find GPS directions when the guy who was behind him in line exited the station.

"East Ridge is straight up Lake Street here, on the right; house is on the right, maybe three blocks in."

Unbelievable. Jake wasn't sure if it was comforting or unnerving to have people be this trusting.

"Oh, but it isn't quite closing time," he said, looking at his watch. "I would check the store first. That'll be up Lake, left on Lincoln."

"Thanks," Jake said while pocketing his phone. He gave the informative stranger a wave before heading to Reynolds' Sport and Tackle.

The Point

He'd lost all track of time. He'd left Commerce City making no unnecessary stops, breaking all speed limits, turning a sometimes ten-hour drive, into seven hours, forty-five minutes, give or take. Now he was in Iron Bay, parked outside of Reynolds' Sport and Tackle. The drive was a blur; it felt as though he'd arrived immediately. *Teleportation, this is what teleportation must feel like,* he thought, as he tried to imagine what it was going to feel like to hold her again. These months without her had left him with nothing but time to plan for, and imagine, this moment. Now here it was.

Chapter 21

Nora sat at the counter of her father's store. It was quiet. That wasn't a bad thing because running the cash register with one hand was tricky. Her left arm had been badly broken in the fall. It was still casted and in a sling, a visual reminder of what had transpired. The blunt force trauma had caused some contusions and uterine separation. Emergency surgery stopped the internal bleeding and repaired her shattered arm.

The damage would have been worse if the shallow water on the ledge hadn't broken her fall. Most of the other physical injuries such as the scrapes, bumps, and bruises had healed over the last five weeks, leaving Nora with a broken arm and deep emotional scars.

Dane had proven himself to be truly demented. His actions had indeed soured Nora's feelings about having his child. She wasn't saddened by the loss of the pregnancy; Dane was right. He did something truly wicked, and she didn't want his baby. She didn't know that was his plan, and he didn't know his plan had been successful. Not that it mattered; he took care of that little situation when he pushed her.

Sitting at the counter, her eyes were fixed on the case of hand-tied fishing flies. Her thoughts drifted to that terrible day when she'd lost all faith in men and love. All she ever wanted was to find the kind of love her parents had shared. *Is that too much*, she wondered.

She thought that's what she'd found with Jake, and what she hoped she'd found with Dane. Not only had Nora misread one, she rationalized the other, until it nearly killed her.

The Point

Being abandoned by Jake was now even more difficult. All she could think about were the Ifs. If she'd just confirmed with Jake the love they'd shared, she'd never have gotten tangled up with Dane Buchman in the first place. If she'd have listened to that little voice in her head; if she had just run, that day...

She was hollow: only a shell of the person she once was. The light had gone from her eyes, and its absence broke her father's heart. It was the same look she'd had when her mother passed.

Nora continued to stare at random objects in the shop, drowning in the past, while Jake exited his car and anxiously skipped across the street. He'd been worried when she hadn't returned to school but, in his excitement, he hadn't revisited the idea that something might be wrong.

He was giddy at the thought of seeing her, the scene all played out in his mind. He would charge in, plead his case, and declare his love. *Nora will be so happy to see me; she'll forgive me and promptly accept my proposal.*

Jake stood at the door to Reynolds' Sport and Tackle. He smoothed his hair and cupped his hand over his mouth and nose, breathing out in short bursts, "hahaha," checking his breath. "Not too bad," he shrugged.

With his left hand gripping the ring box in his pocket, he pushed open the door with his right, causing the bell above to jingle. Nora looked up to see who was crossing the threshold.

His guts were swimming as they pulled him toward her, a wide, warm grin on his face.

She was in disbelief and, suddenly, overcome with emotion. Tears began to pour from her wide, blue, lightless eyes.

Something's wrong, he thought. The look on Nora's face, paired with the arm that was casted almost to her shoulder, slowed Jake's stride. The grin slowly dissipated. "My God Nora, what happened to you?"

She bawled. She didn't get up, or look down, or cover her face; she just sat there, her gaze unbroken, tears streaming down her face.

He ran around the counter and wrapped his arms around her. He didn't hesitate, just reacted to her despair. " Oh my God. What, what happened?"

She cried; she couldn't stop. Her face was now buried in his chest. The fabric of his shirt sucked into her mouth and nose with each inhale of her heaving, grief-filled sobs.

"I should've been here for you. I'm sorry, I didn't know you were hurt." He reeled back, looking her over. "Why didn't you call me?"

She stopped crying as she pulled away, tears running silently. "I didn't know you were interested."

"Oh, oh, I know. I'm a shit; I had to appease my father. I didn't mean to leave you cold. I just didn't want to make a promise I couldn't keep."

"I loved you, I thought you loved me, why didn't you say something? Why didn't you just tell me you were trying to deal with your father? It would've saved me so much heartache," Nora croaked between sobs. She could feel the guilt and anger creeping in.

He continued to try and explain. "I just wanted to please him, complete all the things he wanted of me, so I could come to you and offer myself completely." Jake reached into his pocket and placed the small, black velvet box on the counter.

She eyed the box with disbelief. *Could this really be a proposal?* she thought to herself. *Now...why now?*

He slid the box toward her and flipped it open. A golden engagement ring was nestled in the satin. Its single princess-cut stone sparkled in the fluorescent lights of the shop.

She felt flush as the guilt washed over her. *The way I carried on with Dane, the sex, the pregnancy, the goddamned violence... How can I ever explain it,* she thought. *All while he was spending his summer working to satisfy his father—so he could propose to me?*

She was mad. She was mad at herself for not telling Jake how she felt. She was mad at Jake for not communicating with her about his father. She was angry that she gave everything to Dane and had nothing left to offer Jake.

Once again, she broke down, her sobs shaking her as the grief of what she'd truly lost came crashing down around her.

"What, what is it?" he questioned, obviously hurt and confused.

"You don't want me, I'm broken... all used up."

"You were hurt in some sort of an accident? Tell me about it, it's okay." He tried to comfort her.

"I fell."

"Is that all? It seems like much more." He was perplexed.

She couldn't begin to explain her animal attraction to Dane or her desperate, stupid behavior. All she felt now was guilt over her obvious betrayal of Jake and herself. "I'm recovering from something terrible. I'm not the girl you loved in college."

"Of course you are, I see her right in front of me," he tried to assure her.

"No, I can't...I'm not ready, I'm broken."

"We'll get through it together; I just want to be with you. I worked so hard to get here," he pleaded.

"Please, just go. Just go home, Jake."

"You don't mean it, Nora."

"I've done a terrible thing, and I know you'll never forgive me." She held his hand. Oh, how she missed the way he felt.

"Whatever it is, we can work through it," he promised her.

She was overloaded. If he'd loved her so much, why wasn't he honest and open with her about his father? *Why didn't he just discuss a plan for appeasing his father with me, working toward us being together? Why all the secrecy?* Nora's mind raced.

Dane hid things, played games, held me at arm's length for his own convenience. Is that what Jake did, to some extent?

Did he just tell me that he didn't want to make a promise he couldn't keep? That he had to appease his father before he could commit to me?

The horror over the similarities between Jake and Dane, whether real or imagined, fell on her with a crushing blow. Falling to her knees, she began to shake uncontrollably. Her face turned a deep red as she screamed, "Get out! Get the fuck out!"

"What's wrong? Don't do this, you don't mean it!" Jake was frightened; he couldn't believe this was happening. He'd strolled into the shop, his hopes high

The Point

that they'd walk out engaged, on their way to make love, overjoyed by the prospect of being together.

Now Nora was screaming, on the verge of collapse, and insisting he go.

"Take it and get out, go back to Commerce City and your shit of a father!" she shrieked as she hurled the velvet box at him. It bounced off of his chest and landed at his feet, wobbling on its rounded top.

He stood before her, his mouth wide and tears of disbelief running down his cheeks. Dragging his shirtsleeve across his tear-streaked face, he turned and headed for the door. He walked out, the bell above the door announcing his departure.

She collapsed, her cheek now meeting the linoleum. She blinked, squeezing the tears from her eyes as she looked at the velvet box, now at eye level.

He was gone and she was broken. Broken by the loss of her baby, broken by her own stupidity, broken by the death of her dog, broken by the justice system that let Dane off, broken by the hope of being loved.

She continued to fall apart, her cheek still pressed against the cool vinyl flooring, when her father arrived to help close the store. He rushed, pulling her from the floor and holding her in his arms. " Oh, oh my! Are you all right? What happened, Nora? What's wrong?"

"Jake... Jake was here," she stammered through the sobs.

William looked around. "Where did he go, did he hurt you?" He let go of his daughter and ran toward the door. He flung it open, the bell jingling in complaint. He scanned, searching the street for the man who'd left his daughter distraught on the floor.

"He's gone, Dad. I sent him away," she said sniffling from behind the counter.

"What did he do?" her father asked as he closed the door, locking it with a resounding "click."

"He proposed," she said as she pointed over to the box on the floor.

He picked it up and placed it on the counter. He flipped open the top. They stood and stared at the ring nestled in its satin bed.

"Take me home, Dad," Nora stated coldly, her tone hushed as she gawked at the ring.

"Okay, hon," he replied as he rubbed his little girl on the back.

William closed up shop while Nora stood at the window, looking out longingly, watching the townfolk pass by. The ring was in her grasp, and she rolled the velvet box over and over in her hand. She realized the only man she could trust was her father.

"From now on, it's just you and me, Dad. It's just you and me."

Chapter 22

Jake had pulled up at Reynolds' Sport and Tackle today, confident he'd exit with Nora at his side, soon to be his blushing bride. Instead she rejected him, her violent emotional outburst pushing him out the door.

What could have caused her to feel this way? he wondered to himself. *What terrible event could have damaged her so deeply?*

Jake decided to head back to Commerce City, his progress only halted when he spotted Nora and her father walking toward their truck. William had his arm securely around his daughter as he led her to the passenger door.

I'm not giving up so easily, Jake decided. Throwing the car into park, he jumped out and ran toward Nora's father, his arms extended in a gesture to halt.

William closed Nora's door.

"I think she already told you to go," William reminded the approaching young man.

"Mr. Reynolds, my name is Jake McAllister. I'm in love with her, sir, and desperately need to speak to her."

William felt for him. He did look sickened—green, in fact. No one could fake how heart-broken he appeared. *Dane never looked that ate up*, William thought.

"I'm sorry, son, but she doesn't want to talk to you."

"I don't think you understand how badly I need her... I mean, need to speak to her. I really need to understand what's going on, what happened to her? I love her and want to be with her," he pleaded desperately.

William found himself getting sucked in. *Whoa, he thought, not again. I won't be duped this time, no matter how lovesick he seems.*

"Nora's had enough attention from scheming young men. She might never recover from the damage that's already been done. Just go home, son, find someone else."

"What damage?" Jake called. "Damage by who?" he questioned, as William slammed the driver's side door.

Nora looked at Jake as her father pulled away, grief clearly masking her face. Jake kept eye contact as long as he could, knowing in his gut that she still loved him.

He returned to his car and drove back toward the Vacation Gas Station, the last stop on the way out of town. He figured he'd top off his gas tank and purchase a few snacks for his long trek home. He reached for his wallet. It was in this moment that he realized all he'd worked and hoped for was gone. His front pocket was empty, and so was his heart. It was just minutes ago that he was filled with anticipation and now he was a cavernous void. The void's gravity pulled Jake to a dark place. He sobbed, his head on the steering wheel, crushed by the hurt over Nora's rejection. He cried like he hadn't since he was child, mucus running down to his shirt's first few buttons. Just as he was wiping his nose on his sleeve, there was a knock at the window.

He looked, trying to man up, pausing his grief. The friendly face of the station attendant was peering through the glass. The fuzz on one of the fish flies hooked in his hat was splayed against the glass. "You alright, Mister? You look pretty upset... been out here

The Point

awhile, just wonderin' if I can help ya," his muffled voice asked through the glass.

Jake rolled down the window and tried to explain. "I got some bad news. I'm just taking a minute to compose myself before I head back to Commerce City." He faked a smile then waved, trying to dismiss the attendant.

The attendant ignored Jake's body language and continued to hang around. "Does it have something to do with the Reynolds family, because what happened to that girl has been quite the talk around here?" He nodded as to accentuate the sincerity of his point. "I remember you were quite eager to find them when you were in here earlier."

"I was close to Nora in college. When she didn't return to school, I rushed up here to find her. Something terrible must have happened." Jake shook his head, tears welling in his eyes.

"Yeah! She'd taken a terrible fall from the bluff at the lighthouse. I guess she blamed her boyfriend, said he dropped her. She was supposedly pregnant... lost the baby."

"No, there must be some mistake," he said in disbelief. "She wouldn't have... I mean, really?" he finished, searching the guy's face for clarification.

"Yeah, that's the word around here. Though, that's just talk, Mister. They didn't print all those details in the paper."

"Oh my God!" he gasped. Floored by the development.

"Thanks," Jake said as he shook the attendant's hand vigorously, his lure-studded hat bouncing on his head. "Thanks so much, Uh, Jerry," Jake added as he scanned for a nametag on the attendant's shirt.

He left the station and headed for the nearest hotel. *I'll get to the bottom of what happened to Nora; she deserves that much. What will I tell my father*, he thought. *To hell with my father, he'll get over it.*

Jake circled town looking for the best lodging. He settled on the Regency Inn. It was just a few blocks down from the Reynolds' store and directly across the street from a quaint looking diner, the Light House.

He checked in, leaving his checkout date open-ended. He kept his transaction with the receptionist brief, anxious to get to his room and open up his computer.

"Local Woman Plummets from The Point" was the headline in the *Bay Journal*.

"Holy shit," he gasped before reading on.

A local woman was transported by ambulance to Iron Bay Memorial Hospital late yesterday afternoon after falling from the Point at the Iron Bay lighthouse. Nora Reynolds, 21, was rescued by the coast guard after plummeting to the rocky ledge below. "She was hypothermic and unresponsive when I got to her," Dr. Peter Johnson told authorities at the scene. "I just happened to be sailing by when I saw a man waving wildly, trying to flag me for assistance. I grabbed my kit and swam over while my wife radioed the coast guard. They just got lucky that I happened to be a doctor." According to a report from a family representative, Ms. Reynolds is in critical but stable condition and is expected to make a full recovery.

Jake spent hours searching, reading all the reports several times. He fell asleep, the laptop still open and resting on his legs.

"Fuck me," he groaned as he tried to massage the crick out of his neck. He looked down at the stock photo

The Point

of the lighthouse still illuminated on the screen. "I think I'll take a drive," he announced to the empty room as he scooted the computer from his lap. "Oh, shit," he complained. "Trying to sterilize myself," he winced. The front of his pants was still warm from the over heated device.

He switched the heated seat on in the Beamer. It was a cold and windy morning in Iron Bay, and the leather seats were stiff and chilly.

The seat warmed, reminding Jake of how he'd already boiled his balls once today. *Better not push my luck,* he thought, as he turned off the seat warmer. Luckily the drive was a quick one, with the site not too far from the hotel.

He climbed the bluff, a little more terrified for Nora with each rising step. He came to the edge, and peered down to the smooth rock shelf below. The fall wind was driving the surf. Lake Paramount was all stirred up, the water choppy. The waves were breaking with a roar as he stood on the bluff, the water splashing violently over the ledge below, his heart heavy. *She fell from this height. She believed the man she was with dropped her? She must've been terrified. No wonder. Who wouldn't be damaged by whatever transpired here: dropped or not, it's pretty far.* He leaned, stretching his neck, really trying to get a feel for how high it really was.

Although hurt, she'd been up here with another man; he was more interested in getting to the bottom of what had really transpired and *if* what they'd once shared was salvageable. Jake wasn't sure what was ahead for them; he didn't know if he could get past her indiscretion or if she'd take him back, if he could. All he knew was that he'd invested an incredible amount of time and energy into getting here, and he wasn't leaving until he'd gotten close to her again, try to mend what was broken between them.

Jake dialed as he walked the path back to the car. " Hello, sir," the female voice answered.

"I'm going to be working remotely from Iron Bay."

"For how long?" the pitchy voice on the other end inquired.

"Indefinitely," Jake asserted.

Chapter 23

Jake ran his hands over Nora's bare shoulders. He gathered her long golden hair into his hand and pushed it to one side. He peppered the crook of her neck with little kisses. His full, warm lips brushed her soft, pale skin, causing her to shudder. Goose bumps speckled her flesh as the fine hairs on her body stiffened in response.

Locking his arms around her back, he pulled her closer. His cologne filled her nostrils as she breathed him in. He kissed her shoulders, his mouth wide and soft, his lips trailing. She relished the feeling of his flesh against hers, his warmth washing over her as he caressed her, kissing her deeply. Jake's hips pressed against the inside of her thighs. "No," she cried out in pain. He had shifted too far forward.

He pushed harder—his hips were digging into her, his weight crushing her. He was smothering her, her face smashed by his heaving chest. She began to hit him, swinging wildly at his back.

She was panicked. Her head pounded as her blood pressure lurched, its rise driven by fear. She kept swinging until her hands were tired and her arms were heavy with fatigue. Jake continued, ignoring her attempts at deterring him.

Finally she was able to turn her head away, gasping for air from under his arm. She screamed out, her voice filled with terror.

He stopped abruptly, pulling back to look at her.

"Nooo!" She shrieked. "Nooo, how can this be?" she cried out. "What are you… Help! Help!"

It wasn't Jake at all. *Dane* was looking down at her with his menacing grin, a satisfied and twisted look plastered on his terrible face.

"What's wrong, sweet tits?" he asked.

Nora screamed as she backed away. Her knees were pulled to her chest as she grasped at the bedding for leverage, the sheets clenched in her hands.

"This can't be happening, this isn't real," she yelled as she reeled backward in horror.

"HELP!!" she tried to scream. "HELP," she tried again, her cries for help stifled for some unknown reason, only squeaks and whispers escaping her lips.

The alarm went off.

Nora was awash in a cold sweat; her skin crawled in waves as the sound of her startled heart pounded in her ringing ears. She was still clenching the sheets, her complexion as pale as the cotton they were woven from. She looked around, searching the room from the safety of her grandmother's quilt.

Relief slowly washed over her as she realized she was in her own bed, looking up at her own ceiling; Dane was nowhere to be found. She reached over to turn off the alarm; it was still screeching its morning alert. She took a moment to shake the emotional hangover caused by this latest nightmare.

Dane was the boogeyman in all of her dreams these days.

Apparently being dropped from a cliff while looking into the face of evil stays with you for a bit; it lingers, squatting in your psyche like an uninvited guest.

Nora reached for the pencil on her nightstand. She used it to try and reach the itch that was aggravating the

The Point

hell out of her from under the cast she'd been hauling around these last weeks.

Thankfully it wouldn't be part of her wardrobe for much longer; she only had a week to go before its removal. Aside from the constant discomfort of its weight and the persistent irritation of the plaster, it was a visual reminder of Dane's recent presence in her life. Every time she looked at it, or struggled to live with it, she was reminded of his violence and the terrible acts he'd committed that fateful day.

She hoped that once it was gone, maybe some of Dane's ghosts would go with it.

Nora spent a few more minutes lying in bed reflecting, digging to scratch the deep-seated itch, moving her feet around under her quilt, and searching for cool spots in the bedding.

Exploring the emptiness of her bed with her feet triggered a pang of heartache. Losing Badger was like having an appendage severed. Amputees often speak of feeling like the limb is still there—well, Nora could still feel the phantom presence of her little dog. Sometimes at night she still felt the weight of his tiny body curled beside her, his head still resting on her shin.

I miss you, she thought, as her feet slid through the space her dog used to be. There were no more excited welcomes. Badger no longer met her at the door, hopping and lunging, demanding his proper greeting.

"Looks like I'll be depressed again today," she frowned, her brow furrowed as she looked at a photo she kept atop her chest of drawers. The picture was taken not too long before her mother fell ill. It captured a wonderful family moment.

William and Elizabeth had just returned from a ten-day fishing getaway. Nora had retrieved the camera to snap a photo of her father with his prize trout. That was when Badger began his assault on her mother. Elizabeth had stooped down to the puppy's level so he could be given his proper greeting. The moment her bent knee touched the ground the rascal began to repeatedly lick Elizabeth's face with his lightning-fast, razor-thin tongue. She'd laughed and tried to hold her hands up to shield herself from Badger's slobbery attack.

Nora snapped the photo and caught the whole ridiculous episode on film. Elizabeth and Badger were front and center in their playful pose. William's hand and the tail of the prized trout graced only the back right corner.

Rolling from the bed, she used her good arm to help prop up her torso, allowing her feet to hit the floor with some balance. She took one more moment to glance at the photo before she commenced her morning struggle to get ready for work. She didn't *have* to work. In fact, her father insisted she take it easy, but she had to keep busy. She knew if she kept busy, kept moving, she wouldn't have to think. She couldn't be left alone with her thoughts; they were too much to bear.

Just as she got to her feet, her phone rang. "She's a man eater," blared from the cell until Nora answered. "Hey, Luce," she greeted, her tone stale and sullen.

"Hey, how's it going this morning?"

"Shitty," she answered.

"Well, that's an improvement over yesterday, when I believe you said, "Why keep going?"

"I guess that'll be the bright spot to focus on for today," she countered in a very sarcastic tone.

The Point

"Let's go to breakfast before you head to the store, we can meet at the Light House—my treat," Lucy offered.

"No, I don't feel like going out... people stare."

People *did* stare. Iron Bay was a small community, and exciting things didn't happen very often. Some people believed Nora's story, that Dane tried to kill her and killed Badger, and others believed Dane and thought Nora was nuts.

"You'll have to face the world some day; why not today?" Lucy tried to be positive, persuasive.

"Maybe at lunch, it'll give me time to psych myself up." Nora was reluctant.

"I'm gonna hold you to that. You need to get back out there. I'll pick you up at the shop, we can walk down to the restaurant together."

She said goodbye to her friend and continued working on motivating herself to function.

She shuffled to the bathroom; her toes peeking out of her pajama bottoms as she inched forward. The weather was already unusually cold. The morning temps were somewhere in the low thirties, and that was chilly even by Iron Bay standards.

Nora was stiff in the morning. Having to sleep in a propped position all night, the cast on a pillow, the pillow on her chest, really put a crick in her back.

She was sure the fall hadn't helped either. For weeks it had felt like every inch of her was bruised. Every shallow breath and every minor movement had been painful for a while.

She stood in front of the pedestal sink, her toes curling against the icy tile as she looked at herself in the mirror. Her hair was stringy and oily. She had bags under her eyes deep enough to pack a bathrobe in. She hadn't tweezed or waxed, washed or primped: she simply no longer cared.

This once-attractive, vivacious young woman was now happily disheveled, uninterested in the attention of the opposite sex, basically uninterested in the daily routine of giving a shit about anything at all.

"You should at least shower; you wouldn't want to offend the delicate sensibilities of the customers," Nora said to her reflection as though she were trying to persuade herself to care.

She forced herself into the shower, her casted arm hanging precariously out of the curtain while she struggled to wash her long hair with her functioning hand. She stood in the shower, the hot water pounding against her back, washing away the fog of her latest nightmare.

She showered for a considerable amount of time, the steam billowing into the small bathroom, streaking the walls, and clouding the mirror. She turned the handles, closing the spigot on her antique fixtures now that the water was running cold. Carefully, she stepped over the lip of the rolled cast-iron tub, her feet landing on the plush white bath mat, red from the heat of the blistering water.

She snagged a towel hanging on the back of the door from the day before. She wrapped her hair, swirling the terry cloth into what looked like a loose and askew turban.

"Now the tricky part," she sighed. Reaching under the sink pedestal, she retrieved a towel from a whitewashed basket. She shook it, undoing its tidy fold. With one corner clenched between her teeth, she reached

The Point

for the other with her right hand. She tucked her chin to her chest, the towel still hanging from her mouth as she pulled the white cotton bath sheet around her torso. Using a twisting motion to pull the towel's other corner, she tucked it tightly, allowing it to hang from her frame like a strapless dress. "Now I can add contortionist to my resume," she mumbled.

Stepping up to the sink, she lifted a gauzy hand towel from its decorative bronze hook. Its cream-and-gray stripes were perfectly coordinated with the bathroom's décor. She leaned, tiptoeing forward, to wipe the steam from the mirror.

The fog cleared, and she stood staring at herself in its reflection. She no longer cared to look. She had once preened, tousling her long twisted locks, pleased with whom she was. Nora no longer felt that way. She felt ugly, disgusted by her own image. Dane had damaged something deep within her. She struggled daily to deal with what she let him do.

"How could you be so stupid!" she scowled at her reflection, her voice elevated and tinged with disgust.

Dropping the towel to the floor, she went to her room to dress. She stood in the open wardrobe, shivering, unable to cross her arms for warmth because of the cumbersome cast.

"Ugh," she grumbled as she scanned the many garments, all so cute and youthful. She shut the doors, uninterested in what the closet provided. The dresser was reserved for the more rugged, and utilitarian wear. Jeans, sweaters, and p.j.'s nestled in its drawers. She rummaged to find something more appropriate, eventually fishing out some old jeans and her favorite camp shirt. It was a well-worn flannel checked with a warm palette, its large plaid print and fall coloring suited for autumn wear.

The problem with Nora's plaid-shirt choice was the cast. She would have to cut open the left side of the shirt and remove the sleeve to get it over the lump of plaster she was cemented into.

She had several other shirts already butchered to accommodate the apparatus, but *they* weren't *her* anymore. *No more pastels, or frills, never again*, she promised herself.

"Who are you now?" she asked herself in the mirror. She hadn't morphed into a beautiful and delicate butterfly. She was transformed from pupa to beetle, its hard shell a shield. She was no longer the vibrant, easygoing girl she'd once been. She no longer wanted to pretend to be bubbly and friendly. No more pastels, or skirts, or care of what was fashionable. She was going to put on her favorite camp shirt, and nothing and no one was going to stop her. She pulled on her underwear and jeans. Her wet, tangled hair bounced along with her bare breasts as she stomped down the back staircase to the kitchen.

She came to a halt in the doorway. Her father was leaning incredibly close to Aunt Sara, as though they were having a deeply intimate conversation.

Aunt Sara was Nora's mother's younger sister. She came to town when William told her of Nora's situation. A divorcee, Aunt Sara had limited attachments back in Green River. Her husband of ten years had recently left her for a younger woman.

"Thankfully, I never procreated with that jerk," Aunt Sara would offer at the end of every conversation about her ex.

The Point

She'd been in Iron Bay for over a month. Nora wondered why she hadn't returned home already; *clearly we could manage by now*, she thought.

Aunt Sara was lonely and enjoyed the company. She was single now, after all.

"That piece of shit bastard," Aunt Sara explained, "He dumped me when he decided he'd rather give it to a girl fifteen years younger than me. FIFTEEN YEARS!" she emphasized, clearly pissed off about it still.

Sara discovered that her husband had been indiscreet with this young woman when she found a note from his paramour in her office mailbox.

Apparently Ashley (the little slut's name) not only was in love with Daryl (the husband) but she was now with child. Ashley's note read as follows:

Mrs. Porter: You don't know me, or about me I'm sure, but my name is Ashley Jamieson. Your husband and I are in love and we have conceived a child from that love. Our baby is due later this year. Please understand that I never intended to hurt you, but your husband loves me and will be leaving you. Again, my apologies,
Ashley Jamieson

The thing that was so hurtful about Daryl's indiscretion was that Sara had forgone having children because Daryl hadn't wanted any, and she was happy to comply. Now she was no spring chicken, single at forty, and childless.

"Daryl is a son of a bitch," she would enthusiastically offer anytime he came up in conversation. "Piece of shit bastard."

Nora loved her Aunt Sara. She was in her late teens when Nora was born and was the source of many happy childhood memories. She took Nora to the beach and camping, and spent many summer weekends with her when William and Elizabeth wanted to spend time alone.

Once again, she helped out when needed, caring for the house and providing emotional support to William while Nora was still in the hospital. Eventually she lent a hand to her niece as she struggled to care for herself, inhibited by her injuries. She brushed Nora's hair and wiped her tears when all of her grief would spill over.

This wasn't the first time Aunt Sara had stayed to help out. She was there when Nora's mother passed, staying to help her brother-in-law, who was devastated by the loss of his wife, and comfort her niece, who had lost her mother.

Although Sara had lost her sister, she found relief from her despair by caring for her brother-in-law and her niece.

Sara stayed; she stayed until it seemed as though they were back on their feet.

Well, here she was again, keeping a promise to her late sister, watching over her niece and brother-in-law. It was a great comfort having Aunt Sara around. Nora hadn't realized it before, but her aunt was a great deal like her mother. It was like catching a rare glimpse of her mom. Whenever Sara turned a corner or was overheard speaking from another room, it was like her mother was there. Aunt Sara seemed to fill a deep and empty space: it was nice.

It seems she's filling a deep and empty space for Dad now too, she thought as she watched the two interacting at the sink. Her father had his hip on the

The Point

counter's edge, with one hand on the lip of the sink and the other clutching a coffee mug, while leaning in to Sara, who was also leaning in toward him. The Kat watched from above, his eyes ever judging.

Nora walked right through. She didn't care at this very moment what was going on between them. She was on a mission to get to the tool shed.

William and Sara drew away from each other as Nora stormed through the kitchen toward the back door. They were startled, like teens caught with their pants down.

"Did you see what I saw?" William asked, double-checking with Sara.

"If you think it was your daughter skulking through the kitchen, topless, and headed out the back door, then yes."

Nora had opened the door to the back porch, which was filled with quite the chill on this crisp September morning. She stepped out and shuddered as her feet hit the cold wooden floor. She pulled a pair of wellies from the boot tray that sat beneath a row of hooks donned with a variety of coats and outerwear.

She moved as quickly as the cast allowed, shoving her feet into the rubber boots. She pulled a scarf from one of the brass knobs, swirling it around her neck the best she could, given the handicap the broken arm created.

Nora opened the door, and descended the stairs that led to the back yard. She stomped down with purpose, her feet squeaking in the wellies as she clomped along. She covered her bare breasts with her right arm as she trudged, the scattered fall foliage crunching beneath her feet as she stormed to the shed through the back yard.

William and Sara were slow to react. They were both still trying to process what they'd just seen.

William ran to the window and watched his daughter barrel toward the shed, shirtless, in only a scarf and rubber boots. He turned and looked at Sara.

"That's it, she's finally snapped! I think she's lost her mind," he stated, his eyes wide and his tone perplexed.

"Well, don't just stand there, let's get out there and make sure she isn't going to hurt herself," Aunt Sara commanded, jolting William into action.

They scurried into the porch, grabbing jackets on the fly, the cool morning air a shock to their systems.

They busted into the shed with a loud crash as they frantically approached Nora.

She had her back to them, standing at the workbench; the sound of a saw squealing and whirring cut through the air.

William yelled at her, his calls going unanswered as the noise from the saw washed him out. He slowly approached her, placing his hand on her shoulder.

Nora turned abruptly, the cutting wheel on the Dremel tool still running on high, a serious but purposeful look, her brow set sternly.

"What!" she yelled at her father over the noise of the saw.

"What are you *doing* out here half naked and using power tools?" he asked loudly, trying to project his voice over the squealing device.

"Ridding myself of some ghosts," she replied as she turned back around and commenced sawing into the cast.

The Point

Plaster dust flew into the air as Nora ran the saw's small cutting wheel along the length of her forearm. She had to be careful not to cut too deep.

"Aren't you going to stop her," Sara questioned in disbelief as her brother-in-law just stood and watched as his daughter removed the cast herself.

"No," William barked. "Let her do it, maybe she needs to take control."

Aunt Sara backed into the shed's corner, sitting on a stack of milk crates as she watched William watching Nora.

Nora pulled the saw's plug from the wall and set it on the bench in front of her. She strained, struggling to split the cast with one hand. William placed his hands on her shoulders and gently guided her to face him.

"Let me help you," he said, his voice hushed as he spoke to his daughter in a loving tone.

She put up her right hand and tipped her chin back and out of the way. Her father grabbed the cast firmly on each side of the channel and pulled. The plaster creaked and groaned in protest as he pulled with all his might. He pried, his knuckles white under the strain as he struggled to release his daughter from the cast's physical and emotional hold. He gritted his teeth, his face a shade short of crimson as he yanked.

Suddenly the cast gave with a crack and a tear. Bits of plaster scattered to the floor. Nora looked at her father's labored face. Tears welled in his eyes as his glance met hers. They stood together, filled with overwhelming emotion. The reality of what they'd both recently faced was finally being addressed. With her aunt peering from the corner, Nora and her father quietly came to terms with the reality of the tragedy they'd both escaped.

William stood and looked at his daughter, knowing that freeing her from that cast had set something free in her spirit.

The light in her eyes shifted. The dim haze of helplessness and depression seemed to lift immediately. A new look washed in. It was a look of indifference. William optimistically viewed it as a new and stronger resolve.

"I didn't think that thing was ever going to let go," he laughed. His relief was not from the removal but from the emotional weight it seemed to lift from his daughter.

Nora quickly shifted to a new topic.

"Did I see the two of you together in the kitchen this morning looking…flirtatious?" she asked as she rubbed her freshly paroled arm.

"We were just talking, right, Willie?" Aunt Sara interjected from the shed's corner.

Nora leaned to the side, peeking around her father, who stood between her and the view of her aunt.

"Did you just call him Willie?" she asked, incredibly amused by the nickname. "It looked like flirting or even close, intimate chatting," Nora continued, giving her aunt an inquisitive look.

"There might be some feelings," William blurted, not knowing how else to approach the subject.

"Can we continue this talk inside, my tits are freezing," Nora bluntly announced as she headed for the shed door.

William looked at Sara and found she had the same look of awe on her face as he did. Nora always had a fun and direct sense of humor, but she'd never been *that* forward before. William held his hand out to Sara, helping her to her feet. He shrugged as he watched Nora trudge forcefully toward the house's back door; she scattered leaves with every step.

William and Sara followed her to the house hand in hand.

They dropped off their coats and shoes in the back porch before entering the kitchen where they found Nora leaning against the sink, her arms folded. She'd thrown on a sweater from one of the hooks on the way in.

"So, are the two of you… you know?"

William and Sara were speechless. They were unsure how to approach the subject. They looked at each other, then at Nora.

"We seemed to have bonded while you were recovering." William was once again flushed; this time it wasn't from the strain.

"We wanted to wait for the right time to tell you, we weren't sure how you'd take it," Aunt Sara added.

"Well, I'll tell you what I think…. I think, whatever. It's about time Dad got back on the horse. At least I like the person he's chosen." Nora winked at her dad. "You shifty devil, how long has this been going on?" she asked, harassing him.

"Just a few weeks," he admitted.

"I think we felt the connection right away but we tried to fight it at first, worrying that maybe it was inappropriate," Sara added.

"Well, I think it's great," Nora said with a satisfied grin. "Besides, sound travels in this old house, the heating registers are all connected. You weren't as sneaky as you thought you were."

William and Sara stood in the kitchen, smiling with embarrassment. Nora walked out of the kitchen and headed to her room to finish getting dressed.

Her favorite shirt was still waiting on the bed. She dropped the sweater she was wearing and kicked it to the side. She slipped both arms through the straps of a bra with ease. "Ahh, it's about time." She sighed with relief. Now the tricky part: she tried to reach behind and close the hooks, but her broken arm was stiff. It had been locked in one position for several weeks, and although large movements were simple enough: taking off a sweater, putting on a shirt… stretching to reach and bend in an awkward position was still a bit tough, but something was better than nothing.

Nora simply turned the bra so the clasp was at her belly, simplifying the hooking process. She took the shirt and pulled its left sleeve over her newly freed arm. *What a wonderful feeling,* she thought, as she watched her hands work in unison to button the flannel. It was funny how an act so simple could suddenly become so profound. "Huh," she uttered, knowing she'd never take anything for granted again.

She returned to the bathroom, anxious to finally do something about her hair. As she stood in the mirror, she found she was still disgusted by her own reflection. The resentment she had for Dane, and the fact that she let him get away with so much, still stared back at her. She quickly ran a brush through her hair, another one of those acts now simplified by the use of both hands. She grabbed her bag and headed downstairs: she was eager to get to work.

Chapter 24

Dane Buchman was bent. He was a dark and twisted soul. Although he was never treated for mental illness, it had often been mentioned to his mother, by teachers and caregivers, that there were red flags. Of course their recommendations fell on psychotic ears... so no action was taken.

He may have skirted therapy and meds as a boy, but he was, at the very least, a sociopath. He'd always acted with his own enjoyment in mind. He cared not for the feelings of others and knew that he was always right, no matter what.

Dane flipped the lights on in his garage. He ran the sleeve of his gray knit sweatshirt gingerly over the front of his Charger, brushing some dust from its obnoxiously yellow hood. He needed to make sure it was spotless before commencing his usual morning workout.

The fluorescent lights of the garage glinted in the paint's shiny surface as he caught his reflection, using his fingers to correct a stray hair at his forehead.

He was eager to get the day's lifting in before he headed to the mountain for a celebratory weekend.

A lot had transpired in the last few weeks and he was looking forward to a little R&R.

Nora had presented quite the challenge when she awoke in the hospital after the incident and started pointing fingers. She blamed Dane for her fall at the lake and even told the authorities that she suspected he'd sexually assaulted her once while she was passed out at her home.

Of course, she was telling the truth: he was responsible for the fall *and* he did assault her sexually, but he looked forward to shirking that responsibility and persuading the powers that be that he loved her and had only wanted to save her.

He held his ground, sitting in the hospital room, a look of shock and disbelief across his face as Nora pointed at him. "He dropped me intentionally, he said he would make sure I didn't have his child. I think he meant to kill me, just like he killed my dog." Tears ran from her eyes as she detailed the events of that day. She coughed as she sobbed, choking on her own fear and grief.

Remaining steadfast, his performance was unbroken. He had everyone convinced that Nora was delusional; everyone except her father and her close friends, everyone who knew Dane had harmed her before.

The Sheriff's Department took her seriously, forwarding her statement to the chief prosecuting attorney, Margaret VanHeusen. Ms. VanHeusen was thorough, a real ball-buster. She was intimidating, with her black hair twisted in a tight-up 'do that seemed to accentuate her severe facial expressions.

Regardless of Ms. VanHeusen's dedication to justice, there were no eyewitnesses to the incident. There was no conclusive physical evidence that pointed to anything other than Dane's account that she slipped and he tried to save her.

The prosecutor tried to explain. "Without eyewitnesses or stronger physical evidence, it's a simple case of your word against his."

Dane grabbed a bottle of water from the mini-fridge that was recessed below the flat screen and set it on the floor next to the weight bench. He loved thinking about the day he was cleared of wrongdoing. Smiling, he pulled off his shirt and flexed his arms in the mirror, knowing those were the very arms that terrorized her and put an end to his *little* problem.

He paid his respects to his powerful and capable appendages with a kiss to each bicep as he flexed, before retrieving the weights from their stand.

"Oh yeah," he huffed as he lifted. "Who's smarter? Who's sexier? No one," he chanted as he curled.

Lifting, he admired his form, admired his angular jaw, admired the precision with which he'd duped not only Nora and her father to trust him once again, but the police and the prosecutor into believing he was innocent of the charges.

Dane pumped, curling each dumbbell, working up a sweat, adrenaline coursing through his bulging veins.

"You're incredible," he grunted as he pulled the weight to his chest, "Unstoppable," winking at his fine form in the large plate-glass mirror.

"You're untouchable," he assured himself, continuing his compliments.

"You deserve this weekend away, you crafty devil." He grunted as he started another rep, focusing on his triceps.

He lifted and admired himself until he was ready to head into the house for a shower and to pack for his romp at the mountain.

Chapter 25

Mt. Hematite was ablaze with the reds and oranges of the changing fall foliage. Dane took in the autumn view from the hotel window as he turned down the bed. The garish polyester bedspread and its floral print were in perfect coordination with the widely striped drapes.

He drew the drapes closed before reaching into his pants pocket to place its contents under his pillow. Stripping down to his shorts, he climbed in.

Reclining, with his hands tucked under the pillow, he felt for the items he'd just stashed there, retrieving a condom. He pulled down the waistband of his silken boxers and gave himself a bit of a fluff so he could apply the prophylactic.

Plunging his hand back under the pillow, he felt for the compass.

He held it in his hand, rubbing its smooth crystal face with his thumb, searching for the chip in its surface.

With his eyes closed he focused on the events that took place the day he received his little trophy. The feelings that the small brass treasure stirred were deep and powerful.

As he continued to caress the compass, his urges were building as he waited for his date to emerge from the bathroom.

This celebration couldn't be trusted to just anyone, so he'd hired a professional. Dane didn't want some whiny girl who would complain or get squeamish, so he'd entrust his fun this weekend to a pro.

The Point

Mindy was the best. She and Dane had partied before, and tonight he planned to fulfill his fantasies. Emboldened by his skillful dodge of prosecution, he was ready to complete acts undone and fulfill a latent fantasy. Invincible, unstoppable, and insatiable, he was fully prepared to take his newfound appetite and bite deeply into every situation.

"Hurry up," he called as he watched the needle float, its point unsettled as he shifted the compass's position.

"You better hurry up and get out here," he yelled at the closed bathroom door. "I'm starting without you, there's no tip at the end of the night if I have to start without you."

"Just a minute," Mindy yelled from the other side of the door. " I just want to make sure I'm looking extra-special for you, sweetheart."

The door began to open and Dane looked on as Mindy emerged, wearing the sundress he'd provided. Its cut and pattern were eerily similar to the dress Nora had worn.

Mindy's hair was hanging loosely, with a beachy wave twisted through the long, light-brown strands.

"You need to go back into the bathroom and splash water on the front of that dress," Dane explained.

"It's chilly in here… but you're the customer," she sighed.

She returned, the dress splashed, but far from wet enough. He jumped from the bed and wrapped his arms around Mindy, walking her to the sink, his erection prodding her along.

"Nice pup tent," she joked as he led her to the bathroom sink, his penis stuck in her back like a gun at a hold-up.

"No joking," he barked, his mood suddenly dark.

He reached around her, forcefully twisting the handle, the spigot blasting cold water with more force than the shallow sink bowl could handle. The icy water sprayed on the walls and over the bowl's edge, pooling on the floor.

Using his left arm to hold her in place, he used his right hand to bring the cold water to her breasts, splashing her in quick, forceful bursts.

Cupping the pouring water, he brought his hand to Mindy's breasts, again and again.

"Dane, it's cold, my breasts are getting sore from the pounding."

"Turn around," he commanded.

Lessening his grip, he held Mindy's shoulders, guiding her to face him.

He ran his hands over her nipples, obviously stiffened by the encounter with the cold water. They were poking through the thin fabric of the dress, her entire breast clearly visible.

"That's what I was looking for," he mumbled with a low breathy tone.

Grabbing her hair, he pulled her head back to expose her neck.

Pulling at the dress, he exposed Mindy's breasts. He ran his tongue, hot and velvety, down the length of her neck, straight to her erect nipples.

Tantalized, he bit down. "Stop!" she shrieked, crying out in pain. She struggled to pull away from his hold. Heat radiated though her left breast as the trauma of his cruelty took hold. He pulled back to view his handiwork. Her nipple was split on both sides, a small trickle of blood running along the side of her breast.

The Point

"Jesus Christ, Dane, not so hard!" she griped while giving him a dirty look. "Sorry, just got carried away," he smirked apologetically. "Just wondered what you tasted like."

He grabbed Mindy's shoulders and eased her to the tiny bathroom's floor. The small gray tiles were submerged beneath a puddle created by the overflow of the diminutive sink. Dane laid Mindy into the water, the cold ceramic sending a shiver through her thin frame.

"I want you to lay on your side, with your left arm under your head at the elbow."

"I've had some weird requests, Dane, but that one is really bizarre."

"The customer is always right," he reminded his date.

She lay down, her arm positioned as he requested.

He ran his hands through the water on the floor and then through Mindy's hair, in an attempt to give it a wetter appearance.

"Finally," he murmured. "Perfect." He'd set the stage, but had one final request for poor Mindy. "I want you to hold very still, as though you're unconscious."

"That's fuckin' weird, Dane," she said as she started to sit up.

"No, lay back down, trust me, I'm not going to hurt you. I just want to act out a little fantasy." Doing his best to turn on the charm, he tried to smile and put her at ease.

She returned to her submissive position, left arm tucked beneath her head.

He began to run his hands over her, feeling her cold flesh, brushing the soaked fabric of the sundress over her hardened nipples.

She winced as Dane bumped the injured breast.

"Sorry, forgot." He gritted his teeth with an apology.

He always treated Mindy with respect. This was a business transaction; it would be rude to mistreat her on purpose (the bite to the nipple aside).

She went back to her limp and unanimated state; he was aroused. He could remember that day after Nora fell. How her nipples looked under the drenched sundress. The way the fabric clung to her unconscious body. The way the compass pointed to her motionless form. He could still picture the way her hair floated in the constant push and pull of the shallow water on the Point's ledge.

"I'm going to move you now," he warned her. "Keep still, stay limp."

She did as she was told. He picked her up and pulled her to him, her relaxed body flopping just like Nora's did that day when he cradled her in his arms. Today would be different though, because today he would have his way with her. He didn't have enough time then, but he did now.

He positioned Mindy over his lap, his right arm supporting her back, as her shoulders and head hung over his forearm. He used his left hand to pull up the dress, its wet cloth clinging to her body as he shifted it past her breasts.

He ran his hand over her, exploring her, enjoying the way her cold wet skin felt under his outstretched palm. He hesitated, cupping her bare abdomen with his palm. "I got ya... finished you off, you'll never see the light of day." She peeked, concerned about the dialogue he was having with her lower half. His sexual tastes had often been extraordinary, she figured this was just one of his games.

The Point

Am I getting turned on, she thought with dismay, Dane's strange, sick game appealing to her as well.

He shifted, positioning himself.

She held as still as possible while he worked, pulling her again and again. He was deep in thought with his eyes closed, his lips pursed tightly… he was somewhere else.

He relived that moment at Lake Paramount when he sat with Nora's unconscious body, aching to molest it. Dane found his release and pulled Mindy to his chest, where he held her. He whispered in her ear, "Thank you, Nora."

His eyes popped open. The trance was broken and he found himself suddenly and acutely aware that he had Nora to thank for his newfound power, for the discovery of the parasite that grew within him. It was at the Point that day that he discovered who he really was. It was at that point in time that he discovered the true depths of his darkness.

He'd been playing his little games of dominance with stupid girls for years. He'd spit on them and forced them into embarrassing situations and assaulted them every which way.

His needs were more complex now; his desire had escalated. Making dates uncomfortable would never be enough again—he wanted more. *I needed to push the limits. I'd never felt the way I had with Nora that day, I need to feel it again.* Sitting deep in thought, his hand found its way to his abdomen. The parasite calls.

He scooted back, shocked by the sudden sense of self-awareness he was experiencing.

"I'm sorry," Dane said, apologizing in Mindy's direction.

"No worries, love, johns call me by other girls' names all the time."

He looked at her, a vacant stare planted on his face,

"I need you to get out," he barked.

"Alright, love, where's the cash?"

"In my wallet. Take an extra fifty for the nipple," he directed, his tone now flat as he stared at the bathroom wall.

She took off the sundress and draped it over the back of the chair tucked under the desk–TV stand combo. She pulled on an overcoat and proceeded to rummage through Dane's wallet for her fee, plus fifty.

"See ya later, hot stuff," she twittered as she headed for the door. "Maybe I can pretend to be conscious next time and do that thing you like with my tongue."

"Get out!" he yelled, his patience wearing thin. "There isn't going to be a next time."

Mindy scrambled out the door, giving Dane the finger while cursing him under her breath. "Good, you fucking weirdo—the whole corpse thing was a bit much, anyway."

He sat in the bathroom alone, his bare behind in the pool of recently splashed water, his thoughts reeling. He had a hunger that needed feeding, and he would need to feed it soon.

Dane pulled the spent condom from his now-flaccid penis, leaving it crumpled on the floor. Its freshly ejaculated contents oozed from its rolled opening and spilled onto the carpeting.

Chapter 26

Jake sat at the Light House diner, slowly stirring cream into his coffee. He watched the dairy swirl as the spoon clinked delicately on the sides of the old ceramic cup.

He'd been in the café a few times now. It was located conveniently across the street from the Regency Inn. He'd been waiting to approach Nora, wanting so badly to discover what had happened to her. He'd heard rumors and read the reports; but he wanted, no needed, to hear her side of it. He couldn't let the situation rest until he did.

He had knocked on her door a few times; her father would send him away. He would catch a glimpse of her from her upstairs window from time to time.

Jake set down his spoon, and grabbed a menu. It was wedged between the caddy of condiments and the napkin holder.

The laminated cover was tacky to the touch. Years of poorly wiped grime had accumulated on the curled and yellowed plastic. The menus in this establishment were clearly as old as the rest of its contents.

"I guess the old dishes and outdated décor are part of its charm," he thought to himself as he handled the laminate with the very tips of his fingers.

While he was perusing the menu Lucy was headed to Reynolds' Sport and Tackle to retrieve her friend.

Nora was standing at the register, her festive fall flannel a rugged shift from her usual dress. She was ringing up a transaction at the register, checking the price tag on a box of shotgun shells with her left hand while typing in the amount with her right.

"Nora," Lucy waved excitedly from the door as the bell jingled its familiar tune. "Holy shit, you got your cast off! How does it feel?"

"Just a second, Luce, I'm with a customer," she said, pointing one finger to the ceiling signaling she needed a moment, while focusing on the items before her.

Lucy put her hand down, the enthusiastic wind knocked out of her sails by her friend's short response.

She continued to ring up the order, her head down, fiercely focused on the task at hand.

"That will be $58.95," she said as she bagged and organized the items. The attractive stranger retrieved his wallet from his back pocket and presented her with his credit card.

Lucy was admiring this fine male specimen. He was tall, dark, and handsome, six foot four, and in fine physical shape. Lucy glanced at his firm behind and looked up at Nora as if to say, *did you see that.* Nora kept it professional, never even hinting to Lucy she was interested. The good-looking stranger was obviously trying to flirt. He kept trying to look her in the eyes, ducking to make eye contact. His high cheekbones and a wide white smile offset his angular jaw. Lucy was mesmerized, but Nora couldn't care less.

"Thank you," the fine guy nodded as he picked up his bag, his hand grazing Nora's. She pulled back abruptly.

"You're welcome," she returned, trying not to sneer. "Come again."

The Point

The handsome stranger seemed put off by her reaction; *but maybe he shouldn't be getting so fresh with women he just met,* Nora thought.

"What a creep," she shouted when the door jingled the customer's farewell.

"He was so attractive. Why not just be friendly?" Lucy wondered.

"It only leads to trouble," Nora assured her friend. "Besides, why does he think it's okay to touch my hand? He doesn't know me. What motives does he have? I look like hell, how was he even attracted to me?"

"You're a beautiful girl, makeup and hairspray just accentuate what's already there. He just liked what he saw."

"Dogs!" Nora shouted at the door. "Men are all dogs. Wait, I take that back. That's an insult to dogs everywhere: all men are bastards!"

"Are you ready to head to the diner?" Lucy asked. "Where's your dad, shouldn't he have popped out of the back when you were disparaging men and their character so loudly?"

"He hasn't come in yet. I suspect he is tangled up with Aunt Sara at home."

"Holy shit!" Lucy laughed. "I didn't know the old guy had it in him. Oh, but how do you feel about it, you aren't taking it too hard, are ya?" Lucy asked, realizing it might be a sensitive subject for her friend.

"No, it's okay. I love Aunt Sara, I know they'll be good to each other."

"Good. I'm glad it isn't causing you any grief. I don't think you need any more stress."

Nora appreciated her friend's concern but was tired of being treated like a china doll. She didn't want to be viewed as some fragile child ready to break.

She reached around to the back wall and flipped off the main bank of lights, only leaving the counter illuminated.

"Come on, I'll just close up for lunch. If Dad wanted it open, he would've been here by now."

Nora escorted Lucy to the front door and flipped the Open sign to Closed.

They strolled up Lincoln Street arm in arm toward the Light House Café.

It's great to be out without the cast, Nora thought, *it's cutting down on the number of looks I'm getting.* She looked down at her feet as she and Lucy walked and talked. She was wearing a pair of utilitarian brown boots, which she watched shuffle along the gray concrete of the city sidewalk. They were feminine for boots of the sort, but stood in stark contrast to the delicate and rather elegant footwear of her good friend. Nora preferred to focus on the view below. She felt it was better than having to see all the curious faces stare at her as though she should be wearing a scarlet letter on her chest.

"I wish these people would mind their own fucking business," she whispered out of the side of her mouth to Lucy.

"Let 'em stare. We should just wave and smile, that'll put them off," Lucy suggested as she looked out to the passing onlookers, waving her hand as though she were in a beauty pageant.

She looked up and found Lucy waving to the townsfolk, some of who felt obligated to wave back.

The Point

Laughing, she realized there weren't as many stares as she thought there'd be, and clearly the fine people of Iron Bay were good-hearted enough to return a wave to Lucy, who just seemed to be waving like a demented beauty queen at this point.

"You're crazy, Lucy," she laughed as she nudged her friend, causing her to stumble to the side. Lucy returned the nudge as they continued their walk to the diner.

When they arrived at the Light House, Nora's spirits had lifted. Not enough to admit she was out of the shadows and back to her old self—she might never be her old self again—but just enough that, for one minute, she felt there was a bit of hope.

The two young women stepped through the door into their favorite gathering spot and took a seat at their favorite booth. The booth was to the left as you entered the diner, fourth booth out of the six that lined the row of plate-glass windows. This booth gave the best view of the street and the many people who would scurry by. Nora and Lucy loved to people-watch, and this was the place to do it.

Lucy lifted two menus from their resting place between the napkins and condiments, and handed one to her friend. They both opened and began to peruse the fare.

"You know, I don't understand why we still read the menu; we have the damn thing memorized," Nora commented as she closed her menu and proceeded to tuck it back between the table's objects. "Not to mention how disgusting they feel."

"Tradition," Lucy shot back matter-of-factly, as she dropped the menu.

Lucy looked up to find Nora staring over her shoulder, her cheeks suddenly flushing.

"What is it?" Lucy asked, as she quickly turned to see what was behind her that was so deeply affecting her friend.

"Jake's behind you, two booths back. What the fuck is he still doing here?"

Lucy looked on, while Nora made eye contact with him. He stood and moved toward their booth. Nora was clearly shaken by his presence.

Lucy had never seen Jake before. She'd been given a description by her friend, even seen a photo on her cell once, but it didn't do him justice. He was five foot ten, maybe a little less. He was athletically built, not like Dane or Cooper, but still had that strong, virile look to him. His hair was thick and wavy, a dark brown that made the blue of his smiling eyes really pop. Lucy was charmed already.

"I can't believe I'm running into you here. I've been trying for days to see you." He was genuinely happy to see her. There was a longing in his voice. Lucy felt for him.

"I shouldn't see you, Jake. I told you—go home."

She was firm but calm.

"Please, just talk to me, tell me what happened, I'm sure we can work it out."

"Even if I could forgive myself, or you, for being too stupid to just talk about what was going on between us, you might not be able to get past the things I've done," she explained.

"You have to at least give me the chance. You regret we weren't more open before, so let's be open now." He

The Point

was practically begging, his voice quivering with emotion; he was ready to crack.

He was about to sit down to hear Nora's tragic tale, when the waitress arrived. She was dressed in the usual uniform: a white-buttoned shirt (which coordinated perfectly with her pale complexion) and black slacks. She had a black apron that was pulled over her neck and tied around back. There was food crusted to the waist, and the nametag on her pocket read *Bambi*. Bambi had warned Nora about Dane. Nora eyed her, now sorry she'd dismissed the waitress's warning.

"What can I get for you today," she asked, her familiar monotone voice accentuated by her large, vacant, saucer-like eyes.

"Just coffee for now," Lucy answered for everyone.

Nora was locked to Jake's gaze, preparing herself to divulge all her secrets.

The waitress departed, her shuffle as slow as her synapses seemed to fire.

"Fine," Nora blurted. "Now that the waitress is gone, let's spill it all. Sit down next to Lucy and I'll tell you the whole sordid tale." She gestured to the seat next to her friend.

"I could leave, the two of you clearly have a lot to talk about." Lucy began to stand as though she were going to slip out.

"No, you should stay. I need you to stay." Nora looked at her friend, her eyes saying it all.

"Okay, I'll stay."

"So, what do you know already?" Nora asked Jake, wondering how much info he'd been able to extract from local gossip.

"Only what I read in the papers. They were vague, mostly eyewitness reports and legal findings," he confessed.

"Holy shit, Nora, that's right! You broke your father's rule…you got your name in the paper!"

"Thanks for pointing that out at this moment Lucy," she snarled.

She returned her attention to Jake. "What do you want to know?" she asked him.

"Start from the beginning, and end at the point where you got pissed and told me to get the fuck out," he suggested.

"Fine." Nora took a deep breath. She hadn't started talking; yet she could feel the sting of tears already burning her eyes.

"We parted ways. I was hoping you would say you loved me and we would see each other during the summer. As you know, we didn't talk about our standing, and you didn't want to see me."

"That's not true, I told you I had a lot to do."

"You should have been more specific." Nora was starting to feel the same anger she'd felt at the shop that day.

"Fine, I was a bit short-sighted, please go on." Jake clasped his hands in front of him, waiting for her to continue.

"I came home missing you, wondering where we stood, too stupid and caught up waiting for you to make the first move."

"I didn't know, I'm sorry." Jake was concerned: he could see now that Nora was paving the way for a monumental blow.

The Point

"I met someone when I was visiting my mother at the cemetery. He gave me a ride when my car wouldn't start. If I'm going to be honest, I was immediately attracted to him. He was incredibly sexy. Tall, built, very charming."

"Are you sure you want to get into all the details, Nora; Jake is starting to look a little green." Lucy patted Jake on the shoulder, trying to help put him at ease.

"He wants to know, so he can hear it all." Nora was stern, ready to tell the whole tale.

"Dane is his name, and we had a brief, passionate moment in his office that first day, but I felt guilty, so I stopped him and then tried to avoid him."

"Then you saw him at Cooper's party," Lucy chimed in.

"That's right. Lucy invited me to a party her boyfriend Cooper was throwing. Well, guess who happened to be there... Dane. Apparently Dane and Cooper are first cousins, their fathers are brothers."

"Goddamn Iron Bay... Everyone is related." Lucy chuckled. "Three degrees of separation instead of six," she joked while nudging Jake's shoulder. Nora nodded in agreement with Lucy's observation, then continued,

"Dane and I had a few drinks with everyone, and by this point I had already talked to you on the phone and you seemed distracted by your father's assistant. So, I had that swirling in the back of my mind. Anyway, the night wound on, and I found myself with my bare ass in the sand as Dane and I ..."

"I don't know if I want to hear any more." Jake dropped his head and buried his face in his hands, "I can't believe you let him... I can't even say it."

"That isn't even the worst part," Nora assured him.

"Spare me any more sex details, I know you are mad at me, but you don't have to twist the knife." Jake was now holding his stomach as though he could actually feel a dagger twisting his guts into a painful knot.

"Dane and I had many interludes. Then, just when I started to question his motives, he declared his love for me. In hindsight, that's when he started toying with me."

"What do you mean?" He leaned forward, no longer holding his stomach, his hands flat on the table's flecked surface.

"He would play games, hurt me, or play tricks that were demeaning." Nora became flushed again. The memory of Dane's cruelty began to bubble up; her anger began to rise.

"I can't believe what I let him get away with." She choked up, realizing the scope of her previous denial. Sitting in the booth at the Light House had brought from the shadows just how foolish she'd been. No wonder she felt such disgust when she looked at herself in the mirror.

"I let him have his way with me when I should've been running... then I got pregnant."

"What? What was that last part? How fucking stupid could you be?" Jake was pissed.

"I might have been able to forgive the infidelity...the idea of some other guy inside of you was hard to take but probably forgivable, but some other guy's baby, it's too much to bear." The thought of him fucking her, and coming inside of her... Jake's blood was beginning to boil.

"Oh my God, I thought I could handle it, I thought I could, but the thought of him touching you, fucking you unprotected, how could you? The one first we were going to share, you gave to him. I thought I would marry you

The Point

and we would start a family, but you already had his child inside of you…?" Jake didn't know he could feel this way.

"I thought you wanted to know what happened. You insisted we talk, I tried to tell you it was terrible, to go away, but you pushed. The story isn't over yet, so sit back down!"

Nora was on her feet, forcefully commanding Jake, while pointing toward the bench of the booth.

He returned to his seat. Nora returned to her twisted tale.

"For the sake of time and your delicate sensibilities I will condense and move right to the part where I end up in intensive care."

Nora was visibly shaken; tears were welling up in her eyes. Lucy reached across the table and placed her hands on her friend's, trying to provide some support.

"Take it easy, it hasn't been that long. Only talk about it if you want to." Lucy's words were soothing, her smile a moment's reprieve from the dark place she was entering.

"Dane found out about the baby and decided he would use my little dog Badger to persuade me to abort his bastard. He tortured my dog and lured me to the top of the bluff at the lighthouse. He held the dog over the edge. I tried to grab Badger, so he dropped him. I fell, clinging to the rock, I begged him to help me. He reached down; I thought he was going to pull me up. That's when I saw it, the darkness and the evil within him. He made me fall. He said he would be sure to get his way and he did. I didn't die, but the fall caused a miscarriage. Weeks later, you walked into my father's store and found me with my arm in a cast."

"Holy shit!" Jake exhaled as he stood up with both hands pushed against the table's surface, "What a fuckin' psycho!" He sat back down with a plop. He was sweating, his mouth agape; as he tried to mentally file all of the info Nora had just given him.

"What were you thinking? And you just followed him up there...for a dog? It was just a dog, you could have been killed." He couldn't believe she fell for *and* fucked that psycho. *Not to mention carrying his bastard, and actually wanting to keep it.* Jake hated her *and* felt sorry for her. He doubted his own judgment and at the same time felt guilty for not just telling her the truth at the semester's end.

Looking across the table at the girl he once loved, he searched her eyes for some semblance of who he once thought she was.

"She isn't in there anymore," Nora assured him, realizing he was searching her eyes for recognition.

"I told you that before, I was broken, and my pieces are now askew and misplaced. I'll never be the same again."

"I can't believe this is the end for us. I won't believe it," Jake stated firmly.

"Why didn't we communicate? Why did we purposely leave a distance when we parted? If I would have just declared my feelings for you instead of waiting to hear it from you first, or if you had just been honest and told me how important I was, and that you had to appease your father, we wouldn't be sitting here, confused about our situation." She was exhausted. "I was a naive girl looking for a fairy-tale prince to run to me and declare his love," she continued. "Instead, my prince

The Point

chose to work all summer in a secret plot to launch a sneak attack."

"I just needed to get things in order." Jake said looking sheepish.

"If we were so in love, if I was so important, you would have wanted to see me or at least tell me the whole truth," she insisted.

"I... I was involved with my father's assistant," he blurted.

"She's the daughter of one of my father's associates; we were to be married. I knew I loved you and wanted to be with you, but I had to get rid of her first. OH, I can't believe I'm going to tell you this," Jake said, as he wiped his face with his hands pulling at his cheeks.

"I was *with* her that night you called, because I was a coward and couldn't tell her."

"So instead of telling her about us, or just not seeing her, you felt obligated to continue fucking her," Nora said flatly, her tone steady, her voice unwavering.

"You cocksucker!" Lucy yelled into Jake's ear. She turned and faced him, her nose to his. "You've been sitting here, making my best friend feel guilty for falling for some schmuck, while you were out fucking around anyway." Lucy gave Jake a shove. He slipped off of the booth's maroon vinyl and landed flat on his ass, right in the center of the diner's aisle.

Jake looked up at the girls, who were glaring down at him. He bit his lip as he stood up and brushed the floor's debris from his behind.

"I'm sorry, I wanted you. I just didn't realize it entirely until I had returned home to Susan." Jake was defeated.

"How did we get here, Nora?" Jake asked, as though there would be some concrete answer that would fix the situation and send them running into each other's arms.

"I'll tell you how," Nora said as she stood up. "You're a lying coward, and I was a naive girl who idealized her parents' relationship. But I'm not that girl anymore."

She stepped into the aisle and headed toward the door.

"Sorry, Luce, I'll talk to you later," she said as she walked off, a sense of purpose in her step.

"Are you happy now, you shit?" Lucy asked Jake, who was still sitting next to her, a dumbfounded look on his face.

"No," he replied as he buried his face into his hands once again.

"Well, when I saw you in here today I thought maybe you would say some magic phrase and she'd find her smile. But no, instead you doubled down on why men are slime."

Lucy began to rummage through her purse for her wallet so she could leave a tip for the waitress, who had no doubt fielded a few complaints about the shouting coming from booth four.

"I know her summer fling was my fault. I planned to let it go. I didn't realize the depth of the problem. She was going to have his baby. How do you ever move past something like that?" Jake was looking to Lucy for some answer.

"You both fucked up, and either you love her or you don't. If you really want her, you'll let it go. Technically, you cheated first. Remember, you were involved with someone else the whole time you were together; she wasn't. Don't be such a shit, Jake, try to see it from her point of view."

Lucy gestured to Jake that she'd like to depart the confines of the booth.

He stood up and moved out of her way. She apologized to the spacey waitress on her way out of the restaurant. "Sorry for the commotion," Lucy said, handing the waitress a twenty.

"You know I warned your friend," she sniped with that *I told you so tone in her voice.*

"Yes, I know," Lucy agreed as she exited in pursuit of Nora.

Retrieving her phone from her purse, she sent her a text: *Hey, where'd ya go?*

She stood, scanning the windows of the local businesses, waiting for a reply. *Maybe she returned to the shop,* Lucy thought as she turned and headed back toward Reynolds' Sport and Tackle.

Chapter 27

Nora had left the Light House hell-bent for change. She was tired of who she was, and she was going to do something about it.

Storming across the street, she waltzed right into the Frothy Goat. The Goat was an English pub popular with the college crowd. She parked her ass on the stool closest to the bartender and demanded he "line 'em up."

He grinned as he approached, drying his hands on his apron as he contemplated the age of the petite blonde.

"I'll need to see some ID," the bartender said as he started lining up the shot glasses. She retrieved her license from her back pocket and handed it to him.

"Well, Miss Reynolds," the bartender started, as he inspected the card for her birthdate, "it appears you are indeed of age. What shall I fill these with?" The bartender playfully motioned to the three shot glasses resting before her.

"Tequila," Nora said with stern certainty.

"Tequila it is," the barkeep returned.

He reached down and grabbed the tequila bottle from the rail. Just as he was about to pour she stopped him. "Whoa, the good stuff," she added as she pointed to the riser on the back wall.

"As you wish." He returned the bottle to its home in the bar's underbelly and reached to the wooden shelf lining a decorative mirrored background. The long mahogany mantle was lined with bottles and decanters. Pulling the bottle of Patrón from the riser, he quickly poured, filling the glasses with the precision of a veteran bartender.

The Point

Nora watched the tequila sparkle under the warm glow of the pub's overhead lighting. Before the bartender could provide her with salt or lime, she'd already imbibed all three shots.

She tipped her head back, her eyes closed, as she focused on the warmth from the liquor running down her esophagus, its burn trailing to her stomach. She realized what she needed was a change; something so monumental that when she looked in the mirror, she'd no longer be viewing her old self.

"What do I owe ya?" she asked as she stood up.

"Twelve bucks," the bartender answered.

She set a twenty on the bar and strolled out the door. She squinted as her eyes adjusted to the afternoon sun. She walked toward the shop, scanning the street, taking in the many sights. She eyed passersby, clothing stores, and gift shop windows. She was still a block south of her father's store when she found herself in front of the Superior Salon. Posters of the latest trends in hair and nails were pinned up along with a sign that read *Walk-ins welcome*.

I think I'll do just that, she thought... *walk in*. She entered to find the salon having a rather slow day. A squat but bubbly woman, whose nametag read "Ramona," clicked over in her kitten heels and asked, "What can I do for you today, honey?"

"Cut it all off," Nora replied.

Ramona flipped her own hair over her shoulder and inquired further, "Are you sure that's what you want? Your hair's so beautiful, how 'bout a trim instead?"

"No," she replied. "I want it all gone. I want to look in the mirror and see a new me."

"Alright, hon, follow me."

Ramona led her to the back, where she seated her at the washing station. The tequila swirled around in her head as Ramona massaged the shampoo into her hair.

"So," Ramona began, as she commenced making small talk, "how was your summer?"

"I was led on by a man who said he loved me, and then when I told him I was pregnant, he dropped me from a cliff," Nora quipped, in a dry but sincere tone.

"Wow, okay... Uh, at least you seem okay now, right?" she returned, shocked by Nora's answer. Trying to act nonchalant Ramona added, "Seems like you had some excitement."

"Yes, and now it's time to turn over a new leaf," Nora said, nodding beneath Ramona's washing hands.

Ramona rinsed and toweled before leading Nora to her chair.

"Would you like to look at some pictures, try to find something you might like?"

Nora scanned the posters in the shop. Above the front door was a picture of a girl with a short pixie crop. The back was snipped to the nape of her neck and the front was heavily fringed and longer, swept to one side.

"That one," she said as she pointed to the poster's example.

"Alright, if you say so. I just want you to be sure." Ramona added, "I can't put it back."

"I'm positive," she assured her.

Sitting in the chair, every muscle in her body was relaxed from the tequila. She closed her eyes and listened to the snipping of her long golden locks. She could feel the weight of her hair lessening as Ramona sheared and clipped.

The Point

She lost track of time, as Ramona quietly worked. Business was slow, and the other woman was just sitting in the corner reading a romance novel.

Nora snapped back to reality with the roar of the hair dryer. She opened her eyes and looked to find her long blonde hair was now cropped above her ears. The color now appeared darker due to the lightest parts having been snipped off.

Although her long hair had been beautiful, her large blue eyes really popped now that her short 'do accentuated them.

"Wow," she said under her breath. "Incredible." She was very pleased. Where long tendrils once passed by her face, high cheekbones were now present. The short playful fringe of the haircut's front was pushed to one side by a wide parting, and the hair sat softly in a lovely angle above her brow.

"Incredible change," Ramona chimed. "I wish a haircut would do that much for my looks."

"Thanks, thank you so much, it's fucking amazing!" Nora exclaimed, somewhat shocked by the drastic change. "Oh, sorry about the F-word there," she apologized.

"No worries, hon, you're right—it's fuckin' amazing," Ramona assured her.

Standing up, she leaned forward to look at herself very closely in the mirror. She ran her hand through her hair. It was *so* short. It felt *so* weird. Her hair had been long since she was a child.

"Huh," Nora said, as she continued to inspect her new 'do.

She suddenly remembered she needed to get back to the shop. Lunch was running a little long today, and she hadn't even eaten.

"Ahh shit, I need to go, how much?" she asked as she walked toward the sales counter.

"This one's on me," Ramona answered. "It was my pleasure to provide a change so daring."

"Thanks," she said, leaving a twenty as a tip for the generous stylist.

She took one last look at her long hair as the other employee began sweeping it up. Each change today made being Nora Reynolds a little easier.

She walked toward the shop, her thoughts clouded by booze and beauty choices. She would often catch her reflection in store windows, enjoying the view of the new her.

When she returned to the store she found her father there with Lucy.

"Where the hell were you… Holy shit, what did you do to your hair?" Lucy was floored. She ran over to her friend and ran her hands through her hair.

"Wow! All I can say is, wow!"

"Amazing, all I had to do to make you speechless was cut off all my hair," Nora joked.

"Yeah," Lucy agreed with a one-word answer.

"Well, that's a nice change, sweetie," William said as he tried to sound complimentary.

"Yeah," Nora answered abruptly. "Well, you know, I just didn't like what I saw in the mirror anymore. After I saw Jake, I went to the bar to compose myself with a few shots and on my way back here I decided to rid myself of all that hair."

The Point

"I was worried sick, Nora! I texted, you never answered. Your father and I have been here waiting, wondering where you got off to." Lucy was peering at her with great concern.

"I'm fine. I really need everyone to lay off. I'm not going to fall apart, or get kidnapped by strangers!" She was irritated, tired of being babied.

"Why were you so late getting in, Dad?" Nora questioned.

"I was just going over something with Aunt Sara," William answered sheepishly.

"I bet you were," Lucy winked.

William blushed.

"So, let's just get it out on the table," she said to her father. "What *exactly* is going on between the two of you and when did it start? I'm not a child, I can hear the two of you giggling and carrying on... let's have it, spit it out."

"When you were in the hospital... She was there comforting me, and you. There was a tension building between us; we were both aware, but trying to ignore it. One night, she was heading back to the house; I was going to stay with you. I escorted her to the hallway to say goodnight, She leaned in and kissed my cheek... my cheek became my lips, the rest is history."

"That's enough," Nora chimed in. "I get the picture."

"I'm sorry if this hurts you, my dear. Aunt Sara and I have been torn between what we want and what we think would be best for you."

"Jesus Christ, Dad, I'm an adult. What's best for me is that you're happy so I can feel like I could leave the house someday. I might not be in the market for a man right now, but someday my prince will come. Then I should fly the nest."

"So glad to hear you say that. You really *do* seem good today."

"Yeah, shots and a haircut have really changed your tune," Lucy added.

"Is Jake gone?" Nora asked Lucy.

"I don't know?" she answered. "I didn't see if he left or where he went. I left the restaurant and he was still there. I'm not sure what he was planning to do." Lucy shrugged, "Maybe he decided to head back to Commerce City."

"Yeah, I'm sure I finally scared him off," Nora said, returning Lucy's shrug.

Chapter 28

Dane had returned from his stay at the mountain only to realize he had desires that no call girl or girlfriend could ever fulfill. Trying to kill Nora had awakened something in him, a yearning, a drive to push the limits.

He sat in his living room, his bag from the weekend still on the floor by the entryway.

What exactly will quench my thirst, he thought. Dating was way out of the question. *The fuck-up with Nora's pregnancy proved that.* Plus, it was exhausting to pretend to care for someone. He needed his victims to be one-night stands. *Of course, it will be difficult to avoid the law repeatedly, so a plan will need to be followed. A script for keeping myself out of jail.*

Although Dane had avoided prosecution in his case with Nora, local law enforcement did issue him a verbal warning (while smashing his face into the pavement with their knee in his back). It was along the lines of, "We know something happened up there, and we might not have the evidence to make it stick, but if we even as much as suspect you are up to something, we'll have your ass."

It didn't help the situation that the deputy to the town's sheriff was an old high school rival.

Doug Sanders had been dating the cheerleading captain Emily Trenton. Although Emily wasn't the prettiest girl in school, she was fit and popular. Doug and Emily were very close; they had big plans for after high school. Doug played receiver for the high school football team and Dane was the quarterback. They were teammates on the field, but off the field was a different story.

Doug was a gentleman; he'd been taking it slow with Emily. They'd been dating for many months and he'd just recently rounded third base. One night at a bonfire out at McKinley Cove, Doug had to go home early (some family function) and Dane, who had acquired a bottle of whiskey, charmed his way into Emily's pants, something Doug, or anyone else for that matter, had never done.

Let's just say Doug had yet to let that go. Surely Dane would have thought twice about violating Emily if he'd known that Doug would someday become Deputy Sanders and have the authority to arrest him.

Dane did a few chores and unpacked from his weekend before settling into bed. His mind strayed as he contemplated all the titillating possibilities. *I need to set my alarm,* he thought, picking his cell off of the nightstand. *Early to work tomorrow, I'll get ahead so I can find time to play.* Just as he was about to set it back down, he thought of Nora. He scrolled through the few photos he had on his phone: Matt and Brian at the Silver Dollar with their hands up the skirts of their dates; his dad at his birthday; and, finally, Nora, zip-tied to a radiator. Dane rubbed his thumb over the image. He closed his eyes, concentrating, reliving that incredible moment in time.

He was aroused, inspired.

He hopped out of bed and threw open his closet. This once two-bedroom craftsman bungalow was now a bachelor's dream home. Dane had the entire place gutted and re-done, including using the space from the adjacent bedroom to create a walk-in closet any girl would die for.

The Point

The entire closet was lined with wooden shelves and drawers stained a dark espresso. His shirts and pants were hung tidily on the right side, lined up by size and color. This space was a testament to fine design, with drawers and shelving custom-built to fit the designated spaces perfectly.

"What shall I wear out on the town?" he wondered while seated in his tufted leather chair. Just like the rest of Dane's house, this closet was spotless and orderly like a photo from a magazine.

"Casual but classy," he decided as he threw on his best jeans and a tight button-up shirt. After selecting a pair of short leather boots from the shelf, he opened one of the narrow drawers exposing a row of watches all nestled in a plush gray lining. "You," he decided with certainty as he snatched a watch from its nest and snapped it on his wrist. He was going trolling in the bars and wanted to look his best.

Dane stopped in the bathroom on his way, checking his hair before rummaging through the cabinet for the Vicodin he was given when he'd injured his leg at the Point.

He took two pills, ground them into a powder with the back of a spoon in the kitchen, and then folded the powder into a small piece of paper.

Checking his pockets one last time, "Wallet-check, mints-check, compass-check, Vicodin-check."

Stepping out into the cool autumn air, he walked the four blocks west to the Village, where he started his rounds at the popular college bars.

Monday was typically a slow night at the bar in the summer, but now that school was back in session, it was standing-room-only in every establishment on Third Street.

His favorite was a place called the Elbow Room, probably because there wasn't any.

College students were mixed in with the old-timers and the local barflies, asshole to elbow. Dane squeezed his way through the crowd and bellied up to the bar, where he ordered a club soda, not wanting to dull his senses with any alcoholic libations.

He stood, surveying the crowd for any possible victims. He could feel the weight of the compass shift with his movements. *Are you calling to me,* he thought, perplexed by his sudden awareness of its position. Retrieving it from his pocket, he held it face up in the palm of his hand. He rubbed the chip in its crystal surface, coveting it, while watching the needle float and dance its way to its desired location.

The needle settled, and Dane turned to see whom the point chose. A young woman was leaning against the frame of the bar's main entrance. *She's kind of squat, average looking at best, are you sure?* he thought, mentally questioning the compass's choice.

Her brown hair was barely to her shoulders, and it was somewhat flat. Her best feature, by far, were her ample breasts. "Are you sure she's the one…All right," he quietly conceded while jostling the compass in his hand. He decided he would trust its decision and pursue this unsuspecting woman.

He approached the short brunette, strolling with a swagger as he made eye contact with her. He nodded, his smile causing her eyes to light up.

Oh my God, she thought, *he's looking at me, he's coming over here.*

The Point

"Hello, my name is Mike," Dane said to his captivated victim.

"Stephanie," the brunette replied as she held out her hand for him to shake.

"I was just standing at the bar and noticed you over here and wondered if you'd like to have a drink with me?" He grinned, his smile wide, his eyes twinkling in the bar's low light.

Do whatever he wants, she thought before answering. "Yeah, that would be great," she giggled awkwardly, giddy at the thought of catching the attention of this incredibly hot guy.

He took Stephanie by the hand and led her to the back corner of the bar. She looked over her shoulder at her friends, tossing them a "can you believe this guy chose me" sort of look. They had to quickly hide their expressions of disbelief to smile and wave, pretending to be happy their frumpy friend had struck gold.

In truth, she was just their decoy. The unattractive friend chosen to make everyone else in the group look better.

"He must have beer goggles," Stephanie's pretty blonde friend offered as she waved. The other girls in the group emphatically agreed.

"What would you like," Dane asked leaning in, making sure to get very close.

"Whatever you're drinking," she said, still captivated.

"I'll be right back, don't go anywhere."

There is no chance of that, she thought.

He touched her hand and made sure to look into her eyes before turning toward the bar.

"Vodka and club soda," he ordered, figuring it would look just like his drink except it would be filled with booze—and two Vicodin.

"Three dollars," the bartender barked over the roar of the crowd.

"Keep the change," he replied as he dropped a five on the bar.

Pulling the folded paper from his pocket, he slipped the powder into her beverage.

This should make you compliant, he thought as he slid her the drink.

"Wow, this is strong." She coughed as she sipped from the tumbler.

"They pour a stiff drink in here," he replied.

"So, Mike, do you go to school here?"

"No," Dane replied, "I'm in construction. Just here for a building project."

"Oh, what are you building?" She asked.

"The new theater behind the mall." He got closer and stroked the side of Stephanie's face. "You are stunning," he said gazing into her eyes.

Stephanie melted. Her body language became overtly sexual. He was charming a defenseless young woman. Not only had she never been wooed by someone as beautiful as Dane before, the booze and pills were taking hold and she was becoming very malleable.

"How much longer before it's done?" she asked, referring to the theatre.

"Not much longer, I think," he answered, referring more to her level of intoxication than the progress on the new theatre. He felt so clever. There really was a new theater being built, just not by him.

The Point

"I would really like to spend some time alone with you, Steph; want to get out of here?" He leaned in, putting his arm around her.

She could feel his strength, the firmness of his toned muscles through his shirt. His dark eyes were piercing and his scent was almost as intoxicating as her cocktail.

"I've never left the bar with a guy before…"

(Dane thought she was about to listen to that little voice of reason and turn him down.)

"Just let me tell my friends." She grabbed his hand and led him back to her group of clucking hens.

"We're gonna get outta here. I'll see you all later." Stephanie was gleaming. She was gleefully rubbing Dane in their faces.

Just as he was about to clear the doorway with his victim, he could hear a familiar voice calling his name from inside the bar.

"Dane! Dane! Back here!" He turned just enough to glance at who was calling. It was Brian.

Stephanie sensed his slight hesitation and turned to see what was wrong. She was afraid he realized he was leaving with the wrong girl.

"Who's Dane," she asked, "Do you know him?"

"No, I just thought I forgot my phone, but it's in my pocket."

He hurried Stephanie out of the door, quickly turning right, heading east back toward his house.

"Where are we going?" she asked.

"I'm renting a house about four blocks from here. I thought we'd get to know each other… have a quiet drink."

"Oh," she answered sounding pleased and a little nervous.

He walked, strolling romantically through the fall night. He made his victim feel like the only woman in the world. Gently, he held her hand while leading her to his home, the full autumn moon shining on the crisp fallen leaves.

By time Dane and Stephanie reached the house, the Vicodin and vodka had started to take effect.

"Wow, I'm really feeling the alcohol," she slurred.

"Well, let me help you to the sofa," he offered.

"Thanks, I really should stop drinking so much," she said as she slumped back, her chin pressed into her chest.

"How much is too much," he joked.

"Well, I had a few before you showed up," she replied with a hiccup.

He hadn't considered the amount of alcohol she might have consumed before he arrived. Any decent person would have worried that all that liquor mixed with two Vicodin might be too much for a small woman, but not Dane. His only concern was that she might die while in his custody, leaving him trying to dispose of a body. *Maybe the construction site over at the new theatre would be a good place to hide a body,* he thought, *in case of the worst.*

"I'll make us some coffee," he said as he scuttled toward the kitchen.

"Thanks, Mike," she gurgled from the sofa.

He turned to see if she was still conscious as he entered the kitchen, only to find she'd passed out. Her limp body had shifted to its side, her head on the throw pillow, her feet still planted firmly on the floor.

He jogged over to her and shook her. "Steph, you awake?" She was out. A bit of drool was running from the corner of her mouth. "That's attractive," he sneered.

The Point

"I better work quick or I might journey into necrophilia inadvertently," he joked to himself.

He threw her over his shoulder. "Christ, woman, what do you weigh?" he groaned as he carried her down to the basement.

It was a finished space. A pullout sofa sat in the center of the room, facing the back wall where a small television sat on an old steamer trunk. He dropped the girl on the floor so he could open the bed hidden in the sofa. Moving her to the sleeper's freshly sheeted mattress, he stood before her unsure where to begin.

Dropping to his knees, he started to work toward disrobing the unsuspecting girl.

He probably could've gotten this girl into bed when she was sober, but surely she wouldn't have condoned what came next. Pulling the television from the trunk's top, he flipped its lid, pulling a toolbox from its depths. In the box were several of his toys. He'd used some of the usual gadgets on a date here and there, but this is where he kept the really weird stuff. The toys in this case weren't made of latex or silicone. In fact, stainless steel was the main component of these tools.

He started with some zip-ties, a tool he'd used and enjoyed recently in the past. Dane lifted Stephanie's limp arms above her head. He felt along the top of the mattress, searching for the edge of the sleeper's metal frame.

With a quick zip, he fastened her wrists together and then to the bed frame.

Next he lifted the top tray in the toolbox, looking for just the right instrument for his pleasure.

He extracted a few gadgets from the base of the box. They were frightening. Any casual observer might have seen these toys and thought they were intended for an invasive medical procedure, or perhaps torture in a horror movie.

He probed and twisted, delighted he was able to finally enjoy these implements with a guest. These were special tools he'd only ever used on himself. He indulged himself, and thoroughly tortured the poor thing while she slept. On occasion, if an act was particularly uncomfortable, she would shift or flinch, but she never awoke.

"You will be sore on both ends… if you wake up tomorrow," he whispered into Stephanie's unconscious ear. "You must be uncomfortable, yet you haven't moved. Are you still with me?" he asked as he reached his hand to her face, checking for breath. He pulled it back, thankful to find she was still with the living. "I was worried we might be taking a ride to the new theatre," he joked.

"Picture time," he called, before flipping Stephanie to her stomach and bending her knees so they were pushed toward her chest. He pulled out his cell and snapped a photo. *One more for the album*, he thought.

"What will I remember you by, sweet tits?" he asked he as he rummaged through her things.

He noticed she had a charm hanging around her neck. It was perhaps Celtic in origin and suspended from a long, finely braided leather cord.

"Perfect," he exclaimed as he yanked the trinket from her neck. The cord gave at the clasp with a snap.

Once again he stood over his victim, his palm to his stomach, relishing the feeling he was left with—satisfaction. "I feel satisfied, Steph," he admitted to her. "I feel satisfied and that is thanks to you." The parasite

The Point

was fed. He pulled on his jeans and then put the cord through the loop on the compass's case. It was just long enough to slip over his head.

He pressed the compass, relishing the way its cold brass felt against his bare chest. "Thank you for this," he said as the brass warmed against his skin. It had pointed the way to his success with poor Stephanie, and he was sure it would point him in the right direction from now on.

~~~

"So much for getting to work early," Dane scoffed as he waited for his date to awaken.

"Ugh," Stephanie groaned as she palmed her aching head.

"Hung over?" he asked as he sat at her feet on the living room sofa.

"I feel like I've been hit by a fucking truck," she barked as she tried to pull herself to a sitting position.

"Did we... you know, do it last night?" she asked with a cringe, worried they did and she couldn't remember.

"No, we got back here and you passed out. I just left you to sleep it off, here on the couch." He was enjoying himself. She had no idea that he'd spent a large portion of the evening enjoying her in many deviant ways.

"Do you have some aspirin or ibuprofen or something," she asked.

"Sure, I'll go grab some for ya." Dane got up and headed to the bathroom medicine cabinet. He was giddy. He felt like skipping to the pain reliever.

Stephanie on the other hand was taking stock of her current physical condition. She remembered having a few drinks at the Elbow Room, but not enough to warrant this hangover. She swung her legs over the sofa's edge to the floor. A searing pain shot through her pelvis and exited her rear end.

"Something's wrong," she murmured quietly to herself.

She slowly stood, the pain now traveling through her abdomen and around to her lower back.

He returned with the aspirin and a small paper cup of water.

"Thank you," she said as she took the items from Dane. She tossed back the aspirin and chased them down with the water.

"Where's the bathroom," she asked, her hand on her stomach.

"Down the hall, to the left," he pointed.

She stepped slowly, walking gingerly toward the hall. Stroking his chin, he grinned with delight at the obvious discomfort she was displaying. He dropped his hand and placed it on the compass, feeling its weight under his shirt. Rubbing his palm over its form, he caused the shirt's fabric to shift over its crystal face with each pass.

Stephanie's stroll to the bathroom was excruciating. The pain in her lower bits pulsed with every beat of her heart.

Dropping her pants, she slowly lowered herself to the toilet's cold white seat, her physical discomfort exasperated by the sterile and institutional atmosphere of Dane's contemporary john.

"Jesus," she winced as she tried to urinate. Looking down she noticed her yellow cotton underwear had a small spot of blood in the crotch.

The Point

"What the hell," she wondered as she stood to search herself for other signs of injury. She pulled up her shirt and spun around, trying to view her back and sides. There were no visible marks. She frantically felt each leg and arm, examining them for sore spots and bruises, but there weren't any.

"You need to find a nice boy and settle down, you stupid cow," she whispered to herself in the mirror.

This was the moment she realized that her necklace was missing.

"Shit," she grumbled, disappointed to find herself at a stranger's house, hung-over, and without her favorite trinket.

She returned to the living room eager to ask Dane a few questions.

"You're sure we didn't hit it last night Mike?" she inquired, feeling quite sure something happened based on the experience she'd just had on the toilet.

"Nope, we got here and you were out like a light." He used his most convincing tone.

"Did I fall, maybe, because I have some serious pain and my necklace is missing." She placed her hand on her chest as though she could still feel it hanging there.

"You did take a little spill on the way up the stairs, but I haven't seen a necklace. What did it look like?"

Stephanie went on to describe it, and Dane pretended to listen. He knew damn well what it looked like because he was wearing part of it right now.

"Listen, I have to go out," he lied ready for his guest to depart, "But I've called you a cab, it's waiting outside."

She stepped to the window and peeked between the slats on the wooden blinds.

"Oh... well, see ya then, she stammered, disheartened and confused. *Mike's the first really attractive guy to pay attention to me, and now he's sending me packing. Mom was right, nobody buys the cow when they're getting the milk for free*, she thought.

"Do you want my number or something," she asked awkwardly, secretly embarrassed by her desperation.

"Got it," he lied, "You gave it to me last night."

"Oh, well, I'll see ya then," Stephanie repeated clumsily as she opened the front door.

"Yeah, great meeting you." He gave a little wave as she descended the stairs.

Just as he sat at the kitchen island to drink some coffee and relish his conquest, his cell rang.

"Hey man, is that frumpy chick still over there, or did you send her packing already?"

"I'm alone," Dane asserted.

"Yeah, now maybe, but I saw you last night. What were you picking her up for? You always get the best-looking broads. It's Matt and I that always end up with the dogs. But, vag is vag, I guess, even for you."

Brian was chipper. It was great to see Dane with an ugly girl.

"I was home all night, you must've seen my twin," he joked.

"Fine, you don't want to admit you fucked that ugly girl. I'll leave it alone, but I know what I saw." Brian couldn't wait to tell Matt that Dane went slummin'.

"Listen, I gotta go." Dane hung up abruptly.

Brian looked at his phone, amused by his friend's behavior.

Rummaging through the junk drawer, he searched for a note pad and pen.

The Point

He sat at the island realizing that he'd have to map his behavior and follow the directions every time to avoid incarceration.

Dane realized what he wanted, no, needed to do. The fun he wanted to have would require distance from prying eyes. "I can't just bring girls back to the house," he planned aloud. "One: they might remember where I live, and two: eventually one might tell the authorities."

He wasn't exactly hoping to bring 'em home and just make love to them like some schmuck. These girls would be pawns, food for the parasite, nourishment for his cravings—and that would require extreme privacy.

"I can't troll bars in my tiny hometown," he said as he tapped the pen on the granite. With this fact spilled freshly from his lips he realized he would have to make some drastic changes in his lifestyle to accommodate this new venture.

"What I desire to do will require discretion and privacy. I can't pick up college girls at local bars, be seen, and then walk them back to the house; there is too much risk."

Dane numbered the lined sheet:

1. Troll for "dates" in surrounding towns
2. Find remote location, something private
3. Get a different car, something low profile
4. Quit job, focus on fun

He realized what he needed to do: Sell his house and move out of town. The parasite did a flip. He needed to get away.

If he moved south into the deep swath of wilderness that lined the lakeshore, there'd be a steady supply of tourists at the remote dive bars.

If he went west toward the mountain, he could frequent his usual stomping grounds but avoid suspicion from family and friends. He often visited the Hematite Mountain area, and no one would think his relocation to that area would be particularly strange.

Chapter 29

Time heals all wounds.

Jake laid low while trying to process his encounter with Nora at the café. He struggled with the complex feelings their meeting had left him with. "If you love her, you'll let it go," Lucy had said. It didn't take him long to realize she was right. He loved Nora, and his behavior with Susan made the situation a wash.

Jake had done drive-bys, peeking in the shop window or walking her street.

He'd even spoken with William on a couple of occasions, who informed Jake that he needed to address his daughter in person. Which was hard to do when she kept slamming the door in his face.

"By the way," William said to Jake, "I thought you might want this back," as he handed him the ring.

While Jake sat and tried to muster the courage to approach her one more time, Lucy couldn't get over Nora's new 'do.

"Holy crap, I cannot get over that haircut. It really was ballsy. You look awesome!"

Lucy had been looking at the haircut for a week now and still found herself in awe of her best friend's new look.

She shot Lucy a smile from behind the sales counter. They chatted, until Jake interrupted them.

"I'm sorry," he blurted as he burst through the shop door.

"I'm sorry I'm a shit!" he added.

Jake did a double take. Nora's appearance was quite the shocker.

"Wow, acted impulsively after we ran into each other, eh?" Jake was floored by the change in her appearance.

"If you don't like it, please take my previous invitation to get the fuck out!" she shouted.

She looked over to her father. "Sorry, Dad."

"That's quite alright, honey, sometimes certain things just need to be said."

William looked at Jake, his mild contempt fueled only by the fear that this guy might try to hurt his little girl as well.

"Do you want me to force him to get the fuck out?" William asked colorfully.

"No, I'll take care of him myself."

"Let's just take a minute to sort some stuff out," Jake suggested.

"Are you sure you can deal with the hair?" she asked sarcastically as she pointed at her head.

"Yes, it's fine," he said, just glad she was willing to talk.

Approaching Jake, she led him outside, pulling him by the elbow to his car.

She'd found herself hoping to see him; his drive-bys and evening strolls hadn't gone unnoticed, and the last time she slammed the door, she did feel a bit bad.

They convened at the trunk of his BMW, leaning on the car, which was parked right outside of the shop.

William and Lucy crept over to the window and peered from its corner, trying to catch a glimpse of the interaction between the couple.

"I wish we could hear what they were saying," William whispered to Lucy.

The Point

"I know," she replied. "I think Nora secretly wanted his attention. She asked me if I knew where he went after we left the coffee shop the other week. "

"Interesting," William whispered. "Do you think he's a decent guy, I kinda feel for him?"

"Yeah, he's no Dane," Lucy assured William, patting the top of his right hand.

They continued to peek while Nora and Jake leaned against the BMW's trunk, shoulder to shoulder. Their arms were folded across their chests, trying to fight off the brisk afternoon air.

" I know I lied and treated you like a criminal for whatever it is you were mixed up in this summer, but I love you and rushed here, ring in hand, only to be told to fuck off."

"We were both wrong, I know that. In some ways it lessens my guilt to know you were still involved with that other woman." Nora was angry he lied but relieved she wasn't the only one who seemed to stray.

"I'm not like Dane," Jake asserted. "You compared me to him the other day, and I realize I used my father as an excuse, but please don't lump me in with him. I really do care for you and wouldn't want to fling you off the Point for having my child."

She leaned her head onto his shoulder, still looking forward, then said, "I did worry I would never see you again after I stomped out of the coffee shop, and I did regret that last time I slammed the door in your face. I'd like to give you credit for not giving up. I'm really glad you stuck around."

"I'll continue to stick around, we'll take it slow." He was smiling; he could feel the uncertainty lifting as they stood there, the cold afternoon seeping through the fabric of his shirt.

"I think I can handle that," she smiled as she nudged him playfully.

"I just want you to know that I often thought of you and never would have gotten myself into the mess with Dane, had I known how you felt," she continued.

"I'm sorry I was a coward. I was twisted with guilt myself; I returned home and faced Susan. I had long ago realized she wasn't what I wanted, and that you were."

His words were heartfelt and sincere. She suddenly realized how artificial Dane's words had been. Jake's tone had a depth, a weight, that Dane's never had. She'd been a fool looking for love in all the wrong places.

She turned and stepped in front of him.

Leaning in, she kissed him.

Lucy and William had their foreheads pressed to the glass. Lucy's jaw dropped open as William slapped her on the back. "Holy shit!" William clucked. "I guess I can worry less about irreversible damage to her psyche."

"Yeah, looks like she's on the mend," Lucy added.

The two turned away, giving the lovebirds some privacy, feeling they'd done all the spying necessary for their needs.

Jake quickly reacted, wrapping his arms around Nora. He ran his hands up her back and planted his hands in her short hair. He pulled his fingers through the freshly cropped locks.

He looked into her eyes, once again seeing the girl he left back at school.

"Feels awesome, doesn't it?" she questioned, as she quickly looked upward, the tip of her head suggesting she was referring to her hair.

"It's really grown on me. It feels amazing." He continued to run his fingers through it, once again pulling her in for another round of kissing.

Just a week ago he didn't know if he could get past her previous situation. But he'd stuck it out and manned up, showing her he meant to stand by her by simply waiting faithfully at a distance. Now her warm lips were pressed against his, and all that dark history was fading into the light.

They quietly agreed that each of their actions had cancelled the other's out. From this point on, they would work to repair what they'd left behind when they parted for the summer break.

Chapter 30

While Dane planned for his upcoming move out west, Nora and Jake were slowly moving back into each other's lives. He said he wanted to stay and take it slow, and that was exactly what he'd done.

They'd been seeing each other a few times a week since they connected outside her father's store.

Nora thought she'd never want to be touched by a man again after what Dane had done to her, but she could feel her desire for Jake growing. She could feel the pull when they were together; but, as always, he was waiting for her cue. She had a new appreciation for his sensitivity since her experiences with Dane.

She was preparing to spend the weekend with Jake at Cooper's family cabin. Lucy was giddy over the idea of the two couples spending a weekend at the mountain. The foliage had peaked and the colors would be truly spectacular this time of year.

Nora was packing her overnight bag. Standing in her room, she had clothing scattered on the floor and spread across her bed as she tried to choose the right outfits for the weekend.

She'd cleaned out her wardrobe and dropped half of her clothes off at the Goodwill. She never wanted to wear anything she wore while seeing Dane ever again.

Luckily, life in Iron Bay meant a wardrobe for each season. Since her saga with Dane occurred in the summer, she only had to cut loose her warm-weather garb.

I think I'll go with all my favorite stuff, she thought. A cable knit sweater, which had a wide crewneck in a

The Point

dark cream, her favorite flannel, and an extra pair of jeans. She knew Jake wouldn't care if she wore an old tarp: he was just happy to be with her.

She briefly contemplated shoving something sexy in her bag, just in case, but she decided that her cotton Fruit of the Looms would have to do. She wasn't interested in spicing things up; she wanted to get back to basics. Her naked form would have to be special enough if the need arose.

"I've become quite the slob," she admitted as she kicked some of the strewn clothes under her bed and stuffed the rest in her dresser.

"Toothbrush, deodorant, shampoo—check," she said as she grabbed her packed bag and flipped off the light. She smiled as her feet hit the kitchen floor. Finding pleasure in something as simple as the back stairs made her realize that the darkness had lifted. Dane's hold was almost completely gone.

"Good morning, Nora," William practically sang as she set her bag by the back door.

"Good morning, Dad, you're certainly in a fine mood this morning," she said, suspicious about her father's behavior.

"Yes, yes, I am," he retorted, as he rubbed the shoulders of Aunt Sara, who was grinning foolishly from a chair at the kitchen table.

She stood eyeing them both, deciding if she dare ask why they were both so weirdly chipper this morning.

Her dad continued to stand behind her aunt, his hands gently rolling over her shoulders as they both grinned madly at her. He glanced up at the Kat, his eyes quickly moving back to his daughter.

"What is it?" she asked, with a "spit it out already" tone in her voice. "Why you looking at the Kat? Is he judging? Feel guilty about something?" she said, giving her father a hard time.

"I've asked Sara to marry me, and she said yes."

"Holy shit!" Nora exclaimed, shocked but strangely pleased by the news.

" Why don't you have a seat?" Aunt Sara suggested.

"I know the two of you have been flirting and fooling around, but I wasn't expecting this. Wow, you decided to just go for it, hey Dad?"

"Yeah, I sure did," he answered.

Nora realized that aunt's expression had begun to change, her excitement giving way to worry hidden behind a smile.

"What's going on?" she asked as she processed the change in her aunt's demeanor.

"Please sit," Sara said once again.

"Oh shit," she mumbled as she pulled out the chair. "It must be bad if things have soured so quickly."

"What's with the language lately," William asked. "You used to be so foul-mouthed. What happened to...?" William stopped himself; he was going to say his sweet girl, but he knew what happened: she was abused and dropped from a cliff. *That would probably harden you a little bit*, he considered.

"Is that what you wanted me to sit down for, to tell me that my language has become too foul. I apologize, I'll try to work on it." She smiled, finding her father's discomfort with her swearing cute.

"That wasn't why we wanted you to sit," her father went on.

The Point

"I didn't realize how difficult this was going to be until just now," he mumbled.

"Here it is: we are going to have a baby," William blurted as he dropped into the seat next to Sara, his hand on hers as they both looked at Nora, waiting for a reaction.

She just sat looking at them, uncertain how to react. *Are they worried I can't handle it because of my loss, or because of my mother?* she thought to herself.

"How'd this happen? When did this happen?" she asked, more perplexed than angry.

"Sometime in the last few weeks," her aunt replied as though she were apologizing.

"We just weren't careful," her dad added. "I'm in my fifties and Aunt Sara is also older; we just didn't think about it. It's a miracle, really," he said as he tried to rationalize the situation for Nora's sake.

"Wow, fucking wow!" Nora repeated. "Crazy, this is crazy."

"Are you mad?" Aunt Sara asked, obviously very concerned that it just might be too much for her niece to process.

"I'm really sorry," Sara continued, "I don't want to hurt you."

Nora smiled. She really wasn't angry or hurt. Her mother had passed six years ago, and her father hadn't dated in all those years. *He should be happy*, she thought.

"Well, I hadn't seen you smiling, or skipping or humming, in a really long time, not until you took up with Aunt Sara anyway. I love you both so much, I'm nothing but happy for you." She got up and hugged her father.

He wrapped his arms around her, never getting up from the chair. Nora pulled back and grabbed her aunt's hand.

"I couldn't have asked for a better person for Dad to choose," she assured her aunt, "I'm not angry; you haven't hurt me. I'm excited: a wedding and a baby. I'm going to be a big sister!"

William had tears in his eyes as he smiled at his daughter. She could've been devastated that they were having a child so soon after she'd lost so much. What they didn't know was, Dane was truly wicked, and she was happy she'd never have to peer into the face of evil and know it was her own child.

"I'm going to go; Lucy and Cooper are expecting me out at the cabin." She grabbed her bag and pulled open the back door.

"I'm sure Jake is eager to see you as well," her father jabbed, teasing her about how smitten she'd been lately.

She shot him a look before giving him and her aunt one last wave and a smile.

"See you Sunday night *or* Monday morning," she said as she shut the door behind her.

Once in the porch, she pulled on her gray anorak and her trusty brown hikers. She had a red wool hat that her mother had made for her when she was about ten. October was colder than usual this year and, with the short hair, Nora was certain she'd need the extra warmth.

Chapter 31

Deer Lake was a tiny, rural north-woods town miles from anywhere.

It was common for small towns on this northern peninsula to be named after any nearby landmark of significance, mainly because there was nothing but trees otherwise.

Deer Lake, the town, was named for the nearby body of water bearing the same name. Its founder, some frontiersman from the 1800s, probably named the lake due to the high prevalence of white-tailed deer. Then, of course, the town that followed was granted the same creative moniker.

Dane had spent a great deal of his buy-out from the family business on his house. Some of it was left, and he'd also been saving to start his own landscaping business. Now he would just use it to make the move to his new life. He didn't need to make money from the sale of his house; he just needed to get out from under it.

He had once fussed, gutting and perfecting the small craftsman he'd called home these last few years. Now he would leave that meticulous life behind in order to feed the monster living beneath his skin.

Dane was at work, going through the motions, trying to wait patiently for his house to sell and things to get moving. Feeling restless, he decided to get out of the office and take a drive. He pulled the keys to one of the work carts and slowly cruised the many dirt roads that crisscrossed the large rural cemetery. It was a beautiful place. Large, old deciduous trees lined lanes that divided the cemetery's many sections. Bright gold and orange foliage drifted from the trees above as Dane drove. He cruised the plots, trying to take his mind off of the stress of waiting.

Rounding a corner he realized he'd come to the Reynolds' family section. He parked the cart and walked the sites, reading the stones. Nora's grandparents were side by side. At their feet was Elizabeth Reynolds. This was the very spot he'd met Nora just those few months ago.

He ran the toe of his work boot along the base of her headstone.

"Your daughter was a *good* time, Elizabeth," he assured his ex-girlfriend's dead mother.

"I bet she gets that from you, your husband seems like quite the dork."

Dane smirked. He was really enjoying his walk down memory lane. Pulling his cell from his pocket, he began to scroll through his photos when his phone rang.

"Hello, Mr. Buchman. Good afternoon," the pleasant voice greeted him.

It was the Realtor. She was a falsely bubbly and extremely irritating woman, but he hired her because she was the best in town.

"Hello," he replied. "Do you have some news for me?"

"Yes sir, I do," the Realtor proclaimed. "You have an offer, and..."

"I'll take it," he interrupted.

"Why don't you come in to the office, and we'll look it over," the Realtor suggested, concerned he was ready to accept it sight unseen.

He looked at his watch. "How about forty-five minutes?"

The Point

"Alright, Mr. Buchman, I'll be expecting you."

Dane bid Elizabeth Reynolds farewell and rushed back to the office to park the cart.

He hummed a pleasant tune all the way to the realty office. When he arrived his Realtor, Mary Tillman, greeted him. "How are you today, Mr. Buchman?" she asked, her fake smile shining.

"Fantastic, now that I have this offer," he answered.

"Let's walk back to my office and look it over."

Mary led Dane down the hall, her short blonde bob swinging just as wildly as her wide, plump ass.

She was probably in her mid-fifties and in fairly good shape. Well, except for her ass. Dane found it entertaining that her manner of dress and hairstyle was younger than she was. It was as though Mary were wearing a disguise from her own age.

He sat at the dining-table-sized desk while Mary presented him with the offer. It didn't matter to him what it was, as long as it cleared his mortgage.

"It's a little low, but they're also asking for the kitchen stools, all the appliances, and the television in the kitchen. They feel the stools at the island are an integral part of the kitchen's design, and the television is mounted, so they insist it's a fixture. There is also the television and the refrigerator in the garage."

Mary searched Dane's face for agreement that the offer was too low compared to the requests the buyer had made.

"Good, let's sign. When can we close?" He was eager and matter-of-fact.

"Within thirty days, but an earlier closing could be your counter-offer on their requests."

"Good, great, let's nail them down." He stood up, signed on the dotted line, and waltzed out of the office. *Things are moving now,* he thought. He stopped at his house and grabbed a bag of clothes and some bathroom essentials. As he began to pull out of the driveway, his neighbor flagged him down.

Dane stopped and rolled down his window.

"I see you got the place for sale, any luck," the old guy asked.

"Yep, sold it today," Dane divulged, trying to stem his curiosity.

"Aren't you Walt Buchman's kid?"

He'd lived in this house for a little over three years, and *now* this old bastard wanted to have a conversation.

"Listen, I've really gotta go," Dane explained as he rolled up his window while simultaneously backing out of the driveway.

"That's exactly why I need to move out of this fucking town," he complained to himself as he drove west.

"This is the moment I've been waiting for," he chortled as he pulled out his cell and hit his boss's number. He was ready to take the next step and tell Bob where he could shove that shitty job. "No more digging, no more dirt, excellent!" Dane's house was sold and his plan was underway; it was time for his boss to know he could fuck off.

"Hello, Dane," the booming voice answered.

"I quit, Bob." He smiled while he said those words. It felt great.

"I'm to consider this your two weeks then?" Bob asked, confusion in his voice.

"No," he replied, "Effective immediately."

The Point

"I need to find a replacement, you can't just leave." Bob was now audibly flustered.

"Don't fuckin' care, Bob." He ended, hanging up and continuing his drive.

He hummed, his sinister heart filled with joy over the adventures that awaited him out in the northern woods.

Mary had referred him to a Realtor in Deer Lake. This Realtor was not a falsely pleasant woman in denial of her age. The buyer's agent he was about to meet was an old grizzled guy who had been selling camping properties for the last three decades. Mary Tillman assured him that Greg Pelto knew his way around the north woods like the back of his hand.

Dane wanted something with modern amenities like running water and electricity, but would settle just for the water, if need be. He could heat with wood and get power from a generator if the property had what he was looking for functionally. Seclusion was more important than being on the grid.

He arrived at the Buckhorn Bar. He walked into the backwoods' dive and immediately enjoyed its relaxed atmosphere. It was easy to embrace how rural and unassuming the establishment was. It felt a lot like the Silver Dollar at the mountain but with more critters mounted to the walls.

He snagged a table and waited for Greg Pelto to arrive.

"Hey there, you must be Dane," Greg said as he held out his hand. "It was easy to pick you out of the crowd," he joked, as he looked around at all the empty tables.

Dane stood up and shook it.

"Wow, anxious, I like it," Greg smiled as he sat down.

"I've printed some flyers of the different properties available in the area. You mentioned wanting to be north of the mountain and on or near Deer Lake, if possible."

"That's right," he affirmed.

Greg handed Dane the flyers. He flipped through them, sorting them into two piles: maybe and not at all.

While Dane perused the flyers, Greg waved over the waitress.

He looked like the kind of guy who'd enjoyed a drink or two in his lifetime. His sparse grey hair provided spotty coverage of his bulbous, shiny cranium. He was a stout man with an aged look about him. His nose was veiny and bulbous, and wonderfully accentuated by several pockmarks.

"I'll have a Jack and Coke," Greg said, "Want anything, Mr. Buchman?"

Dane shook his head. "No, I'm good, maybe just some water."

The waitress shuffled off to relay their order to the bartender. He watched her ass as she walked away; she reminded him of Nora.

"I would like to see these," he said, handing Greg the stack of fliers in the maybe pile. Trying to re-focus his attention on the properties and away from the waitress's ass.

"Sounds good, I'll just suck this down and we'll head out."

Mr. Pelto inhaled his lunchtime whiskey.

"Let's get going." Greg stood up and pushed his chair in.

The Point

"We're looking today?" Dane said with a hint of excitement in his voice.

"Yeah, these camps aren't anyone's permanent residence, so they're all open for viewing."

He was thrilled. It felt like it was meant to be. The whole plan had come together so easily, he couldn't wait to get a place and break it in. He took one last glance at the little blonde before following Greg outside.

Greg took Dane and drove him to places deep in the forest and off of the highway. Greg shuttled Dane all over the western end of Paramount County.

He'd viewed many fine places, but the final property was on the backside of Deer Lake.

There were many turns, and the winding dirt roads had many disorienting forks and old logging roads. It could be very confusing to get in and out of there if you hadn't been there before.

"This is promising so far," Dane blurted as the two men wound their way to the cabin.

When they arrived he was sold. The camp was an attractive old cottage. Its running cedar siding was wonderfully aged. It had a hipped roof that sat on its top like a wonderfully pointed hat.

"Great curb appeal," the Realtor remarked as they exited the vehicle.

Dane followed Greg up the stairs. Greg took a key from the ledge above the door and unlocked the house.

The entry door was a wonderfully wide French door, its many lights allowing for a view of the thick forest in front and, once inside, the back of the house had another wide French door, framing a view of Deer Lake now visible through the scarcely leaved fall trees.

Strolling through the house, Dane was pleasantly surprised by its condition. There were wide plank floors that had been painted a deep brown. A large rustic fireplace was centered on the right wall of the house. It was constructed of sandstone and had a heavy wooden mantle constructed of what looked like half of a wide tree trunk.

The whole place, although rustic, was well done.

"What's this place going for," he asked, feeling that it must have a heavy price tag for the shape it was in.

"Um, let's check the sheet, " Greg said as he shuffled through the stack.

"Seventy-eight thousand."

"I'll take it," Dane announced, feeling like it could be snatched up any minute.

"Are you sure, there isn't any electricity."

"Is there plumbing?"

"Yes, a well and septic. But you'll need to fuel a generator to run the pumps and lights in this place, not to mention the amount of firewood you'll need to stay warm in the winter." Greg knew this place was cute and on the water, but couldn't imagine why anyone would want to live out here full time.

"It really isn't meant to be a permanent residence. There's no mail delivery or snow removal." Greg was doing his best to try and talk him out of it.

"It's also for rent; perhaps you could just rent a while, be sure you want it first."

He continued to try and sway him toward another property.

"You know, that one off the highway had electricity and water. You'd be closer to town."

The Point

"I appreciate your concern, but I'm sure... This is the one." He nodded, trying to assure his reluctant Realtor that he knew what he was doing. He wandered outside, excited about the view from the back.

A short set of wide stairs led down to an opening between two groups of trees. There was a clear view of Deer Lake below. It was waterfront property in that you had a direct view of the water, but the lake's edge was a steep drop, maybe twenty feet or more.

Dane walked around to the front. He found a shed and a stamped concrete patio. In its center was a large, recessed fire pit.

This was obviously utilized for large parties. Five large benches with a rustic log construction and a faux cedar color were placed around the fire pit's edge. The bench legs were anchored in the concrete, a permanent fixture.

Greg approached Dane. "I believe they used this house in the winter for snowmobile parties."

"That explains the oversized fire ring. I imagine you would need quite the blaze to keep warm out here in the dead of winter," Dane said. "You could stoke an inferno in that thing," he went on, drawn to the idea of a massive blaze.

Mr. Pelto shot Dane a sideways glance, somewhat unnerved by the way he was pining over the fire pit. He cleared his throat and quickly changed the conversation.

"Whatever contents are still remaining in the house are included in the sale price," he conveyed to him.

"Wonderful," Dane said, "bonus material."

Chapter 32

Nora had never been up to the cabin but instantly understood why Lucy raved about it.

Finely hewed maple floors and a soaring, vaulted ceiling greeted you as you walked through the front door. She now knew why Dane spoke of this place with such resentment—it was spectacular; there were few houses in Iron Bay as nice as this cabin.

"Cooper, I'm green with envy," she remarked as she walked around, running her hand along the fine furnishings.

"I bet this chair cost more than my car," she joked as she plunked herself into it.

"That's not saying much—your car is worth about five bucks," Lucy joked.

"Very funny," she said as she faked a laugh at her friend's attempt at humor.

"Why on earth would you drive yourself up here in that piece of shit when your boyfriend owns a Beamer?" Lucy asked sarcastically, her hand planted on her hip.

"I don't know why. To be in control of my own transportation, I guess."

She hadn't realized she'd potentially alienated Jake by driving herself. Nora was pretty sure Lucy and Cooper had come together. She hoped she hadn't hurt Jake's feelings; it wasn't her intention.

"So, what's for dinner?" she asked, trying to move the conversation along.

"Let's ask Cooper," Lucy said as she turned toward the men who were standing in the kitchen, beers already in hand.

The Point

"Drinking already," Lucy scoffed, her green eyes wide.

"You know what they say, my love, it's five o'clock somewhere." Cooper walked over and kissed Lucy sloppily on the lips, making a smooching noise at its conclusion.

"Yuck, Coop!" she exclaimed as she laughed and wiped her mouth on his shirtsleeve.

"I have something special planned for dinner," Cooper said with a sly smile crossing his lips. "I hope you all brought something nice to wear."

"Oh," Nora gasped, "I'm afraid I didn't come prepared for a fancy affair."

"No worries," Jake jumped in. "It'll give me a chance to play the doting boyfriend and spoil you a little."

Jake grabbed Nora's jacket and whisked her out of the door.

"How do we get to town from here?" he asked as he helped her into the car.

"We wind down the hill and take a right," she explained with a swirling gesture.

"Alright, let's shop." He was looking forward to buying her something lovely.

"What a beautiful drive," he commented

"The views are really lovely this time of year," she added. "So serene, so peaceful. There's something so calming about the falling leaves."

The winding road was awash in the beauty of the autumn leaves. When coupled with the clear blue sky, the drive to town was breathtaking.

"Where can a guy buy his best girl something nice in this tiny town?" Jake asked Nora, his gentle smile warming her heart.

"Park here and we'll walk, it's a beautiful day."

Once the car was parked, they linked hands and strolled along, quietly enjoying each other's presence.

They passed the Silver Dollar Bar and crossed the street. Johnson's General Store was adjacent to the small boutique. "Northern Trails," she said, reading the shop's placard. "Most of its patrons are tourists, but it's probably the only place nearby to get some new clothes. There's a thrift shop a block over if you'd rather try there first," she explained, not wanting to take advantage.

"I think it looks charming." He added, "Let's see what they've got for you."

The selection could only be described as north-woods chic.

"That looks sexy," Jake said as he pointed to a finely knit sweater dress. It was a soft, warm gray; it had a wide, cowled neck that sat off of the shoulder and was accompanied by a brown leather belt.

"Okay, I'll try it," she said.

Pulling one from the rack he asked, "What size," as he slid the hangers scanning the tags.

"Medium maybe, a six or eight," she answered.

He rummaged, finally finding the right dress. She disappeared and returned, the dress hanging loosely from her small frame. Her shoulders were exposed; her satin-like skin a fair contrast to the dress's smoky color.

"You look amazing," he complimented.

She stood before him in the lovely knit dress, her cropped coif wavy and to one side. The hair's short length elongated her neck, which created a dramatic slope

The Point

to her collarbone. Jake's glance fell, as he surveyed her beauty.

"It is lovely," she agreed.

"We might need to do something about those boots, though," he added as he motioned to her feet with his eyes.

"Take those off," he commanded as he walked over to a display of women's footwear.

"Nothing too high," she insisted, "I'm petite, and really high heels make me look like I'm playing dress-up in my mother's shoes."

He located a pair of long, brown leather boots. The zipper followed the inseam, and they sported a heel of a sexy but sensible height.

"We'll need a pair of these in the young lady's size," Jake called to the sales associate.

"Looking glamorous now," he complimented, satisfied that he'd adequately dressed her for the evening's events. "Shall we?" he asked as he offered her his arm.

"Thank you." She hooked her arm to his.

Nora leaned on his shoulder, her arm locked in his, as they strolled back toward the car. They were unaware that while they shopped, Dane had left the Realtor and was now skulking around Mt. Hematite, frequenting the local bars.

He was walking across Main Street, the Silver Dollar his target. *Is that her*, he thought as he surveyed the familiar face.

"Oh man," he said to himself, "She's really lost it, the crazy bitch chopped off her hair."

He continued to have a chuckle at her obvious meltdown, *not that she looked bad.* In fact, the more he stared, the more certain he was that she looked better than he remembered.

Jake and Nora had already crossed the street, taking a moment to stop at a small park nestled between two of the old storefronts. The term "park" was a bit generous. There was a wooden bench beneath a large apple tree. A few apples still clung to the tree's nearly bare branches. A statue of the town's founder looked out onto Main Street from a planting bed filled with once-colorful perennials, now cut back in anticipation of the harsh winter that would soon arrive.

They sat kissing as Dane watched Jake hold Nora tenderly. He was looking longingly at her, while stroking the back of her short hair. Dane realized that even his best acting never achieved the depth of character that Jake's did.

His insides began to twist. He reeled as a deep pang of jealousy grew in the pit of his stomach. He watched Jake with his hands and mouth all over her, and something deep down in the recesses of his gut squirmed. The parasite beckoned.

He placed his hand to the compass, which was still at rest beneath his sweater. *What should I do?* he wondered as he rubbed it. *I know. I know what you want,* he silently acknowledged. He simply wanted to use her to once again experience the surge he'd felt that wonderful day at the Point.

Jake stood and held his hand out to Nora. The lovebirds walked to the car, their fingers entwined.

He didn't want to let her go; he needed to see her some more.

Trotting back to his car, he proceeded to follow the black BMW as it wound its way up the mountain pass.

The Point

He knew this road all too well, and soon realized that they were staying at his cousin's snotty cabin.

"I should've known that these two were staying at Cooper's with his redheaded cunt of a girlfriend," Dane sneered, his hateful words bouncing around his car as he tailed Nora and Jake up the mountain.

The Beamer turned off the main road as it entered the drive to the Buchman's cabin. Dane continued past the driveway, parking a bit further up the road to avoid detection.

He hiked, cutting through the woods, his sights set on the lights of the stately vacation home.

"A cabin," he scoffed sarcastically. "Only Uncle Hank would call that pretentious monstrosity a *cabin*."

Creeping through the brush and towering pines, the leaves crunched and twigs snapped as he slogged along the mountain's varied hillside.

The distant glow of the house grew closer as he hiked, his view only possible because of the drop of the autumn leaves.

He crept up to the house's base, his back flat against the siding, as he hid amongst the shadows cast by the towering residence.

Dane could hear the couples chatting and laughing as they prepared to sit down for dinner. He observed an extra vehicle parked in the drive: it seemed to be a catering truck of some sort. He rolled his eyes. "Cooper is showing off, what a dick."

Lucy was still gushing about how wonderful Nora's new dress was. "You look so lovely, I still can't get over what an amazing change that hair cut has been. And while you were gone the caterer arrived. Cooper has quite the evening planned, he's such a scoundrel." She finished by giving Cooper's ass a playful squeeze.

Dane was tall, over six feet, but he still couldn't see into the bottom floor of the cabin without a boost. He wedged his toes into the sandstone foundation and gripped the window's ledge to pull himself into position, jockeying to take a look at the goings-on inside.

He peered across the open floor plan of the house's great room. There was an extravagant stone fireplace on both ends. One was positioned on the living-room side of the cabin; the other was the glorious backdrop of the dining table, which was handcrafted from bird's-eye maple. It was finished to the same rich hue as the expansive wooden floors.

He observed Cooper and Lucy ready to dine, their guests in close attendance. The table was set with all the best glassware. A sure sign that it was a special occasion. It was the same set of china Aunt Babs used when she would host the Buchman Christmas parties up here.

He watched as the four friends sat around the beautiful table laughing and eating their gourmet meal. Jake was seated next to Nora, and his hand rarely left her thigh as he whispered into her ear and kept close to her, a hint of intimacy to his posture.

Dane felt his temperature rise in spite of the cold October air. He was strangely affected by the site of Nora being manhandled by this stranger. *I bet this is the college guy*, he thought, *the guy she told me about when we were together.* "Together... huh, what am I thinking," Dane said to himself in a hushed tone. "We were never together, I used that gash for my own kicks and nothing more." He nodded as though to reassure himself of the

The Point

facts. Still, it didn't quash the bizarre feeling twisting in his gut.

To his dismay, his fingers began to betray him, causing him to drop to the ground.

Eager to find another viewpoint, he circled round back to the screened porch. He peeked through the rear windows, which were catty-corner from the dining table and the back fireplace. This vantage point allowed him to sit and watch from a more comfortable position.

He squirmed in his seat as the friends carried on, eating and drinking. Each couple was tucked tightly together, with loving gestures and intimate glances. "It's enough to make you sick," Dane whispered. "Fucking fakers, as if anyone really feels that way."

The syrupy outpouring of romance and tenderness was harder to swallow than a bottle of castor oil. He began to feel squeamish.

"Maybe they'll throw their dates on that barn door of a table and nail them instead of eating dessert," he chuckled, hoping for something more exciting to happen.

Excitement was about to be delivered. A server arrived at the table's edge with a cart graced by a delicate white cake. It was decorated with white frost that swirled and danced around its edges. What appeared to be a satin ribbon was tied in a billowing knot. There was a glint—a sparkle in the bow's center that danced in the firelight of the dining room.

The server sliced a giant piece of the cake and placed it on Lucy's plate. The ribbon and its gold charm were sitting atop her served piece. Cooper pushed his chair away from the table.

Oh no, Dane thought, already aware of what was coming next.

Cooper dropped to one knee and pulled Lucy's chair so she was facing him. She already had her hands on her mouth. *Oh my God*, she thought, *this is it*. Acutely aware that the pose her lover had struck could only mean one thing.

He placed his hands on her legs as he looked up at her from his station on the floor.

Dane couldn't hear what his cousin was saying but knew from the scene unfolding before him; he was proposing. "Well, welcome to the family, you fiery bitch," he quietly scoffed as he looked on. He had only been in Lucy's presence a few times while he was playing with Nora. Lucy was a hot piece of ass, and he knew his cousin couldn't possibly be scratching every itch *she* had; he was just too straight-laced.

Cooper eventually ran his finger through the icing, pulling the ribbon free from its sugary hold. Slipping the ring from the ribbon, he placed it on his future bride's finger. She'd obviously said yes, because Nora and her date had hopped to their feet to congratulate the newly engaged couple.

"I guess there'll be one more Buchman at the family gatherings from now on," Dane said as he stretched his neck.

Jake leaned in and whispered something to Nora. She responded by grabbing his hand, leading him to the back porch. Dane slid off of the stairs and underneath the porch's windows. He peeked up from below, only his eyes visible from the screen's bottom.

"I just want to be alone with you," he said to her, her hands in his, her arms stretched in front of her.

"Seeing Cooper propose to Lucy saddens me a little; we could be engaged right now."

The Point

Jake sounded forlorn, as though he was asking a sad question.

"I was in a bad place when you asked," she replied, recalling how distraught she was those weeks ago when he blew into town with the engagement ring.

" I still want you," he assured her. "You can put that ring on anytime. I love you and want you, no matter what."

She was close to tears.

He pulled her in, kissing her.

"Yech," Dane groaned a little too loudly.

"What was that?" she questioned, looking to Jake as though he were the culprit.

"It wasn't me," he assured her as he turned in the direction of the sound.

Oh shit, Dane thought as he quickly crawled to the house's corner. His heart throbbed in his ears as he ran through the yard, triggering the floodlights that were operated by a motion sensor. Nora pulled away from Jake, startled by the sudden wash of light in the yard.

"What was that," she asked again, startled by the activity.

"No worries," Cooper consoled as he called from the dining room. "Probably just whitetails running through the yard."

Dane scurried back up the wooded hillside, climbing into his car awash with feelings he had no experience with. He squeezed the steering wheel, his knuckles white from the strain as he tried to steer the emotions he had bottled in his twisting gut.

"I want her," he stated, somewhat confused by the shifting the parasite did. "I want the feeling of her," he said with correction, the creature within helping him to clarify his feelings.

"Deer Lake—the Buckhorn, there is bound to be an unsuspecting victim bellied up to the bar at that shithole."

That waitress, he thought as he sped down the mountain.

Chapter 33

"I can hear you thinking," Emily Sanders commented as her husband sighed quietly into the dark.

"Just work stuff," he assured her. "Bad people doing bad things."

Deputy Doug Sanders rolled over and brushed his wife's cheek, hoping his touch would wipe away her concerned look.

"Anything I can do to help you?" she asked. "You need some water or a sleeping pill maybe?"

"No worries, hon, I'm just thinking. You're the one who needs sleep. The kids will eat you alive if they sense any weakness," he joked, pulling the blankets up over her shoulders.

He gave his wife a peck on the lips as she closed her eyes.

"You're right, I'll sleep while you think," she agreed groggily.

He watched as his wife dozed. Her sweet face lit by the glow of the street lamp, its light filtered by the delicate weave of the window dressing.

I know it was him, he thought as his mind churned over the events of that day.

Stephanie Lewis had come into the office convinced she'd been drugged and violated by a man she'd met at the Elbow Room some weeks before.

She gave a description and said his name was Mike. "I can't remember how to get to his house exactly," she'd informed them, "But I remember turning right past the bar into a residential neighborhood."

"Could you describe it?" he asked.

"One-story, I think. Maybe—I don't know; I was pretty out of it. I would definitely remember the bathroom if I saw it again." She'd never forget it: high-end but sterile.

Stephanie was sent for testing at the local hospital, rape kit included. *Why didn't you come in right away*, he thought as she pulled out of the lot. *There is no evidence left, just your word against his, and you don't even know who he is.*

With Ms. Lewis off on her errand with one of the female deputies, Doug took a drive.

"Would you look at that, the resident psycho has decided to relocate." The deputy scrawled notes into his little book, making sure to note the Realtor and her number.

Doug knocked on the neighbor's door, hoping they might have some idea of where Dane might have gone.

He'd been slippery in the past, but he would get him eventually. He was sure of it.

~~~

While Deputy Sanders tried to build his case, Dane was in Deer Lake filling his needs.

He sat at the bar, his devilishly good looks attracting glances from the many aged and weathered barflies, who were no doubt regulars at this fine establishment.

He was disgusted. *You are all unsatisfactory*, he thought as he shopped. He couldn't have any fun with these women. Not after seeing Nora. She was young and fresh, pretty and inviting; these women had no redeeming physical qualities. Even Bev, the buxom delivery woman, had a great body, just a so-so face.

The Point

Dane slammed his drink and was about to blow the bar when a young blonde came traipsing in.

"Hey," she called to one of the older gals. The older woman looked up. She was draped over some guy who was just as weathered as she was.

"Are you ready to get home, Ma?" the girl asked.

"Not now," the haggard woman replied. " I was just getting comfortable," she joked as she rubbed up against the ragged man to her right.

"Yuck," the young woman exclaimed as she looked at her mother, "that's quite the bag of shit you're cozied up to."

"Mind your own business," the mother snapped before slamming the last of whatever clear liquid graced the bottom of her tumbler.

Dane had caught the young woman's attention. She smiled at him from the other side of the bar, before continuing to deal with her mother.

"Fine, stay here with the bag of shit then, I'm going home without you."

"Go ahead," the woman said as she waved her daughter off.

The young woman shook her head disapprovingly as she walked toward Dane.

"I saw you working here earlier," he said as she stood before him. He passed his hand over the compass, pressing it against his chest.

"So," she said. The short word was smeared with contempt. He snagged the waitress by the arm as she passed. He smiled, his charm holding her attention.

"Can I buy you a drink," he asked, hoping to liquor her up and get her pliable.

"Yeah, but not here," she answered as she walked toward the front door. He continued to hold her arm, following her to the front walk.

"Where does one get a drink if not at this fine establishment?" he asked trying to sound charming."

"The lake," the girl replied, keeping her answer short. "Where's your car?"

"This way." He led her to his vehicle.

" Should we stop by the store on the way," he asked, "Buy some drinks maybe?"

"All set," the young woman responded as she tapped the side of her rather large purse.

He drove toward the lake while his passenger began to drink steadily from the bottle of whiskey she'd procured from her handbag.

"What's your name?" he asked.

"Becky," she replied. "What's yours?"

"Mark," Dane replied.

He could tell that Becky was on the same path as her mother. She'd be a gnarly barfly: three kids with three different fathers, your usual north-woods white trash.

"So," Dane began, thinking she might need some small talk.

Becky interrupted, " Save it, let's just drive."

"Okay," he answered, pleased he didn't have to dig for something to say.

"Just so you know, it's fifty for handys or blow jobs and one twenty-five for anything else."

"Okay," he answered, pretending to have known that Sweet Becky was an experienced working girl. *Does it matter*, he wondered. *Does it matter if she's overly experienced*?

The Point

He dropped his left hand from the steering wheel and checked his stomach. His palm pressed into his diaphragm.

"You all right?" she asked. "You're not gonna be sick are ya? I thought we were gonna have a good time?"

"All is well," he stated with cold certainty.

They arrived at the turn-off to the lake, when he realized they weren't too far from the house he was purchasing. *Perfect*, he thought, *it's empty and I know where the key is.*

"Hey, I know a place we can go—I'll give you three hundred for the whole night."

"Let me see it first," she demanded.

He lifted his ass off the seat as he drove, fishing his wallet out of his back pocket. He was about to toss it to Becky, allowing her to retrieve the cash, when he realized she might glimpse his ID and realize his name wasn't really Mark.

He pulled over and grabbed the right denomination from the wallet's leather pocket.

She fanned the cash, tapping it on her chin. She reveled in her windfall, and he double-checked his choice with the compass.

"What you doing with that?" she asked as he watched the needle point in her direction.

Just making sure I'm on the right path," he grinned.

"Okay, Mark, take me where you will."

Dane pulled back onto the road and proceeded to take the many turns to his new house.

He was surprised by his ability to find it again on the first try—and in the dark, no less. He walked to the passenger side and helped her from the car.

"What is this place?" she asked as she surveyed the cottage's exterior. "You hunt out here?"

"Something like that," he replied. "I fulfill my manly urges."

"Yeah, lots of guys are out in these woods doing that," she agreed, like she had some experience with the matter.

He retrieved the key from above the doorframe and led Becky to the living room. The little house still had a few furnishings (obviously easier to leave than move from this secluded property).

"So, is this your place," she asked, a bit of a slur now present.

"I bought it today," he responded as he tried to light a lantern left in the kitchen pantry.

"No electricity?" she inquired.

"No, I need to purchase a generator."

The lantern finally lit, emitting a low hiss, filling the room with its warm glow. Becky slid off her pants and sat with her legs spread wide on the old chair. She was a pretty young thing. Dane wondered how old she really was.

"So, how old are you?" he asked, wondering if the simple act of fucking her would be a crime.

"Twenty," she answered. "Don't worry, I'm legal, I just look young."

"Good," he answered, not that it really mattered. He wouldn't want to violate a child, but sixteen or above was fair game.

"How long have you been a working girl?" he asked.

"Well, I realized I was fucking guys for free, and it occurred to me that instead of hooking up and getting

The Point

nothing, I could charge, and save them and myself the trouble of trying to pretend."

Oh, Dane liked her. She was pragmatic.

He walked over to her and unzipped his pants. Becky got right to work. He closed his eyes and tried to think happy thoughts… Nora tied to the radiator, Stephanie unconscious in his basement, Nora dangling from the ledge, pleading with him for help—

He grabbed her hair and jerked her head away from the task at hand. She looked shocked, as her head snapped back, her hair clenched in his hand.

"Ow! What the fuck!" she yelled. "Was I biting or something?" She winced as she reached up to her head, her hair straining at the roots from his tight grasp.

"Christ, let go." She struggled as he twisted, stepping behind her.

He needed to cook up a scenario capable of getting him off, of satiating the parasite that was now lurching restlessly. Unfortunately for poor Becky, it would mean something unpleasant.

Rubbing the small of her back, he knelt behind her contemplating his next move.

"Everything okay back there, stud," she asked, trying to make light of the situation.

"Yeah, just thinking," he replied.

"Thinking about what?" she dared to ask.

"What to do to you next," he answered honestly.

"Take your time," she said. "You paid for it."

"Have you ever heard of auto-erotic asphyxiation?" Dane asked while rolling his hands over her shoulders.

"Is that where you choke yourself while getting off?" she answered with a question.

"Right!" he answered, pleased she knew.

He wrapped his hands around her neck and began thrusting. She went with it at first, but started to squirm when she realized that Dane was the one getting off, not her. He squeezed, her flesh bulging between his spread fingers. Reaching back, she was swinging wildly, trying to pry his hands from her neck. She clawed, gouging bits of skin from his knuckles with every swipe. Dane was fueled by her panic. He relished fucking her while she fought, while she tried to survive her date with "Mark."

"Oh, how good you feel, Becky," he said as he choked and thrust, his pleasure heightened by her fear and fight.

Just as Dane found his release, Becky went limp.

"Oh, did I get too rough?" He pulled back; Becky was face down in the chair's seat, her arms hanging to the floor. He discarded the spent condom and pulled up his pants as he looked at her slumped posture.

He pressed his ear to her back, she wasn't breathing. He turned her head, and felt what could only be described as popping and crunching.

She was dead.

He pulled his phone from his pocket and snapped Becky's photo. Her pose was like that of Nora's and Stephanie's. Her back was to him, her knees bent, her bare behind out and ready to receive. He sat on the floor, trying to feel anything, unable to conjure an emotional response to poor Becky's death.

"Did I want to kill her?" he asked himself out loud.

A familiar warm tingle spread through his torso. *Yes,* he thought, *satisfied once again.*

He sat with Becky, enjoying the high she'd provided. The precious moment was only ended when he realized what he'd done.

The Point

"Shit!" he exclaimed, suddenly realizing he now had to dispose of her body.

It was dark. Not city dark, where light pollution and street lamps provide illumination, but north-woods dark. A pitch black, can't see your hand in front of your face, kind of darkness.

He took the lantern and walked outside, searching for a solution to his little problem. He approached the shed, hoping to find some tools, a shovel or axe, anything useful. He flung open the doors to find it empty.

He eyed the fire pit but knew it would take a large and sustained blaze to eradicate all evidence. *A blaze that size might draw too much attention, even out here.*

The lake. That's it, Dane decided. *I'll tie her to a rock and sink her.*

Just as he returned to the house to commence his clean-up, the lantern started to sputter.

"Shit! Not now, not fuckin' now."

The lantern faded out, the scraps of fuel no longer sufficient to keep it burning.

He pulled his phone from his pocket and used its glow to return to the house.

"You still here," Dane joked as he nudged Becky's butt with his foot. She wobbled back and forth, finally collapsing to the floor.

"Stupid bitch. Who drives off with a stranger into the woods?" He was amazed at how easy it was to get these girls alone.

He climbed into the chair and checked his weather app for tomorrow's projected sunrise.

"I think I'll sleep in the car, it's really musty in here. You don't mind do you?" he asked poor Becky while nudging her with his foot.

He used his cell as a flashlight to navigate his way to the Charger, while accepting the fact that no one was as clever or as witty as he was. He reclined in the front seat and closed his eyes, contented by these recent acts and the fact that he was more intelligent than any one he'd ever known.

"I can't be stopped now," he whispered to himself in the dark.

Instantly he was whisked away by a turbulent dream about his mother. She was cruel and overly critical, desperate to be in control of every aspect of his life. He seemed to dream of her more now, her presence heightened by the strength of his expanding darkness. Sharon came to Dane in his dreams and flogged him, whipping him with her braided leather belt while he sobbed, the heartbreak of his mother's cruelty far beyond that of the physical pain.

It seemed like he had been trapped in her hell for weeks when the alarm sounded. He shot up, a cold sweat trickling down his back, the nightmare about his mother still fresh in his mind.

He wiped the driver's side window, which was fogged by the labored breathing of his haunted slumber.

The dark of night had begun to clear, as the faintest light of the morning sun became apparent.

Tired but ready to clean up, he stepped from his car to complete the task so he could return home.

He entered the house and dressed Becky's body, returning all her garments to their proper place. He threw her over his shoulder and carried her down the back stairs, setting her on the ground.

The Point

"Rope," he said to himself as he verbalized the tools he needed, as though saying it out loud would help divine them.

He returned to the house and scanned its interior. He was short on time; he needed to dump her before it was too light and the few other houses across the lake began to stir.

Dane walked into the bedroom. It was small, but had a queen bed pushed against one wall and a bunk bed against the other. Clearly this setup was meant to sleep several people at once, probably for hunting parties. The bedding was straight out of the seventies. Brown, green, and gold prints graced the worn bed linens.

A fitted sheet was still covering the double bed. He pulled it free and returned to the back stairs. With his car keys he started a tear from which he could pull the sheet into strips. He tied Becky's purse to her body. Three hundred dollars was still tucked in its front pocket. "I should take that back," he said eyeing the cash. He removed it and fanned it out as she had, tapping it to his chin while he thought. "But, you did earn it... You know what, sweet tits, you keep it." He pulled back the collar of her striped button up and tucked the cash into her bra.

She continued resting in the back yard, while he searched for a suitable weight.

"I really need to plan better next time," he complained while scrambling to sink her before the sun breached the lake's surface.

"Aha! Found it," he divulged to her lifeless body. A spare cinder block had been wedged under the footing to the stairs. He figured it was his house now, so no one would notice if it was missing. "Besides, I plan to replace the entire back deck anyway," he assured her.

Dane secured the block to Becky, binding her with strips of the fitted sheet. Once she was tied up, the block fastened to her chest, he rolled her to the edge. He hesitated. *What if I push and she becomes wedged in the trees? What if the water wasn't deep enough to conceal her, sinking her from sight?*

The sun was peeking over the horizon now, and Dane could see the windows of a distant house. *You'll have to take the chance,* he thought.

He shoved her. Her thin body rolled quickly, her bottle-blonde hair whipping wildly with every tumble.

He watched eagerly, hoping she'd fall in and sink out of sight.

Becky hit the water's surface with a splash. Her hair floated, twisting in the water as she was pulled under, just as Nora's had that day in the wash of Lake Paramount.

As she sank, her pale face was locked in a haunting gaze; her frozen expression looked up at him. He felt nothing but thankful that she was drifting deeply enough to be obscured by the lake's amber waters. Soon her pallor was no longer visible and the bubbles of her descent were no longer rising. Dane backed away from the edge and returned to the house.

"This place really is perfect," he commented pleasantly as he put everything back in its place. He was sure to tie a knot in his discarded condom and place it in his pocket.

It was shaping up to be a pretty good day. He breathed deeply, letting the fresh air of this autumn morning fill his lungs. He'd given the new place a trial run and found it to be everything he'd hoped and more.

Dane thought he'd buy this place and satiate the parasite with the occasional woman, but now he knew he could enjoy so much more. He realized that out here, he could do anything to anyone, anytime.

Chapter 34

"How ya doing, Dane?" Deputy Sanders asked as Dane arrived home from his romp at Deer Lake.

"Good, and yourself?" he asked in return, trying to keep cool under the pressure of this ambush.

"Not so good," Doug admitted. "I had a young woman come to the station and file a complaint about a sexual assault." He searched Dane's face for any recognition wile keeping close watch for any shift in his demeanor.

"That's awful," he responded. *I hope that sounded sincere,* he thought, knowing he often sounded sarcastic when it came to being sympathetic.

"We both know it was you, Buchman," the sheriff's deputy blurted with concrete certainty.

"Let's not get nuts," Dane said, trying to put out Doug's fire. "At the very least I'm innocent until proven guilty—do you have some proof?" he asked while trying to seem stunned by the allegations.

"YOU are the only sick fuck I know," Doug insisted. "Emily, Nora, Stephanie, who else has been the victim of your twisted desires, Buchman?" The deputy stared at him; his gaze focused enough to burn a hole in steel.

"Why, I'm sure I don't know what you're talking about," he insisted, doing his best to sound coy.

"Of course you don't," the deputy followed up sarcastically.

"Are you here to charge me with something?" Dane asked.

The Point

"I'm watching you, Buchman," the deputy said as he pointed, sticking his finger into his face.

He watched the deputy as he walked back to his car. *I wonder if they will link her to me?* He ran his night with Stephanie over in his mind, slightly worried she'd pinned him.

"It's fine," he said trying to reassure himself, his hand resting on the compass hidden beneath his fleece pullover.

He didn't realize it yet, but he was in a tailspin. His demented desires had hurled him into fast forward. He'd jumped the gap between harm and murder without batting an eye.

Dane's new appetite for violence and sex was a vice more powerful than heroin. He showered, once again admiring his anatomical gifts by aggressively pleasuring himself. The pressure of his grip was second only to the fevered frenzy in which he pulled.

A deep gasp escaped his lips, as he dropped to his knees. Exhaustion gripped him as the hot water turned his muscles to rubber, his release the last of his starch. Climbing from the shower, he dried off, patting his firm physique with the white towel while gazing blankly into the mirror. He blotted without looking, shifting down to his thighs, wiping until he experienced a sharp and sudden discomfort. He looked down to find a bruise the size of his fist spread out on his right thigh. It was a deep purple, surrounded by a wide red ring.

"Oh shit," he hissed as he inhaled through the pain. "I've tenderized my own leg."

A Ziploc bag full of ice provided some comfort as he lay in his bed, the weight of the compass resting against his chest. He stared up at the ceiling, watching as the afternoon sun cast shadows of maple leaves onto the chalky white ceiling. He was tired, but at peace. His adventure the night before, his feast on poor Becky, had appeased the parasite. *And once again the compass pointed the way,* he thought as he drifted off.

At first his current contentment produced a sweet dream, one scene drifting into another, a blend of memory and fantasy.

It's summer at the lake and he's terrorizing his friends, one cruel prank after another; he's chasing Matt. He runs through the woods at camp, searching for his friend and finds Chelsea Jensen under the bleachers at school. (It had actually been another girl, but he'd always wanted it to be sweet Chelsea.) He violates her, his hand beneath her skirt, each squeal of discomfort getting him hotter, until the ground falls away and Chelsea is hanging from a cliff. He's watching her dangle, hoping she'll fall. He looks into her terrified eyes, but it isn't Chelsea's terrified face pleading with him now, it's Nora's. He places his hand on hers. He can feel her muscles straining under his grasp. He tries to pull, and her body suddenly becomes weightless. His force causes her to vault, her body sailing overhead, landing with a thud behind him. Something is unsettling. The landscape has darkened. Heavy pendulous clouds have obscured the sun. He turns slowly, his heart pounding so loudly he can no longer hear the water hit the rocks. "You're sick!" His mother's voice screams. "I hate you, you're as useless as your father!" He clamps his hands over his ears and falls to his knees trying to protect himself. She keeps screaming; her hair on end, her eyes glossed over and bloodshot. Her form is twisted and evil. Demonic shadows grace her face as her eyes stretch wide with each new breath. Terrified, he clamps his eyes shut and begs, no prays, for her to go away. Silence. **My prayer is answered,** *he thinks as he pulls his hands away from his face, but they aren't hands he recognizes, they are smaller. He's twelve, just a child again. He finds himself crouched in a dark corner, "I'll fucking kill you," his mother screams, her shrill voice lined with a deep guttural growl. She storms toward him, swinging wildly. He tries to shield his head as his mother whips him with his father's belt; his bent knees are the only things protecting his naked body. Saliva falls on him like a fine rain as Sharon screeches, her face now red and sweaty.*

Dane bolted upright, inhaling with a loud gasp as he tried to pull himself from the grips of this nightmare. The room had darkened; evening had begun to fall. A heavy layer of perspiration had broken out and was now soaking his sheets. He flipped on his lamp, hoping the light would wash away the fear coating his flesh.

He'd gone to sleep feeling satisfied, but he'd awakened with a new and growing hunger. The parasite was roused by the horror-filled dream and was ready to feed.

Desperate to satisfy the creature that now stirred, he hopped up, the closet his first destination. *Jeans and a hoodie,* he thought, as he made his selections. He donned a pair of running shoes carefully selected from one of his tidily organized shelves and jogged out the door. His pace was hurried as he scanned the streets on his way to the harbor. He was hoping to find an unsuspecting woman on an evening stroll or a college girl wandering out of one of the establishments down at the water's edge.

Skulking, his pace was frenzied. He flipped up his hood, shielding his face from view as he hunted. Dane ducked into the shadows of Prell's fish market. Lurking, he waited; watching the people ambulate as they passed between the many bars and restaurants lining the harbor's edge.

Right girl at the right moment, he thought as he plotted. *Timing will be everything.*

Darkness finished falling, blanketing the landscape, finally creating the proper cover for this dirty deed. His patience wore thin while he surveyed the many passersby. *Come on,* he thought, his hand stroking the compass under his shirt.

Like a wish granted, the perfect target exited the Dock Side Bar and Bistro.

"See you next weekend," Allison Bennet called to her friends as she crossed the street to the bike path. He felt the familiar lurch, the parasite, his *twisted traveler,* taking control as he watched her cross. He slipped from the market's shadow, one hand to his gut, the other clenched around the compass. *My navigator will lead me,* he thought as he recognized the purpose of the creature he perceived within. *Stupid cow. You are just like all the others in town, blind to the dangers lurking in the shadows. It usually would be safe*, he thought as he watched her, *that's if I wasn't on the prowl.* Usually it would be safe to walk the streets in the middle of the night in this small quiet town, but that was before— before Dane had tapped into the anger and darkness of his psychotic break. Before he let *the navigator* guide the way.

The Point

He followed the lovely young woman, watching the loosely knotted bun of her light brown hair bounce as she walked, her arms crossed to combat the chill of the crisp fall night. She was moving with purpose, not from fear but from the intent to get home quickly and get out of the cold.

Crossing his own arms, he shivered as he followed his newest victim. A surge of adrenaline coursed through his veins as he tailed her, no plan, just acting on impulse. Like a hunter after prey, he stalked, ready to lunge.

His hood up and his head down he followed, now watching her heels click forward as they walked the bike path along the harbor.

"Look out, someone's gonna get you," he whispered playfully to himself. "Oh, something stirs down below," he mouthed as he adjusted his crotch, now crawling with anticipation.

She was just ahead; he could smell her perfume wafting back as he closed in. He readied himself to snag her, planning to haul her under the stone bridge that topped a small tributary emptying into the lake. His heart pounded in his ears, his juices flowing as he prepared to dig in.

The bike path was about to split, the left passing below along the running water, and the right climbing, passing over the bridge's surface. Dane sprinted and wrapped his arms around the woman. He proceeded to clasp his hand over her mouth and haul her under. The slope to the creek's edge was rocky, and he struggled with his footing.

"Good evening," he greeted as the young woman wrestled, swinging and kicking, trying to wriggle free of his hold. She couldn't breathe. Her screams were stifled by his large hand, which was blocking her mouth and nose. She gasped, sucking in as she hyperventilated, creating a tighter seal between her face and his hand.

She was tall and thin. Her slight build allowed him to handle her with ease. Her kicking tripped him up, but he could swing her legs out of the way without much difficulty.

"I've got ya, now what should I do with ya?" he asked, his voice wavering under the strain of her struggle.

He wasn't thinking when he decided to snatch someone this cool October night: he just knew he had an itch to scratch and he couldn't stand the feeling crawling under his skin.

Traipsing down the rocky-river bank, he hauled his victim into the darkness. "I'll find some cover for us under this charming stone bridge. It's quite the romantic spot isn't it, sweet tits?" His lanky victim was slipping as she squirmed, her right arm falling from his grasp. His large hand continued to muffle her screams, her saliva oozing between his fingers.

"I really need you to calm down, no one can hear you. All you're managing to do is slime my hand," he stated trying to remain calm as he passed his words through gritted teeth.

The young woman began grasping nearby structures, trying to snag anything to gain some control of this situation. He continued to twist and yank, her limbs flailing as he tried to keep her from grabbing hold of any sticks or rocks.

His arms began to tire from the constant struggle and just when he'd decided to try and adjust, regaining some control of his wriggling prey, the panicked woman planted her leg, wedging it in the stones of the bank.

The Point

Dane stumbled, tripping as her sudden stop hurled them both forward. The young woman's leg snapped under the pressure of their forward momentum. He landed on top of her as they both spilled to the ground, her head striking a rock on impact.

"Now look what you've gone and done," he gasped as he crawled on top of her, pushing her now disheveled hair from her face. She moaned, slipping in and out of consciousness.

"Let's have a look at you." He surveyed her features.

"A bit pointed for my taste," he whispered to her as she lay beneath him, his weight pinning her to the rocky bed below. "But," he continued, "My compass has never misdirected me before."

Dane could feel her, her warm body still, as her shallow breathing labored under his weight.

"Oh, am I crushing you, sweet tits?" he asked as he stroked her hair before tucking it behind her ear. He pressed his cheek against hers, her soft skin pressing into his.

"I'm a bit aroused," he divulged with a bit of comedic inflection. He reached down and lifted his hips just enough to unzip his pants freeing the erection brought on by this latest act of brutality.

"Let me help you with that," he whispered as he reached under the bottom edge of the long coat the she'd tightly belted to keep out the chill. He explored until he found her waistband. The pale flesh of he exposed rear now giving off a soft glow in the shadow under the bridge.

"Lovely," he whispered as he rubbed, caressing each cheek.

Dane forced himself on her, relishing this act of stolen intimacy. He began to thrust forcefully, his full weight pressed into her back. He broke into a sweat, his exposed flesh sticking to his victim's. His cheek, pressed to hers, was pulling, causing her face to shift with every push. She was now awake, hoping he would finish and leave her.

Lurching above her he swayed, the pain of the violent penetration was masked by the snapped leg as he continued to grind her flesh against the rocky bank.

Saliva trickled from the corner of his gaping mouth and along her bottom lip. She could feel the warm liquid dripping from her chin as it fell to the ground.

"Ooohhh," he groaned, his bottom lip quivering against her cheek.

Unaware of her newly alert state, he whispered to her, "Very satisfying, sweet tits."

She stayed still, hoping he would just leave now that he had what he wanted. He stood and turned, trying to keep steady on the uneven ground. "Better get myself together," he announced zipping past a wet spot on his jeans. " Huh," he uttered as he realized, "It would seem that in my haste I've forgot to use protection...I hope you're on the pill," he joked. As usual, pleased with his rapier wit.

"Not that it matters, because I plan to take care of it right now."

All hope that he just wanted to rape and run instantly dissolved. Allison gathered her courage.

The young woman jolted to an upright position, a rock firmly grasped in her hand. Her movement was sheltered by the rolling waves and Dane's self-indulgent banter.

Fueled by adrenaline, she choked back her fear and moved swiftly despite the serious injury to her leg. Without hesitation she struck. The rock met his skull with a satisfying crack.

Chapter 35

Nora arrived home from her weekend at Cooper's cabin with Jake in tow. He'd stayed on for dinner and now was conversing with Nora's father like they were old pals.

"The biggest I've ever caught was just over five inches... had to let the poor thing go, catch and release. Not much of a fisherman, I'm afraid," Jake admitted. "Not like you, I hear you're quite the outdoorsman."

"Oh, practice makes perfect," William offered, trying to sound humble. "I've caught some whoppers, though." William put up his hands, spreading his palms apart in a comical gesture to accentuate the length of his "whopper." "I'll have to take you out sometime, show you all my secret fishing holes."

Nora stood at the kitchen sink helping her aunt wash up, while her father and Jake sat at the kitchen table chatting and chuckling about William's tall fish tales.

She listened to the banter behind her and glanced over to her aunt, who was smiling while she wiped plates and listened to the boys getting on together. Nora realized right then that she was happy.

There she stood, her hands plunged into the very sink where Dane first assaulted her, and she was smiling warmly at the joy she felt. She could've continued to be bitter and guarded (Dane had certainly given her the ammunition), she *could* spend her life wrestling with a damaged psyche—*but I absolutely refuse,* she thought as the happy sounds in the kitchen freed her from the past.

She pulled her hand from the sink and dried it on her jeans before placing her arm around her aunt.

The Point

"I love you, and I'm really glad you're here. You've made Dad so happy."

"Oh, Nora," Aunt Sara said as she put her arms around her niece, engulfing her in a tight embrace.

"I love you and your father, I really want us to be a family."

"We already were." Nora assured her aunt. "And now I'll be a big sister *and* cousin, weird," she said jokingly, rolling her eyes at her aunt. "Oh," she added, "When you marry Dad, does that make me my own cousin?" she joked, her father turning and giving her a sideways glance.

"Very funny," William retorted. "You must get your sense of humor from me."

"That's a knee-slapper," Jake added with a mocking dry tone. As he delivered his line the clock caught his attention. He pointed, suddenly changing the subject. "That cat has the most peculiar expression on its face. It's not really a smile— it's more of a grin, like it's wryly pursing its lips in judgment."

She smiled at him. He fit right in. It felt so natural. Nora knew that Jake was *the one*, and so did her father.

"My wife hung that clock there years ago. Its been judging us ever since. We joke about it all the time. It's watching over us, keeping us in line." William gave it a casual salute before returning his attention to their guest.

"So, Jake, were you still hoping to make an honest woman of my daughter?"

"Yes sir," he said as he stood up. "If she'll have me."

He walked over to Nora and pulled a familiar velvet box from his pocket. He'd carried it around all weekend, wondering if there would ever be a moment where it would seem right.

She held out her hand and watched as he pulled the ring from its satin bed. Jake handed the box to Aunt Sara, allowing him to hold Nora's hand while slipping the ring into place. He didn't propose, he just held her hand, looking deeply into her bright blue eyes.

"I love you, Nora."

His declaration was proposal enough. She beamed, her smile wide and honest. Lost in the moment, she lunged at him, eager to start a new chapter as Mrs. Jake McAllister.

She kissed him hard and long, full on the mouth, right in the kitchen, right in front of her dad and Aunt Sara.

"I guess that's a yes," William chimed as he watched his daughter assault her suitor. "Funny, that was the same response your aunt had when I asked her to marry me."

Sara slapped at his hand. "You silly thing," she flirted.

William put his arm around his pregnant wife-to-be and smiled warmly at his daughter and her fiancé. He was very pleased that their lives had taken this new turn. They'd moved away from a terrible recent past and headlong into a bright future.

Although their recent family developments were healing in nature, he was nervous about wandering into fatherhood again. *A father again, at my age*, he thought. *Not to mention the heartache and worry a child can bring...* But, he was overcome by his love for Sara and watched as his daughter's eyes once again sparkled.

The Point

Perhaps a new baby is just one more blessing... a blessing that will help heal old wounds.

"I think this calls for a toast, let's crack open the good stuff," he suggested.

"I would love to stay and celebrate, but I have to rest up for my drive back to the city tomorrow." Jake informed them. "My being up here for so long has my father in a twist, and I have to head home to tie up some loose ends at work."

"You won't be long, will you?" Sara asked, concerned for Nora.

"No, not at all," he assured everyone. "I've had a wonderful evening," Jake said as he shook William's hand. "And thank you for a wonderful dinner," he continued as he waved to Aunt Sara. She'd retired to the sofa, her legs swollen from being on her feet in the kitchen all afternoon.

"You are so very welcome, Jake," she returned from her reclined position. "We hope to see you here for dinner again real soon. I expect you to be a regular fixture now that you're marrying our sweet Nora."

"I'll be back on Wednesday," he assured her.

"Are you checking in and out of the hotel?" William asked.

"No, I'll just keep my room so I won't run the chance of losing it," Jake replied.

"How much is *that* costing ya?" William asked somewhat rhetorically.

"It doesn't matter. I wanted to be here for Nora, and there aren't any month-to-month rentals in Iron Bay," Jake responded.

"You're family now. Bring your stuff, you can crash here from now on."

"I wouldn't want to put you out," Jake replied.

"Nonsense. Sara is with me in my room now, and unless you're planning a long engagement, I assume you'll be rooming with Nora soon anyway." William smiled, trying to persuade Jake to bite.

"That's truly wonderful of you. I'll check out in the morning and then drop some of my gear off before I head out of town." Jake was humbled by William's generosity. "I'll see you in the morning, and thanks again," Jake said as he stepped onto the porch with Nora.

William and Sara gave one last wave and bid Jake a goodnight.

"I'll miss you, and therefore be motivated to hurry back," he admitted as he held her in his arms while swaying her back and forth.

"Glad to hear it," she said as she looked up at him, her chin resting on his chest.

"Brrr," she snuggled in deeper trying to find some hidden warmth in Jake's embrace, "It's really cold out here, feels like it could snow."

"It has been a bit chilly lately," he agreed. "I'm going to go now, but I'll see you in the morning. Will you be up?" he asked.

"Of course," she answered. " I wouldn't want to miss out on seeing you off; besides, I'll be getting ready for work."

"I should be over about seven so I can get on the road nice and early."

Jake gave Nora one last kiss before pulling away from her grasp. She walked over to the thermometer mounted to the pillar on the side of the porch.

"Thirty-six," she called to Jake as he opened his car door.

The Point

"Yikes," he replied. "Looks like winter wants to come early this year."

He blew her one last kiss before driving off.

Nora watched as Jake drove down the street. Her arms were crossed at her chest as she tried to combat the chill sneaking through her sweater. Her breath billowed into the cold clear night. She turned and headed in, eager to ready the guest room for her fiancé's return.

Chapter 36

"Hello," Deputy Doug Sanders answered, mumbling into the receiver.

"I need you to get your ass down to the emergency room ASAP. I've gotta girl down here who's been roughed up by some sick fuck. We've got a real mess on our hands."

"Yeah, on the way." Fumbling around in the dark, Doug hurried to don his uniform. He grabbed his gun, badge, and keys from the dresser top, and kissed his sleeping wife on the cheek before walking out the door.

"Be careful, I love you," his wife, Emily, mumbled from her pillow. A veteran cop's wife, she no longer worried—as much.

"I will," he smiled. "Love you too."

Jumping into the prowler, he hurried to the hospital to assess the situation. As Doug arrived his uncle greeted him.

"Why can't crime occur in the afternoon?" he complained, his eyes bloodshot. "Fucking criminals and nutcases! They must sign an agreement to only wreak havoc at night."

Doug placed his hand on his uncle's shoulder. "So, what are we looking at?"

Sheriff Grant led his nephew to the bay that Allison Bennet was in. She was scraped up, her face scratched, a large gash on her forehead.

The gash topped a swollen eye, and her leg was wrapped in an inflated compression device. The device was suspended from a sling mounted to a metal bracket, which was attached to her bed frame.

The Point

Doug and his uncle approached her bedside.

"Allison," Sheriff Grant started, "this is Deputy Sanders, please tell him what you told me about your attack."

"I was walking home from a gathering at the Dockside Bar when he grabbed me from behind, dragging me under the bridge. We got tripped up and I fell onto the rocks, hitting my head and then blacking out."

She began to cry. Silent tears streamed down her face as she relived the terror she felt at the hands of her perpetrator.

"What else can you recall? I know it's hard, take your time," the sheriff reassured her.

"I awoke and he was raping me. I was still face down, so he couldn't see that I was awake. I just held still, hoping that he'd finished and leave. I overheard him joking, he said something about birth control, then he said he was going to take care of it. That's when I hit him with a rock and ran, well, limped to the road. My leg, I had to drag my leg. I climbed up the hill, I thought I was going to pass out from the pain, but I had to get away—I had to."

Allison sniffed, her nose now running along with her tears.

"Is there anything else, maybe a characteristic, or something he said, scars, or tattoos…" The sheriff trailed off, waiting for Allison to reply.

"Why didn't I fight? Why did I just let him…Oh God, I should have tried to stop him, why didn't I stop him?"

"You did the right thing. Whatever you did saved your life, you're here to tell the tale," Doug tried to reassure her. "He was an animal, unpredictable. You were just acting on impulse, any outcome where you're alive is a good one." The deputy was taking notes as he talked to Allison, making sure to record every detail, but feeling certain he already knew whom to visit when he was done recording the victim's interview.

"He talked to me when he thought I wasn't listening, joked around at my expense. He called me *sweet tits*." Allison pulled tissues from the box resting on her lap.

"Can you say about how tall he was?" Deputy Sanders asked.

"Tall, over six feet, with an athletic build," she answered. "I'm five six, and he was at least a head taller than me."

"What color was his hair?" the sheriff asked.

"Not sure, he had his hood up." She gestured, as though she were pulling up a hood as she said it.

"A sweatshirt hood? Do you know what color?"

"Something dark, black or gray maybe." She tried to remember.

"Is there someone we can call for you, Miss Bennet?" the sheriff asked.

"The nurse called my parents, they're on the way from downstate."

"Alright, we're going to let you rest. Give us a call if you think of anything else or have any questions. Hospital security will be keeping an eye on your room, you are safe now." Sheriff Grant patted her hand.

"We're very sorry that this has happened; we'll catch this guy," Deputy Sanders said reassuringly before placing his card on her table.

"I know who did this," Doug told his uncle as they walked the hall to the elevator.

The Point

"Who would that be, I'd like to pay him a visit for making me get out of bed **IN THE MIDDLE OF THE NIGHT!**" Doug's uncle took a moment to compose himself, running his hand over his sparse gray hair. "Just for once, could the bad stuff happen after lunch? I always feel best after lunch."

Doug raised his eyebrows, shaking his head in response to his uncle's entertaining emotional liability.

"I like Dane Buchman for this. He has a long history of complaints, his behavior seemingly escalated. I would like to go check on him, see if he has a rock-induced headache."

"Yeah, pay him a visit. See if he's sleeping, THEN POUND ON HIS DOOR!"

"Will do," Doug answered. "Looking forward to it."

The sheriff wiped his brow, once again trying to calm down after this latest flare-up. "I'll pull the files on related cases, particularly Nora Reynolds, seeing we are both thinking Dane is our resident weirdo." The sheriff raised his eyebrows when he said the word *weirdo*, as though that somehow emphasized it. Doug just thought it made him look like a loon.

The sheriff went on to fill Doug in on Allison's injuries.

"Her leg is fractured. The doc said it'll need surgery...probably pins. The ER attendant said it was a miracle she was able to haul herself to the road." The sheriff took his hat off and rubbed the top of his head vigorously.

"How about the rape kit?" the deputy asked.

"It's being processed, they're running the DNA. They'll send it to the city for processing, we're looking at several days at the least." The sheriff sounded frustrated.

"Was Dane's DNA collected when the Reynolds girl was pressing charges?" the sheriff asked his nephew.

"Yeah, we did standard processing on him and her," the deputy assured his uncle.

"Good, get going now, we have work to do; this degenerate made me get up at an unholy hour and that is just one more reason to nail him."

"Is the crew already down at the bridge?" he asked his uncle.

"Yeah, they're on their way down to process it now."

The two men parted. The sheriff headed back to the station to pull the Reynolds' file along with any others that might be pertinent, and the deputy was going straight to Dane's house to see what he was up to.

Did you even make it home yet, Doug thought. *Are you hiding in some hole or maybe still face down?* "Hope you're in a lot of pain, you sick son of bitch," he sang, hoping Dane was suffering.

The deputy drove over and parked a block down. He slowly pulled the keys from the ignition while surveying the street. The lane was empty as he walked over to the property. The house was dark. The deputy strolled carefully as he walked around the garage. Peeking into the windows, he checked for vehicles, activity, or anything that would give him probable cause.

"I don't want to approach the door alone," he whispered to himself, not wanting to confront a possibly desperate suspect alone—"that's how you get dead."

"On the other hand, let him try something," Doug posited as he placed his hand on his pistol.

He walked up the front stairs and pounded on the door.

The Point

"Dane Buchman, open up, it's the Sheriff's Department."

Chapter 37

"Fuuuck," Dane winced as he breathed through the pain coursing through his head. He reached up, exploring for the source of the ache. Blood had soaked through his hood causing the fabric to feel tacky. Just the brush of his fingers against the wound caused a burning pain to radiate through his skull. "Shuhhh," he inhaled, his teeth clenched as he tried to breathe through the sudden wave of discomfort.

Chilled to the bone, his limbs were stiff from the early stages of hypothermia. Still mildly disoriented from the shot to the head, he struggled to pull himself to his feet. It took him a moment to find the sense of urgency needed to remove himself before the sheriff and his shit of a nephew arrived.

Dane felt for the compass. Pleased to find it still tucked in his shirt, he began to run. His head thumped with every strike of his foot. Doubling back along the harbor, he hid in the shadows, weaving in out of the risers on the ore dock.

She got away filled with my DNA, he thought to himself.

Panic surged as he became acutely aware. *I won't get away with this one.*

"Fuck me," he whispered, watching his breath swirl in the frigid night air.

He could see the lights of the patrol cars bouncing off of the nearby buildings. He could hear the muffled voices of the authorities as they searched the area he'd used earlier to satisfy the navigator.

The Point

He crept from under the dock, worried that they'd start to search the area.

"The little bitch no doubt spared no detail."

He was fairly sure she hadn't seen his face, *at least not when I was still conscious.* "She probably didn't look, just ran for her life," he mumbled quietly as he scurried, looking for somewhere to go. *If she didn't look, they can't tie me to the crime until they process the DNA and that'll take weeks in this Podunk town,* he thought, as he tried to hatch a plan of escape.

Deciding he'd walk home, he crossed through yards and alleys, avoiding sidewalks and main roads. His house was just blocks away. If he could get home and into his garage he could head out to Deer Lake and lay low. He kept a spare set of truck keys in a jar of screws mounted to the workbench. "I'll just sneak out of town, before the authorities are crawling all over me." He mumbled, vocalizing his plans.

After several minutes of crawling and creeping, he'd had finally slunk to the alley that ran behind the houses on his block. Lurking behind his neighbor's shed, he tried listening for the squawk of police radios or the hushed voices of impending justice.

Nothing, he thought as he continued to creep forward, inching along the inside line of his nosey neighbor's cedar picket. He got to the corner that faced the street. He could see two prowlers from the Sheriff's Department parked under the maples across the road.

He dropped to the grass, resting his forehead in the newly settled frost. His head was still pounding and he thought he could still feel blood trickling through his hair.

Slowly, carefully, he pulled himself up to have a peek over the fence. *I need to see where the officers are posted so I can get out of here,* he thought.

Just as his eyes cleared the top of the four-foot fence, he could see Deputy Doug standing on his steps waiting for the other officer to exit his car.

Dane dropped back down, slipping in the process, and rattling the fence. Fear gripped him as he clung to his neighbor's frosty lawn. *Did they hear me?* he thought as he slowly backed away, expecting them to come down on him, weapons drawn, at any moment.

He crawled, slowly creeping until he made it back to the alley, amazed they hadn't heard his brush with the cedar planking.

Trying to hatch a plan, he racked his aching brain. He needed to get out of the cold and rest a moment; he couldn't think clearly with his head pounding and bleeding, his body working against him. Slipping quietly through the night, he walked, weaving through yards and occasionally ducking behind cars, paranoia commanding his every action.

I need to rest, he thought. *Help me,* he beckoned, his hand on his gut hoping the navigator would show him the way.

He looked up and realized he'd dodged and weaved his way to Nora Reynolds' yard.

Dane was standing in the shadow of her garden shed. He stared at the back of her house. Oh, how he wished he were tucked in that hokey metal bed of hers, sleeping heavily after a rousing game of grab-ass.

His crotch began to tingle.

I couldn't very well sneak in and have one last romp for old times sake, could I?

The Point

His hand to his gut he walked, eventually finding himself with his nose to the screen of the back porch door. The hand he'd had planted to his abdomen swiftly found its way to the small cast iron knob. He twisted to find the door unlocked.

He stepped into the porch, pleased to be out of the cold night air. Slipping through its narrow paneled corridor, he ran his hand along the row of jackets and scarves dangling from the many brass hooks. He let his hand glide from the outerwear to the knob gracing the door into the Reynolds' kitchen.

"Time for a little closure," he quietly sneered as he cracked open the door and stepped inside. The kitchen was a landscape of shadows and dark angles cut by the ambient light of the moon. He tiptoed through the space, acutely aware of every creak and shuffle. Once at the table he paused to appreciate the warmth and take stock of the pounding in his head.

"Hello," he mouthed, suddenly distracted by the swish of the Kit Kat's tail. It rolled its eyes, seeming to survey the intruder. "What are you looking at?" Dane questioned in jest while pointing, his index finger jabbing in the clock's general direction.

The clock seemed to lunge from the wall. Dane lurched forward in an attempt to catch it. He watched helplessly as it crashed to the stove below. The burners of the gas cook top rattled against the ceramic-coated steel with a spectacular clamor.

"Did you hear that?" Sara asked William who was already upright and scooting toward then end of the bed.

"You stay here, I'll check it out," he whispered.

Nora met her father in the hall. He motioned for her to remain quiet. She nodded in agreement before placing her hands on his shoulders. They both crept down the back stairs.

Dane had already fled, and was once again lurking in the shadow of the Reynolds' shed. He watched as the lights flipped on, *no doubt the patrol to see what the racket was*, he thought as he watched Nora and William through the kitchen window.

Nora picked up the clock, turning it over in her hands. William shook his head.

"Saved by the attack cat," Dane scoffed. "It wasn't the attack dog, I made sure of that." He grinned, as he recalled the pleasure of dropping Badger to his death.

"Sheeesh," he inhaled as the ache in his head escalated, the excitement caused by his brush with the clock having antagonized his condition. Watching, he waited while the two putzed around, finally turning out the light.

The bite of the night air combined with the bite the rock took out of his skull was taking its toll. *What am I going to do?* he thought, trying to work through the thickening fog of his head injury.

Falling to his knees, he crawled around to the front of the shed. *Please don't be locked*, he prayed.

"Thank Christ," he mumbled as the door swung open.

On his knees, his head now cradled in his cold stiff hands, he tried to collect himself. Desperate for some respite from the agony, he scanned the shed with the dim light of his cell phone for any source of comfort.

The flicker of a faint blue flame became apparent in the darkness. To his relief there was a gas heater mounted on the wall a few feet to the left of the door.

"Thank god, oh thank God," he repeated, suddenly finding himself broken down and near tears with relief. He knelt in front of the heater. The grate was lukewarm from the pilot light, but in Dane's chilled state it was not warm enough.

Once again using his cell as a light, he tried to read the instructions printed on the heater's face.

"Push knob and turn clockwise until you hear a click," he quietly read to himself.

"Next, push firing button to ignite heater."

He read on, inspecting the buttons and knobs located on the top of the unit.

"Finally, turn knob counter-clockwise to adjust temperature."

He proceeded to follow the steps, anticipating the simple pleasure of being warmed.

The heater hummed as the blue flames danced behind the glass. He scooted closer, his butt sliding along the wood floor as he leaned in, trying to absorb the warmth radiating from the small grate.

As he warmed his hands, his joints loosened, with full function slowly returning. "Fuuuck," he groaned as he pulled back his hood. The cotton had dried to his bloody hair, yanking at the tender wound as he tried to separate the two. Once again, the burning pain radiated, bending him in half.

Still trying to separate the hoodie from his mangled scalp, he worked to liberate a few strands of bloody, sticky hair at a time. The process was grueling: each attempt brought another wave of agony. Tiring of the prolonged discomfort, he decided to do something bold.

"It's like a Band-Aid," he said, "One, two, three…
"Mmmmwaw," he yelled through tight lips while ripping the hood free.

Kicking his feet, he squirmed, his heels scraping the floor as he bit his fist trying to stifle his scream. Tunnel vision guided him to the floor followed by a flash of bright stars, then darkness. His already tender skull hit the wood floor with a dull thud.

The spell didn't last long. He came to, a wave of nausea washing over him. He breathed deeply, trying to stave off the vomit rising in his chest. "No, no, no," he chanted between breaths, worried that hurling would only worsen the pounding in his head.

A slow trickle of blood was dripping down his neck. He kept breathing through the pain and nausea as he searched the shed for something to stop the bleeding.

Trying to keep the noise down while he rummaged, he once again used his phone as a flashlight, scanning drawers and shelves for towels or a first aid kit or an old shirt, anything at all.

In the far right corner there was a small utility sink. He turned the faucet, but the tap only offered a trickle. "Frozen?" he quietly questioned before catching what he could on his tongue. Forgetting the open tap, he reached for some paper towels stored on a shelf above the sink.

Dane pulled a long swath of toweling and pressed it to the back of his head. There was an old flannel shirt hanging on the back of the door. He grabbed it before sitting, returning to warm his chilled body.

With the glow of the heater easing the pain, he pulled the paper towel from his head and placed the now-crimson wad on to the outstretched shirt. He positioned

The Point

the toweling over the wound and tied the shirt's arms at his forehead.

With the heater hovering just above him, he slowly shifted, curling up on the floor. He rested his head on the inside of his forearm, pulling his knees to his chest. Curled in the fetal position, he choked up. The sting of tears filled his eyes as the anxiety induced by his compromised state took hold.

Cold, wanted, and concussed, Dane tried to doze. The tranquil sounds of bubbling water trickled into his psyche. The bubbling became a roar, the noise invading his slumber, hurling him into a torrential nightmare—falling, drowning, being swept out to sea. "NOOO!" He shot up, his heart racing, his head pounding.

Water was rushing from the tap, its trickle now a gush.

The shed had heated up considerably and Dane was now both warm and parched. "Feels like I've been breathing sand," he coughed, the pounding in his head now exacerbated by the heat and dehydration. He squeezed, applying pressure, trying to alleviate the pain filling his cranium as he lumbered to the sink. He dropped and pulled himself to its edge, scooping handfuls of the rushing water to his mouth in gulps.

He closed the spigot and fell backward. He untied the shirt, and slowly peeled back the paper towel. He explored the wound—*seems like it stopped,* he thought, upon finding a dry crusted mass. The bleeding had subsided, but a considerable lump had formed at the site of impact.

A wave of nausea washed over Dane like a twenty-foot swell as he stumbled, scurrying to crack the shed door. He fell to his stomach and breathed deeply at the narrow opening, staying low, trying to keep cover while beating back the urge to barf. "No, no, no," he pleaded, in fear that vomiting would only worsen his already miserable state. "Heee, ahhh," he wheezed as he breathed in and out in measured bursts.

It was still dark. He watched his breath billow in the chilly morning air as he inhaled and exhaled, trying to Lamaze away the pukey feeling.

He reclined onto the floor, pulling the door closed, laying his head to one side while trying to avoid the tender knot that now seemed to occupy the majority of his cranial surface. Each beat of his heart was followed by a wince. "I wish I could find that bitch and finish her off. I bet that miserable cunt is up at the hospital all safe and comfortable, while I'm down here suffering."

Denying his anxiety, he stayed on the floor trying to clear his head and come up with a plan. *I can't give up, I've already done so much…it would be such a waste; I've come too far. I need to get to the mountain.* He stretched his fingers and reached for the flannel. Gingerly, he brought himself to a standing position. Once he gained control of his legs, he wrapped the flannel around his neck, transforming it from the bandage it had been, into a scarf. He tucked the sleeves into the collar of his sweatshirt then secured the hood, pulling the strings tight, hoping to protect his wound from the cold air.

Rummaging the shed for anything that might be of assistance, he scored some brown polyester work gloves he found tucked into the top of a coffee can that was filled with stray nuts and bolts. They were well worn, and smelled a bit like grease. "Phew," he gasped, the smell making his stomach turn.

The Point

"Heat off, phone, compass," he rattled, checking the list before attempting to sneak out and on his way.

The cold, morning air was still. It felt heavy against his face, as he peeked through the door making sure the coast was clear. His feet crunched loudly as they landed on the blanket of heavy frost coating the Reynolds' lawn.

Taking each step cautiously, he crept behind a large oak to the right of the shed. He unzipped his fly and proceeded to relieve himself. He arched his back, sending the urine into a high arc. "Ahhh," he stretched, quietly yawning. This early morning piss came as a great relief, "Oh yeah," he groaned as his lengthy urination steamed in the frosty a.m. air.

I feel like a new man, he thought as he tucked himself back into his jeans. He stood behind the tree, contemplating his next move. He peered around its massive trunk as he tapped at the bark, searching for answers. He pulled the compass from the cover of his shirt and looked down at its face. The yellow glow of the nearby streetlight was just strong enough to illuminate its surface. He stood, lurking behind the massive oak, waiting for the compass to point him in the right direction.

Chapter 38

I wonder if she'll want a winter wedding, Jake thought as he whistled, sorting his belongings into two piles: one to travel with, and the other to drop at Nora's on his way out of town.

He shoved enough clothes for the short trip into a small leather bag and topped off the wad with his few necessary toiletries. He piled the rest of his clothes and miscellaneous items into a garbage bag and one cardboard box. The box was filled with files and random office supplies, all the items he'd been utilizing in his makeshift office at his hotel desk.

He glanced at the digital clock, its icy blue glow lighting the surface of the table below.

"Better get a move on," he ordered himself. "Get the car loaded and take this hotel up on one last free breakfast."

The inn wasn't quite four-star, but what it lacked in style it made up for with terrible cooking. The restaurant off of the lobby, which supplied the guests with a free breakfast, had to make it complimentary—no one would willingly pay for what came through that kitchen door.

The Light House *was* across the street, but he was in a hurry and the popular spot often meant a wait time. He knew that the greasy spoon within the hotel would have no wait at all.

After some questionable fare, he entered the lobby ready to check out.

"Did you enjoyed your stay, sir?" the bouncy brunette asked as she clicked the computer keys.

The Point

"It was fine," he answered as his complimentary breakfast swirled around in his gut.

"Is there anything else we can do for you?" the young woman queried as she handed him his invoice.

Antacid, perhaps, he thought, before answering, "No, I'm all set."

"Thank you, Mr. McAllister, hope you'll stay with us again."

Jake nodded an ambiguous answer before exiting.

It was early, still dark. The air was quite cool this mid-October morning. He had to scrape the frost from his Beamer's windshield with his jacket sleeve.

His nose ran as he rubbed the frosted glass.

"Goddamn, it's cold out here," he shuddered to himself, his teeth chattering.

Giving up on the scraping, he hopped into the car, wiping his nose on the same coat sleeve he'd used to clear the windshield.

"Argh," he complained, as the frost-caked sleeve passed across his already-cold face.

He gave the car a minute to warm, allowing the windows to clear before heading toward Nora's. He grinned, filled with happiness over the way things had turned out for them. He went from one extreme to another and back again, and knew that she was the only girl he'd ever really loved.

Sorry that things had been so screwed up, he now knew that he'd love her and never look back.

Turning toward the Reynolds' house, his stomach fluttered with excitement. He was really looking forward to holding her and making sure she knew how much he loved her. *I'll never let her wonder how I feel again,* he thought as he pulled onto Nora's street.

Dane lurked, compass in hand.

Just as the point on the needle settled, Jake pulled to the curb.

He nodded to the compass in compliance. *I must move swiftly,* he thought. *The navigator's restless.*

Blissfully unaware of the danger lurking in his fiancé's yard, Jake turned off the car and stepped onto the street. Whistling a merry tune, he fumbled with the fob, opening the trunk. Still whistling, his airy tune rushing between his teeth, he reached into the cars recesses.

"Crap," he grumbled pleasantly. "Come on you…" he coaxed as his fingertips grazed the box of files that had shifted during the drive. He leaned in deeper, one foot planted on the asphalt and the other extended behind him like the toe point of a dance move. "Oh, come on," he sighed as the box slid forward just a bit more, seeming to elude him.

Dane approached, moving swiftly. He surveyed the street, as he skulked, taking advantage of the circumstances that were unfolding before him. *You are making this too easy,* he thought as he moved in. He lifted his arms as he took the last few steps toward the BMW. With his hands planted quickly and firmly, he slammed the trunk onto Jake's head.

"Ooohhh," he mocked, watching his victim collapse from the crushing blow. "That looked painful, my friend."

Frisking, he searched Jake for the keys before flipping his now-limp body into the trunk. Dane looked down at him, his head cocked curiously to one side as he surveyed his handiwork. "Nothing personal, man, I just need *you* to get *me* out of town."

With his getaway secured, like the body in the trunk, he whistled Jake's happy tune as he drove away.

Chapter 39

"Mrs. McAllister, Mrs. Nora McAllister, Nora McAllister," she repeated into the mirror as she pushed and pulled, coaxing each strand of her short 'do into place. The stone of her ring glinted in the vanity light. She looked at the princess-cut gem positioned on her left hand and smiled widely at the thought of a life with Jake.

One last look, she thought as she passed the guest room her aunt had recently vacated. *I want everything perfect.* She smoothed the comforter with a swat, pushing one last wrinkle over the bed's edge. She scanned the space once more, making sure everything was ready for Jake's arrival.

"Good enough," she asserted with a nod finally feeling satisfied by the room's appearance. She skipped down the front stairs and stopped at the door. Pulling the lace curtain from its window, she checked for Jake.

She exhaled, blowing her fringed bangs from her forehead. She checked the clock on the cable box as she crossed through the living room. *Maybe he's running late,* she thought as she pulled her phone from her pocket hoping to find a missed text or call.

"Jake here yet?" William called to his daughter from the kitchen.

"No, I was just about to give him a call," she answered.

She did just that... no answer.

He's on the way and can't pick up, she concluded as she put the phone back in her pocket.

The Point

"I'm frying some eggs," he informed his daughter as she entered the kitchen.

"Good, throw one on for me," she ordered.

"Will do," he said with a nod.

Just as her fork pierced the yolk of her eggs over easy, the bell rang. She abandoned her fork, ready to throw her arms around her love.

"It's about time, I was so... Oh, hello," she said, quickly changing gears.

"Good morning Miss Reynolds," Deputy Sanders greeted. "Expecting someone else I see."

"Yeah, my fiancé." She brandished her ringed finger, taking the opportunity to finally wave it at someone.

"Shit, is something wrong. This isn't about Jake, is it?" she asked, suddenly flooded with worry over the presence of the lawman at the door.

"No, no, no, I was hoping to speak with you about Dane Buchman," the deputy said, calming her fears as he removed his hat.

"Oh, of course. Please come in," she gestured, pointing toward the sofa.

The deputy sat in the center of the aging couch, sinking deeply into the well-worn cushions. He placed his hat on the coffee table and retrieved his notebook from his inside jacket pocket.

"I was hoping to ask you a few more questions regarding your ordeal with Mr. Buchman."

"I gave a full statement at the time, " Nora assured the deputy. "I believe you were there, in fact."

"Yes, but I was wondering if there were any details about your relationship with Mr. Buchman that might help me deal with a new case."

"You suspect him of hurting someone else," she said, a question in her tone.

"We've had a complaint, but the victim wasn't sure who the perpetrator was. His description matched Dane's build." The deputy was visibly agitated. He was trying to remain professional but was finding it difficult.

"Just between you and me," the deputy continued, "I know it was him. I believed you when you said he dropped you off the Point. He has a twisted past."

"How can I help," she asked, hoping she had something he could use against Dane.

"Did he have any unusual behaviors, anything can be important, even the smallest detail." The deputy leaned in, his pen at the ready.

"I don't know," Nora started. "He liked to be in control. He'd play games of domination, humiliate me for his own entertainment."

She still couldn't believe she let him get away with it as long as she did. *How embarrassing to be so brainwashed by an idea that you were willing to rationalize any behavior to make things work.*

"Well, that is something," Deputy Sanders commented while scrawling in his notebook, his pen scratching wildly. "Thanks for your time, and congratulations—it's good to know you didn't let him get to you."

The deputy stood. "Thank you for your help with this matter." He furnished a business card. "Please call if you can think of anything else, or have any questions or concerns."

He left the Reynolds residence mildly disappointed. *I have to find something, a way to get him*, he thought as he returned to the station.

The Point

"I believe he's the guy as much as you do," Sheriff Grant assured his nephew. "But the prosecutor isn't going to give us a leg to stand on without something more concrete."

Doug knew his uncle was right and wanted to dig up some more dirt.

"I think I'll take a drive out to Deer Lake and ask a few questions, snoop around a little," he informed his uncle the sheriff.

"All right, but stay out of trouble, I know you have it in for Buchman, but you're an officer of the law first," Grant reminded as he lectured his nephew. "Don't let your personal feelings interfere with the job."

He assured his uncle that he'd act accordingly.

"Any info come in from the other sources?" Doug asked, wondering if there were any more leads.

"No, nothing new, your girl was the only one."

"Alright, hopefully I'll come up with something out west."

Doug placed a few calls before making the drive.

"Tillman Realty, how may I help you," the chipper voice on the other end answered.

"This is Deputy Doug Sanders with the Paramount County Sheriff's Department, and I was wondering if you could provide me with some information on a Mr. Dane Buchman?"

"Mr. Buchman is working with Mary Tillman, I'll forward you to her office."

Doug tapped his pen on the base of the phone while he waited for the transfer.

"Good morning, this is Mary."

"Good morning, Ms. Tillman," he returned. "This is Deputy Sanders from the Paramount County Sheriff's

Department. I was wondering if I could speak with you about a Mr. Dane Buchman? He's a person of interest in an investigation and I was hoping you might know what his relocation plans were?"

"I'm not sure I'm comfortable, or legally required to divulge that information," she dodged.

"I understand your hesitation, but it would be a great help if you would assist me. He's believed to be dangerous and is currently unaccounted for."

I was alone with him—he was looking at me. What if he has ideas about me? Mary's sudden sense of self-preservation nudged her to kowtow to the Deputy's request. "Oh dear, I hope he didn't do anything too terrible. I was alone with him quite a few times; he isn't dangerous, is he?" By this time she was clutching her neck in a subconsciously defensive manner.

"I'm sure you're safe," Doug assured the nervous Realtor.

"I don't know what his plans are, but I could put you in touch with his buyer's agent out west. I referred him to Greg Pelto in the Hematite Mountain area." She continued to rub her neck.

"Thank you, that's very helpful."

Chapter 40

"A man that can cook! I'm truly blessed," Lucy beamed as she took another bite of her Eggs Benedict.

"I don't want to go home today," Cooper announced. "I think we should stay out here all week, then invite our families for dinner Saturday and announce the engagement."

"How wonderful," Lucy agreed. "We can drive into town and start the party planning." She clicked, excitedly making a list on her phone.

"I'll need to do some work from here today, but you head in and shop while I get some stuff done." Cooper pulled a credit card from his wallet. "Get whatever you need."

She placed her hand on the card pulling it and Cooper toward her. She kissed him firmly on the mouth. "You're sexy when you give me money," she joked.

"Very funny, Lucy Jane," he batted back, planting a sloppy kiss on his future bride's cheek.

"I'll be in the office upstairs, let me know before you leave."

He ascended the stairs to the loft while Lucy rinsed the breakfast dishes. She watched her ring sparkle under the warm water as she finished the cleanup.

She was excited about shopping for her engagement party and wanted her best friend to help. She called, unaware that she was reaching out at just the right moment.

Nora had called Jake's cell several times. The voice mail would break in, "The person you have reached…"

then she would hit End and then call again. "Don't do this, please don't do this," she pleaded, now defeated to the point of being physically ill.

She paced, tapping her phone to her lips while wondering where he could be. She peeked out of the front window every time she heard a car drive by.

Did Jake run, afraid to tell me he changed his mind? Perhaps he overslept and his phone is on silent.

Convinced that must be it, Nora grabbed her bag and headed out to the Rover. She hurried to the Regency Inn, sure she'd find him fast asleep in his room. Trudging through the lobby, she entered the stairwell. She ran the three flights to Jake's floor, lunging, skipping steps. He'd given her a key, "Just in case you feel the need to pop in sometime," is what he'd said. Well, she didn't need the key; his door was ajar.

"Where's the guy who was staying here," Nora asked the housekeeper she found tidying the room.

"He must have checked out, hon," the woman replied. Her expressive eyebrows were lifted high, colliding with her shiny forehead. Nora watched in disbelief as the rotund woman covered Jake's bed with clean sheets, her flabby arms wobbling with each tuck and pull.

Grief washed over her, she ran; her heart was broken.

"You bastard!" she shouted, pulling her hair as she slowly came apart.

Not wanting to upset her father, she skipped the shop and went home to bed. Curled up under the familiar patches of her grandmother's quilt she sobbed, she sobbed loudly. No one came to comfort her. Aunt Sara had gone to the shop with her dad. Her little dog was

The Point

gone (murdered and apparently lost at sea), and her mother had been silent for years.

Lucy's call was the answer to Nora's cries for comfort. Lucy was the light in Nora's darkness. She could have ignored her friend's call and let depression pull her under, but she wasn't going to let another man manipulate her feelings.

"Hello, Lucy," Nora answered, trying to sound positive.

"You okay, you sound stuffed up. You're not getting a cold are you, because Cooper and I are staying out here all week then having a party to announce our engagement. I want you to help. I can't have you sick during this important time for *me*." Lucy's "it's all about me" humor was usually appreciated, but right now Nora just found it troublesome.

"I'm fine," she answered dryly. "I'm just tired. Of course I would love to help, I'll get out there as soon as I can."

"Fabulous! Try to think 'theme' on your way out here. All good parties have a hook."

"Isn't the theme already predetermined?" she asked, wondering why engagement wasn't its own theme.

"No silly, it has to be *more.*"

"Well, let me go so I can get there some time today," she barked.

"Yes ma'am." Lucy responded with her best recruit impression. "Oh, will Jake be back in time for the party?"

"Maybe, if he's cleared everything up by then," she lied, his sudden absence twisting the knife of betrayal once again. "I'm gonna go and get ready, see ya soon," she said before hanging up.

Nora lathered her face with hand soap and rinsed away the smeared eye makeup. She applied a new coat of cosmetics and plastered a pleasant look on her face.

"I am happy for Lucy," she told herself in the mirror.

She jotted a note for her father:

Going out to the Mountain to spend time with Lucy.
I'm staying the night so don't wait up.
Love ya, Nora

She climbed into the Rover and choked back the tears. "Suck it up, suck it up right now!" she commanded of herself, refusing to give Jake any more thought. "In fact, I'm turning you off," she declared while powering down her cell. "I'm taking a peaceful drive to see Lucy, and I won't be interrupted by you."

Chapter 41

Dane pulled off and snaked down a gravel road, driving deeply into the thick and towering pines.

"I just need some privacy to assess our situation," he talked into the back seat. "This is a really nice car by the way. Classy. I'm more of a muscle car guy myself, but to each his own, right?"

He sniggered. It was fun talking to the guy in the trunk.

The sun had risen but was obscured by the steely gray of the heavy autumn cloud cover.

Once pulled over, he exited the vehicle ready to see what was happening in the back. He searched the road, *I need a weapon,* he thought while scanning its surface for a rock that comfortably fit in his hand.

He hit the trunk button, and hoisted the rock to a ready position. It slowly lifted, revealing the fleshy cargo. Jake was motionless. Dane kept his eye on him, his rock still elevated. He stooped to grab a narrow branch that had been discarded by one of the many pines hanging over the road's edge. He nudged him with the stick, poking hard at his shoulder. Jake didn't budge.

He dropped his weapon and poked Jake with the stick one more time just for good measure: still no response.

Dane disposed of the stick and began to nudge him with his finger instead. He planted his palm on his back and pushed, looking for any movement. He rolled forward; that's when he saw the blood. He felt for a pulse, placing two fingers on Jake's neck.

"I wasn't really trying to kill you with the trunk, but it would save me the trouble of doing it later," he said in jest. "I do have a long list of to-do's for the day, and killing you might just not fit in." He was enjoying himself, faking as if he were looking at a watch as he joked about not having the time to kill his passenger later.

"Sorry about the head," he apologized sarcastically, "I was cracked in the skull last night myself... hurts like hell. It would really hurt tomorrow, if you were going to see tomorrow."

He searched the trunk for something to tie his hands with. There was nothing.

"You're less of a man than I am," Dane joked. "These hicks jab me all the time about being a townie, but at least I have duct tape in my car."

Dane pulled the flannel from around his neck. He hadn't realized how much of the chill it had been blocking until its absence. He gripped the old shirt in both hands and pulled at its tail until the plaid fabric gave. He kept ripping, pulling the shirt into several strips.

After binding his hands and feet, one strip remained. "I think this one will be a gag, just in case you come to and decide to start singing."

Once satisfied that his cargo was sufficiently subdued, he searched his pockets for some cash. In the first pocket perused was his cell. Dane scrolled through the contacts. He wondered how upset all the names listed would be when they heard the bad news of Jake's unfortunate disappearance. "They'll never find you, ya know. I'll make sure of it." He quietly assured his passenger.

"There are quite a few missed calls here from sweet tits," he passed on to Jake's comatose body. "Someone

The Point

really wants to get ahold of you," he joked while counting the missed calls from Nora.

"I know that sweet piece of ass of yours. You know," Dane continued, "speaking of her ass, I have a photo of it. I took it when I had her zip-tied to a radiator." He chuckled to himself, amused by the situation. "You're in the trunk, captured by me, the current lover of the woman who set me free when I let her go." He was amused. "I think there's an angle there."

Exhausting the phone's entertainment value, he kept rolling and patting Jake, his hand sliding and rummaging over his person and through his pockets.

"Finally," he uttered as he stumbled across Jake's wallet; it was tucked inside his sport coat, which was under an overcoat.

"Had to practically molest you to find this," he ribbed as he flapped the wallet in Jake's face, his voice tinged with irritation.

After slamming the trunk, he climbed back into the driver's seat. He unfolded the wallet. It was a deep brown, fine grain, leather—obviously hand-crafted.

"Nice," he complimented while flipping it over, once again talking into the back seat. He pulled it open, spreading the wallet wide. A stack of cash was tightly wedged into the fine leather pocket. He rubbed the edge of the cash with his thumb, causing the bills to shuffle.

"Huh," he uttered, " five hundred… you shouldn't carry this much cash, someone might roll you for it."

Continuing to explore, he rifled through the collection of credit cards. A variety were on display, each nestled snugly into its own sleeve, which was mounted to the right end of the wallet's interior.

On the other end were photos of what he presumed were his passenger's family. He pulled out a photo of what were probably Jake's parents and their three kids. The tallest one looked exactly like Jake.

"Is this your mother," he asked, flicking the photo with his middle finger. "She's got great tits for an older gal."

He tucked the picture back in its plastic sleeve, then turned and thanked Jake.

"Very nice spread," he complimented, his head once again turned toward his human cargo.

"This will do nicely. I appreciate your generosity."

He tucked Jake's wallet into his back pocket, adjacent to his own. He turned the car around and headed toward Hematite Mountain. "I'm gonna grab a bite and purchase supplies. I suppose I need to call the Realtor as well," he informed the body in the back. "Just want to keep you abreast of the day's plans." He had a chuckle, amused by his relationship with Jake. "I think I shall borrow your identity today," he added as he wound toward town.

"You won't mind, though, because you're tied up in the trunk and, well, close to death." He smiled as he drove the BMW toward town, scanning the channels for a decent tune. "This is my favorite song," he announced before jumping in and singing loudly, "At the Copa, Copa Cabaaanaaaa...." he howled, his pitchy tone no match for the music stylings of Barry Manilow. "I love Barry, I love him. I have his greatest hits at home," he admitted with a nod.

He pulled into the Hematite Mountain branch of the Vacation Gas Station with his hand to his head. "I

The Point

shouldn't have sung so loudly," he quietly admitted to himself.

The blood dried in his hair now felt crunchy under his hand. The pounding had begun to subside; it was faint but still present.

"Got anything good to wear in here?" he asked his passenger as he pulled Jake's bag from back seat. He perused the contents and decided to bring the whole thing to the restroom.

"I'm going to freshen up, don't you go anywhere."

"I'll need this too," he announced, as he grabbed the jacket that had been hanging over the passenger side headrest. "It looks like it might snow."

Keeping his head down, he made his way to the men's room. *Make it sneaky, you don't need any attention from these people,* he thought as he shuffled shiftily through the convenience store.

"Sheesh," he uttered at the sight of himself when he stepped in front of the men's room mirror. He reached and locked the door, his eyes still fixed on the creature before him. "You're looking rough," he whispered to his reflection as he pulled at his cheeks with the palms of his dirty hands.

Thankfully, Jake's bag was a treasure trove of clothing and toiletries. Dane utilized its contents, trying to remove all evidence of the kind of night he'd had.

After some wincing and quiet profanity, the blood and dirt had been removed from his hair and elsewhere.

"That's better, now let's see what there is to wear." He pulled Jake's clothes from the bag with abandon as he searched for something warm.

"Really," he complained as he produced flannel-lined jeans and a merino wool sweater. "Orange. Burnt orange. And these jeans... too small for one thing, I must have four inches on you, not to mention this sweater. We're going to have words when I get back to the car," he promised, as he negotiated the application of the hideous garment.

The sweater was a poor fit. Dane was a larger mammal than Jake.

This will take some negotiating, he thought as he held the sweater to his chest, realizing it would be a tight fit. Stretching and yanking, he manipulated the knit until he'd pulled it into a shape better suited for his form. His efforts paid off; he'd given the sweater a little extra room.

One hand to his gut and the other on the compass he gazed into the reflection. "Rest," he whispered, "I'll take care of everything."

Dane placed the bloodied sweatshirt deep into the station's trash and headed back to the car.

He scanned the vicinity for prying eyes before knocking on the trunk, "Still asleep in there?" He asked. "We're going to have a talk about your clothing choices. Who buys an orange sweater?"

He rubbed dust from the metallic paint with a swirl. "Let's continue this inside, best not draw attention."

Tossing the bag into the back seat, he pulled on the jacket before climbing in and taking the wheel.

"Fashion is important to me. Clean lines, crisp, cool colors. I prefer it in my wardrobe and my home. But this," he demonstrated by yanking at the front of the sweater, "this is an Eddie Bauer– LL. Bean nightmare come true. Shit, stuffing you in that trunk was a public fashion service." He paused, squeezing the bridge of his nose while gathering his thoughts.

The Point

"Alright, lecture's over. We need to do so some shopping.

He hummed a Manilow montage as he steered his way to the general store, eventually parking along Main Street and across from the Silver Dollar.

Eyeing the sign of his favorite establishment, he briefly entertained the idea of a drink and a quick date. Dane conferred, his hand on the compass. He remembered he had errands to run and someone spoiling in the trunk, so he walked into Johnson's General Store instead.

Wasting no time, he grabbed a cart and started filling it with all means of supplies: food, fuel, rope, a shovel, everything and anything one would need to live, or stop people from living.

Ernie was, as usual, manning the register, his hat ever present—flaps down (cold weather was here) as he rang up Dane's transaction.

He knew he'd seen him in there before. Ernie was good with faces. Decades of running the only store in a small town made you familiar with families and their physical structure. He knew something fishy was up when Dane handed him a credit card that said *Jake McAllister* on it. *Looks like a Buchman,* he thought as he took the card. *I'll play along, you varmint, but I'm calling the sheriff as soon as you leave.*

"By the way," Dane asked, "what about a generator?"

"Have to order one, two weeks," Ernie said, as usual, a man of few words.

"Great," he answered snarkily, his mood soured at the thought of weeks at the lake without power. He felt a familiar lurch, as the parasite twitched. His hand found its way to the compass. *This peninsula is too small for my appetite, and the sheriff is likely closing in. I best be moving on sooner than later.*

Chapter 42

Dane was entertaining the rumblings of the navigator while loading Jake's vehicle with his fraudulently purchased merchandise, as Lucy arrived and parked just two spots behind him.

"What on earth is he doing out here," she mumbled as she exited the car.

Nora *said he was in the city this week*, she thought, absolutely certain that the black BMW in front of her was Jake's. She approached, eager to see him.

Dane got in, unknowingly ducking out of sight just before she caught a glimpse of him. He began to pull out.

"Wait, Jake!" she shouted. She brandished her cell and called Nora while plotting her next move. Nora's phone was going straight to voice mail.

He just didn't hear me, she thought as she got back into her vehicle and followed. *I'll just pull up to the passenger side and flag him down.* Pulling up, she smiled brightly ready to greet him, but to her horror she found Dane driving what she knew must be Jake's car.

She pulled back. *I hope he didn't see me.* She was panicked, her call to Nora had gone straight to voicemail. *What if he had her? What if Dane had hurt them?* Lucy's thoughts turned dark as she contemplated all the worst scenarios.

She tried to call Cooper as she followed him.

"Hey hon, how's the shopping?" Cooper asked as his pen continued to scratch at the notes he'd been taking.

"I'm following Dane; he's driving Jake's car." Lucy whispered as if Dane could hear her.

"What?" Cooper asked, confused by that info.

"Dane has Jake's car, it's a black BMW with Commerce City tags. Nora hasn't responded to me. I'm worried he's done something terrible to them."

"Don't follow him, he's dangerous." Cooper was worried.

"I have to, what if he gets away and she's in the trunk or something."

"Come get me, we'll look for him together," he suggested.

"There are too many hiding places out here, we might never find them again. I won't let him see me, I'll just tail him and see where he's going, then phone the authorities." Lucy's plan seemed solid.

"Please be careful, I'm really uncomfortable with you following him. I fear he could be dangerous if cornered."

He was right, Dane was dangerous; he didn't want to believe how dangerous.

She did her best to follow closely enough to keep him in her sights, but without seeming too obvious.

He headed north past the mountain before turning off, navigating the many turns and forks before arriving at his new but temporary home.

His arrival was met with feelings of melancholy. He pulled in front of the house, parking the car to the far side of the shed, well out of Lucy's view.

The sight of this wonderful place filled him with a wash of confusing emotions. He'd had so many plans, but now realized that he'd fouled it up by letting his urges dictate his actions. *Was I led astray?* he thought, the question fleeting as he reached for the compass. *No, I was navigated to exactly where I'm supposed to be*, his hand now groping at his gut.

The Point

His hasty bit of fun the night before had cost him location, but nothing more. *I'll take care of the problem in the trunk, regroup and plan my escape from this miserable peninsula.* He placed his hand on the compass, wondering if his prized treasure had been to blame. *Did some force point me in the wrong direction, knowing it would lead to my downfall?*

Doubt cracked the door in Dane's fractured mind as he thought of the Kat. For a split second he wondered…

"Nonsense!" Dane shouted at his reflection in the rearview. He shook his head and with a fake smile called himself an idiot. "I'm losing it. My dick led me into trouble; as usual, the navigator helped bring direction to my situation."

As Dane tried to smother his demons, Lucy scouted a place to park.

This looks promising, she thought upon discovering an overgrown logging road. Its opening provided a fine spot to pull in and camouflage Cooper's Chrysler.

Leaving the safety of the vehicle, she trekked right, creeping through the woods. *Where are ya,* she wondered as she crunched along, her heeled boots a poor match for the terrain, as she searched for an opening through the forest to Dane's location.

Bracing herself, she gripped the bark of the closely grown trees, as she inched closer to the yard. She could see the shed now, and the house just beyond.

She had no clear view of him; the shed shielded his activity. She could her him talking to someone, but couldn't quite follow the conversation from this distance. The wind was creaking through the forest and rattling the dry and falling leaves. His words were obscured by their constant hiss.

She turned left following the tree line to the bank that hovered over the water's edge. The thin line of trees, and their heavy shed of foliage, provided little cover for Lucy and her flaming red hair. She covered her head with her gray scarf. *Thank God I didn't walk out the door in my red wool coat this morning,* she thought as she worked to be inconspicuous.

She could now see him; he was up to his elbows in the trunk. He was having an intense conversation.

Perhaps he is just talking to himself, she thought, unable to see anyone else in the vicinity.

Hiding, she peered from behind the trunk of a large maple, trying to discern what he was up to.

"I've had a good time with you today," Dane told Jake, who still hadn't regained consciousness. "Unfortunately I have to drop you off, and get some other chores done."

He reached under Jake's arms and pulled him from the trunk. He propped him on the bumper and then stooped to get him over his shoulder.

With a fireman's-type carry, he hauled him to the back of the house and laid him down on the cold ground. Lucy gasped. She began to back up; fear was running along her spine in a clammy wave.

Jake was pale, his lips and eyes dark. She could see blood had soaked into his hair and collar.

She kept inching backward, not wanting to turn her back to Dane, afraid he would sneak up from behind. She moved quickly along the ledge, holding branches and limbs trying to steady her footing on the slippery, damp leaves and uneven ground.

While she nervously shifted away from Dane, Cooper had been nervously watching the clock. He

The Point

hadn't heard from her in over an hour. He picked up his cell.

"Shit," he said, before dialing her number. "What was I thinking, she shouldn't be out there following him alone."

He selected her number from his contacts and hit call. His stomach flipped as the phone rang; he was saddled with worry.

Lucy had avoided detection so far. She just wanted to get back to the car and call 911. Dane had Jake's car packed to the roof with supplies. He was unpacking, first Jake, now everything else. She could see him carrying some things to the shed, and setting other things on the porch.

She kept her eye on him, carefully moving backward. She'd almost cleared the ledge, when her phone rang. It rang loudly, perhaps more loudly than it had ever rung before.

She dropped to the ground, her feet hanging down the slope toward the water. Clinging to a sapling, she used her free hand to fish the phone out of her pocket.

The ringing halted Dane's activities. He pulled out his phone and then Jake's. He quickly realized the ringing hadn't come from his pockets, but the ledge above the water. He walked slowly toward the tree-line that bordered the top edge of the slope. Slowly placing the phones back in their respective pockets, he crept toward the shrill ring. *What, or more importantly, who shall I find lurking*, he thought as moved forward.

She ended the call, holding the power button until the phone switched off. Her shaking hands had betrayed her, allowing the ringing to go on entirely too long.

Just as he reached the crest, the ringing stopped. He could hear the faint sound of labored breathing.

Petrified, her rapid, shallow breaths drew the scent of the fallen and molding leaves into her nostrils as she clung to the sapling for dear life. She tried to dig her feet into the loose debris on the slope. Her left foot finally found another small tree to brace against. Looking down, she peered under her arm at the drop below.

The sound of Dane sneaking up on her was obscured by the sound of her panic. Her palpitating heart, combined with her position, had her preoccupied.

Her scarf was still obscuring her red hair, so when he grabbed her and began to haul her up the bank, he didn't realize whom he'd snagged.

"Well, well," he sneered, with that familiar wide and menacing grin on his face. "Aren't you a pleasant surprise."

She struggled, twisting and kicking, wildly trying to break free.

He smacked her across the face. "Calm down, for Christ sake, there's nowhere to go, and screaming won't help."

She screamed. "Help! Help me! Somebody help," she screamed until her voice gave out and turned into a sob. He just stood there, holding her by the arms. He remained still and amused while she bucked and howled.

"Are you done yet," he asked during a moment of silence. "You weigh what, a hundred pounds. I can do this all day."

Dane watched as Lucy's pupil's dilated, the realization of her situation finally registering.

The Point

He leaned in, resting his cheek against hers. He pressed his lips to her ear, licking them, making sure they were moist before he whispered,

"Let's go into the house so I can slip into something more comfortable."

Lucy felt her muscles give. She'd lost all control.

He carried her quivering body toward the house, her diminutive form tucked snuggly under his left arm. He snatched a roll of duct tape out of the box on the porch on his way in.

"I won't lie, it was quite the shock to find you lurking out here. How *did* you find me, no wait, let me guess. You saw me in Jake's car and just had to know what I was up to. I forgot you and Coop were shacked up out at the cabin. I probably should've been more discreet, but look what my carelessness delivered to me."

"That was Cooper who just called, he knows everything." She tried to sound persuasive, but he knew by the look in her eyes that she was bluffing.

Dane held two fingers up on his right hand, then turned them down and pointed them at Lucy's eyes. "You can't lie to a liar, we know what it looks like."

She shed silent tears. They ran down her cheeks leaving streaks in her perfectly applied cosmetics. Her heart was heavy with defeat.

He led her to the bedroom and guided her to the surface of the dusty queen set. He took out the duct tape.

She was being pleasantly compliant. *Just stay calm, get the upper hand,* she thought as he made his preparations.

Looking at her as though she were a long-awaited meal, he licked his lips as he unrolled a long strip of tape.

He leaned over, "See, isn't it nicer when you're calm and compliant?" he asked while working to bind her hands.

I'll show you compliant, she thought as she threw her head forward smashing him in the mouth. Her forehead split his lip on contact. He was knocked backward, landing flat on his ass. His lip was busted wide open. Blood poured to the floor as he tried to pull himself up. He was still fighting the distant ache of that concussion and was slow to get to his feet.

"You fucking bitch," he growled.

Lucy bolted. She took off the instant her head found his front teeth. She wiped the blood from her eyes as she ran, her blow to Dane splitting her head open just above the brow.

She put her hand on her keys, sprinting toward the road, knowing her car was parked just beyond the drive's opening, only a hundred yards to the right.

Even with a generous head start, she was no match for Dane's size and strength. He ran and caught her with little effort.

He jumped, driving her into the ground. She struggled under his weight. Her head was pounding from the impact. Her senses swam as she tried to process her surroundings. Everything was happening so fast. He was on her, and then he was in her.

She knew she was struggling, wrestling him, but was this real? Was he really in her? Was this really happening? Defeated, she stopped fighting, her only movement caused by Dane's thrusting.

Lucy stared at the cold gray sky, her mind wandering, trying to protect her by focusing on the snowflakes that had begun to fall. Concentrating, she

The Point

focused on the feeling of the flakes as they melted on her face. While he pushed on, the snow gently, silently dusted them.

"I had wondered what it would be like to fuck my cousin's redheaded cunt of a girlfriend," he said as he stood up, his pants still around his ankles. "When you ran, it really turned me on. The sight of your narrow ass fleeing in fear was a great aphrodisiac."

He stood over her and with his hand on his hips. He flipped his still erect penis back and forth, a fine stretch of semen hanging like a string from its end.

"Does it look like Cooper's? I bet mine's bigger." He grabbed himself and thrust his hips forward.

Turning her head away, she covered her face with her hand, refusing to entertain him.

Shuffling farther over her, he dropped to his knees, landing at her chin.

"Take a good look you fuckin' bitch." He grabbed her red hair and pulled her head up, pressing her lips against his perfectly positioned penis.

"Lick it," he commanded.

Lucy knew she was going to die. Dane wasn't going to let her live. So, she smiled, and did as he asked.

"More?" She asked.

"Yes," he said as he controlled her by her hair.

Lucy gave him more. She gave him more than he bargained for when she clamped down, her teeth sinking deeply into his most prized possession. He wrapped his hands around her neck, squeezing, trying to get her to release. She remained clenched until she lost consciousness.

He pulled back, Lucy's dental impressions clearly pressed into his sensitive flesh.

"Fuuuck!" Dane yelled into the sky as he clutched his maimed manhood.

Scrambling to tend to his wound, he opened a bottle of water and poured it over the bite. "Holy shit! Fuck me!" he screamed, his string of profanity hardly adequate in expressing the amount of pain he was in.

His pernicious behavior had come back to bite him for the second time in the last twenty-four hours.

Chapter 43

Nora was eager to share in her friend's excitement. *Focusing on Lucy will be a great distraction,* she thought.

As she pulled into town, she gave Lucy a call. *Pick up, I'm here. Where are you*? She thought as she scanned the main street for Cooper's car.

"Christ, town's only so big, where are you hiding?" she asked as she listened to her friend's phone jump to voicemail once more.

Nora called Cooper. He jumped on her. "Have you heard from her?" he asked frantically.

"No, and hello to you too," she replied.

"Where are you?" he asked.

"In town, parked on Main Street," she answered, worry starting to build. "What's going on?"

"Lucy saw Dane driving Jake's car. She thought that maybe he'd done something terrible to you. I'm worried, she should've called already; I haven't heard from her, her phone is going to voicemail."

Nora sat in disbelief: *Did he say Jake's car?*

"Why would Dane be driving Jake's car?" she asked, unable to wrap her mind around what that would mean.

"I think it would mean that Dane stole it," he answered, somewhat irritated. "I need you to come get me. We can track her phone's location with mine. We need to find her," he urged, the distress in his voice tangible.

I'm on the way," she promised as she started out to the cabin.

"Please let her be all right," she prayed as she raced to Cooper. "Please, Please, Please don't let it be Jake's car. It has to be a mistake."

She was still pleading with the powers that be as she and Cooper started the drive toward Deer Lake.

Trying to navigate the back roads with his phone as their guide to Lucy's aid, Nora made a suggestion. "We should call the police."

"We will, as soon as we find her. I don't want to waste another minute." He leaned forward, his gaze shifting from the cell's screen, to the road, and back again.

"He wouldn't hurt her," Nora said, more of a question than a statement. "He only hurt me because of the situation, right. He wouldn't hurt her, right, Cooper?"

"I think he would, Nora. I think he would."

She kept driving, taking directions from Cooper, hoping that this was all just some weird misunderstanding.

"This is really out here," she said as she scanned all of the dense pine encroaching the road.

"How will we ever find our way back out of here?" she pondered.

"I think that was the idea," he responded, with a sudden understanding of why his cousin would choose this remote location.

"We are close now," he pointed, the two points on the phone about to collide. "Let's find some where to pull over, we'll walk in."

Cooper scanned the area, motioning to a spot level enough for them to park.

The Point

As they walked the narrow dirt road, they looked for any sign of Lucy or his car. They walked a quarter mile, when they spotted it tucked away.

"Oh my God there it is," he yelled as he ran to the vehicle. "Lucy, Luce," he called, hoping she was near.

He pulled open the door searching the Chrysler's interior before popping the trunk. He walked around back. With his hand on the car he looked up, his eyes meeting Nora's. She looked away, afraid of what he'd find.

Nora stood on the road, her sights fixed on her feet.

"She's not over there, let's keep walking." He ploughed on, determined to find her.

Oh thank God, Nora thought as she trotted to keep up with Cooper.

The driveway was long and narrow. Cooper peered down the wooded corridor, "We're almost on top of it now," he stated, referring to the signal.

Chapter 44

"The card said Jake McAllister," Ernie explained, "but I'm certain that the guy was a Buchman."

"How can you be sure, sir?" the voice on the other end questioned.

"Because I know faces, and he had the face of a Buchman. Buchmans have been traversing the mountain, shopping in my family's store for decades, and *I've* been standing at the register. He has that angled jaw. The Buchman jaw."

"All right sir, I'll pass it on to the sheriff, you have a good day."

"Yahoo," Ernie griped as he hung up the phone. "Departments full of yahoos."

Deputy Sanders wasn't a yahoo. He found it very interesting that Dane planned to relocate to the very area that the stolen credit card had just been used. He knew the name Jake McAllister sounded familiar.

"Is this the man who used the card?" Doug asked as he slapped a photo of Dane onto the counter. "Yeah, that's him alright, with the Buchman jaw."

"In the report it says the name on the card was Jake McAllister, is that a name familiar to you?"

"No sir," Ernie answered. "But I saw the car he was driving, it was a black BMW. Ya don't see those around here very often. Come to think of it, I think his usual car is one of those muscle type cars, kind of an obnoxious yellow."

"Did you happen to catch the plate?" The deputy asked.

The Point

"No, but he bought a lot of supplies, everything and anything. That's how I noticed the BMW. I saw him loading stuff into it."

"Interesting," Doug responded, knowing all too well that Dane had planned to hole up at the Deer Lake property that Mr. Pelto had just given him the address to.

"Well, thank you for your time, give me a call if you think of anything else." The deputy finished by giving Ernie his card.

Doug sat in his car, staring at Jake's name. *Where have I heard your name before,* he wondered. He brandished his little notebook and flipped through his notes.

"Nope, nope, nope," he repeated as he flipped each page. "Aha!" he exclaimed as he passed the notes he'd scrawled at the Nora Reynolds interview: *Engaged, no other developments.*

"Her fiancé, her goddamned fiancé, is Jake McAllister."

His phone was already in his hand and dialing Nora's number.

"Jesus Christ," Cooper winced, "Answer it before it rings again."

"Hello," she mumbled, her voice practically a whisper.

"Hello Miss Reynolds," the deputy greeted from the other end. "I wanted to ask you a few questions, is now a bad time?" he asked, picking up on the stress in her voice.

"Sort of, can it wait?"

"It will only take a moment, please, it's important." The deputy sounded pressured.

"Okay, make it fast," she said without considering whom she was talking to.

"Who is it," Cooper mouthed wondering why she would take a call at a time like this.

"It's Deputy Sanders," she mouthed back.

"This morning we talked about your fiancé, what was his name again?"

"Why?" Nora asked, her heart in her throat.

"I just couldn't remember, and I was wondering if I knew him from somewhere."

"Jake McAllister," Nora answered. "His name is Jake McAllister."

"Are you with him now? He did show this morning?" he asked, she could hear it in his voice, something had happened.

"Something happened to him, didn't it?" she questioned.

Doug struggled to construct an answer.

"Don't worry until I give you a reason to."

Nora hung up.

"Turn it to vibrate," Cooper whispered. "And why didn't you tell him we were out here—to send help?" he asked.

"Because we're going to take care of it ourselves," she said ready to take matters into her own hands, as she started to sprint down the drive. Cooper took chase, running up alongside her.

"Dane has Jake and probably Lucy too," she whispered through labored breath. "That's why Lucy saw Dane in Jake's car, and that is why the deputy just asked me if Jake showed up at my house this morning. The deputy wanted me to remind him what Jake's name was,

The Point

why would he do that unless he knew something had happened."

Cooper knew what his cousin was capable of; he just never wanted to admit it. Nora knew what he was capable of and now would make him pay for it.

They crept onto the property, while the deputy was slowly patrolling the back roads trying to find his way with the Realtor's directions.

Doug drove deeper, knowing that the only reason you'd live this far out was to get off of the grid.

How many women would lose their lives out here? the deputy wondered as he meandered the many back roads of Deer Lake.

Chapter 45

Cooper kept Nora tucked behind him, his arm extended as a shield.

Dane watched from a post behind the shed, as Cooper and Nora patrolled the yard.

He rolled his eyes; *such a sappy prick,* he thought as he witnessed his cousin's attempt at chivalry.

Suddenly Dane was stricken with a bout of guilt. *Getting rid of you, sweet tits, should be easy enough, but cousin…it pains me.*

He considered how it had been Nora who'd opened the door to the navigator. She awakened the parasite and provided the compass, but he didn't care for her. Dealing with Cooper would be difficult. He was the one person Dane had ever cared for. They were close as children, and Cooper was always the first to stick up for him, even if he'd done something mischievous. Cooper never viewed him as a problem like others did.

Memories continued to plague him as he watched his cousin guide Nora past the massive fire now burning in the large ring recessed in the patio. The glow of the flames bounced off of the surrounding benches in the gloom of the heavy cloud cover. The occasional squall of snow would break in on a burst of wind, which interrupted the otherwise gently drifting flakes. Cooper watched as the snow melted on contact with the concrete patio, its heat radiating the entire perimeter.

Cooper stopped Nora, silently pointing toward the BMW parked to the far side of the shed.

She quickly slipped past Cooper, running to the car. She was overcome by a strange convergence of emotions.

The Point

She was instantly and simultaneously relieved and grief-stricken by the sight of her fiancé's car.

Pulling the handle, she yanked the door open. He wasn't inside, but she could see that he'd packed his things with the intention of showing up at her house. Tears of fury streaked her face as she pushed the button to pop the trunk.

"What're you doing?" Cooper whispered, trying to stress the carelessness of her actions.

Nora responded out loud. "What if he's in the trunk?"

He knew she'd lost it. "Keep it down, he might hear us," he tried to shout in a whisper.

"Good," she continued. "Let him come out here, I'm tired of his shitty games."

Cooper approached her, wrapping his arms around her. "Let's just keep it down until we find them, then we can call him out and confront him okay, safety in numbers?"

With her face buried in Cooper's chest, her resolve quickly dissolved.

"Let's take a look inside," he said as he led her up the steps.

They peered in the door. "I don't see anyone," she said her voice hushed.

"Let's go in, take a look around," he suggested.

He selected a stick of firewood from the pile at the front door as they entered, "Just in case," Cooper explained tapping the wood in his hand with a batting motion.

Dane crept to the back yard and waited patiently as they snooped around the house. He knew they wouldn't find what they were looking for in there. *I can't wait until they work their way outside for the real surprise.*

Cooper ran over to the kitchen table. On its worn wooden surface he found keys and two cell phones. "Come over here," he called.

She stepped to his side, "That one is Jake's," she said as she pointed to the black iPhone. "That one's Lucy's," he concluded, the rhinestones giving it away.

They continued their search. The small house was quickly turned over.

Cooper looked out of the back door at what might have been two bundles of something lying on the ground. He wiped the moisture from the glass pane in front of his nose. The windows were fogged from the dampness stored in the old house.

He took another look, and stepped back, his expression suddenly bizarre, stricken.

"What?" Nora asked, acutely aware that he'd seen something unsettling.

He slowly opened the door, his hand shaking on the handle. She followed him, her insides churning with a terrible anticipation as they both stepped outside.

They descended the stairs together, every step bringing them closer to the forms lying motionless in the yard.

Nora clung to Cooper's arm, the pit in her stomach drawing her toward what she knew were Jake and Lucy.

They were coated in a thin blanket of snow, the print from the shrouds of aged bedclothes barely visible through the fluffy white ground cover.

They stood with their hands clasped, both acutely aware that the deafening silence was second only to the stillness that pressed down on them at this very moment.

The Point

Cooper dropped to his knees and began to frantically unwrap the smaller bundle. Lucy was swathed in an old sheet, the silver of the duct tape criss-crossing the brown and green of the late seventies floral pattern. He scooped her up, cradling her tiny frame in his arms. He stroked her pale face with his thumb, pleading with her to wake. Nora watched in horror as he pulled her to him, cupping her head then pressing his lips against her cheek. He looked at her red hair as it sat woven between his fingers. Closing his eyes, he ran pictures of her through his mind. Her bright smile, her brilliant green eyes... Cooper rocked her, his grief inconsolable. He kissed the flesh of her cold cheek one last time before returning her to the ground.

Nora leaned over Jake. She began shaking him, asking him, no, begging him, to be all right. She tore at the tape trying to pull the aged fabric from his head. The sheet parted exposing his dark hair. *He loved me. He was on the way over. He was just interrupted.*

She dry heaved as she sobbed at the sight of her best friend and her fiancé, dead and left on the cold ground. Their expressions were as flat and stiff as the ground they were resting on.

On all fours she heaved, convulsing violently as she vomited. Saliva ran from her screaming mouth as her howls shattered the heavy silence.

Cooper crawled over, pulling her to his chest. Holding each other, they swayed as they cried, each having a friend and a lover dead beside them.

Dane watched on from the back corner of the cottage as the two fell apart, more than pleased with their reaction. He reached for his groin with a wince. *Had Lucy not so maliciously mauled me earlier, I might find the sight a bit arousing.*

"What a scene you two," he said while applauding his grief-stricken company. "Oscar-worthy performances from you both. The wailing may have been a bit much, but I applaud your commitment to the role."

Cooper was on his feet and lunging at Dane, ready to end his reign of terror. Driven by grief and anger, Cooper had the upper hand.

He railed on his cousin, wrestling and swinging wildly to the point of exhaustion.

Dane didn't realize he could lose. He may have been injured, but his ego wasn't. Finally able to gain control, he flipped Cooper end over end and began pummeling him, grinning at his cousin's bloody and beaten face.

"Killing you will leave me with a bit of heartburn," Dane explained to his favorite family member, "But I imagine the pain will fade with time. Looks like this is the end for you, cousin," Dane chortled.

Cooper looked up to find Nora standing behind Dane, the discarded stick of firewood in her hands. She swung. The wood met Dane's head with a dull thud. The cut covering his already injured skull split wide open.

He collapsed, the blow rendering him unconscious.

Nora pulled Cooper to his feet. They both stood, looking over Dane's body, his head bleeding into the thin layer of snow that was covering the fallen leaves.

Chapter 46

"How will we cover this up?" Cooper asked.

"We'll figure it out as we go along," Nora stated coldly while twisting the roll of duct tape around her wrist she was now wearing like a bangle bracelet.

"Oh shit, I didn't see this coming," Dane admitted as he surveyed his circumstances. He coughed and heaved, spitting a blood clot toward the fire.

"Got a little carried away with the tape, don't ya think?" he commented sarcastically, his hands and feet bound tightly in front of him.

Cooper sat him up and dragged over, leaning him against one of the benches.

"Tape," Cooper said as he reached toward Nora. She stood and pulled the roll from her wrist. Cooper ran the roll around Dane's chest and through the slats on the bench's seat, making it so he couldn't shift, move, or lie down.

He sat in front of Dane, motioning for Nora to join him.

"We want to talk about what happened today, and if you cooperate we'll make sure you suffer as little as possible."

"Planning to torture me, are you," he chuckled, as though he didn't believe they'd do such a thing.

"Hammer," Cooper ordered, his hand outstretched.

Nora scooted, her bottom never leaving the cement. She pulled a box back with her, reclaiming her position next to Cooper.

Reaching into the box, she pulled out a hammer that Dane had purchased it at the general store earlier that morning.

"Your boyfriend bought me that hammer," Dane joked.

Nora bypassed Cooper's outstretched hand and swung it. It connected with Dane's kneecap with a loud and gratifying crack.

He howled in pain. She bit her lip, not wanting to smile, worried it would seem disgusting to Cooper. Cooper patted her on the back. "How'd that feel?" he asked her with a grin. "It looked therapeutic, I think I'll give it a try."

She was pleased he wasn't disgusted by her morose delectation of Dane's misery. She handed him the hammer and joked, "Take a crack at it, it feels great."

He held the hammer, palming the foam grip, enjoying the weight of the tool in his hand. Dane looked up from the first blow to see Cooper ready to swing. He tried to move, squirming, trying to pull his legs out of the way. There was nowhere to go. The hammer connected with the left kneecap; it broke like a china plate.

They watched him suffer like a cat watching a maimed mouse.

Cooper placed the hammer on the concrete and reached for Nora's hand. He held it, her fingers entwined in his, while they waited for Dane to regain his composure.

"How'd you get Jake's car?" she asked.

"Well, you see, sweet tits," Dane started, "I hid in your shed overnight. I originally thought I would sneak up on you, and have one last romp for old times sake, but that fucking creepy clock of yours decided to sideline my

The Point

plan. And seeing I'm wanted by the police, I ducked into the shed. In the morning Jake arrived right when I needed a ride out of town."

"Why'd you kill him, why not just take the car?" Nora was tearing up and visibly angry.

"I cracked him in the head with the trunk and pushed him in. I think I hit him pretty hard, he never woke up. I guess maybe the blow combined with exposure might have ended him; I only hit him the one time, but it was pretty cold today."

Nora felt a wave of nausea wash over her again. She heaved and grabbed her stomach, trying to hold it together.

"What about Lucy?" Cooper asked.

"Now, that's a more interesting story. She was hiding, spying on me, and then her phone rang. I found her on the bank above the lake, and pulled her up. She did try to run, but I caught her. I bet you can't guess what we did next."

Cooper shifted in his seat, the hammer once again clutched in his hand.

"Oh, it looks like you might have some idea," Dane smirked, his right eye winking. "I told her I always wondered what it would be like to fuck your redheaded cunt of a girlfriend."

Cooper dropped the hammer and went straight for Dane's neck. He squeezed, all his strength wrenching at his throat.

Dane squirmed and shifted, defenseless against his attacker.

Nora watched on intently as Cooper attempted to squeeze the life from Dane's body.

"Freeze," a voice called from the distance. "Paramount County Sheriff, freeze!" he declared once again.

Cooper kept a tight hold; his only plan was to end Dane's wretched life.

"I said freeze," the deputy said, this time cocking his gun in earshot of Cooper.

Reluctantly releasing Dane, he backed away.

The deputy waved the barrel of his gun, motioning for them both to step back.

"What's going on out here, Miss Reynolds," the deputy inquired.

Pointing a shaky finger she said, "Behind the house."

"Don't move," the deputy ordered as he walked sideways toward the house. As he turned to walk around the cottage's side, he glanced past the back stairs and saw what looked like two bodies lying in the distant, dim light of the fire.

"Did he kill them?" Doug asked as he returned.

"Yes," Cooper said, his voice calm and measured as if that one word explained why it was okay for them to kill Dane.

Deputy Sanders lowered the hammer on his revolver and placed it back in his holster.

"Get out of here," he ordered. "Go home. You were never here."

Cooper walked, watching the deputy eye Dane as he snagged Nora's arm. They took a few steps backward with hesitation, waiting for the deputy to change his mind and place them under arrest.

"Go, leave in the car you came in, before I change my mind!" he yelled.

The Point

They sprinted to the road, slowing to a fast walk when they cleared the driveway. They kept peeking over their shoulders, trying to catch a glimpse of what the deputy was doing.

They returned to the Rover and sat silently in the dark front seat. Turning the car over, she let it run. It needed to warm, the windshield was crusted with snow and she hadn't put the scraper in her car for the season yet. Minutes passed in silence as they sat waiting, clutching each other, numbed by the madness of the day's events.

Nora released Cooper's hand, put the car in gear, and backed up to the road. The Rover's wide tires cut two ruts into the freshly fallen snow. The headlights burned through the darkness illuminating the flakes floating weightlessly in the air, as they slowly drove down the secluded dirt road. They'd just arrived at the first turn-off when they heard it.

Double tap, Cooper thought with satisfaction as the shots pierced the frosty northern air.

Chapter 47

Cooper got out of the car and walked to the driver's side door. He held his hand out, "Let's go inside."

As they strolled up the walk to the cabin's front door, Nora's cell rang.

"Report Lucy missing, do it right away. You and Cooper will awake tomorrow with a visit from me and another officer, act surprised." Nora agreed to do what the deputy ordered then hung up. She relayed the info to Cooper.

They sat on the sofa and held hands. They didn't sit close, a whole cushion between them.

His touch was reassuring. She leaned over, placing her head on his shoulder. She closed her eyes, her thoughts drifting to her friend and her husband to be. She could picture Lucy's red hair perfectly in place as she gave her little wave; hand next to her cheek, fingers wiggling, that silly smile on her face.

"Her mother will be devastated," Nora whispered.

He didn't answer, he just placed his hand on her arm and gave it a gentle rub.

I called. It's my fault he found her, he fixated, guilt swelling in his brain.

While he struggled with guilt, she sobbed quietly, choking back the deluge of emotion.

Tipping back, he rested his weary head on top of the sofa. He closed his eyes, squeezing pooling tears from his eyes, forcing them to run down his cheeks. He continued to rub Nora's arm, his own eyes running, as she shook silently, trying to stifle her grief-riddled sobs.

The Point

The pair drifted off, their sleep heavy with heartache.

Their troubled slumber seemed brief as they awoke to a knock at the door. The sun was barely up as Cooper and Nora rose, the reality of what they'd experienced the day before rushing back to them.

She stood at the kitchen counter as Cooper opened the door.

"Hello, are you Mr. Buchman?" the deputy asked Cooper.

"Yes, how may I help you," he answered, playing along.

"May we come in? We have something important to discuss with you."

Cooper stepped back, allowing the deputy and his associates to enter the cabin. Cooper led them to the living room where he offered them a seat.

"Can I offer you a beverage," he asked.

"No thank you, I think we should get right to it," Deputy Sanders replied.

Nora took a seat in the armchair next to Cooper.

Doug began, as he was the lead on the investigation.

"I'm afraid I have some terrible news for you, Mr. Buchman," the deputy began.

Cooper leaned in, his hands clasped in front of his face. "What is it," he asked. "Is it Lucy, did you find her?"

"Yes, I'm afraid we did. It seems your cousin Dane had abducted her, and, well... we're terribly sorry."

Cooper was visibly angry. Acting was unnecessary.

"We won't know the exact cause of death until the autopsy is returned." The deputy sat back to take a breath before getting to Jake.

The news was just as devastating the next day. He was clenching his fists with his teeth gritted. Tears were streaming down his crimson face.

Nora tried to touch his hand but he pulled away.

"I'm interested to find you out here, Miss Reynolds," the deputy disclosed.

"Lucy had asked me to come out and shop with her, we're best friends. When my fiancé didn't show yesterday morning, I figured I might as well come out and focus on Lucy." She was tearing up; the news of Lucy's passing was hard to hear, and she already knew Jake was next.

"It would seem that your beau didn't arrive because he was carjacked by Dane Buchman. The theory is that he'd been hiding in the neighborhood and just happened upon your fiancé as he arrived at your residence."

Nora already knew all of this, but it was so terrible that shock and despair came easily.

"We are terribly sorry for your loss, please feel free to contact me or the department if you have any further questions."

"What happens to him now?" Cooper asked. "What will happen to my cousin?"

"Unfortunately, a struggle ensued, and Mr. Buchman was shot and killed."

Deputy Sanders had tied up the whole thing, leaving the two of them out of it.

"Again, very sorry for your loss, we'll see ourselves out."

Cooper dropped to the floor, his hands in his lap. Nora walked past him, getting ready to leave.

The Point

He grabbed her as she walked by. "Don't go. We're the only ones who know what we know. We need each other to get through this. *I* need you to get through this."

Sitting on the floor next to him, she hadn't considered that she'd lost someone close to her before and Cooper hadn't. Losing your mother is one of the hardest things anyone ever goes through.

Dane had been a villain; his death seemed justified. Lucy's death was difficult and would prove to be a crushing blow for Cooper.

Nora adored her friend and loved Jake, but she was hardened. She'd formed a callus. These losses were painful, but they weren't her first. She was already prepared to put grief in its place. She didn't want to give Dane any credit for her new and improved strength. She was sure her mother's passing was the seed that bore that fruit, but Dane definitely helped to fertilize her resolve.

Nora comforted Cooper. She happily played the role of caregiver. It was great to be the strong one, the one being relied on. She no longer felt like the fragile child she'd been treated as so often before.

Chapter 48

Deputy Sanders sat in his prowler scrolling through the photos on Dane's phone. He was disturbed to find dozens of photos of young women in compromising poses. He continued on, each becoming more disturbing than the last. He recognized a few of the victims, but many of the women in the shots were yet unidentified. Doug hoped they were lucky and still alive, only Dane's sexual victims, not his murder victims. Doug tucked the phone back into the box of evidence and pulled out the compass.

He knew it was Nora's, and it would be returned someday, but right now it was evidence of Mr. Buchman's maniacal process.

Not only was he wearing the compass, but it was strung around his neck by Stephanie Lewis's leather cord. *Trophies,* Doug thought. *My resident sick fuck was working toward being a full-blown serial killer.*

"Enough of this," he grumbled, tossing the compass back in with the evidence. "He's dead, job done."

He'd had been awake for nearly forty hours and wanted to kiss his wife and hug his kids. He locked up his cruiser and ascended his front steps.

His three children rushed to meet him at the door of his modest home.

He scooped up the two-year-old and tousled his brown hair as his five-year-old daughter clung to his leg. They shouted a chorus of "Daddy's home, daddy's home," as he walked through the house.

The Point

"You made it for dinner," his wife said, a warm smile on her beautiful face. *Just as lovely today as you were when we were kids*, he thought as he admired her.

Doug strapped the baby in the high chair and sat his daughter at the kitchen table. He wrapped his arms around his wife, who was standing at the stove boiling something that smelled delicious.

"I love you, Emily," Doug whispered into his wife's ear.

She could tell by his tone that he'd had a bad couple of days.

"Is everything alright?" she asked.

"It is now," he answered, as he held her, kissing her passionately.

"I'm going to check on the little man," he announced as he left his wife to her cooking and walked into the family room. His oldest son was parked in front of the TV. Doug sat on the floor and watched as his son looked on intently, the cartoon lighting his face as it flashed across the screen.

The young boy looked up at him with his dark brown eyes, while placing his little hand on Doug's leg.

"Glad you're home, Dad, I missed you. Did you catch the bad guy?"

Doug placed his hand on his son's blond curly hair; it was such a strange contrast to his dark and serious eyes. He resembled his mother in small ways; gestures, some structure, but he had a very distinct jaw-line.

"Yeah, he won't be able to hurt anyone anymore."

~~~~~~~~~

"Coop, could you get that," Nora called from the living room. "I'm nursing and can't get up."

He trotted to the door.

"Just thought I would stop by and see that baby today," his mother gushed on her way through the house.

"Grandma," a tiny voice called.

"There's my boy," Babs sang as he ran into her arms.

"Are you here to see the baby again?" little Jake asked, mildly disappointed.

"Yes, but you first, my handsome little man," she assured her grandson.

Nora buttoned up and commenced to burp Lucy, sure that her mother-in-law would want to begin cuddling her as soon as possible.

"Is she done?" Babs asked her daughter-in-law.

"Yep, she's all ready for you."

Jake ran off to get back to playing, happily driving his red and yellow car over building blocks in the living room.

Nora stood, handing over the baby.

Barbara instantly became a babbling, cooing idiot. It was quite the sight to see this poised, refined woman, standing in her heels and chiffon blouse, flapping her lips with such enthusiasm.

"When are you going to have another one?" Babs asked with a straight face. "She's three months old already, she's almost too big to cuddle."

"Maybe when she's two we'll try again," Cooper announced.

"Don't I get a say in this?" Nora jumped in.

"This is a big house, we need to fill it," he said as he scooped her up in his arms.

The Point

"Maybe two years is too long, maybe just another nine months," he joked. Nora smiled; he was cute when he talked about having more babies.

The couple shifted to the sofa. They watched as Babs *oohed* and *ahhed* over their precious daughter while their son scooted around the large family room in his cozy coupe.

"Did you show it to him?" Cooper asked as he tucked a stray hair behind Nora's ear.

"Of course," she replied as she recalled her morning with her little brother.

~~~

"MWR," Mitch said as he held the compass in his small hands, "those are my initials."

"Yes, they are," Nora assured him. "You're named after our great-great-grandfather, Mitchell William Reynolds. Dad will save this for you, and when you're ready to go to college he'll sit you down in the kitchen and give it to you."

Mitchell was a little disappointed he had to wait. "I don't wanna wait that long, I want it now," he pouted, mesmerized by the floating needle.

"Dad will keep it in his room, but he'll show it to you if you ask; that's what he used to do with me when I was little. Then, one day when you are grown, it will become yours, and he'll tell you it'll help you find your way."

***